"*Sixty-One Nails* is a *Neverwhere* for the next generation. The pacing is spot-on, the characters engaging, and the world fits together beautifully to create a London that ought to be. I stayed up too late finishing it."

– *C E Murphy*

"Mike Shevdon strikes sparks from the flinty core of English folklore, as a hero every reader can relate to finds he's part of an incredible and scarily believable parallel realm. If you've been thinking urban fantasy has nothing fresh to offer, think again."

– *Juliet E McKenna*

MIKE SHEVDON

Sixty-One Nails

**ANGRY
ROBOT**

ANGRY ROBOT

A division of HarperCollins*Publishers*
77-85 Fulham Palace Road
London W6 8JB UK

www.angryrobotbooks.com
Mine

First published by Angry Robot 2009
1

A catalogue record for this book is available
from the British Library.

ISBN-13: 978 0 00 733399 8

Set in Meridien by Argh! Nottingham

Printed and bound in Great Britain by
Clays Ltd, St Ives plc.

for Leo

ONE

I was staring into space when it happened, so I didn't really see. I could feel the wind as the tube train buffeted towards the platform and hear the grinding and squealing as the driver applied the brakes. I was part of the crowd waiting for the train. There was no sign that the guy beside me was in any distress. He just stood there with everyone else, until the train was yards away. Then he stepped forwards, leaned over the edge and toppled onto the tracks.

I reached out my hand, pure reaction I suppose, in a futile attempt to pull him back. He fell away from my empty hand.

The electrical flash filled my eyes with vivid green spots and the screech from the train intensified until I was deaf as well as blind. The train juddered past me, finally stuttering to a halt fifteen or twenty yards down the track.

There was no chance he'd survived.

I stood on the platform, numb, while people pushed past me. Some were trying to get a look at what had happened, some trying to push past to the exit. No one asked me what I had seen. No one asked why I hadn't stopped him. I didn't even know what he looked like.

"We are sorry to announce that there will be no further trains on the District or Circle lines until further notice. This is due to…"

There was a significant pause while the announcement system sorted through its list of possible reasons and selected one.

"…a person on the line. London Underground apologises for any inconvenience this may cause to your journey."

I looked at the small group of ghouls crowded around the front of the train. Were they trying to see or were they just making sure it wasn't anyone they knew?

Personally, I could sympathise with someone who had reached a point in their life where they just wanted to flash out of existence with no chance of reprieve. It had a brutal simplicity to it, though you had to feel sorry for the crews that cleaned up afterwards. The Underground staff had arrived and were pushing people away. Nothing to be done. Nothing to see here. They helped the driver from the cab. His face was white and he couldn't stop his hands shaking.

I shook myself to clear my head, then turned away, walking back up the stairs from the platform and used my card to exit the barrier. The ticket hall looked out over Embankment and I could see a sharp shower had blown in, soaking cars and commuters alike. With the rain, the cabs would all be taken and the buses full. If I didn't want to get drenched then the best bet would be to use the covered walkway to Charing Cross Station, get the Northern Line up to Tottenham Court Road then take the Central Line into the City. I would have to be incredibly lucky to make it to the office in time for my morning meeting.

Running up the steps across from the station entrance, I wheezed towards Charing Cross. I wasn't fit enough for this. I'd only just caught my breath by the time I reached the entrance to the main concourse. I pushed through the swirls and eddies of the commuter crowds, heading for the entrance to the Underground.

As I reached it, I saw the sign hastily chalked onto the board next to the stairs leading down. It said Tottenham Court Road Station was closed due to a suspect package left on the platform. I swore and kissed goodbye to my morning meeting.

Flicking open my phone, I hit the first speed-dial. My day was going to be spent playing catch-up and there was no way I was going to be able to leave early to collect my daughter from my ex-wife that evening. It was unusual for me to have Alex from Thursday, but she had Friday off school for a teacher training day. Katherine had arranged for me to have our daughter so she could go away with some friends for a long weekend. At least, that had been the plan.

The phone rang and rang. I was about to disconnect when she finally picked up.

"Hello?"

"Katherine? It's Niall."

"Sorry, I was in the garden getting the washing in. It was such a nice day and then the rain came down. Now it's all wet again." She sounded breathless and annoyed.

"I'm ringing about tonight."

"Alex has her bag packed and ready and is looking forward to the long weekend with you. What's all that noise?" The station announcements boomed around me so I had to wait for a lull to speak.

"I'm sorry, Kath, but I haven't even made it to the office yet. Some guy committed suicide on the tube line and I'm going to be really late. I'll have to work tonight. Can I fetch her in the morning?"

"Don't do this to me, Niall. You promised."

"A guy died, Katherine. I was right there."

"So take some time off."

"I have taken time off. I have all day Friday. I just can't be there this evening to collect–"

"You're doing this deliberately, aren't you?"

"What?"

9

"You're just doing this to spoil my weekend. You can't bear me having any time to myself."

"Now you're overreacting."

"I am not overreacting!" her voice rose in pitch, "You promised weeks, no, *months* ago, to keep this weekend free and to collect Alex after she got home from school so I could have a weekend away."

"I know, but it's not my fault. The trains are really–"

"It never *is* your fault, Niall, that's your problem."

"That's not fair. Look, I've got to go, otherwise I'm never going to get there."

"That's right, run away. Leave me holding the baby. Again."

"Katherine, I haven't got time for this discussion now, OK?"

"Just ring me when you're leaving the office. It doesn't matter what time. Alex can stay up late. It's not like she's got school tomorrow, is it?"

"OK, I'll ring you. I promise."

Today was going to be a very long day. I closed my phone and took the steps downward two at a time and trotted along the passages into the underground station and looked at the tube map. If I took the Northern Line to Leicester Square then I could probably get a train from there that would get me into the City. By then the rain might have stopped and I might just get into work in time to salvage something from my morning.

I waved my card over the ticket barrier and it flipped open. Taking the down escalator, I pushed my way past the column of people standing to one side. Hearing the announcer on the platform ahead telling everyone to mind the closing doors, I dodged past people into the tunnels at the bottom and raced for the platform. I pushed my pace harder and made it just as the Doors Closing alarm started. Ramming myself through the gap between the closing doors, I forced them to re-open and then slam closed again under the resentful gaze of my fellow passengers.

My breath wheezed in my chest. Indigestion grumbled in my stomach, the result of coffee, no food and being wedged into an airless carriage. We rumbled down the tunnel for the two minute journey to Leicester Square. As soon as the doors opened, I joined the mass of people trudging down the platform into the echoing passage to the Piccadilly Line.

The commuters around me kept the same steady pace, unconscious of my need to hurry. Their footfalls resounded against the tiled walls like the march of a ragged army, their steps coming into time then falling out again. My attempts to squeeze past were met with glares of disapproval and a wall of cold shoulders until I resigned myself to yet further delay. I could hear the train arriving on the platform ahead and feel the warm rush of displaced air as it clattered onto the platform. I heard the announcement as the carriages halted, the words booming along the corridor. The press of people ahead bunched and slowed as they approached the platform entry, bringing us all to a shuffling halt.

The indigestion came back. It twisted into a stomach cramp and I bent forward involuntarily, earning a push backwards from the dark-suited man in front of me. Tingling started in my fingers and I lifted my hands to look at my palms, mottled and slick with sudden sweat.

The crowd shuffled forward, penning me in. My head felt light and a sudden nausea had me swallowing hard. The tingling numbness crept up my arms and tightness banded round my chest, leaving me panting for air. My jaw ached and my mouth went dry. The numbness spread to my tongue so it felt fat and useless in my mouth.

A gap opened up ahead and the crowd surged forward, spilling down the steps onto the platform. The stairs wrong-footed me and I grabbed out sideways to steady myself, only to feel the shoulders to either side shrug me away. Unbalanced by the sudden space ahead of me I tumbled down the steps, rolling into the ankles

11

of the people in front. Cursed for my clumsiness, I sprawled at the bottom of the steps as people stepped over me.

I finally realised what was happening: I was having a heart attack.

I tried to reach up and catch hold of one of the coats floating past my fumbling fingers. I could hear acerbic comments made over me about drugs and drunkenness. I wanted to tell them I was sick, that I needed an ambulance, but my tongue wouldn't form the words. It flopped uselessly in my mouth, producing only incoherent groans. Why didn't one of them stop? Couldn't they see?

Fear clamped around my frantic heart as I realised I was going to die before anyone called for help. A wave of pain crushed the breath from me. Panic seized me, churning my stomach. My vision blurred with unshed tears. I couldn't get enough air.

If you're ever going to have a heart attack, don't do it on the Underground. Pick a back street; you'll get more help from passers-by. As they walked on past, the darkness swallowed me and the world fell away.

My final thought was for my fellow commuters.

Bastards.

I heaved air into my lungs and threw my head back, arching my spine. My throat burned and my eyes shot open. Watery colours in London Underground livery swam before me as I tried to focus and failed. I held that breath then let it out in a wretched coughing gasp, collapsing back in a series of choking sobs.

Shivers racked me. Cold and fear coursed through me. My heart hammered in my ears, its beat loud and irregular. Cramps knotted in my stomach, leaving me breathless with pain. Somewhere in the back of my head part of me was evaluating this calmly, telling me *Just breathe, idiot,* while that same quiet voice informed me that I should be dead by now, actually, so no matter how painful, this had to be an improvement.

I would have been thrashing on the floor, but for the person knelt sideways behind me, leaning over and pressing their warm hand against the cold bare skin of my chest, holding me tight against the side of their thighs. I ceased struggling and worked on breathing.

The face above me came into limpid focus. An old lady with pale skin sprinkled with faded freckles was addressing a blue-jacketed attendant from the Underground.

"I know," she said, "but I can hardly move him in this condition, can I? Just give him a moment."

The public address system drowned out his reply with an announcement: *"Due to intermittent power problems on the platforms, this station is closing. Please make your way calmly to the nearest exit. There is no cause for alarm."*

Another cramp twisted in my stomach and I curled around it, gasping as the light dimmed around me. I screwed my eyes shut and ground my teeth while she spoke calmly over me.

"I am a doctor, and I know perfectly well what I am doing. I'm quite capable of dealing with a minor emergency like this one."

I tried to tell her I was having a heart attack and needed the ambulance but this was interpreted only as further groaning.

"It's on its way, madam," he replied.

"Tell them to cancel it. He has no need of an ambulance. By the time they get here it'll be too late."

He held her stare for a moment then turned away to issue instructions into his handheld radio. I finally managed to get enough oxygen inside me to be able to say something.

"I think I do need an ambulance," I croaked.

I lay on my side in the recovery position, her open hand resting on bare skin beneath my shirt. She leaned across, bowing her head over me, giving us a moment of relative privacy.

"Tell me truly. Are you from the other lands, yes or no?" Her words were quiet but insistent.

13

"Other lands?" I coughed.

"Yes or no?"

Her question pressed on me in a way I didn't understand. I felt the answer worming its way out of my gut until I blurted it out. "I live in London. I was born in Kent." It seemed to be a relief to tell her.

"Very well."

She sat upright and the light faded. For one terrible moment I thought I was having another heart attack. Then I realised that the fluorescent tubes along the platform had dimmed and were pulsing with greenish light as they flickered uncertainly. A murmur rose among the people waiting to exit the platform and the attendant looked around. He began talking rapidly into his radio, only to find that it too had failed. He tapped it against his palm, pressing the talk button.

There was a distilled moment, crisp in every detail. The floor underneath me was suddenly chill in contrast to the spreading warmth in my chest and I noticed tiny droplets of condensation forming on the hard tiles. A breeze whipped down the tunnel, plucking an abandoned newspaper from a seat, strewing broadsheets down the platform. The gust pulled at coats and hair as people turned their backs. I assumed a train would follow it and hurtle onto the platform, but the breeze died again just as suddenly, leaving sheets of newspaper floating gently down onto the tracks as the lights flickered back to brightness.

The heavy pressure subsided and she took her hand away and moved so I could roll gently onto my back.

"An ambulance?" I suggested, looking up at her.

"Nonsense, young man, you feel better as every moment passes."

I was about to protest about the chest pains, the cramps and the tingling, when I realised that I did feel OK. The numbness had gone, there was no frantic heartbeat, no tightness in my chest and no indigestion. Could I have imagined it all? Could it be a hallucination brought on by stress and low blood sugar?

While my mind fought to rationalise the situation, the lady fastened my shirt buttons. I lay there stupidly while she carried out this act of decorous sensibility until she stood in one easy movement and offered me her hand. I sat up gingerly, expecting any moment for the clamping chest pains to reassert themselves, finding instead only how cold I had become on the floor.

Two men ran down the platform towards us. From their uniforms I would guess the attempts to cancel the ambulance had been unsuccessful.

"That's all right, madam, we'll take over now."

For an odd moment I thought I heard the old lady swear under her breath, but then she turned to face them, all smiles and praise for the speed at which they had arrived. One of the men knelt down beside me.

"How are you feeling, sir? Any dizziness, nausea?"

"No, no. Nothing now."

"Any chest pains, sir? Any tightness of breath or pain in the arms?" He held a stethoscope against my chest and listened to my heart. "Are you on any medication? Any pills?"

"No, no. I'm not taking anything."

"Any history of heart disease, diabetes, strokes, epilepsy?"

"No, nothing like that."

"Has this ever happened to you before, sir?"

I shook my head. "No. I'm fine now."

The platform attendant filled in the gaps. "We saw the gentleman collapse on the monitors in the control room and I was asked to assist. By the time I reached him the lady doctor had turned up."

I looked around for her, wanting to thank her and explain, but she'd gone. Where did she go?

"She was here a minute ago."

His colleague looked up and down the empty platform. "No one here now."

The man beside me looked down, assessing me.

"You feel OK?"

"Yes, the lady helped me."

"We'd best get you to hospital just in case, sir. You're going to need a check up. Nothing to worry about but better safe than sorry, eh?"

"I'll be late for work."

"Better late than never, as they say. Can you walk?"

"I think so."

"It's probably easier to walk you up if you feel up to it. Any sign of dizziness or nausea, though, and we'll bring the trolley down for you. Mark, keep the oxygen handy. What's your name, mate?" He helped me to my feet then to a nearby seat.

"It's Niall."

"Excellent, Niall. I'm Joseph and this is Mark. Just sit there a moment and get your breath back."

"I told you, I'm fine."

"No sense in overdoing it, is there? Take your time."

Mark draped a blanket around my shoulders while I sat there feeling like a fraud and the crew chatted with the platform attendant. I was just thinking that now I really had got an excuse for turning up late for work and that Katherine was probably going to think this was just another way of spoiling her weekend, when I heard a train coming down the tracks.

As the noise grew, my eye caught the movement of one of the tiny grey underground mice that dwell in the cracks under the platform. It scurried quickly under the rail and bolted for cover as the train rattled onto the platform. As it crossed the open space between the rails, a long grey arm shot out from under the platform, snatched the mouse and vanished. The train rushed in, then slowed along the platform in a squeal of brakes. Passengers looked out from behind the glass as it slowed to walking pace, their expressions turning from hopeful to disappointed as the train accelerated again off into the tunnel without stopping.

"Did anyone else see that?" I asked.

"See what?" said Joseph.

I looked at where the mouse had been. "There was a mouse, under the train. And then–"

"Don't worry about them, sir. They live here all the time. They only come out when it's quiet."

I thought about trying to explain about the grey arm, then thought better of it. Maybe I really did need a check-up. "Can we go up now? I think I'm ready."

They helped me to my feet and walked me to the escalators at the gentlest of paces, accompanied by the attendant. The escalator was still working and carried us up to the ticket hall, where we were escorted through the side gate and around to the street exit. Up the stairs at street level the mesh gates had been pulled closed, but were pulled back to allow us out into the listless crowd waiting for the station to re-open. Mark cleared the way while they helped me to the waiting ambulance.

Inside, the ambulance was white and sterile. They insisted that I lay down and was strapped in before driving off. Joseph stayed in the back while Mark went to the driver's seat and used the radio to inform his controller that they were en-route with a conscious patient. Joseph belted himself in and then we were away, siren blaring as the ambulance forced its way into the traffic. We accelerated in a short burst then braked hard as the traffic failed to clear out of the way. The siren wailed at the jammed cars.

Without warning, another stomach cramp twisted violently into my gut, I gasped and squeezed my eyes shut against the pain, pulling against the restraints and grinding my teeth. Then, just as suddenly as it had arrived, it passed. I opened my eyes and the lady was standing over me. She was undoing the belts.

"What are you doing?" I asked her.

"I am trying to get you out of these wretched straps."

"Stop that. I'm supposed to be going to hospital." There was a sound like a low groan coming from the ambulance.

17

"You're not going anywhere. The ambulance is dead, can you not hear it?"

I propped myself up on an elbow as she loosened the webbing. Joseph was slumped against the seat belt, Mark had collapsed over the steering wheel and the ambulance siren was making a sound like a stranded white whale.

"How did you get in here?"

"I followed you. I didn't have to walk very far with you in here. As soon as you had a spasm, all the power died and the ambulance stopped. That noise is the siren using up what little power remains. I would turn it off, but I don't know how."

"You're crazy. What have you done to Joseph?"

"He'll be well enough." She grabbed hold of my lapels and hauled me up to a sitting position with surprising strength. "Look, I don't have much time. I need to you to come with me now, away from here and away from the hospital. I don't want anyone looking too closely at you." She flung open the rear door of the ambulance and gestured for me to exit. The sound of car horns blared through the opening from the blocked traffic.

"You're crazy! What are you talking about? I'm not leaving. I'm sick."

"You're fine, you have my word. What are you called?"

"My name is–"

"I didn't ask you what your name is, I asked you what you were called."

"It's the same thing," I told her.

"No," she said, "it really isn't. I shall call you Rabbit."

"I don't care what you call me. I'm going to the hospital."

She shook her head. "No," she said quietly, "you're not."

She grasped my hand in hers. There was a sense of vertigo and a momentary blinding headache.

* * *

When I opened my eyes the ambulance had gone. It was almost dark, the threat of dawn glimmering through the overcast clouds. I looked around, but found only rolling grassland fading away into the darkness. I wiped my long hair back from where it clung to my face in the damp air. Fine rain drifted around me.

Twisting around, I half expected to see the ambulance behind me, but found only empty grassland and patches of boggy turf in near blackness. Apart from the wind, there was no sound at all. The breeze was fickle and gusty, tugging at my buckskin jerkin and linen shirt.

I couldn't see more than twenty feet in the dim light. I stuck my hands out around me, trying to break what must be an illusion. The cold breeze twisted through my fingers. Water started seeping into my boots from the soggy turf.

Where had the lady gone? Where was I?

A sound came. It drifted down the wind, too low for a wolf, too long for a bear. All the hairs on the back of my neck stood on end. It howled, long and low, and the primitive part of my brain that knew about caves and monsters kicked my feet into motion.

I found myself stumbling through the darkness away from that sound. My instinct said, *Hide, make yourself small*. I looked around as I stumbled forward but there was no cover, just stringy tufts of grass and rolling hummocks.

I started running and the howl came again, rolling down the wind after me. Tripping on a tussock of grass, I went down on my knees. Panic brought me up again, my fingers scrabbling in the wiry turf to get up and away. My heart started pounding in my ears as I accelerated away, the long howl louder now as it gained on me. I sprinted, every ounce of energy focused on getting away. Then the headache came again and blinded me.

I crashed into something and went sprawling on the concrete. I was surrounded again by the smell of wet pavement, the distant urban drone of diesel engines and motorbikes. My breath came in harsh barks while my heart drummed a staccato rhythm in my chest. I lay on my back, only thankful that the ground under me was hard and the sound of the hunt had gone. I had beaten it.

A shadow crossed my face and I opened my eyes. It was her.

"I'm so sorry," she said. "It took me a moment to catch up with you."

"What in hell did you do?"

"I used what I called you to create a certain type of reality for you."

"You mean it was real?"

"As real as you made it."

This was insane, but still... "What would have happened if it'd caught me?"

"The same thing that usually happens when wolves run down a rabbit."

"There was only one," I told her.

"You only heard one."

"And it was too big to be a wolf."

"Suddenly you're an expert on how big a wolf can get. Tell me, Rabbit, where did you come by such wisdom?"

I squinted up at her then rolled onto my side, still breathing hard, trying to gather my wits.

"Ah, more cautious now," she said. "Maybe there is some wisdom here after all."

I looked up at her. The harmless old lady look was beginning to wear thin.

"What are you, some kind of witch?"

Her eyes hardened and her expression soured. She reached down to me. I scrabbled backwards to the wall away from her, avoiding her questing touch.

"*That* word," she followed me until my back was against the bricks, "is not a kindly word where I come from."

20

"Sorry, sorry. I didn't mean anything by it."

She withdrew her hand. "I'll thank you not to use it again."

"Fine, whatever you say." She relaxed again, allowing me to look around. "Where are we?"

"Away from the ambulance and the hospital. In an alley. You collided with a dustbin and ended there. It was just as well you came back to yourself or you might have been trapped."

"I was fine until you interfered," I told her. "I was going to the hospital."

Another bout of pain erupted in my abdomen. I curled around it for half a minute or more, immobilised by its intensity. It faded gradually. "Oh God. I'm having another attack. Can't you see?"

"I told you, you are not going to die of a heart attack. Here, let me help you up." She offered her hand.

I looked at it, mistrustfully.

"Have it your own way," she said, withdrawing the hand.

"Who are you?"

"You can call me Blackbird."

"Blackbird? What kind of a name is that?"

"It's as good a name as any I have ever had and it will serve me nicely, thank you."

Her tone was acid, but I didn't care. "What do you want from me?"

"From you? You're not in a position to offer me anything, just now."

"Then why did you follow me? What are you after?"

"When I revived you earlier, I acquired a degree of responsibility for what happens to you."

"I was fine. The ambulance men said I was OK, I just needed a check up."

Another of the stomach cramps twisted inside me and I bent over, momentarily breathless.

She was unconcerned. "Just try to breathe. The aftershocks will diminish shortly."

"Is it my heart?"

"Gracious me, no. Your heart is as strong as an ox and will stay that way for many years to come, should you live that long."

"I thought I had a heart attack."

"You don't remember?"

"Remember what?"

"You were on the platform of the Underground. Your heart failed. You died."

I searched my memory. Those last seconds were curiously blurred, as if my brain didn't want to register what really happened. "I can't have died. I'm here."

"I brought you back. I healed your failing heart and summoned you back into your body, to keep something else from entering and using your corpse. If you were not dead then that other thing could not enter and I would not have to deal with it."

"What kind of 'other thing'?" This was crazy.

"The sort of thing you don't want roaming around in someone else's skin."

"You're talking about... possession?"

"I am talking about reanimation, but yes, in this case they are essentially the same thing. Unfortunately you were already dead and it gained a foothold. I had to heal your heart and summon you back into your body. For a moment I was not quite sure which one of you I had rescued."

"That's what you were asking me, in the tube station – *are you from the other lands?*"

"Had it succeeded, I would have killed it quickly while it was still weak from the crossing."

"But it was me."

"It was you. By the time I reached you, though, it had gained a sense of you. It will know you. It will have some of your knowledge, some of your memories."

"What will it do with them?"

"It will use them to find you."

"And then what?"

22

She looked at me. "It will kill you."

"I don't understand. Why would anyone want to kill me?"

"Because you are not entirely human." She said it so plainly, like it was something she said every day.

"Are you mad? Of course I'm human. What else would I be?" The old woman seemed rational, but then started talking nonsense. Was she serious? She looked serious.

"Here," she said. "Let me help you up. I promise I'll not harm you." She offered her hand again.

I waved her hand away and pushed myself to my feet. I felt light-headed. Perhaps it was from being alive when I ought to be dead.

"You have something on your trousers. It looks like it came from the bin with which you collided."

The sight of my trousers brought me immediately back to earth. "Oh no. This suit was just cleaned. Look at it, it's ruined." There were patches of damp and the dark stain of something putrid was smeared into the knees.

"It is the least of your worries, believe me. If you let me buy you a coffee, I will try to explain."

She walked to the end of the passage, to where it met the street, and waited while I tried to remove the worst of the stain with some half-used kitchen towel that was protruding from a lacerated bin-bag. I wiped the slime from my hands with the remaining piece as best I could.

She turned down the street and walked away suddenly, and I ran to catch up with her. I fell into step as she walked along. Mercifully, the rain had stopped, leaving the streets shiny in the autumn sun.

"Why are you doing this?" I asked her.

"I do not like loose ends," she answered. "They cause difficulty. Are you married?"

"I was. I got divorced last year." It was an old wound, but nearly dying made it freshly painful.

"No children." She made it sound like a statement.

"I have a daughter."

She stopped and stared up at me. "A child?"

"Yes. She's nearly fourteen. I'm picking her up from my ex-wife's tonight. We're going to spend the weekend together."

"A daughter? Well, well." She turned and continued walking, momentarily lost in thought. I followed, crossing Long Acre and heading down St Martin's Lane towards Trafalgar Square.

"What did you mean when you said I wasn't entirely human?" I asked her.

"Somewhere in your family tree there is one who is not human, but something else."

"What kind of 'something else'?"

"A creature of power. A member of the Feyre, a race far older than humanity."

"I don't... The...? Is this some kind of wind-up?"

"You tell me. Did you have a heart attack? Were you cold and dead? Are you a corpse on its way to the mortuary or walking along beside me?"

A faint smile touched her lips. Was she mocking me?

"I think... I think I would know if I wasn't... wasn't human."

"Without Fey blood in your veins, the creature would not have been able to enter your body when you died. It was using your dormant power to bridge the gap between this world and the one it comes from. When I revived you I called to your power, the core of magic within you, and used it to mend your failing heart and bring you back."

We strolled past people on the pavement while she talked in level tones about magic and creatures. Nobody paid us the slightest attention. It was unreal.

"How did you... I mean, what...?" It made no sense. "This is... Why should I believe you, any of this?"

"There was a creature waiting for someone like you, in another place nearby but entirely separate. It was waiting to cross over into our world. It was already in

24

the process of taking your body when I found you. By bringing you back, I prevented it from completing the crossing, but it will have gained a sense of you. It will know you and will be able to predict where you will go and what you will do. Now it knows you, it will come for you, sooner or later."

"What does it want from me?"

"I told you, it wants you dead."

"Why? What did I do?"

"It wants you dead because of what you are, not what you have done. It knows what you are. As I do."

"So we're back to that. You think I'm... not human."

"The only reason you are not lying dead on the floor in the Underground station right now is because you have an ancestor who was Fey. It is the reason you are alive. When I intervened, I took a degree of responsibility for you and for what happens next. If you were to just wander off then things might become... difficult."

"What do you mean?"

"The magic I woke in you was dormant, but having woken it, it will not sleep again. It is alive in you now and will stay with you until you die, which unfortunately may be quite soon."

"I don't understand. First you tell me I'm healthy, then you tell me I'm going to die. You're not making sense. Which is it?"

"It's both. You're alive because one of your ancestors was not human, that much is certain. The creature that was trying to take your body will know you and will try to find you, that is also certain. It will not be able to cross the gap between our worlds again for some while. It will need a little time to recover, then it must wait for an opportunity to slip across, but when it does it will come for you – and for your daughter."

"My daughter? What has she got to do with this?"

"Rabbit, if you have a Fey ancestor then your daughter does too, of course. You don't need to be a geneticist to work that out. It will want her dead as much as it does you. That is why you must stay away from her, at least for a while. Don't go near her and don't discuss her with anyone, no matter how harmless they appear. You do not want to lead it to your family."

It was bizarre, as if somewhere, at some point in my morning, I had taken a wrong turn. I found myself sifting back through her words looking for the loose strand that would unravel this elaborate tale. Is that how she got her kicks, conning middle-aged men into believing the unbelievable?

"What does it look like?" I asked her.

"A better question would be 'who does it look like?'. The Untainted don't enter our world directly unless they have to. Instead, it will find a host, another body with enough of a thread of magic in it to sustain the crossing. It could be anyone: young, old, fat, thin – anyone." She gestured at the people around us as we crossed the street at the bottom of St Martin's Lane.

"So how am I supposed to know which one is trying to kill me?"

"So you believe me now?"

"Let's say I'm humouring you."

She sighed. "Their perception of our world is governed by their own time, so they will appear a little uncoordinated, as if they were drunk, or hungover. You will have to be watching carefully to notice the difference, though." She suddenly changed her pace and led the way to a coffee and sandwich shop. I followed her inside and she ordered for both of us, two strong coffees, mine with sugar and hers without.

I rested my hand on her arm. "How did you know I took sugar?"

"I didn't, but it is good for shock – and dying counts, do you not think?" She glanced up at me then took a small purple purse from her bag and paid the girl, all in coins.

The coffee shop was crowded and noisy with nowhere to sit, so we took the coffees outside where the staff were wiping down the chairs and tables. The lady held the door open while I carried the tray. She led the way to the table furthest away from the few other people where the broad pavement sloped down to the dominating presence of the church of St Martin-in-the-Fields. I put the tray on the table and she handed me my coffee as we sat down opposite one another.

I took the opportunity to look at her more closely. She was around retirement age, one of those silver-haired ladies who have worked and now have the resources to lunch in the city whenever they please. Ladies like her were common around the National Gallery and Covent Garden, and I would not have picked her out as anything unusual.

She wore a wool coat with a tweedy texture to it which looked well worn, but not worn out. At her neck was a paisley patterned silk scarf that was wrapped inside her coat. Her hands clasped the cardboard cup. They had the soft texture of liver spots and freckles that you associate with older ladies with fair skin. Her eyes were clear and blue-grey, and her hair was grey in a short but elegantly soft style. She watched me, removing the lid from her coffee and holding the cup underneath her chin, allowing the steam to rise around her face.

"If you knew somehow that you only had a single day left to live," she asked me then, "what would you do with that day?"

"What? A single day?"

"One only," she nodded.

"I'd spend it with my daughter doing all the things you should do with your children before you die: wild rides on the fairground, eat too much ice cream, paddle on the seashore…"

"What if you could not be with your daughter? What then?"

"I don't know. Hmm. Maybe just carry on and have a normal day."

"Just carry on? Is there no one else you would spend your last day with?"

"You needn't look like that. I have responsibilities. My job is important, and not just to me. My team rely on me. That's why I have to go to work."

"You are failing to understand me. If you go back to your job, your life expectancy can be measured in hours. More importantly, what are you going to do there?"

"What I always do: manage my team, work on my projects–"

She burst out laughing. "Oh, Rabbit, you are precious."

"What's wrong with that? It's my life!"

"It *was* your life." She considered me for moment. "I need to show you something, but I need to use the facilities first." She pushed her chair back and stood. "I will be back in a few moments."

"Will I be safe here, all by myself?" I was suddenly conscious of how exposed I was, sat at the edge of the open square.

"That depends. If this is a trick of some kind then you'll be as safe as ever you were. If this is real then no, you're never going to be safe again. Get used to it."

TWO

She turned and walked away across the pavement, slipping her hands into her pockets as she walked up the steps into the coffee shop, leaving me alone at the edge of Trafalgar Square.

I looked around nervously. People walked across the square as they always did in the rarer moments when we were blessed with autumn sunshine. They talked or just stood around taking in the view, caught up in the mass of humanity.

I sat back in my chair and tried to compose myself. Her story had spooked me, I had to admit, and left me feeling paranoid. I was much more conscious of the people around me, those that appeared to be going somewhere and those wandering aimlessly. They were probably tourists, visitors to the capital enjoying a day of autumn sunshine. I watched them anyway.

A fair-haired couple, she with coloured ribbons tangled in her hair and he with matted dreadlocks, wandered arm-in-arm past the tables. They didn't look very typical, but they could be Australian, or mad, or in love. They didn't look like assassins from another world – but what would an assassin look like? Slightly drunk or hung-over she'd said, so that only included about ten per cent of the population of central London.

My scan of the crowds caught a young woman emerging from the coffee shop. She made her way down the steps carefully, her high heels precarious on the polished surface. She hooked her bag over her shoulder and strode out though the tables, heels clicking and glossy smile flashing as she negotiated her way past one of the staff clearing tables. I noticed the men behind her checking out the rear view as she passed. She was quite something. Her coat was caught together with only one button and fell over the flared skirt that stopped well short of her knees.

She walked right past me and I had to agree, the guys weren't wrong.

She stopped and looked over to Nelson's Column, then back up towards Leicester Square. Taking a piece of paper from her coat pocket, she consulted it. I tried to keep my eyes on the scattered wanderers around the square, but she was very distracting.

She turned to look back at where I was sat and said to me, "Is Leicester Square in that direction?" She pointed a finger towards Charing Cross. Her voice was deeper than I had expected, but it hit the right notes. She had a mass of tangled red curls framing her face. That colour couldn't be natural, could it?

"Excuse me?" she said again, speaking more slowly and distinctly. "Is Leicester Square—"

"In that direction? No. Sorry, I was miles away. That's so rude. Please forgive me." I realised I'd been staring, my manners coming to the rescue at last.

"I thought perhaps you hadn't heard me."

"No, it's OK. I was… Never mind. It's that way, I'm afraid." I pointed in the opposite direction, past the National Portrait Gallery.

She turned one way then the other. "Oh, I thought I knew where I was. Do you mind if I sit for a moment and get my bearings?"

"Well…" I looked around. There were plenty of free

seats, but there was no sign of Blackbird returning yet. In fact, I wasn't even sure she was ever coming back. "Sure. Take a seat."

"Are you alone?" She stepped back to the table and turned a seat sideways to sit down, crossing her legs with a whisper of nylon and placing her bag on the table.

"Yes. No," I added.

She smiled at my confusion, the same glossy smile she'd used before, the heart-stopping one.

"That is, I was with someone." Disappointment crossed her face. "An older friend I was having coffee with. She went to powder her nose."

"Oh, well, if I am interrupting–"

"No, no, it's OK. She'll be a moment or two, I expect."

Her perfect lips curved into happy acceptance and she dipped into her handbag, extracting a small mirror and a lipstick. She checked her make-up, which she must only have done moments before, because it was perfect. Nevertheless, she added a little more gloss to her lips then tucked the items back in her bag.

"You must be local," she commented.

"Sorry?"

"To know where everything is," she explained. Her eyes were green, but not the pond-weed green you sometimes see. This was the sort of sparkling green you find in emeralds. Was she wearing contact lenses?

"Yes, well, not really," I replied, finding myself unable to frame a coherent sentence.

"Do you live nearby?"

"It takes about forty-five minutes to travel back to my place from here, so not exactly nearby, no."

"Do you live alone or with family?" she pressed gently, smoothing invisible flecks of dust from her skirt and showing off glossy nails.

This was closer to territory I wanted to avoid, no matter how distracting she appeared. Blackbird had said not to discuss my family with anyone, no matter how harmless. Was she some sort of spy? If so, I was betting I could run faster than she could in those heels.

"I live alone," I admitted, avoiding mentioning my family. The safer option also happened to be the truth. "I have a flat."

"A flat? It must be nice having space of your own and being able to live as you want, to do whatever takes your fancy." The breeze caught in the organized tangle of her hair, lifting it from her shoulders momentarily. She shifted her chair around so it faced me.

"Do you live with someone else, then?" I asked her.

"Yes, my housemate. She is so untidy." She smiled again, lifting her chin and shaking her head, leaning forwards on the table. Her blouse was casually open at the neck and I could just see the hint of dark lingerie. "You would not believe it."

"I probably would. I'm not the tidiest person, I'm afraid."

She looked at me, making me feel as if I was being sized up for something. Maybe she was deciding how untidy I was.

"I can imagine," she said. "Clothes scattered everywhere. Very untidy." Her lips curved upwars slightly, amused.

Understand that I am not an unattractive man, but my ex-wife will explain at length, given barely half a chance, how unperceptive I can be around women. This, however, was definitely seduction. Her expression made it personal. It was not my clothes that were scattered untidily, but ours.

"You know, it would be lovely if someone who knew the area was prepared to guide me around. As someone who knows his way…"

The suggestion was an offer, and she was incredibly attractive. She watched me considering. The thing was, I wasn't even supposed to be here. I'd only come for coffee because of what had happened and now this woman was propositioning me when I should be going to work.

It really was the strangest morning.

"I'm really sorry," I told her reluctantly, "but I am waiting for my friend and then I have to get to the office."

She gave me that smile again, the one that made my trousers uncomfortably tight. "Well, Rabbit, if you are sure there's nothing you can be tempted with?" She coiled a twist of hair around a delicate finger.

"I'm sorry, but I'm quite– *What* did you say?"

"I asked if there was nothing that could tempt you." She leaned forward over the table, displaying more than she had before, laying her hands flat on the table and meeting my gaze with those cool green eyes, levelly, calmly.

"You called me Rabbit," I accused.

"Is that your name? How amusing." She smiled, looking away, but there was more to that smile than I had first thought. She was playing with me.

"What do you want?" I glanced sideways, reconsidering whether I could really outpace her.

"What do I want? Now that's a big question." She leaned forward conspiratorially, lowering her tone. "I want you to believe me, Rabbit. I want you to understand that what you see is not what you get, not anymore, not now, not ever. I need you to understand that appearances – yours, mine, and theirs – can be very deceptive."

I struggled to unravel what she was saying, trying to make sense of the words emerging from those beautiful lips.

I looked back to the coffee shop to see if Blackbird was returning, but there was still no sign of her. Looking back at the young woman in front of me, I searched for something that would help me understand what was going on. I was beginning to feel as if I was standing on the edge of an invisible abyss.

Trying to keep my voice down, I asked, "Tell me who you are."

"Who do you think I am?" There was a mischievous curve to her lips.

"Did you meet Blackbird? Did she put you up to this?"

"You're still not getting it, are you, Rabbit?"

"What don't I get, exactly? Who are you?" I was preparing to run for it, readying myself to get away from the wrongness of it all.

"I told you," she said quietly. "You know who I am, but you don't want to accept it. You know who you are, but you don't want to accept that either. You keep denying the existence of anything that doesn't fit within your cosy little world-view."

"Blackbird... But... If you're Blackbird, how come you're wearing the body of this young woman?"

"*How dare you!*"

For a second, I thought she was going to slap me, her words ringing out across the tables, attracting more attention than I thought we wanted. "How *dare* you suggest I would do such a thing?" She sat back and moved her chair sideways again, cheeks flushed, her breathing harsh as she controlled her anger.

I was distracted by sniggering from the group of guys near the door and my cheeks flushed in response. They obviously thought I'd suggested something quite different. I gave them a dirty look and they made a minimal effort to compose themselves. We were making quite an impression. I turned back to Blackbird, or at least I was beginning to think it was Blackbird, and found her grim and unhelpful.

"Look, just tell me. Are you Blackbird or not? You still haven't answered me."

"Of course I'm Blackbird. How obvious do I have to be?" She sounded petulant, sulky even.

"More obvious than you are being, plainly."

She cast me a disdainful look.

Exasperated, I kept my voice low to avoid being overheard. "OK, so I accept that you're Blackbird, but looking like someone much younger. What was I supposed to think? You've just gone to a lot of trouble to explain how the body-snatching thing works, after a close personal experience on my part, I might add, then you turn up looking like…"

"Like what?" She softened, her mood brightening like the clouds moving off the sun.

"Like a high…" her expression shadowed, "mainte-nance, fashionable… girl, out for a day's sightseeing." I adapted my words in a feat of mental juggling I hadn't realised I had the skill for. This was like walking a verbal tightrope.

"Do you not like it?"

It was the same question as "Does this make me look fat?" and I had never mastered that one.

"It's maybe a little overdone, isn't it, for someone your age?" As soon as the words left my mouth, I knew I'd said the wrong thing. So much for verbal juggling.

"My age? And what exactly is my age, Rabbit?"

"I'm sorry, I just meant you look a lot younger than… before." I tailed off. I looked back over to the coffee shop, still hoping that Blackbird would be coming down the steps, exposing whoever was sitting opposite me as an impostor.

"Well?" She had me skewered on the question.

"About fifty-five or maybe sixty?" I really couldn't win at this.

I was surprised when she burst out laughing.

"Bless you, Rabbit. I am *far* older than that." She flashed that heart-stopping smile at me again and I shifted uncomfortably. My heart had stopped enough for one day.

I turned back to her. "Can't you change back or something?" I was disconcerted, both by the knowledge that Blackbird didn't look the way she should and also by the fact that I had been considering letting her seduce me. The idea of spending intimate time with someone more than twenty years my senior was disconcerting.

"You don't like me this way?" She was about to sulk again.

"No, in fact it's quite the opposite, it's very distracting."

"Are you sure you would not like a little distraction, just for a while?" She twisted the curl around her finger, smiling wistfully.

"Look! I really can't deal with this teasing. I'm not in the mood."

"You were in the mood earlier."

I dropped my voice back down to a reasonable level, having suddenly become aware that I had raised it. "Would you kindly change back to the way you were so we can continue this discussion in a civilised manner?"

"All right." She collected her bag from the table and stood up, stepping around the table and leaned down to whisper close to my ear. "Give me a moment. I have to slip into something a little more comfortable. For you, that is."

She turned and walked back towards the coffee shop, skirt swinging with her walk, legs long and ankles slim, heels clicking on the hard paving. As she approached the glass door, one of the guys at the table nearby got up to open it for her. She smiled, exchanging small words of thanks and entered, lost behind the reflection of the glass. The guy went back to his mates and there was a degree of ribald teasing as he joined them.

If only they knew.

He didn't sit down again, but they stood up around him, gathering their things together and ribbing one another as they moved past the table where I sat.

"You've got your hands full there, mate," said one as he passed, grinning.

"Wish I had," remarked the one who'd opened the door.

"In your dreams." The last one passed me, addressing his comment to his friend's back.

I watched them go, as they nudged and jostled each

other, laughing. I had never had friends like that, never felt comfortable or at ease in the shifting rivalry of peer groups. My early managers had said I was not a team player, but I had made a career out of playing with teams. My ability to see through the mire of conflicting information, to focus effort on the elements that represented paydirt, had made me successful. I was well-off, if not actually rich, and while I was sure it wasn't just wealth and status that had attracted my ex-wife, I knew it had played its part. What I had perhaps been slow to understand was that being successful couldn't sustain a relationship. My success had given me power and influence, but marriages weren't built on power, they were built on trust. And power trusted no one.

Still, I had my daughter. She was power incarnate as far as I was concerned. I was coiled around her little finger and she knew it. Unfortunately, my ex-wife knew it too and it was a constant source of friction between us.

"What on earth possessed you to buy her those?" she'd demanded, when we returned from one of our weekend jaunts with her showing off sequinned hipster jeans with laces down the front.

"It was what she wanted," I would always say, which would spark the age-old row about the difference between what she wanted and what she needed. In my view, what she needed was at least one parent who would occasionally give her what she wanted. The problem was it was never my ex. She always ended up fulfilling needs, not wants.

It wasn't fair, but then none of it was. My ex-wife played single parent while I played absent father, roles neither of us wanted.

Thinking of absence, I realised that no one knew where I was and I had meetings organised for today. My team would be wondering what had happened to me. I pulled my mobile phone from my pocket, intending to call the office, but then stopped when I couldn't think what I would say to them.

If I called and said, "Hi, I've just had a heart attack, but I'm fine now" they would want me in a hospital for tests, assuming they believed me. Blackbird had told me my heart was fine, so why wasn't I at my desk, doing my job?

I looked at the signal on my mobile, showing a solid connection with the network. It wasn't my phone that was disconnected. It was me.

Blackbird returned, looking exactly as she had before, prompting me to look again to see whether there really were two of them. She sat down opposite, putting her bag at her feet and leaned her forearms on the table.

"Who are you calling?" Her eyes were back to their natural grey.

"I was going to call work and let them know I'll be late."

"It would not be a wise thing to go into work, Rabbit. The Untainted are patient and they will wait their chance, but if someone gets in the way they will just kill them. You'll be putting the lives of your colleagues at risk."

"I still don't understand why they would want to kill me. I know you said it was because I had this... Fey blood, but why?"

"It's complicated."

"Try me."

"There are no simple explanations. I can't begin to explain it all."

"So I just have to take your word for it, do I?"

She sighed. "The Untainted are pure-bloods. They fought to keep the blood-lines of the Feyre free from the taint of humanity. Half-breeds like you and I are a symbol of their failure to maintain that purity. We are the reason they were exiled, the source of their pain, the justification for the continuing conflict between the courts. Simply by existing you are a thorn in their side, and they will pluck you out."

"So will they come for you too?"

Her expression darkened. "They would if they could. I stay away from them, try not to get involved." She looked meaningfully at me. "Unfortunately, as I said, I gained some responsibility for what happens to you."

"So maybe I could stay away from them too? Like you do."

"I told you, it gained a sense of you. It will be able to find you."

"So what am I supposed to do? It's not just me, there's my daughter too. She doesn't even know they'll be looking for her."

Blackbird paused, considering. It left me wondering how far her responsibilities went.

Finally, she spoke. "I can take you to see someone, someone who may know what to do. Maybe if you can join one of the six courts then it will help. The courts provide justice and protection. Any Fey who is not a member of the courts does not receive their protection. If you're killed then it is just unfortunate. No one will avenge your death or demand blood-price for your heart."

"My heart?"

"It is a figure of speech."

I was relieved to hear it.

"Mostly," she added as an afterthought. "But the point is that the courts may be able to protect you from the Untainted and from other Fey who wish you harm, at least for a while."

"And my daughter? What about her?"

"She's as safe as she can be at the moment, as long as you stay away from her."

"Will the courts protect her too?"

"They may, but meanwhile neither of you are bound to any court and therefore receive no one's protection."

"Not even yours?"

She paused, then continued, "There is a way you may receive my protection. You could bind yourself to me as my servant for nine-times-nine years of your life, during which time you will do no one's will but mine. Is that what you want?"

"Eighty-one years? I'll be dead by then."

"You may be dead a lot sooner than that. It is one way to survive. By binding yourself to me you would receive the court's protection as it extends to me and I would be responsible for your life. But when I say you would have no will but mine, I mean it. Any power you possess would be mine to command and if I told you to stick your head in a bucket of sewage and breathe in, you would do it."

"And what about my daughter?"

"She would have to take her chances, as you did."

"Then I can't. You understand?"

"It is a wise decision. Wiser than you know."

"I'm sorry? If you knew I shouldn't do it, why tempt me with the offer?"

"Life is full of choices. If you did not know it was a possibility then you could not choose. As you have chosen, your life may be short, but it will be your own. Had you decided to bind yourself to me then your life would be mine for the next eighty-one years. You will live longer than that, if you survive, but those years would have been mine, not yours. You would probably never see your daughter again."

"Then I made the right choice."

"Perhaps. We make the choices we make. For as long as you live, your will and your power will be your own."

"My power? You mean I'll be able to do magic too?" This whole conversation was starting to freak me out again.

"Don't get excited. Your gifts may be quite small: a talent for lighting fires, perhaps, or a way with growing things."

"Like green fingers?"

"Without knowing your heritage there's no way to predict what it will be. You will find out in the next couple of days, if you live that long. It will take a little time

40

to manifest properly. Your body adjusts quicker than your mind, especially as you have come into it so unexpectedly."

"How will I know when it happens?"

She shook her head. "Each individual's experience is different, Rabbit. It could be that you will find that you can make things disappear in plain sight, or that you develop an intuition for how things should work and ways of fixing them. It could happen suddenly or develop slowly over weeks, months maybe."

"Is there a way of making it happen faster?"

"It isn't a matter of making it happen, Rabbit. It's already happened. The power is there within you, all you have to do is reach for it. Your mind, though, will not accept it. Like suddenly having an extra sense, your mind ignores it because it does not know what to do with it. Once you make that connection you will be able to bind your power to your intent, to make things happen because you want them to, bend reality around your will. But until you make the connection it will remain inactive. How long that takes depends on how much you believe in it, and how much you want it."

I laughed.

"What's so funny?"

"Me. I'm sitting here talking about magic powers as if they're real. I'm about as magical as this table."

"There you are, you see? As long as your mind denies your power, your magic will remain quiescent, unsummoned. The truth is that long before your gift can flower, the Untainted will come for you. You need to be prepared."

"Maybe I can use my power to defend myself?"

"This is not the first time this has happened, Rabbit. You are not the only one to come into their power in the middle of their life. I helped another in your position. She wanted to fight."

"What happened to her?"

She scanned across the crowd, as if in search of a familiar face. "I never saw her again. Maybe she is out there somewhere, never staying anywhere long, always moving."

"You don't believe that."

She shifted her attention back to me, looking straight into my eyes. "No, I don't. If she fought then she died. If you fight, you will die also. These are full Fey and they are old. Magic responds to need, that's true, but the Untainted are among the most feared and powerful of the Feyre, creatures of nightmare. When they come for you, do not try and fight them. Run."

"Where to?"

"It matters not. Wherever you go they will find you. Just keep running and hope they do not catch you."

"And if they do?"

"Then it's over. You will die."

THREE

"So what am I going to do? I can't keep running for ever."

"I'll take you to someone who may be able to offer you counsel. In the meantime you should call your office and tell them you won't be in. If you make it to Monday you can think again but that's a long way away, right now."

It was Thursday. How far away could the Monday be? Still, she had convinced me to make the call to work. I extracted my mobile from my jacket pocket and flipped it open to get the number from the speed-dials.

It rang twice. "Good morning, Project Management Office."

"Hi, Jackie."

"Niall? Is that you? Where are you?"

"Hi, Jackie, sorry I've had some problems this morning and I'm not going to make it into the office. I need you to do a couple of things for me."

"But I've got the electrical engineers downstairs in reception waiting for you and there are a pile of phone messages from the site manager. He's been calling since seven-thirty."

I had made the mistake of calling her without any clear plan of what I would say.

"Jackie? Sorry, I know there are problems. Look, I've had a death in the family."

"Are you all right? Are Alex and Katherine OK?"

"They're fine. It's not them, thank God, but I'm the only one who can deal with it. Apparently there are circumstances and someone has to sort out the affairs."

She reminded me of a host of commitments I had made and asked me what she was supposed to do with them.

"I'll have to deal with them next week, if I'm back."

"If you're back? You have the fourth floor conference room booked for the heating and lighting review on Monday morning. What am I supposed to tell them?"

"Ask Jim if he'll talk to them." I named my deputy and second-in-command. "We only need an estimate at this stage. We can confirm prices later."

"So when will you be back? Jim is going to ask." She was right, he would.

"I don't know how long. A few days, I guess. I'll probably be back sometime next week. Could you tell Human Resources I'm taking unexpected leave? Anyone else, just call them and put them off for me. If there's anything that looks really urgent, ask Jim if he'll step in and cover."

"I'll ask him, Niall, but he is already complaining that he's over-committed."

"Thanks, Jackie." I was about to say I had another call waiting, but the lie stuck in my throat. It was a ruse I had used many times to cut short awkward calls, but I just couldn't say the words. I settled on an alternative. "You're a treasure. I don't know what I'd do without you."

There was a stream of further questions that I couldn't hope to answer without a lot more time.

"You're just going to have to cope, I'm really sorry. Ask Jim if you're not sure. OK. OK, bye. Bye." I closed the connection and sighed.

"That is something else I wanted to tell you," said Blackbird. "Lying isn't the same any more. The Feyre can tell when someone else is lying and they don't lie themselves. It's too…"

"Uncomfortable?"

"That's a good description. It's not that you couldn't lie, but it provokes a sense of discord that rankles in your heart. The more you use your magic, the stronger it will get. You're much better off telling the truth. Magic and truth are siblings, which is why true names have power."

"You might have mentioned it before I called the office," I suggested.

"There's so much I haven't told you, Rabbit, so much you need to know. I don't entirely know where to begin."

I was beginning to realise that, as much as I found that untruth rankled in my own heart, the words of others also held the same note. Blackbird wasn't lying. In fact it threw everything she'd told me into a new light. It briefly occurred to me that this might be yet another layer to this elaborate deception but I had felt it for myself. I knew it was so.

"You should make one more call before we go," she advised.

"Go? Go where?"

"We can't stay in one place for too long, Rabbit – or rather you can't."

"OK. Who should I call?"

"Your ex-wife. Tell her you can't come and collect your daughter this evening."

"Blackbird, I can't tell her that. We've already had one argument about it this morning."

"Do you value your daughter's life? You'd be putting them both in danger. Is that what you wish?"

"You know it's not, but what can I say to her? She already thinks I'm unreliable, unpredictable and a host of other words beginning with 'un'."

"Find a version of the truth she can accept," suggested Blackbird.

I opened my phone again then placed it on the table, looking at it. I really didn't want to make this call, though in my heart I knew I had no choice. I couldn't look after my daughter in these circumstances. I picked up the phone and stood up, excusing myself from Blackbird for a moment and walked a little way away across the open pavement to gain some privacy.

I took a deep breath and rang her. The phone buzzed for a while without answer. Finally she picked up.

"Yes?" Her voice was cold and curt.

"Kath, it's Niall."

"I know who it is. Your number comes up on the phone."

"I need to talk to you about tonight, about the weekend."

"We've had this discussion, Niall. You're coming to collect her after you finish work, whatever time. That's what we agreed."

"I know, and you know I hate to let you down."

She paused, then said, "I know you're going to."

"Kath, this is more complicated than you realise. Something happened this morning."

"Was it something more important than your own daughter?"

"It concerns Alex as well."

"What do you mean?"

"I mean, if I come and get Alex, I'll be putting her in danger."

"What do you mean? What kind of danger?"

"There are some people after me."

"After you? What kind of people? Niall, have you been drinking?"

"I'm quite serious, Katherine, and no, I haven't been drinking. I'm very sober right now. Look, I know it sounds preposterous but you have to believe me. It isn't safe."

"What are you talking about? You just think you can make up some story and it will all go away, is that it?

Good ol' Kath. She's always there when I want to go gallivanting off somewhere. She doesn't mind. She's used to being the housekeeper, the drudge, the domestic. Is that it?"

"No, it isn't like that. Something happened to me on the underground this morning. I nearly died. There was an ambulance. I had to be revived."

"Where are you now?"

She could probably hear the traffic on the Charing Cross Road.

"I never made it into the office. I'm not going in. There was a woman, she rescued me."

"I might have know there'd be a woman involved."

"Oh, please. She's about sixty, OK?"

"Well, I suppose that's a bit old, even for you."

I sighed. Despite Katherine's accusations I had never been unfaithful to her. "Look, she's a doctor. She revived me. I collapsed on the platform and she was the only one who helped."

"Where are you? A hospital?"

"No, I'm in Trafalgar Square."

"Well, it can't have been that serious then, can it?"

"Listen, Kath. I need you to understand. I've got involved in something unexpected. There are some people who are trying to find me. I can't go to the hospital and I can't have Alex with me."

"Are you in trouble with the police?"

"No. There's no police involved."

"Then go to them. They can protect you."

"It isn't like that. The police would think I was nuts."

"They're not the only ones."

"This is *serious*, Kath. Do you want Alex to be in danger? Do you want her harmed?" The other end went silent. "I can't be with her, Kath. I'd be putting her in danger and I can't do that."

"What have you done, Niall?"

"Look," I took a deep breath. "I just need you to explain to Alex that I can't be there tonight. She'll be expecting me and I don't want to let her down, but—"

"Oh, so you don't want to let her down."

"Or you, OK? It's too dangerous. These people may be following me and I don't want them anywhere near the two of you. In fact," an idea occurred to me, "could you go away for the weekend?"

"What? I was planning to go away. Remember?"

It was suddenly apparent to me that she was lying. Her words sounded sour, somehow, filled with deception. Why would she lie to me about something like that? I shook myself. It didn't matter. I just needed her to look after Alex.

"I know, I know, but for me, could you take her away with you? Take her to the coast, maybe somewhere in Europe?"

"Europe? I haven't got that kind of money and you damn well know it, Niall Petersen."

"I'll pay for it," I volunteered.

"Well, I'm very pleased that you can afford to spend weekends swanning off to Europe, but we have other priorities in this house." Her voice had taken on its familiar sarcastic tinge. I couldn't afford to get tangled in this well-rehearsed debate right now.

"I can afford it if it means Alex doesn't get kidnapped," I stated coldly.

"What do you mean, kidnapped?"

"I mean taken away from you, and me. Hurt. Harmed."

"You're not serious?" She sounded frightened now. "What kind of trouble have you dragged us into, Niall?"

"I don't know. I'm just trying to be very careful with the people I care about and I care about the two of you." I think some of the emotion in my voice travelled down the phone line because it went very quiet. "Are you still there?"

"Yes. I'm here." There was a further pause. "Where can we go?" All of a sudden she was taking me seriously.

"I don't know, and don't tell me. It's better I don't

know." Echoes of my conversation with Blackbird came back to me. "Use the internet, book one of those last-minute city breaks somewhere, go today."

"I can't just drop everything, Niall."

I knew she could. "Yes you can," I insisted.

"You really are serious, aren't you? My God."

"Yes I am."

"What do I tell Alex?"

"Tell her it's a surprise trip."

"Not about that, about you?"

"Tell her I love her." My voice broke at the end of the sentence and I had to stop and breathe for a moment.

"Niall? Niall, for God's sake, what have you fallen into?"

"I don't know and I don't want either of you involved. Take your mobile with you and I'll call you in a few days." A thought occurred to me. "When I call, I'll ask about the dog, understand?"

"We don't have a dog."

"I know. If I don't ask about the dog, don't say anything. Especially, don't say where you are or what you're doing. In fact, just hang up. And if you see me, make sure it's me, understand?"

"What do you mean, make sure it's you?"

"I mean these people, they can make themselves look like other people." I was sounding a bit strange now, even to myself. "Look, just get me to remember something only we would know, to make sure I am who you think I am."

"Who I think you are?" She was starting to sound sceptical again.

"Just do it for me, OK?"

"Niall? What are you going to do?"

A little part of me was glad she still cared enough to worry what happened to me.

"I'll be all right. I'll have it sorted out in a few days. I'll call you on the mobile when the coast is clear. OK?"

"OK."

"And if I don't call, don't come looking for me. Understand?"

"If you don't call me, I'm going to the police."

There was an edge of determination to her voice that made me feel momentarily proud of her. "OK. You do that." Maybe it would do some good.

"Niall…?" Everything that remained between us, despite all the harsh words and hurtful silences, hung in the pause after that word.

"I know, Kath. You take care of each other."

"Bye."

"Bye."

The connection closed, leaving me standing alone and apart.

I walked back across the paving to the table where Blackbird waited. She looked up as I approached.

"All settled?"

"Yes. She's going to take her away for the weekend."

"That would probably be for the best, Rabbit. Are you ready?"

"What for?"

"A little walk, and then perhaps an introduction or two. It is about time you met some of your new brethren." She stood up, tucking the chair neatly back under the table and leaving the paper cups at one side where they could easily be collected.

"Is this the person you said could help me?"

"Perhaps. They will at least be able to offer you guidance. Whether you act on that guidance is up to you."

"Another one of your choices?"

"Life is choices, Rabbit. We are defined by the choices we make."

I stood up and followed her to the edge of Trafalgar Square and then back up St Martin's Lane.

"So what does one do when one is introduced to one of the Feyre? Shake hands?"

"Touch is an intimate thing amongst the Feyre. You don't touch another Fey unless you're invited."

"But you touched me." It wasn't meant as a criticism, but she gave me a hard look.

"The other circumstance when one touches another Fey is when one is using power, Rabbit, or when fighting or killing. That is why it is considered discourteous."

"So you touch someone to do magic on them... to them?"

"Some of our gifts require touch, and touch can enhance other gifts, making them stronger. Some of it works without touch, or even presence."

"You can use power over a distance?"

"Some can. The spell that binds each Fey to their court works regardless of distance, or even presence. A Fey who broke that spell would risk their life, even if they were a world away, like the Untainted."

We continued along our route through the back lanes and side alleys of Covent Garden. There would appear to be a dead end then we would turn a corner and find a gate or the way through a fire escape. People didn't leave their back entrances open in central London because they didn't want drunks or druggies hanging around the fire escape, yet all of these opened to her hand.

"Are you using magic to open these gates?" I asked her.

"Stick to the path, Rabbit. That way is safer." She hadn't answered my question.

We wound our way in a loose spiral around Covent Garden, with me catching occasional glimpses of landmarks I knew and several times finding myself walking in the opposite direction to the one I thought we were going in.

"Do we have to come this way?"

"The straightest path is not the shortest," she said.

"What does that mean? Are we talking some mystical geometry here? Surely the shortest path between two points is a straight line?"

"That depends on what is between you and your destination."

"So what would be between us and our destination?"

"This way is safer," she said. "Believe me."

She squeezed her way past a fence post and around the back of a huge wheelie-bin into the rear courtyard of an office block. Two curious smokers, ostracised to the outside, watched us thread our way through and then along the back of the building and through a hole in the fence to the next.

"Now they've seen us, the hole won't be there next time."

"Yes, it will. They won't remember seeing us."

"Why? Did you do something to their memories?"

My voice fell to a hush as she approached the corner of the building more stealthily. Two pigeons were strutting around each other in a doorway, but there didn't appear to be any other hazard to be wary of.

"I didn't do anything to their memory. I used my glamour, the part of my magic that affects my appearance, to make us unremarkable. By the time they've finished their cigarettes, the conversation will have moved on to something else and they won't think enough about us to mention it to anyone. "

"So are you using your... glamour to affect my appearance too?" She was walking slowly up behind the pigeons.

"Glamour is the least of Fey magic. It allows us to alter our appearance to suit our surroundings or our circumstances. It's all a matter of knowing how you look and willing it to be so. It's a bit like driving, it takes practice, but once you know how, you don't even think about it. As far as they are concerned you are standing in my shadow, in a manner of speaking. The impression it leaves can spill over."

She took a soft brown sack from her bag, then reached down and lifted one of the pigeons off the pavement. The other looked bemused, as if its playmate had vanished. After a moment it flew upwards towards the strip of sky overhead. Blackbird eased the docile pigeon into the sack.

"Why are we catching pigeons?"

"It's a gift."

"Do you mean the catching of them, or that the pigeon itself is a gift?"

"It's bad manners to turn up on someone's doorstep when you haven't seen them for months and not have something to offer." She opened the door, stepping out onto the edge of Covent Garden Piazza. "Which reminds me, you need to do a little shopping."

"I do?"

She opened the alleyway door and strolled out into the open square as if we hadn't just been furtively sidling around the back of offices. I followed and the door slammed shut behind us, an anonymous doorway in a row of Georgian houses.

"Oh, I've missed this. It's one of the old places." Her mood lightened as she crossed onto the cobble stoned plaza.

I corrected her. "It's not as old as people think, actually. The flower market is only late nineteenth century."

"And why do you think they built a flower market here?"

"Well, I guess it was part of the original settlement. Maybe there were market gardens here once?"

"Oh, there were gardens here, convent gardens actually, and there was a market here long before Christianity and for much more than flowers. Herbs and potions, talismans and wardings, you could buy anything here, once." She stepped up onto the paving around the covered market and breathed in as if inhaling a heady scent.

"Blackbird, if you don't mind me asking, how old are you, exactly?"

"Didn't I tell you it was rude to ask someone's age?" She arched an eyebrow at me, but I was prepared for her evasion this time.

"No, I don't think that's actually what you said. I think you asked me what age I thought you were and then, when I told you, you laughed and said you were a lot older than that, but you never told me how much."

"Perhaps I thought you were being nosey." The comment was not harshly made and left just enough of an opening for me to ask once more.

"Are you going to tell me?"

"No, I don't think so, except to say I have rolled in the buttercups here and come away dusted in their pollen. I have slept here under the stars on the solstice and been gifted with dreams of the future and I have fought for my life here and come away bloodied, but unharmed. It is a place that has been special to me for a long time." Her words hung in the air despite the milling tourists that passed us by, unaware of her reminiscences.

"Buttercups, huh?" I mused.

"Trust you to latch on to that." But the smile she flashed me was one that hinted of the young woman in the square.

She walked through the meandering tourists and I followed her, walking past numerous stalls until we came to one selling semi-precious jewellery. We stood waiting while an elderly couple debated the merits of a haematite pendant versus a pair of olivine earrings.

The stallholder was a middle-aged woman with fair wavy hair which fell around her shoulders. She wore a peasant skirt and a bronze top with an open neck. Her earrings were made from coloured feathers and beads and her belt was a band of interwoven colours with more beads strung from it. If this were the Sixties then she would have been one of the flower people. Her face was lined as if care-worn and she looked pensive; worried even. Then she smiled and twenty years vanished. Her eyes were alight with humour and her creases became laughter lines.

We waited until the couple had made their decision and their tiny gift-wrapped parcel was handed over. She wished them a good day and turned to us.

"Hello, Blackbird." To my surprise, she walked around the front of the stall and embraced Blackbird with affection, which Blackbird returned. She had told me that the Feyre didn't touch others, but here was Blackbird greeting this woman like a sister.

"How's everything?" she asked Blackbird. Her voice was deep for a woman and had a worn quality, as if it had once been soft and low and someone had taken sandpaper to it.

"Things are good," said Blackbird, holding onto her hands for a moment. "I would like to introduce you to someone. This is Rabbit. Rabbit, this is Megan."

She turned to me and extended a hand in greeting. "Pleased to meet you, Rabbit."

I took her hand, figuring that if Blackbird had embraced her then it must be OK. Her hand was warm and, like her voice, had a delicate roughness to it.

"Pleased to meet you too."

Closer to her, I realised that what I had thought were beads were actually polished stones. Her necklace, earrings and even her belt were adorned with small stones, carefully matched for shape and colour.

"Megan and I have known each other for some time, haven't we, Megan?"

"It's been a while, Megan agreed, "but it all goes by so fast. I can't keep track," she admitted, shaking her head and leaning back against the stall.

"Anyway, this isn't entirely a social call. Rabbit would like to choose some stones from your excellent selection."

"I would, would I?"

"Have a look and see if there's any that take your fancy," Megan gestured across the selection.

"It is a test of sorts. You cannot pass or fail, but it may tell me something," said Blackbird.

"Is it something you should know?" Blackbird appeared to have my interests at heart, but there were still too many unknowns for me not to ask the question.

"Well said, Rabbit, and by your choice I will do you no harm." She said it as a promise or a vow, and I believed her. After all, if she lied to me I thought I would know.

"How many?"

"As many as you will, and no more."

Megan gave me a complicit smile but offered no help.

I turned to the semi-precious stones set out on the table, searching for obvious clues. They were all nicely shaped, though not completely regular. Megan plainly had a gift for selecting ones that were attractive because they were imperfect.

A stone in a cotton-lined rectangular box caught my attention. It was a lozenge with brown and gold stripes that glowed with an inner light. I lifted it from its box and was slightly startled when Megan held out a black suede pouch for me to drop it into. I let it fall into the soft pocket and she retracted it, waiting for me to choose again.

The second choice was easier as I had more idea as to what I was looking for now. My gaze settled on a lump of minty rock with a sparkly surface. I collected it and dropped it into the proffered pouch. I glanced at Blackbird but she had a watchful withdrawn expression.

My third choice leapt out at me when I spotted it amongst the stones at one side. It was stratified like the first, but had verdant green hardness that stood out amongst the others. It joined the rest in the black pouch. For the next one I struggled, scanning the rows of boxes for some minutes until I lit upon a dark red stone, deeply embedded and sulking in its nest of cotton fibre. I found myself curiously hesitant to touch it. Instead, I lifted the box and emptied it into the pouch. Megan nodded, knowingly.

I would have ended there, but there was a sense of incompletion, of things left undone. I went over the table again, sifting through the boxes with a fingertip, until I passed over a box and felt a nerve-tingling jolt. I came back and hovered over a stone that hummed under my finger.

"What's that one?"

"It's a green fluorite," Megan answered. "Most of them are purple, so the green ones have a rarity value."

I picked it out and dropped it into the pouch with the others. "I'm done then, I think," I told her.

She walked back around the table and laid out a black velvet cloth, tipping out the pouch. She fell into a rhythm and recounted the stones, placing each at five points of a circle.

"Tiger's eye to see beyond and pierce the veil, actinolite for balance and healing, malachite for connection to the spirit, red jasper for grounding and connection to the earth, green fluorite for guidance and self-knowledge."

"You choose well. These will be well received." Blackbird offered the compliment with something of a degree of respect that had been absent before.

"I just chose the ones that felt right."

"Just so."

I turned back to Megan, pulling out my wallet.

"No cards," said Blackbird. "This is a cash transaction between you and Megan. There is to be no intermediary."

"For a friend of Blackbird's—" Megan began.

"It is for a gift and for that it must be Rabbit's to give," Blackbird told her.

At that Megan nodded her understanding and scooped the stones back into the pouch.

"How much do I owe you?" I asked her.

"You owe me nothing, Rabbit, but I will accept ten pounds if you agree?"

I smiled and offered her a tenner from my wallet which she squirreled away in a cash box after handing me the black pouch. It felt weightier than it should.

"Thank you, Megan." If this was a test, maybe I had passed it.

"If I may?" She scanned quickly across her wares and plucked a stone from a box. She held out her closed hand for me to put mine underneath.

I glanced at Blackbird and there was the slightest indication of a nod. I put my hand out, palm underneath her fist. She dropped the stone into it. It was shaped into a tiny pear in a deep glossy blue and had a silver ring attached where the pear-stalk would be. It felt initially cold in my palm but it pulsed into warmth in my hand as if fuelled by some inner heat. It didn't look any different, but it felt somehow alive in my palm.

"Megan, we're not..." Blackbird started to explain then halted. She blushed very slightly. I looked from her to Megan, waiting for some explanation.

Megan looked thoughtful for a moment then offered, "Lapis will aid your physical awareness and perhaps enhance the focus of your power. It has other properties, too, but those are the ones that are important for now."

"Why does it go warm like that?"

I was talking to myself, but Megan thought the question was for her. "It does?" she said, surprised.

"Hmmm," added Blackbird in a tone that told me she wasn't going to elaborate.

"Here, let me." Megan held out her hand for the stone. I gave it her back she took it and turned away for a moment. When she turned back she had threaded a leather thong through the loop, which she tied deftly in a knot.

She passed it back to me. "Wear it close to your heart and may it bring you good fortune."

I didn't know quite what to say so I slipped the loop over my head, loosening my tie slightly to allow it to fall down inside next to my skin. I felt it rest cold against my chest then flare to warmth again before slowly cooling to skin temperature, confirming what I had felt before.

"Thank you, Megan." It felt odd to start wearing rocks around my neck, but the warmth emanating from it told me there was more to this than I had thought, and I needed all the good fortune I could get.

"Megan, it has been a pleasure to see you again, but we must go. Rabbit, it's time we were moving on."

I nodded, acknowledging the gift once again and slipped the black pouch into my jacket pocket. Then I followed Blackbird through the random swell of people out of the market and back onto the cobbles.

"Is she Fey?" I asked Blackbird as we moved out of earshot.

She glanced sideways at me but then continued walking and, for a moment, I thought maybe she hadn't heard me. Then she spoke.

"Megan is an interesting person because she is sensitive to our kind. She can usually tell if a person has Fey blood – she knew you did straight away. And you've seen the skill she has with stones." We were momentarily separated by an American couple with broad Western drawls delighting over the ancient monument of Covent Garden, reminding me that what people considered ancient was all relative.

"But she has no power as far as I am aware," Blackbird continued as if she had not been interrupted. "I came across her when I was looking for a gift for someone and she had the ideal thing for me except that when she searched for it, it wasn't there. Some very light fingers were pilfering her stock. She knew they weren't the run-of-the-mill thief as this wasn't the first time things had gone missing from under her nose but she had not found a way to prevent it from happening."

"And you helped her."

"I placed a simple ward on her stall making it uncomfortable to steal from her, then spread the word that if I caught the thief, I would have the price of the thievery out of their hide." She smiled a grim smile and for a moment there was something predatory there.

"Couldn't you just have them arrested?"

"The Feyre live outside of human law and human law enforcement. There are no Fey criminals. If you've done wrong, you've done wrong. Fey justice, when it is served, is immediate and personal. If someone transgresses against one of us then that one has the right to satisfaction, in blood if necessary. It is our way."

"Your way, you mean."

"No, I meant what I said. It is our way whether you like it or not, and it is a way you will learn if you want to survive. Others will not make the allowances for you that I have."

"I hadn't noticed you making allowances for me."

"That's what's worrying me. Here, we're going down." Blackbird made for the entrance to Covent Garden underground station and waltzed through the barrier without validating a ticket. I fumbled for my card, then waved it at the machine and followed her.

"How did you do that?" I indicated the barriers where the attendant watched people passing through but had completely failed to notice Blackbird walking through without a ticket.

"Do what?"

"You just walked through the barriers without paying."

"The barriers aren't meant for me," she explained as the lift door opened. Thankfully at that time of day most of the people were coming up in the lift, not going down and we had the lift car to ourselves.

"So you just walked through the barriers because you thought you could? Everyone else has to pay."

"I don't, though, do I?" she explained, as if I were a two year-old.

I found myself trying to argue with the obvious. I had just watched her walk through the barrier, so I knew she could do it. If the reason she could do it was because she thought she could then perhaps that was reason enough. It occurred to me that there was an underlying arrogance to the Feyre. They believed they were privileged and because they believed it, they were. It was an arrogance I was familiar with amongst human beings, especially at senior levels within companies, but it translated to the Feyre well enough.

The lift reached the bottom and the doors rolled open to the empty corridor. Blackbird exited and I followed her out and towards the platform, except that she swung right after the lifts. I followed her into the passage that joined the platform entry and exit passages. She halted outside a door marked *Staff Only – No Entry*.

"Here we are." She tapped on the door and entered.

"It said Staff Only," I pointed out, in case she hadn't noticed.

"I know. It's to keep people out."

"Should we be in here then?"

"No one comes in here unless they're entitled to, trust me. And if they did, they would regret it." Inside we took the spiral stairs leading down. A little way down, a passage led off to the base of the lift shaft but the steps spiralled on down.

"Where does this lead to?"

"I think it used to be a service tunnel, but it's been adapted for other purposes now. Here we are." The stairs ended in one of the circular tunnels that are common on the underground, except that this one looked as if it hadn't been used in years. The floor was smeared with something dark in places. Worryingly it looked organic in origin, as if something had decomposed there and left a stain.

Blackbird passed me the brown sack with the pigeon sleeping in it and stepped slowly down the corridor away from the spiral stair. I hung back. The hairs on the back of my neck slowly lifted until I could feel them prickling down my neck. Some instinct was telling me it wasn't safe here and that my best course of action would be to flee back up the stairs as fast as I could.

She paused and cocked her head as if listening for something. The light illuminated only the first fifteen feet, then slowly merged with the darkness beyond, vanishing into featureless grey.

"Are we going down there?" I spoke softly to her back as the distance slowly increased between us.

She held up her left hand with one finger raised to indicate that I should be quiet. She paused then stepped forward again into the edge of the darkness. As she did, a huge shaggy figure coalesced out of the grey and reached out for her.

"Blackbird!" I shouted a warning.

The long shaggy arms closed around her, sweeping her up. I was torn between trying to rescue her and running back up the stairs. My cowardice shamed me, but the thing was immense. Huge hairy arms grasped Blackbird's slight frame. It had swept her up off the floor as if she were weightless and was crushing her against its chest. What could I do?

A long low growl came from the tunnel echoing from the walls as Blackbird kicked her legs helplessly, caught in its grasp. Why didn't she zap it or something?

Torn between staying to watch Blackbird's fate and saving myself from a similar one, I stayed at the bottom of the stairs, hand on the rail ready to run for it when my laggard brain made sense of the low growling emanating from the creature.

"Bbbbrrrraaaacckkkbiiirrrddd." The sound rolled like a glacier grinding gravel.

It knew her name?

I hesitated as I heard another noise. It was muffled, but it came from the figure pressed into the creature's chest.

Blackbird was laughing.

FOUR

The scene transformed as my perceptions shifted.

The arms became a hug, though on a scale that was hard to believe. Blackbird's thrashing became her return of the enthusiastic greeting she was receiving. The growl was speech, though it was slowed and so low that most of it was wasted on my ears and found rest somewhere low in my gut.

The creature was still half-concealed in darkness, though it filled most of the tunnel. Grey shaggy hair covered it completely, sweeping down its shoulders and arms and hanging in loose dark curls where Blackbird was pressed against its chest, her arms buried up to her elbows in fur. Its head was wide where creamy tusks emerged from the darkly lined lips. Its eyes were black inside a ring of burnished gold and they were watching me.

Blackbird's feet descended slowly to the floor, though she clung with her face pressed into the fur for a moment longer before stepping back.

The creature swept its hand up then extended its palm, turning upwards.

"My apologies, Gramawl, I am losing my manners in the joy of seeing you again. He is called Rabbit. Rabbit, this is Gramawl." As she said this, she made a complicated gesture, rotating her middle finger downwards and then indicated me and made a little rabbit with her hands. As she was signing, I realised that the last sentence spoken was meant as a cue for me.

Blackbird stepped aside and I hesitantly stepped forward. I felt a wave of dizziness wash over me. I staggered for a moment, unable to make sense of what was happening. I came to myself, clinging to the rail and finding my knees unsteady. Something washed over me, like waves of disorientation.

"I suppose I should have anticipated that." She turned back to Gramawl who retreated slightly into the dimness. She wobbled her fist and then tapped it sharply against her palm, then made a series of sharp sweeping motions, ushering Gramawl backwards.

Gramawl made a small circle to indicate us both then added an outstretched hand that tipped from side to side. The sensation dissipated and I found myself able to stand again.

"Yes, I know what you thought, but even if that were the case, that is a poor welcome, isn't it?" She pressed the knuckles of each hand together for emphasis. There was a reprimand in her voice, mixed with the sort of fondness reserved for a well-intentioned but overprotective uncle.

The shape retreated further into the dimness.

"Oh, stop it. Come out and meet Rabbit properly." She was both frustrated and amused.

Clearly the creature understood her speech as it came forward, this time fully into the light. As it emerged further I became aware that it was hunched over. Shoulders loomed behind the head, sloped down to fit in the tunnel. I thought it would shamble forward, but its step was light, full of grace and poise, like a dancer.

There was a seismic rumbling, accompanied by a complex bow and ending with an outstretched palm.

"He apologises for his misunderstanding, Rabbit, and offers you welcome, if you will accept it."

I gathered my wits.

"Thank you, Gramawl." I bowed in turn, keeping my eyes on the shaggy form. As he approached I became aware of his scent. I had thought he would smell like a beast, but instead there was the freshness of new-turned earth. I could see, now I was closer, that the shaggy fur was not matted and grey but layered with grey over brown, over black. It had the quality of a finely groomed horse's mane and I wondered who had spent time combing through that mountain of fur.

"I was about to explain that Rabbit had brought you a gift, Gramawl, but now I'm not sure whether he will want to part with it." She was comfortable speaking and signing at once, though Gramawl appeared to understand our speech well enough. Was there some etiquette to this?

Gramawl, lifted and then dropped his arms, pantomiming disappointment. At the same time his voice, if you could use that term, dropped in tone until I could only feel it rumbling in my bones. The hackles on my neck rose. I found myself stepping back.

"Only a little something," she teased, holding out her hand as if swinging a sweet by the wrapper or a tiny mouse by the tail and ignoring the shivering air.

The great eyes flicked back to me, luminescent in the overhead lights. His flat wet nose wriggled, seeking clues.

"Of course, that was before you offended my friend."

"I'm not offended," I interjected, a little too quickly.

He swept away the air with his hand, rubbed one palm against the other and added an opening and closing gesture.

Blackbird translated for me. "He says you have accepted his apology and that it was only a misunderstanding and now he would like to know what you've brought."

Blackbird stepped up to him, smiling, and affectionately stroked his cheek above her head. "I don't know, I bring people to meet you and this is how you welcome them. Why don't you show Gramawl his gift, Rabbit?"

Taking my cue, I reached into my jacket for the stones, but she shook her head. "Those are for a little later. Put the sack on the floor and leave it, somewhere in the open."

I stepped forward, still a little hesitant near Gramawl, and placed the sack on the ground and stepped back.

"You need to open it a little or it's not going to come out," Blackbird added.

"It'll fly off." I hesitated.

"That isn't going to be a problem, is it, Gramawl?"

There was a rhythmic huffing sound and my stomach vibrated to the sound of his amusement.

I stepped back to the sack and opened the neck, letting it fall open around the bird. It hopped out onto the sack in a flurry, getting its bearings. I stepped back again.

The bird was initially bemused to find itself underground. It looked about, putting its head on one side and then suddenly focused, darting sideways as it caught sight of the huge figure. It burst into the air in a clatter of wings.

There was a dull thump, like a pulse in the air. I blinked.

All was silent again. My brain caught up with my ears and I realised that Gramawl had taken it, mid-flight. I hadn't even seen him move.

Gramawl let out a low rumbling that might have been a purr if it had been high enough. He pressed his fist to his chest then touched his lips with his forefinger, opening his hand into a fluttering motion.

"He says it tastes of light and air," Blackbird translated, "and offers his thanks."

"You're welcome," I offered, still trying to figure out how something so big could move that fast.

"Delightful as it is to share such things with you, Gramawl, we really came to see your Mistress. Is she at home?"

He used a two-handed gesture, one hand inside the other, that I couldn't interpret, then placed his palm outwards, rotating it to point at the ground.

"We'll wait here then, while you check." She turned to me. "He thinks she might be sleeping, so we'll wait a moment."

He merged back into the dark and vanished, leaving me staring at the empty sack.

"Do they all eat pigeons?" I asked Blackbird.

"No, but Gramawl is a creature of open twilight and he's been living down here a long time. Bringing him something from the daylight world above is like offering him a taste of autumn sunshine."

"Can't he just leave?" I felt some sympathy for him. I had been stuck on the Underground for an hour once and that was long enough.

"He is tied to his Mistress and she won't leave, so he'll stay with her until she changes her mind."

"Is he bound to her, then?"

"In a way, yes."

"He doesn't need protection, if you ask me."

"He doesn't do it for protection. He does it because he loves her."

"Oh." I couldn't think of how to respond to that.

We stood in the lighted area of the tunnel in silence until my sense of curiosity overcame my unwillingness to break the stillness.

"Are all the Feyre like that?"

"No, most are smaller. Gramawl is a sylvan troll, a creature of twilight. His line goes back to the first trolls. The mountain trolls are a little shorter and their coats are grey and white, but you hardly ever see mountain trolls these days."

"He's very impressive."

"You may meet others like him. There are a few in

and around London, but the majority live out in the forests where they're more comfortable."

"It must be very hard for him to live so far away from woods and trees."

"Well, trolls like caves, and this is only a man-made cave when you think about it. But yes. He wouldn't stay if it wasn't for Kareesh."

"Kareesh is his Mistress?"

"Yes, and I don't think she has been out of these tunnels in many years."

"Is that who the stones are for?" I tapped the pocket of my jacket where the stones weighed in the pocket.

She nodded. "A gift for a gift, Rabbit. She is the one who might be able to show you a way to survive, if she takes a liking to you."

And if she doesn't? That question led me to other thoughts. "What do they do for food and water down here?"

"Gramawl goes outside to forage for short periods, but not until full dark."

"Didn't you say he was a twilight creature?"

"Yes, but twilight in the forest is easily as dark as full night in the city. I doubt he will have seen the sun for years."

"Do they, you know, turn to stone? In sunlight, I mean, as in the legends?"

Blackbird laughed. "No, they don't turn to stone. But, over the years, some may have appeared to vanish leaving only the rocks behind, if they were being pursued."

"I suppose if you were pursuing something that big and it vanished in plain sight, you might be tempted to believe it had turned into a rock," I suggested.

"Yes, you might."

We fell into silence again, me thinking of the vanished pigeon and Blackbird with her own thoughts. I wanted to ask more questions but the sound of our breathing was sufficient disturbance in the silent tiled corridor.

Gramawl materialised from the darkness without a sound. It wasn't just that he moved quietly; in the silence of the passage you could have heard a feather fall but Gramawl made no sound until he reappeared from the tunnel. Blackbird was unsurprised by this and took in the rapid gestures that accompanied his return.

"She'll see us now, Rabbit. You are privileged. She must be curious about you."

"Why would she be curious about me?"

"Because I brought you to her, I expect."

Gramawl stepped back into the darkness and Blackbird followed him. I wasn't sure what to expect now that we were going to meet Kareesh. What would a female troll look like? Were they bigger or smaller than the males? Was she likely to decide I was a self-delivering takeaway?

The darkness eased in behind me and we were climbing slightly. The passage angled left and right and came to a stairway at one side while the passage continued onward into darkness. The metal treads of the steps gleamed dully in the darkness and I noticed a faint glimmer of light coming from above.

There was some unseen exchange between Gramawl and Blackbird and she took the steps upwards. I followed, nodding a blind acknowledgement to the hulking shape in the dimness, guessing that with his huge gold-rimmed eyes he could probably see me perfectly well.

The steps doubled back at the first level and climbed up to an area that opened out, whether into another corridor or a room it was hard to tell, for every surface was hanging with rugs and heavy curtains patterned in muted gold and red. In contrast to the space below, the echoes died immediately, leaving a sensation of muffled closeness.

As we walked forward, we stepped onto rugs with curving geometric patterns that led the eye to wander. Delicate filigree lamps in beaten copper hung from the ceiling, their shape reminding me of Indian or Persian influences. Their light was warm and glowing, and flickered as we passed. A scent of musk rose up around us with an undertone of new-turned earth. It might have been fetid, but it smelled clean, as if it had just rained.

We approached a corner where there were cushions piled around with hangings draped into folds above and to each side making a nest. In the centre of this nest was a figure. Huge almond-shaped eyes, completely black, watched us approach. Her face was long, her chin pointed and her limbs were thin and spindly. Her alabaster skin was pale and translucent, stretched over her frame and showing her bony joints. Is this what female trolls looked like? I glanced at Blackbird but she was focused on the figure in the cushions.

"Greetings, Kareesh. You look well." Blackbird's voice sounded muted in this enclosed space.

"You always had a way with words," said the figure, but she smiled, exposing parallel rows of tiny needle-sharp teeth behind thin lips. "Come and sit with me, and bring your new friend." She patted the cushion beside her. Silver wisps of cobweb hair trailed from her arm, hanging momentarily in the air as she moved.

We approached slowly, Blackbird hunching down to nestle in beside the smaller figure who sat like a grandma pulling her grandchildren in around her for warmth and comfort. I bobbed down onto my haunches and eased sideways to sit on the edge of the cushions.

"So what have you been up to all this time? I've missed you, girl." Her voice was sweet but crackly.

"I'm sorry, Kareesh, I would have come before, but–"

"Oh, I know. You've a thousand things to do and I don't blame you. It's your time, girl, and you'd best make the most of it." She reached over and patted Blackbird's hand affectionately. Blackbird captured the hand gently and held it for a moment.

"And you've brought this one to see me, have you?" Kareesh nodded towards me.

I bowed awkwardly from the seated position. "Greetings, Kareesh,"

"Nice manners," she remarked in an aside to Blackbird, "but still wet from the birthing pool. Have you started taking in waifs and strays, girl?" I bristled at her implication that I was either of those.

"I found him on the Underground this morning; he was being taken by the Untainted."

"Hush, child. Do not speak of those. Too much sadness has come of it and I won't dwell on what's downstream. You stopped it, that's the main thing. It was well done." She pressed Blackbird's hand and looked at me again, those huge eyes unblinking.

Perhaps because she looked so ancient, perhaps because of the cosy quality of the place, her strangeness wasn't as disconcerting as it might have been. Perhaps my exposure to Gramawl's fearsome size and speed and Blackbird's eccentricities had inured me to the fear I would have felt, had I encountered her on any other day.

"You're still hiding then?"

I thought the question was aimed at me and I struggled for an answer, but it was Blackbird who replied.

"It's not hiding, it's blending in."

"And yet you drew attention to yourself this day, if my nose does not mislead me."

Her nose was small, unlike Gramawl's, and would have been dainty if it weren't so flared. She turned back to Blackbird, who looked at her hands in the dim light. I thought I saw the colour rise gently in her cheeks.

"You don't miss much, do you?" Blackbird mumbled, then lifted her chin to meet Kareesh's considering look.

Kareesh nodded, then let the subject drop, turning her attention to me. "So, girl, let's have a look at this rescued waif."

She shuffled around to face me, wrapped in overlapping layers that hung from her frame like a long-sleeved smock. Wiry legs appeared from under her then

71

vanished again under the folds as she repositioned herself.

Blackbird glanced at me, raising an eyebrow, but said nothing. I touched my hand to my jacket over my pocket and she nodded imperceptibly.

"With a little assistance from Blackbird, I have brought you a gift, Kareesh, which I hope you'll accept." I dipped into my jacket pocket and pulled out the black bag.

Kareesh's eyes twinkled as I held out the bag. "Well, then. What have you brought for me?" She took the bag from me without touching my hand, a courtesy perhaps, then tipped the stones out into her palm. For a moment the stones shone in her pale palm, or perhaps it was only that they reflected more of the available light against the whiteness of her skin.

Looking at her hand I realised she didn't have a thumb. Instead, the outer two fingers lagged behind the others. She dipped into her palm with the other hand and I could see the outer fingers were articulated differently, allowing her to select a stone from the cluster. She picked out the dark red one.

"This one hid from you, I think." She laughed to herself with the sound of rustling paper, holding it up in the light.

I remembered that this was the stone I had almost missed as it nestled into its box. It was also the stone I had been reluctant to touch. She held it up to the lamplight and it gleamed darkly.

"It wasn't meant for you, oh no, but you chose well. Yes, a good choice." The stone vanished into the smock and she used the longer middle finger to stir around in between the others. "And this one, well yes, I should have expected you to be chosen, shouldn't I?" She addressed the orange Tiger's Eye as if it were animate. Then she dropped it back and slid them into the bag again, tucking it under her smock with the other stone. Had she kept the red one apart for a reason, I wondered?

"So, young Rabbit, you have a gift for gifts." She laughed at her own joke. "But you would like something from me, yes?" Her grin broadened and I was treated to a full display of her pointed teeth.

"He needs your help, Kareesh." Blackbird spoke on my behalf.

"His gift has pleased me, girl, as you knew it would, and I offer him something in return, but it is up to him to choose. You cannot choose for him now, can you?" She wagged her middle finger at Blackbird.

"I am glad my gift has pleased you, Kareesh, but I would not know what to ask for. As you pointed out, I am very new to this and I have no idea what you might consider a fair gift in return."

"Ooh, *such* pretty manners," she teased. "Perhaps you would choose a talisman to wake you in time of danger?"

I glanced behind her at Blackbird and she shook her head, minutely. I was used to negotiating with vendors where I knew what I wanted and roughly what it was worth. This was different. I chose my words carefully, aware we were bargaining, though for what, I wasn't sure.

"That's a fine offer, but what other thing might you consider worthy?"

"I might consider putting a certain girl over my knee and spanking her skinny behind, as once I did, if she helps you again." She was looking at me but the remark was intended for Blackbird. "You know the rules, girl, as do I."

Blackbird gave me a helpless look, but then looked down at her hands to avoid catching my gaze again. I was thinking of when and why Kareesh might have spanked her when she made her second offer.

"Would you wish to know, then, whether there's a grandchild for you? Your daughter's a mite young yet, but a child may not be too far to see."

"How did you know I had a daughter?" I glanced back

at Blackbird, who was still staring resolutely at her hands.

"Well there wouldn't be much point in having the sight if I couldn't see the things written plain in front of me, now, would there?" She grinned, her teeth showing as ivory glimmers against her pink gums.

"Another fine offer, Kareesh." I hesitated. She was a canny bargainer and she knew how to tempt a worried father. If my daughter was to have children then that meant she would survive, didn't it? Or was she simply offering to tell me of the potential for grandchildren?

I was tempted but I had more pressing concerns if I was going to see my daughter safe.

"Is there something else?" I asked her.

"Are you sure you won't have the talisman? You may find you need it sooner than you think."

Did she know something or was she just pressuring me? She'd gone back to the first offer before moving on, which in my experience meant there was something else she could offer, though I couldn't tell what it might be. Perhaps in Fey culture, as in some human cultures, it was a matter of honour to try and get the best price for your bargain.

"No, not the talisman, Kareesh, but something else, something I need." I didn't know what it was, but I was now pretty sure she did.

"Well then, young Rabbit. Will you accept the sight of something to help you secure your place in the courts? Something that will soon be needed – not far away, but not easily found, no."

I glanced at Blackbird. She was like stone. What did she mean by the sight of something? Not the thing itself, obviously, but a picture maybe?

"Truly a generous offer."

I wanted to ask her, if I was able to secure a place in the courts whether that meant my daughter could also join with me but I sensed that, as with her other suggestions, the offer was what it was and it would be up to me to judge the value of it.

I looked for a sign from Kareesh that it really was as generous as she made it sound but her inhuman face was unreadable to me in so many ways. Was there a reason she had offered me the talisman first? She'd hinted that I might need it. I had turned down her initial offer almost on principle, though that could be a double bluff.

No, Blackbird had said that joining in the courts might provide safety for me and my daughter for a while. That was why she brought me here. I had to trust her and get what we had come for.

"And one I would like to accept," I told Kareesh.

Blackbird let out the breath she'd been holding.

"That's a fine bargain you've struck, Rabbit," Kareesh remarked.

I glanced at Blackbird and she gave me a tense smile. Clearly there was affection between these two, but there was a sense of tension too.

"Come then gauntlet runner, witness and suspect, evader of traps, bringer of hope. Rabbit, you are well-named, but not for always. Another name will be yours when you have earned it. The sun will rise and they shall fall. So say I."

Blackbird looked at Kareesh and her jaw dropped. I was lost, still trying to follow what she had just said. By the look of Blackbird's face she thought it was significant. I made a mental note to ask her about it later. Kareesh, meantime, continued without pause.

"Here, Rabbit, hold out your hands and, when you are ready, rest them in my palms. You can remove them any time you wish and the vision will end. You might find it easier to close your eyes."

"Will it help?"

"No, but you may find it easier to bear that way."

To bear? That was a strange word to use. I repositioned myself on the cushions so I had slightly more support. I had no idea how long this might take so I wanted to be as comfortable as possible. I took a deep breath and let it out slowly.

"OK, I'm ready."

"No, you're not. But then, no one ever is." She showed me her teeth again and I lowered my hands into hers.

Cold rushed up my arms, clamping my heart and seizing the breath in my lungs. Echoes of the heart attack I had survived earlier flooded my veins with fear. The cold wrapped itself around my gut and pooled in my groin, killing all sensation. My eyes flooded with tears and blurred. I couldn't move to wipe them. Lights expanded and shattered into refracted fragments of delicate snowflakes and rushed inwards. I was blind, cold and numb. I think I screamed.

Images hammered into my head: a heavy door that swung ponderously shut, the dull *thud* reverberating; letters carved into pale stone that I couldn't read; a familiar looking building with a roof stained with livid green verdigris; a black cat, ready to pounce, silhouetted against a darkening sky. Autumn leaves swirled around me in a vortex of red, orange and gold. There was a green twig haloed in a sickly light and a room striped with sunlight, bedclothes scattered across the floor. It shifted into a vaulted ceiling like the roof of a wine-cellar, walls lime-washed and inset with dark stones.

I spun upwards like a reverse skydiver, the wind whipping my clothes around me. I recognised the Thames wriggling out below me until I floated momentarily. Then I fell, my eyes streaming with blurred tears as London rushed up to meet me, the river suddenly large and gleaming in dull menace. At the last second, I swerved aside to pass through a heavy metal grating into a brick-vaulted tunnel where I twisted manically, left and right, to a giant hall filled with the sound of rushing water. In the centre was an island with an altar, strung with detritus and misshapen in the darkness.

My final image was of a square iron door in the wall above the water, its edges caked with rust, a keyhole, black at its centre.

Breath rushed into me and I collapsed backwards, rolling off the cushion onto the cold tiled floor, banging my head in the process. The reprise of my experience this morning was not lost on me as I coughed and retched onto the floor, pins and needles prickling my legs as the flow of blood returned. Kareesh and Blackbird watched, waiting for me to recover myself.

After I had calmed and wiped the spittle from my lips with the back of my hand, Kareesh spoke to me.

"Were you ready?"

I shook my head slowly and had the grace to laugh at myself. The gift I had bargained for had turned out to be a thumping headache and a series of fractured images. I felt cheated and somehow soiled by it, as if something dirty had trampled through my head.

Blackbird was more practical. "Did you see what it was?"

I looked up at her from the cold floor. The memory of what I had seen was already indistinct. I remembered the door with the keyhole and the tunnels, and there had been a cat. What was the green twig, and where was the familiar building? It was like remembering a badly edited movie. "I'm not sure."

Blackbird let out a sigh of frustration and turned to Kareesh, but before she could say anything Kareesh held up her strange hand to pause her. "No child, you know how it is."

Blackbird's face fell, but whatever she'd been going to say she kept to herself. She stood up and moved closer to me so she could help me to my feet. I felt as though I had been beaten in the middle of a hangover. My first attempt at standing was unsuccessful. I only made it to my knees. Then Blackbird, with surprising strength, put her hands under my arms and lifted me so I could stand. She kept hold of one arm, supporting me emotionally as well as physically. My mouth tasted of dry ash and there was shimmering in my vision that screamed migraine.

Kareesh addressed her. "Take him somewhere quiet and dark, girl, and he will recover in a little while. He'll sleep well tonight, perhaps too well." She ushered us slowly out onto the head of the steps, patting Blackbird's cheeks affectionately. "Don't be so long next time, girl. And bring an old one some boiled sweets, eh?"

"They're bad for your teeth," Blackbird objected half-heartedly.

"There are lots of things that'll be the death of me before my teeth, girl, and I can always grow new ones."

Kareesh looked up at me, as you might at a curiosity.

"Goodbye, Kareesh, and thank you for your gift," I whispered, my voice unsteady.

"You can thank me later, Rabbit. If you live."

She stood at the top of the steps while Blackbird helped me down into the dark. There was no sign of Gramawl, either in the corridor or at the base of the stairs, though he may have been lurking in the darkness somewhere. My own vision was still haunted by glowing after-images of things I'd never seen.

Using a mixture of cajoling and support, Blackbird got me up the steps and into the lift. We were joined by a group of German tourists who looked distastefully at me when I came close to throwing up as the lift jolted into motion. The lift reached the surface and we let them disperse. Blackbird steered me after them to the exit.

"Do you have your card?" Blackbird asked me.

"Yes, it's in my wallet somewhere." I made a hesitant attempt to find it, but Blackbird walked me forward to the barrier.

"Just know that you're allowed to pass," she instructed, and walked into the gap between the barriers. I concentrated my limited resources on remembering that I was a valid ticket holder and to my surprise the barrier flipped open.

Outside I was confused. The day had vanished into twilight. I looked around, able to support myself now, at least physically. "Where did the day go?" I asked Blackbird.

"We were down there some while."

She guided me over the cobbles and down a side street to a pub that had emptied of tourists and not yet packed with office-workers released from their labours. We entered between floods.

It was dimly lit and although there was a juke-box, it was mercifully quiet. At the back, there was booth seating where Blackbird left me at a table propped against the cushioned back while she went to get me a drink. I closed my eyes momentarily, trying to recapture the vision, then shied away from it when the sense of vertigo returned. It hadn't been the best of days, overall. I had started out dead and now I felt like crap.

I thought of Kareesh sitting in her nest of cushions and hangings somewhere beneath my feet. It was hard to reconcile the waking world around me with the dream-like one she inhabited. I had once had a bad dose of flu with a temperature that made me delirious. The way I felt reminded me of that. The sense of disconnection, of unreality, was overwhelming.

I looked at Blackbird's back, over at the bar. Here she was, shepherding me around, introducing me to creatures I hadn't even known existed a day ago. What did she get from all this? She had said that she'd gained a degree of responsibility for me. How far did that responsibility extend?

She was close to both Kareesh and Gramawl; affectionate even. What was it that was between them? Kareesh said that she was hiding. What was she hiding, and from whom? I hadn't even had the opportunity to ask whether Kareesh was a female troll. She was much smaller and not hairy, but maybe she was just old. All those teeth in their measured rows; I felt cold inside.

And then the thought occurred to me that actually I had no idea what Blackbird really looked like. As I had discovered, she could appear how she pleased. I had a sudden mental image of Blackbird sitting in the booth beside me, rows of tiny sharp teeth reflecting the mood lighting. Could she and Kareesh be related? Is that what Blackbird really looked like?

Had we been visiting an old friend or had I really just been introduced to her mother?

FIVE

My mind was buzzing with the after-effects of the vision Kareesh had granted me and stray thoughts as to Blackbird's true appearance were doing nothing to calm me. My sight shimmered at the edges with the promise of migraine. I closed my eyes in the hope that it might cease, the thumping headache easing slightly.

"Lost, are ya?" The tone was belligerent, but not out of the ordinary in the back-streets around Covent Garden. It was a nice area as long as you stuck to the tourist track. I opened my eyes to view the couple that had appeared in front of my table.

"Sorry?" I tried to focus on them. I was having a bad moment and suddenly felt quite nauseous.

"I said," the tall youth intoned for the benefit of his female companion, "you're lost, are ya?" He grinned at her. He was dressed in gothic style and would have been a punk had it been thirty years earlier. They were the type that always fell in with the darker fashions. He was upwards of six feet tall with strands of long black hair trailing around his face. His T-shirt said "Heavy Metal" in gothic script, visible between the dull gloss lapels of his leather coat. His face was curiously androgynous, clean shaven with eyebrows sculpted in an almost feminine shape. The similarity to his companion made me wonder whether they were brother and sister, or whether the likeness was contrived.

She was wearing marginally more eye make-up than he was, and her lips were fuller than his, though that could have been the purple lipstick. Her skin was deathly pale and I wondered if the pallor was also make-up or whether she simply never saw the sun. Her T-shirt proclaimed "No Rest for the Wicked", which might have been a band or just a slogan.

"I'm just having a quiet drink with my friend, so I wouldn't say I was lost, no." My brain banged on the inside of my skull.

"I think he's lost," he jeered. "If he wasn't lost he wouldn't be here, would he?" His companion apparently followed the intricacies of this negative logic, because she shook her head.

"You've strayed from the path, my lad, and now you've gotta pay." This time she nodded enthusiastically.

I was about to tell him to piss off before I threw up over them when his words about straying from the path rang a faint bell. "Path?"

"Yeah. You're in my stomping ground now, bumpkin, and you're not leavin' till you've paid the price." His companion nodded again. "What have ya got?"

He sat down opposite me, sliding into the empty seat with animal grace, his shoulders rolled under the leather of his coat in a way that wasn't quite human.

"I'm sorry, but I don't have any spare change. I'm clean out. So you'll be better off going and pestering someone else."

"Ya hear that, Carris? He wants to buy us off with coins. Up in town to trade and he reckons he's got nothing, does he? He must take us for bumpkins like he is, eh?"

I was beginning to suspect that this was not the average yob out to intimidate the tourists into making a "donation".

"Look, mate. I don't have anything, so it's not worth your time, all right?" I tried to appear as uninteresting as possible.

"Well, if you've got nothing to give then we'll have to see what there is to take, won't we?" He made to touch my hand, but I snatched it away.

"Stay away from me," I growled.

"Or what, bumpkin? What ya gonna do, eh?"

"He's not the one you want to worry about." The familiar voice came from behind Carris. She spun around, stepping wide to brace herself for an attack, her movements lithe and graceful.

Blackbird walked around her blind side, navigating around the table so she could slide in behind the table next to me. She placed a pint of black liquid in front of me, the head creamy.

"Guinness. It'll help to clear your head." She explained it as though we weren't facing off with these thugs.

She turned back to the youth, who still looked expectant.

"You gonna pay up for him then?" he queried, hand out, making a grasping motion reminiscent of the gestures used by Gramawl. Blackbird made to touch him and it was his turn to snatch his hand away.

"No, Fenlock, I'm not going to pay up for him and you're not going to ask him again. Instead, you're going to apologise to both of us for disturbing our drink then leave us alone."

"And why would I do that?" His companion leaned forward over the table to add to the threat or simply to overhear the conversation.

"Because if you don't, I'm going to shout your true name loud enough for every goblin and nixie for miles around to hear," Blackbird stated calmly.

Fenlock hesitated, calculating, then recovered.

"You don't know it, do ya? Ya can't," he leered at her.

"Don't I? You need to be more careful who you tell it to then, don't you? Once a secret's told then you just know someone will find it out. Perhaps if you chose to mention it to someone who was more discreet...?" Blackbird arched an eyebrow and looked up at Carris, who was still leaning over us. Fenlock's expression darkened.

He spun around, tipping the chair onto the floor and standing in one movement. Carris staggered backwards, caught by the sudden reversal.

"Who did you tell?" His tone was quiet, but darkly threatening.

"Me? I didn't tell her. She's lying, she is. She can't know it. I didn't tell her." Carris eased backwards slowly towards the door. The whiteness around her too-dark lips had paled further and she was suddenly sweating.

"Who? Who was it?" He stalked towards her, accelerating.

She turned and flung herself at the door, Fenlock only a second behind her. The door slammed open then banged shut, leaving the bar in deathly silence. The other customers in the bar watched us for a minute to see if we would deliver any more surprises, then went back to their drinks.

"Drink up," said Blackbird, "We have to be long gone by the time he catches her." She lifted a glass of clear liquid and took a long swallow from it.

I lifted the glass and took a sip through the creamy head. The combination of the strong taste and the cold soothing texture was therapeutic. I took a longer swallow and wiped the foam from my upper lip.

"You don't know his true name, do you?" I called her bluff.

"Oh, I do. But not because of Carris. And if I once revealed it I'd either have to finish him or he'd hunt down everyone who'd heard it and kill them, so it would be a good idea to drink up." She nodded towards the Guinness.

"Doesn't that mean he'll come looking for you?" I spoke my thoughts aloud.

84

"Not if he thinks I won't tell. When he eventually catches up with Carris he won't know whether I really know it or not, will he?"

I had to admire her logic, though in my current state these mental games were too challenging. Instead I concentrated on drinking down the cold dark beer. I was beginning to feel a little better, though whether that was due to the beer or the respite, I wasn't sure.

I tipped the glass up to finish it, finding it had gone down easier than I would have believed.

Blackbird slid around the seat and stood up, so I followed her lead. My vision was steady and my knees weren't wobbly any more. I might drink Guinness more often if it did me that much good.

Blackbird took the empty glasses to the bar and joined me at the door. We exited cautiously, turning back towards the crowds and mingling with the gathering groups around the tube station before passing along the opposite side of the road and heading back towards Leicester Square. I looked nervously around for signs of Fenlock or Carris. The glare spilled onto the pavement from the shops along Long Acre and we had to step around early theatregoers who were checking out menus and taking advantage of special rates as we made our way.

"Are you going to explain what happened earlier?" I prompted.

"With Fenlock?"

"No, about what Kareesh said. What did she mean about my having another name?"

"I don't know, Rabbit. I've never heard her volunteer anything like that before. It's not like her just to come out with things."

Have you known her long?" I edged around the question of parentage as we crossed the junction with St Martin's Lane.

"Most of my life."

Only most of it? "You seem very close to her."

85

"She brought me up; she's the closest thing I have to family."

Close to family, but not family. What did that mean?

"Did I choose correctly?" I shied away from the question I wanted to ask.

"You did well, though I don't know if you chose correctly. Only time will tell us that."

"It was all so confusing, so fast." It was ironic since we had spent half a day down there. "There was a hall, with a high vaulted roof, all in darkness and surrounded by water. In the middle there was this thing, like an altar, only caked in weeds and stuff. What does it mean?"

"The visions are like that. They are fragments from your possible future. They are not precise. That was why I was so surprised when she said what she did, about your name I mean. It's just not like her."

"You care about her, don't you?" It was impossible not to hear the worry in her voice.

"She's very old. Each time I go to see her I wonder if it'll be the last. She was there for me when no one else was."

"So you're not related?"

"No. Whatever made you think...?" She paused. I tried to look interested in a watch shop we were passing but she had stopped and I had to stop too. I had no idea where we were going.

There was a long silence while she just looked at me. I felt as if I was being punished for something out of my control, but at that moment my entire life was out of my control. I didn't know enough to be able to make judgements any more. I only knew how to ask questions.

She sighed as if resigning herself to something, then gathered herself together and straightened her shoulders.

"Tonight you need to clear out of your flat. Remove anything that identifies your daughter or anyone else you care for. Either arrange for your things to be sent somewhere safe and anonymous or else destroy them completely. Don't leave any link that could be taken as a clue. Not souvenirs, nor photographs, nor letters, understand? Nothing that will give you away."

I nodded, feeling cold inside. I recognised the signs, I had been dumped before. She was cutting me loose.

"Sever your ties with the flat and with your current existence. Settle your bills only if you can do it tonight and be out by morning. Take only what you can run with. Carry too much and it'll probably kill you. Take a little non-perishable food with you, you don't know where your next meal is coming from. Leave nothing. Understand?"

"I am to leave nothing." But she was the one who was leaving.

"Head back into central London tomorrow morning. You'll be harder to find in the city."

"I understand." I wanted to say something that would persuade her to stay with me but her expression ruled out any appeal.

"OK. Now go and do it."

We stood there.

"Well go on then," she said.

"Where shall I meet you tomorrow?"

"I'll find you," she said, but there was a hint of something else in her voice: not a lie, but not the truth either.

"Promise?"

"Just go. And watch your back." She was exasperated, impatient for me to leave.

I waited a moment more but there was no sign of the promise I'd hoped for. She had become my mentor and my guide, but she'd indicated from the start that it wouldn't last. My curiosity had led me to push her that little bit too hard and now she was pushing me away.

Reluctantly, I turned and walked towards the tube station. Like Orpheus, who was warned not to look back, I turned to see whether she was watching me go.

There was no sign of her. I hadn't really expected there to be. I was on my own. Well, I could do alone when I had to. I had been there before.

I walked past the open doorways threading my way through tourists and commuters until I made it to the tube station. The rush-hour was starting to build so that the noise in the ticket hall was a constant clamour of voices, barriers thumping closed and announcements that were barely intelligible over the general hubbub. I merged with the stream of people and stepped onto the escalator, letting it carry me down as people too impatient for its steady descent jostled past.

Trying to keep aware of the people around me, I looked for signs of unusual behaviour in the crowds. It was like looking for a blade of grass in a hayfield. So many people in London looked strange, it was impossible to discriminate. I settled for trying to look anonymous.

I took the first train heading south and west. Tired-looking commuters mixed with early evening socialites, packing themselves in until there was no room to breathe. If I was caught here there was no escape. Strangely though, pressed in with my fellows, I felt safer than I had on the backstreets. If someone wanted me then they would have to push past twelve other people to get to me, or at least that's what I told myself.

As the stops got further out, the press thinned, allowing me to take a seat and look around. No one looked remarkable, but as I said, this was London. I found myself thinking back through the day looking for the flaw which would reveal the punch-line, the key to the joke I didn't get. Instead I was left with only a sense of lingering paranoia. At the same time, the day seemed unreal, as if it had happened to someone else. I had met Gramawl and Kareesh, but had I really? Did they really exist? The train rattled down the tracks, but I couldn't help feeling that somehow I was on the wrong line.

A young woman was sitting across from me. She was browsing through one of those magazines filled with candid pictures of D-list celebs and their hangers-on. I found myself wondering if she was what she appeared to be. What if she was Fey too? She looked a little too glossy, a little too perfect to be natural. How many Fey were there? Were they all around us? She looked up. Her eyes were ice blue. Now that I looked closer, you could see that she was not a natural blonde.

"What?" she mouthed at me over the clatter and rumble of the train. Her grimace broke the spell, as I realised I had been calmly examining her while she looked back. I found myself blushing deeply at my breech of tube etiquette.

"I'm sorry, I was… never mind."

"Weirdo!" she mouthed back. Rattling her magazine, she went back to browsing.

I tried not to look at her for the rest of the journey.

At my stop I disembarked and waited on the platform until the train departed and the platform cleared, looking suspiciously at anyone who lingered. I picked out my ticket, climbed the stairs to the barrier and exited into the empty street where late-opening shops tempted the newly arrived commuters to alcohol and convenience foods. Self-consciously I walked past, trying to act like everyone else, to be like them without ever having thought about what that meant. How did you walk? What did you look at? What thoughts were in your head? So many times I had walked this way and had never given a moment's thought as to whether it looked normal or not.

The suburban streets were damp and the street lights did little but highlight the shadows. I followed the route to my flat scanning the gardens along the front of the houses without any notion of what I was looking for. She said that the thing hunting me might know where I would go. Did that mean it might know where my flat was? Could it be waiting for me?

My front door was dark, as I had left it. I turned the key and pushed the door open, hearing only the distant rumble of traffic and the background city murmur. Stepping inside I closed the door behind me. I stood, silent at the bottom of the stairs leading up to my flat, not sure what I was listening for.

Berating myself for making something out of nothing, I spurred myself into motion, stepping stealthily up, avoiding the stair that creaked and staying close to the wall, sliding up to eye-level where the stairway turned a right-angle at the top onto my hallway and checking that the doors were all shut and the flat was as I had left it.

I went to the first door, throwing it open onto my L-shaped sitting room to reveal only the battered sofa and chair my parents had given me, my television and the stereo. The street lights through the window made shadows across the rug. Stomach tight with apprehension, I turned on the lights, then prodded behind the curtains and peered behind the sofa.

Going back into the hall, I moved cautiously along to where the kitchen and bathroom were. I pushed open the kitchen door. Both chairs were still tucked under my self-assembly table so I could get to the kettle and the four-ring cooker. I stepped across the hall and into the bathroom where I threw back the shower curtain. My shaving things were undisturbed on the shelf by the sink.

I had saved my bedroom until last as it backed onto the small garden. I threw open the door and stepped back, letting the light from the hall fall across my double bed. I could see the security locks on the French windows that overlooked the half-balcony were still secure. I clicked on the light and dropped cautiously to my knees to look under the bed. Isn't that where the monsters always hide? I checked inside my wardrobe just to be sure.

The dressing mirror inside the wardrobe door revealed my worried expression. I forced a smile, now I had been all through the flat, and returned to the French window to draw the curtains closed on the tiny back garden. The small patio behind the house that I shared with my ground floor neighbours showed dimly in the lights from the rooms below. The row of evergreens at the end of the garden cast pointed shadows across the small lawn, reminding me somehow of Kareesh's smile. It had been a strange day.

Back downstairs, I locked and bolted the front door, pressing my back against it. I made my way back up to the bedroom and took my suit off, inspecting the mess I had made of it then hanging it up out of habit. I changed into a pair of sweat pants and an old T-shirt, then cracked open a cold beer from the fridge and started packing.

Not knowing how long I would have, I concentrated on putting my rucksack together first, setting aside underwear, shirts, slacks and casual boots, a sturdy belt and several pairs of thick socks. After half an hour I had all this and more packed into a rucksack that I left at the bottom of my bed. I found a long rainproof coat and a fleece in case it turned cold.

In the kitchen, I put together an odd meal of leftover ham, grapes, plain biscuits and fruit yoghurt. I smelled the yogurt as I opened it and consigned it straight to the bin. My stomach was sour enough already. The biscuits were soft, but tasted OK with the ham. I ate the grapes as I went through the fridge, dropping anything that wouldn't keep into the wastebin.

Then I began clearing rooms.

It's funny, it's not until you start clearing stuff out that you begin to appreciate how much you have. I didn't have that much, having recently cleared myself out of the family home and leaving much more behind than mere possessions. Even so, I found postcards from my parents behind the clock and little gifts that Alex had given me in my chest of drawers.

In the bathroom, Alex's hair-mousse was still in the cabinet from her last visit and there was a toothbrush she left with me for the occasional sleepover. I knew Alex's impromptu visits were more often driven by a need for some distance between her and her mother, but I treasured them nonetheless. I tried not to take sides, simply offering tea and sympathy and a place to stay where she was always welcome, always loved. Having her things in my flat was a reminder of her presence. Nevertheless, I binned the items ruthlessly. We could always buy more hair mousse.

Methodically I cleaned each room, looking under the tables, inside tins and boxes and behind anything moveable. Everything specific to my family or myself, I stacked on the kitchen table. The rest I trashed, flushed or left.

When I had finished I went back and cleared again, finding a novelty corkscrew in the kitchen drawer that Mum had bought me ages ago and a letter from Kath which had slipped down the back of the dresser. I put all of the things into padded envelopes on the kitchen table and stuck address labels onto the outside. The first note I wrote to my parents asking them to hold onto the items for me said far too much and I knew it would only worry them. The second told them that I was moving out of the flat unexpectedly and needed them to hold onto things until I found a new place. They would still worry, but it was better than before.

I wrote a cheque to my landlord with enough money to cover three months rent and the outstanding bills, then added an apologetic note that a death in the family had meant I'd had to leave at short notice and wouldn't be back for some time. That much of the truth I could tell him. I asked him if he would mind keeping an eye on the place while I was gone.

The note I wrote to Kath reiterated what I had told her earlier and explained that I didn't know when I'd be able to make good on maintenance. I sent her the card for my savings account and then sent the code in a separate envelope, telling her to use it to support them both until I got back in touch. That would probably scare her more than anything else.

Then I cracked open another beer and sat at the kitchen table, looking at the paltry three envelopes containing anything of significance in my life. The whole process had depressed me. I just wanted to go to bed and sleep but my conscience nagged at me until I went through the whole flat again, finding nothing new this time, and finally came back to the kitchen empty-handed.

Taking stamps from one of the drawers, I split them between the packages, assuming it would be plenty of postage to get them where they needed to go. I didn't put a return address on any of them. I put on the raincoat and, loading the parcels into a plastic carrier bag, walked back out to the strip of shops around the tube station. I had some trouble getting the envelopes into the postbox, but with some shifting and shoving they eventually dropped down inside. At the cash machine I took out all the money from my current account that my card would let me have so my wallet bulged with it.

There, it was done.

Rain spotted onto the darkened pavement, adding its mood to mine. By the time I got back to the flat I was beyond playing hide and seek and simply locked and bolted the door behind me, climbed the stairs and stood in the hallway of the empty flat. I left the damp coat draped over the back of the kitchen chair and went into the bathroom where I stripped off and stood under the shower, letting the hot water wash away the dust and sweat. I had hoped I would feel better after a shower, but I felt hollow, as if it were my life that had washed down the drain.

I packed my wash-gear into a small bag to add to my rucksack after I had showered in the morning and went around the flat turning the lights off. I finally fell naked into bed, dragged the quilt over me and lay in the dark.

Now I was finally able to rest, sleep wouldn't come. I turned the light on and set the alarm for 6am then turned off the light again. I shifted position and tried to relax, knowing that tomorrow would be no easier than today. Shattered thoughts of the day kept wheedling into my brain, pushing aside the sleep I badly needed. Kareesh had said I would sleep well, proving she didn't know everything.

Thoughts of Kareesh brought back fragments of images from the vision with momentary nausea and a dull headache. Oddly the sensation helped to ground me after the strangeness of the day, making it more real.

I rolled and tossed, tangling the quilt around my legs, unable to get comfortable. I felt feverish, too hot with the quilt over me and too cold without it. Flashes of the vision kept jerking me out of slumber. Eventually I fell into sleep, but it wasn't restful.

I found myself walking under a starlit sky. The grass under my bare feet was frosted and brittle, though it wasn't cold. Evergreen trees encroached all around the crown of the hill on which I stood and although there was no moon I could still see the shadows of the branches etched in stark outline onto the grass. There was no wind and the stars were hard and bright against the black of the sky. All was silent.

There was something in the forest. In the dense shadows at the edge of the trees, something was trying to get closer without being seen. I spun around, trying to catch a glimpse of it as it moved. There were only still shadows across the grass. I started to move down the side of the hill, convinced that once I was unable to see beyond the crest, it would slide, unseen, out from under the trees.

I woke with a start, sweating, the dream hanging over into the waking dark. I knew it was much later because the background city sounds, omnipresent even in the outer suburbs of London, had died down to the minimum. The alarm clock confirmed that it was close to 4am. My bladder told me the beer had followed its natural course and I got up in the chilly darkness, still half asleep, finding my way by faint moonlight out to the bathroom to relieve myself. I shook my head to rid myself of the remnants of the dream, flushed the toilet and headed back to bed.

As I reached the bedroom, I stopped. The moonlight in the room was moving. I jumped back, expecting something to leap out from behind the door, but everything remained quiet. I glanced at the window, wondering if I had absent-mindedly left the curtains apart, but they were pulled tight. Strangely, the light was on the inside of the curtains.

My heart was beating fast now and I was wide awake. The unseen pursuit of my dream came back to me and I strained to see what was causing the shifting light. Cold sweat condensed down my back as I tensed, waiting for it to jump out.

But now I looked, the light was with me in the doorway. It was following me around. I went hesitantly back into the bedroom, observing that the strange luminescence accompanied me, falling on the back of the door as I pushed it closed. I turned into the room to find the light dancing on the walls, like moonlight through a leafy tree canopy. It had a bluish night-time tinge and while it wasn't bright, you could make out the whole of the room by it. I turned up my palm, but my hand was dark. How could my hand be dark when everything else was glowing?

I went to the wardrobe and opened it so I could look at myself in the long mirror on the inside of the door. The reflection made no sense. In the mirror, the room around me danced in the faint flickering light, but I was completely dark. I was so dark, even close to the mirror I could see no feature of my face in the strange radiance. What on earth was going on?

I turned around and the light shivered as if it passed through water disturbed by a languid hand. Even when I was completely still it shifted as if rippled by a wind I did not feel. I turned to the mirror and placed my hand upon the surface. Where my hand touched it was completely black but around it the glow intensified as if the glass itself had taken in the light, outlining my hand in a nimbus. When I moved my hand the glow trailed behind it, fading back to normal after a second. Experimentally I wrote "HELLO" on the glass with my finger, but the letters didn't last long enough for the word to show. There was no doubt, though, the glow was connected to me.

I stepped back, perplexed but intrigued. I looked around me and tried to encourage the glow, or at least that was the closest I could come to describing what I did. The glow pulsed and brightened, allowing me to pick out creases in my pillow and the darker pattern in my dressing gown. Then I damped it and it dimmed down until it flickered and died away. I stood in the near dark of my room, but it didn't come back. I turned back to my reflection and noted that even though it was now darker, I could see the features of my face and body in the meagre light leaking around the edges of the curtains.

Is this what Blackbird had meant by my magic? Is this what I could do?

Having done it once, I had to try again. I tried to glow, thinking of the strange light, but nothing happened. I looked at my hand, wishing it dark, but there was no change. Why didn't it do it again? Had I exhausted it? I thought not, but I wasn't sure what had started it. How did one glow when one wanted to? I wished Blackbird were here to see it as I was sure she would know, but then I remembered I was naked and somehow those thoughts didn't mix. She was sixty or something, or a lot older. Either way I could not imagine being naked in front of her. It felt wrong.

I went back to thinking about the glow, putting aside that troubling train of thought. What had she said to me? Magic responds to need? I tried to need to glow, but you can't just need something because you think you can.

I shook myself, shedding my confusion like water.

Blackbird told me that the power was within me, that all I had to do was learn to reach for it. I knew I could do it, I had seen it for myself. What had sparked that connection? The dream?

I closed my eyes and remembered the feeling from the dream, bringing an involuntary shiver. Then I imagined myself standing in my bedroom, with the glow starting dim and building until it flickered over the walls. I made that thought real in my mind, assuring myself that was how it would be when I opened my eyes. Within me, something that had been waiting stirred to life. There was something inside me, something dark and deep. I reached within, and as I did, it reached for me and the connection was there.

I opened my eyes and the room was filled with milky-blue dappled light.

Alarmed, I pulled away and the light flickered and died.

I tentatively reached within myself again. It was there. The connection formed at once. Light spilled out into the room.

I grinned at myself. I had made magic. It was me doing it. I could make a glow. OK, it wasn't summoning lightning or transforming base metal into gold, but I had made a glow.

I relaxed my hold and the connection within me subsided so that the light flickered and vanished. Then I called it back and it returned, quicker this time and stronger, the light brightening until the walls swam like a room underwater. I was so pleased with myself. It was strange and exciting. I couldn't stop grinning.

I released it again, shivering in the pre-dawn chill. My earlier doubts and depression were swept away by my new talent. Maybe I could do other things as well? It made me even more determined to find Blackbird again tomorrow, or later today as I realised it would shortly be. I was tempted to experiment some more with my new-found skill, but I made myself get back into bed and settle down. I needed more sleep if I was going to be able to face the new day. Briefly I summoned it back and made the interesting discovery that the glow wasn't stopped by the bedclothes. It flickered across the ceiling over the bed. It formed around me rather than on me. I was so thrilled, I couldn't wait to show Blackbird. Mind you, she would probably say everyone could do it from the age of three and that I should concentrate on doing something more useful.

With thoughts of what I might say to her tomorrow I drifted towards a deeper, more restful sleep.

That was when I heard the stair creak.

SIX

There are some noises that you immediately recognise. Something about them, the resonance or quality of the sound means that they are unmistakable. My creaky stair was like that. When I'd first moved into the flat it had irritated me. I had kicked it, banged it and knocked nails into it. It still creaked. It didn't creak when the house cooled or when the wind was in a certain direction. It didn't creak when my neighbours downstairs moved around in the lower half of the house.

It only creaked when someone stood on it.

I slipped quietly out of bed and went to the door. It was shut and I put my hand against it, listening intently for any other sound. Maybe it was Alex. Perhaps she'd stormed out after a bad argument with her mother and turned up here for tea and comfort, all hormones and teenage angst. But I had bolted the front door. Alex would have had to ring the bell or hammer on the door to get me to come downstairs and undo the bolt.

The step creaked when you stood on it, and again when you stepped off. I was pretty sure that it had only creaked once. There was absolute stillness. I stood and listened, naked in the dark, starting to feel chilled, but nothing stirred. The memory of the unseen pursuer and chill air from my dream returned to me and I was just on the point of thinking that the creak had somehow been part of the dream when it came again.

There was definitely someone on the stairs. Someone or something.

Could it be Blackbird? A bolted door would be unlikely to stop her if she wanted to come in. She'd said that she would find me, hadn't she? But why would Blackbird creep up my stairs at four in the morning? And why would she stop when the stairs creaked? No, whatever it was, it wasn't good news. She'd told me to watch my back. She'd warned me, "If they catch you, you'll die," and she wasn't joking.

I put my finger on the light switch, then hesitated. It would show under the door and whatever it was would know I was awake. I looked around the darkened room. There was no weapon, nothing I could use to defend myself. Besides, if it was something like Gramawl I was kidding myself if I thought I could fight it and win.

The window was the only option. If I opened the big French windows, I could climb over the railing of the half-balcony, drop down onto the patio and make a run for it.

I moved around the room, trying to locate my clothes in the dark. While it was tempting to just open the window and jump for it, I knew I would be much worse off naked. The delay between stepping on and off the stair told me that whatever it was on the stairs was being cautious. That meant I had a few moments to get my stuff. I fumbled, pulling on my T-shirt and slipped quickly into my underpants. The trousers I had left out for the morning were here somewhere. I cursed silently in the dark. Then I remembered my glow.

I summoned it, but nothing happened. No wonder, my mind was like a butterfly. Knowledge leant me calm and allowed me to focus. I reached within and my glow flickered into life. It was unsteady, reflecting my state of mind. I glanced towards the door and wondered how much time I might have? Not long. If only the door had a lock on it.

Pulling on my trousers, I tried to think of something to wedge in the door to keep it closed. The milky light danced around me. If only I could seal the door.

But perhaps there was a way. Magic responds to need, that's what Blackbird said. Well, I sure as hell needed it now.

I went to the door and put my hand on it, remembering what she told me. The power was there, I just had to believe in it. I knew I could do magic, the light was all around me. I needed to bend it to my will and seal the door.

I focused on the door, thinking, *Yes, I remember there used to be a door here, but it was nailed shut.* I reinforced the thought, feeling an echo of something inside, a pulse of darkness. I struggled to link it somehow with the thought that the door was nailed shut so no one could use it. I opened my eyes, only then realising I had closed them. My glow had gone and the door looked the same, but I knew it was nailed shut. It was no good trying it, because it had been nailed shut long ago. I had to believe.

I went back to the end of the bed and rekindled my glow, fumbling with my socks. Abandoning trying to put them on, I stuffed the socks into the top of my rucksack and put my bare feet into my boots. It would have to do. I pulled the laces tight without lacing them up, knotting them roughly to stop them from tripping me. I heard a tiny sound that might have been something in the kitchen. Damn! That was where my coat was. I'd have to abandon it.

I froze. The door handle on the inside of my bedroom door slowly turned downwards. I frantically reinforced my belief that it was no good trying to open the sealed door and edged towards the window. The handle reached the bottom, but the door didn't open. I grabbed the rucksack and pulled the top closed. Whatever was

101

on the other side of the door now knew I had barred it. I went over to the French window and pulled the curtains back.

The door creaked. I glanced at it while I fumbled one-handed with the security locks on the French windows. Why were security locks so fiddly? I stopped trying to watch the bedroom door, which was nailed shut anyway, and concentrated on the window locks, bringing up my glow so I could see what I was doing. The light swelled and swayed around me, making it more difficult to see what I was doing.

Tiny pings and creaks were coming from the door, as if enormous pressure were building up on the other side. The door bulged inwards as the strain built up. The tips of my fingers were numb with the strain of trying to open the catch when I finally managed to release it and the security lock flipped open. I yanked the catch across and wrenched opened the window. There was a sound behind me and I glanced back. The door had held.

I reached over and grabbed the rucksack, hoisted it over the railing and dropped it onto the patio below as quietly as I could. I didn't want whatever was outside my door to know I was escaping and go back downstairs to intercept me as I came around the front.

A glance over my shoulder revealed dark spots forming on the door. The spots ran together to form a dark stain in the centre of the wood. Each spot had the same flat unreflecting black as my skin when I called my glow. Hesitantly I stepped back around the bed towards the door, fascinated by the spreading blackness. It was like the opposite of my glow, cancelling out any light I could make.

"Brother." The breathy murmur from the other side of the door resolved into words, making the hair on the back of my neck stand on end. "Open the dooooor."

That did it. I went back to the half-balcony and swung my leg up over the railing, finding it uncomfortably tall in awkward places. I fought for a footing on the other side. As I looked back into the bedroom from the far side of the railing I could see black spots spreading over the wood of the door. They spread like drops of water condensing on a surface, running across it, joining and merging into a dark stain. What the hell was that? The spots paused at the edge of the door then swelled onto the wall, running across the wall and up onto the ceiling.

I had seen enough. I took a quick look down to where my rucksack was lying on the patio, squatted down to get as low as I could and dropped from the rail to the paving below. The impact jarred me to the core and I banged my chin against my knee as I sprawled onto the wet slabs made slick by the rain. I pushed myself to my feet. My glow was gone, but I could see my rucksack by the city lights reflected from the low clouds. I grabbed it by the strap, swung it over one shoulder and glanced up at the room, now dark with the window wide open. I would have to leave it like that. What else could I do? The flat had been the one place I could be myself. It was a refuge from work and from life. Now I was being forced to abandon that as well. Anger swelled in me, taking the edge off my fear.

Turning away, I edged up to the corner of the house and peeked around to see if anything was waiting to jump me. There was nothing to be seen. At the front of the house, a quick glance at the front garden told me the way was clear just as a loud dull thump came from the back of the house. It spurred me on and I headed straight for the front gate.

Out on the road, I ran down the street. After an initial sprint, I slowed to a steady jog, putting as much distance between me and the thing in my flat as possible. I'm not a natural runner and the loose boots and rucksack didn't help, but all I had to do was keep moving.

The rain pattered down in steady drops and began to soak through my shirt as I crossed the empty street and turned the corner. Occasional cars rolled past but there were no other pedestrians. I guess four in the morning was a little early, even for the London suburbs. My breath was burning in my lungs as I turned right into a side road, heading vaguely towards the tube station. My rucksack began to pull at my shoulder and I stopped to shift it from one side to the other.

That was when the police car put the blue lights on and pulled over beside the curb.

It crossed my mind that I might run for it, but I was already breathing hard and they were fresh, unencumbered and probably a lot fitter then I was. The last time I had been to the gym had been to fetch Katherine home and that had been a while ago. Both the driver and the passenger got out, effectively cutting off the avenues of escape. I didn't move, but leant over, resting my hands on my knees and wheezing like a steam train.

"Isn't it a little early for jogging, sir?"

That was bad news. They always called you "sir" when they were expecting to arrest you.

My throat burned and I wheezed while I thought of something to say. Unfortunately whatever I told them was going to have to contain at least a portion of the truth. I glanced back down the road for signs of pursuit, but the pavement was empty.

The policemen waited while I caught my breath. The first was tall and heavily built, like a rugby player, and had a slightly crooked nose to match. The other was slight by comparison. His face was narrow and his cheekbones sharp. He wore black gloves and was holding his baton.

"I'm not jogging." I paused to breathe. "I'm running away."

The rugby player took the lead. "Running away, sir?"

"Officer, look I know this is going to sound crazy, but there was something in my flat, trying to get into my bedroom. I jumped out of the window and ran for it." I panted while he looked me over sceptically.

"With your rucksack, sir?"

"I was going on a trip, later," I explained. It sounded lame, even to me.

"Do you mind if my colleague takes a look in your rucksack, sir?" I let the thin one take the rucksack from where it rested against my legs. "Meanwhile you can show me some evidence of your identity, if you'd be so kind."

I patted my pockets. My wallet, watch and keys were still in my top drawer in the bedroom. Good plan, bring clean socks but leave the money behind.

"I don't have them with me. I left them behind when I jumped out of the window."

"So you say, sir."

He glanced at his colleague who was busy rooting though my belongings. "Just clothes, Jim. Some food," he acknowledged.

Jim watched me. "Tell you what, sir. Why don't you get into the back of the car where it's dry and you can tell us all about it?" It wasn't really a question.

His colleague held the door open and they herded me into the back of the car. I was willing to bet the door didn't open from the inside, so I was stuck. They spoke to each other after the door shut and then the thin officer opened the passenger door of the car and deposited my rucksack on the front seat. Jim walked around the back of the car and got in beside me. He easily filled the space behind the driver's seat. I was starting to shiver and my hands were shaking in my lap. He must have noticed because he got out again and opened the boot, returning a moment later with a grey blanket.

"Here, put this around your shoulders. It'll stop you getting a chill."

I nodded, my teeth starting to chatter, partly through cold and partly reaction. I unfolded the blanket and pulled it around my neck, shifting it around to pull it down behind me in the cramped rear of the car. "Thanks."

Was he more sympathetic than his colleague, or was he just playing good cop, bad cop like they did on TV? I had to remind myself that this wasn't a television drama, these were real police and if I came across badly I would end up spending a night in custody. The thought of spending a night locked in a room where the thing in my flat might find me set me shivering again.

The driver slid into the driver's seat in front of his colleague and pulled the door closed with a dull *thunk*. He picked up the car radio and twisted around in his seat.

"I'm going to need to check your ID, sir, if you don't mind. Can you give me your name and address?"

"It's Petersen. Niall Petersen. I live at 145 Cromwell Road."

He nodded. "And how long have you lived there?"

"Just over a year. I moved in at the beginning of September, last year."

Clicking the button on the radio handset he spoke into it. "Control, this is four-two-five-six. I need an electoral check on a householder?"

There was a momentary crackle. "Go ahead, Colin."

"Name, Petersen; first name Niall." He asked me to spell it and repeated it into the handset. "Lives Cromwell Road, number one-four-five."

"Stand by."

He rested the handset in his lap. "Nice place?"

"Sorry?"

"One hundred and forty-five, Cromwell Road. Is it a nice place?"

"I like it." It had taken a while for it to become home after the breakup of my marriage, but in time it had become mine.

The radio crackled. "Colin, I have an affirmative. Niall Petersen, age forty-two, lives one hundred and forty-five, Cromwell Road."

Colin lifted the handset again. "Thanks, control. We have a suspected intruder at that address. Requesting backup, a dog handler, if we can have one?"

"Negative on that, Colin. The dog handlers are all on night-club duty. Will another car do?"

"Affirmative, control. Roger that." He turned to look over his shoulder at me. "Let's take you home, sir, and see what's what."

"I'd really rather not go back there right now." The edge of panic in my voice raised an eyebrow from the officer beside me.

"It's OK, sir. You're quite safe. We just want to check it out."

His efforts to reassure me weren't working. "I mean it." I tried to think of a way to warn them. "Can't you just arrest me or something?" A night in the cells was looking better now.

"We'll see, sir, after we've been to the house."

My reticence to return to the house had sparked off their suspicion again, almost as if there was something I didn't want them to find. In a way they were right, but I could guarantee it wasn't what they suspected.

Colin started the car and did a rapid three-point turn. I wondered whether I could unlock the car doors using my magic and run for it, but then I would lose my rucksack and they would certainly chase me. They already knew my identity and having the police searching for me as well as the Untainted was not a good idea.

The drive back to the house only took a couple of minutes and it struck me that I hadn't run as far as I thought. They parked on the road outside. The house was dark.

"Is it two flats?" Colin asked me, noting the two front doors.

"Yes, the top one's mine. The bottom one belongs to a young couple."

"Do you have your keys?"

"They're upstairs, in my bedroom." I glanced nervously at the front door. "Look, please don't go in there, at least not until morning."

He hesitated.

Jim, the rugby player, answered, "We have to investigate, sir. It's our duty." He pulled the door catch and eased out into the rain.

Colin got out while Jim held the door open and gestured for me to slide across towards him. Colin waited while I reluctantly shrugged off the blanket and shuffled across to get out of the car between them.

"Follow close behind us. We won't let anyone hurt you, OK?" He nodded to Colin and we walked towards the door.

I hung back from them, but then edged closer as the gap opened up between us, leaving me exposed as we went through the gate. The back of my neck prickled. My instinct told me something waited for us but I could see no way out. If I ran for it, I would become their suspect again. Maybe it had gone? Maybe when I ran away it gave up and left?

Colin pushed the front door. "Door's locked."

However it had got in, it'd had the sense to lock the door behind it.

"Is there a back door?" Jim asked me.

"Not for the upstairs flat. Only the downstairs has rear access," I told him, relieved that we weren't going inside.

"Do your neighbours have a key?"

"Yes, a spare. They'll be asleep though," I told him.

"Not for long." He nodded to Colin, who shrugged then went and rang my neighbour's bell.

It took a few minutes for the lights to come on and for my neighbour to come to the door. I could see he was not pleased to be woken at this time in the morning, but that changed as soon as he saw the uniform. His expression altered to one of nervous enquiry.

Colin told him that they needed the spare key and nodded towards me. I shrugged apologetically towards my neighbour. He nodded, looking towards me, recognising but not acknowledging. There was another wait while my neighbour found my key. You can never find these things when you need them. Then another police car turned up, without blue lights or sirens, pulling in behind the other car. Two more officers got out. One of the new policemen came across while the other hung back.

"Evening, Skipper." Jim nodded to the officer who hung back, "Eddie."

The new officer joined us. "What's the situation? Is this the owner of the flat?"

"This is Mr Petersen, Skipper, Niall Petersen. He was running down the pavement with a rucksack and boots with no socks." The expression said the lack of socks was a clear indication of criminal activity. "He says someone was trying to get into his bedroom and he jumped out of the window."

The Skipper turned to me. "Been in the flat long, have you?"

"Just over a year," I confirmed.

"Does anyone live here with you?"

"Only my neighbours downstairs."

"Any other exits besides the front door?"

"The first floor window I jumped out of."

"Did you see the intruder, Mr Petersen? Was there any sign of a weapon?"

"I didn't see anyone, but I could hear someone moving around in the flat."

"Any pets, sir?"

"Pets?"

"Sometimes a neighbour's cat can get trapped in a house and doesn't emerge until later, sir. It scares the wits out of people, but it solves the mystery." He smiled reassuringly.

I acknowledged the smile, figuring that the transition from potential criminal to potential victim was promising. "I don't have any pets and I don't think they do either." I nodded towards my neighbour who had been joined in the doorway by his partner. My expression must have conveyed that I thought it unlikely.

"What's the layout, sir?"

I described the flat to him, including the squeaky stair and fact that I'd left my coat on the kitchen chair, I added that I'd left my wash-bag in the bathroom. I wanted to reassure them I had been fine until someone had broken in. I told them I had jammed the bedroom door shut from the inside and climbed out over the balcony. The new officer was more understanding, but noncommittal. I guessed he was simply extracting as much information as he could before the difficult questions started.

"Eddie, you're with Jim. Go around the back and see if you can see anything. Colin, you're with me. We'll take Mr Petersen inside." Jim exchanged a look with Colin, looking relieved that he wasn't one of the people going into the flat. I guess I had them spooked.

They extracted torches from their belts then went to the corner of the house.

Skipper told me to stick close to them. He took the key and went to the front door. Jim and Eddie slipped quietly around the side of the building.

The two officers went quickly and efficiently inside with me close behind them.

"Police! Anyone in here? Police!"

The stair creaked as soon as they stood on it. Skipper looked back at me and nodded once.

My sitting room was on the right.

"Police!" The officer called Eddie danced his torch beam around the room. "Clear."

Skipper swept his torch down the hall. "Jeez," he said, "what's that?"

His torch hit the black stain that covered the door to my bedroom and the walls around it. It had spread across the ceiling and the smell of it pervaded the air. It smelled of damp and old rot.

I looked at the walls and ceiling, letting my expression show I was as mystified as they were.

The door, walls and ceiling were covered in what looked like damp-rot. It ran over the walls and up onto the ceiling, spreading a smell of pervasive decay. It gave the hall a fetid atmosphere it had never had while I had lived there. My bedroom door was black with mould apart from the gaping hole in the middle where it had burst through like tinder.

We walked forward slowly, the lights from the torches scanning the walls and ceiling.

The radio crackled and Jim's voice came through: "All clear here, Skipper."

Skipper put his hand to the radio switch at his collar. "Roger that."

Colin went down the hall past the bedroom door, being careful not to touch the black stain. He scanned the torch around my kitchen and then the bathroom.

"Clear here too, Skipper. There's not even a scrap of mould in the bathroom or kitchen. It's all clean." His tone said something odd was going on, though he was at a loss to explain what.

"Was it like this before?" the Skipper asked me.

I shook my head, unable to frame an outright lie to the contrary. I was well aware that if I started talking about mould running across the walls like water I would be spending the next three months in a psychiatric unit.

Colin leaned down and used his torch to scan through the gaping hole in my bedroom door. He extracted his baton and used the end to push the door handle down. It was still sealed and didn't move.

"There's no one in there, sir, as far as we can tell, but the door's stuck," he told me. "Is it locked?"

"No." I looked at the ruins of the door. "I just jammed it. Try it again." I felt for the link that connected the seal on the door to me. I imagined it opening at a touch. The link echoed and then faded.

Skipper used his baton to turn the handle down again and pushed. The door scraped, then opened, swinging away from him before casually dropping off the top hinge to land askew. He swung his torch around inside the room and then entered, delicately clicking the light switch on with the end of his baton. The inside was as bad as the outer, dark rot spread over the wall and ceiling. Thankfully it hadn't affected the carpet or furniture, but the smell was awful. It reeked of decay. The damp rainy air from the open windows smelled fresh by comparison.

"Door's had it," Colin remarked.

"And with all the debris on the inside of the room," the Skipper pointed out. "Was there any mould in the flat before?" he asked me again.

"No. I'm sure I would have noticed. I can't explain…" I let my voice trail off as I looked at the remnants of the door and the walls, stained black with it.

"Where are your keys and wallet?" Colin asked me.

"They're in the top drawer, by the bed."

Using his gloved hand, he opened the drawer using the edge of the wood rather than the drawer handle. He lifted out my watch, keys and wallet. "Are these yours?" he asked.

I nodded.

The Skipper clicked on his radio. "The flat's clear. Anything there?"

Jim's voice came back over the radio, curiously echoed by his voice travelling faintly though the open window to the rear. "All clear here, Skipper."

I breathed a sigh of relief. It had gone.

"Roger that," the Skipper replied. He turned to Colin. "Take Mr Petersen into the sitting room," he said.

Colin ushered me into the sitting room, switching on the lights as he went.

I heard the Skipper take a look in my bathroom and then in the kitchen, joining us in the sitting room after a moment. He brought my coat from the kitchen and draped it over the back of a chair.

Colin stood by the door, while the Skipper indicated that I should sit on the sofa. He put my personal items on the coffee table, picking out my wallet and opening it to the photograph of Alex. He ruffled through the money stuffed into the back of it then held out the picture ID from my work pass, comparing my face with the younger image in the photo. It must have been close enough because he put the card back in my wallet and pushed it across the table towards me.

"That's a lot of cash to be carrying about, sir," he remarked as I pocketed the wallet and buckled the leather strap of my watch around my wrist.

"I told your colleague, I was going away for a while. I had my rucksack packed and ready for the morning."

"Where were you going, sir?"

"I have to clear up some family business, personal matters. I wasn't sure when I'd be back. Look, am I under suspicion of something here? I'm the one who was woken up by someone breaking into my home, remember?"

"That's the thing, sir. There's no sign of a break-in downstairs, the lock is intact and opens to your key. There's no indication of an intruder and yet your bedroom door looks as though someone has taken a sledgehammer to it. Then there's the mould..." He let that sentence hang.

"I told you. It wasn't like that before."

The radio cut across me. "Skipper. We think we've found someone."

The Skipper paused, then clicked on his radio. "What do you mean you think you've found someone, Eddie? Either you have or you haven't."

There was a burst of static and then Eddie's voice. "I dunno, Skipper. I could have sworn he wasn't there a minute ago. He's under the trees at the end of the garden. Jim's trying to coax him out now."

I could hear Jim's voice in the background. You could just make out the words, "Police! Come along out, sir. We just want to have a word with you."

The Skipper walked to the door and through into my bedroom to look out over the balcony. I stood up, but Colin held up his hand. "Just stay there, sir."

I could feel all the hairs on the back of my neck rise. It wasn't some old guy they'd found, it was the

Untainted, come for me. I wanted to warn them, to tell them to leave it alone, but I couldn't think of what to say without appearing insane.

Colin's radio buzzed and crackled. "We're going to pull him out. Jim's just..." There was a weird sound in the background, like a woman giggling hysterically but with a man's deeper voice.

The radio died. The light bulbs wavered, dimming to a yellowish glow.

Colin clicked at his radio. "Say again, Eddie." The radio was dead.

I looked at Colin. I couldn't let this happen. I yelled through to the Skipper. "Tell them not to touch it. Tell them!"

A scream came from the back of the house. It was Jim's voice. "Get it off me! Get it off! Get it off!"

The Skipper thundered out of my bedroom. "Officer down, get an ambulance!" He ran down the hall and bounced off the end wall, taking the stairs down two at a time.

Colin shouted. "Stay here! Don't open the door 'till I say." He ran after his boss.

From the back of the house I could hear Jim. "Oh God! It's in my eyes! My eyes! I can't see!"

The manic laughter rose in pitch. The lights winked out, leaving me in darkness. I grabbed my coat on the way past the chair.

Shouted commands came from the back. "Stand where you are! Police! Don't move!"

I ran towards the stairs as Jim's screaming subsided to a gurgling, choking sound. I wrenched the front door open and ran out into the rain. I sprinted straight past the startled Colin who was talking urgently into the car radio in the open door of the car. He shouted something as I ran out into the road. I fled that sound, lengthening my stride and pushing myself, not caring that my heart hammered in my ears or that my feet were sore where my boots chafed my bare feet. I had to get away. I ran on into the night, knowing what was behind me if I stopped.

I took alternate right then left turns as I met each junction, working my way towards the tube station where there would be other people, other human beings. I needed to lose myself, and fast.

Adrenaline fuelled my pace and kept me moving until I finally came to a halt at an empty bus shelter. I leaned against the inside for a moment, my breath raw in my throat, then shrugged into my coat, thinking it would be easier to run while wearing it than holding it. My chest heaved and my heart hammered. I couldn't keep this up indefinitely, I just wasn't fit enough. I needed a plan.

I pushed off the bus stop and started running again. There was a minicab service near the tube station. If I could make it to there I could get a car into London. As Blackbird had said, I would be harder to find in the city.

A glance backwards showed a light like a bright star rising in the sky in the direction I had come. Shit! No one told me it could fly! Then the sound caught up with me. The jittered thumping meant the police had called in a helicopter. A beam of the light stabbed down onto the streets behind me. Were they looking for me? Why? I was the victim. I was the one who was being pursued by the thing in the garden. They should be dealing with that, not chasing innocent people.

Except I wasn't innocent. I had known what was back there and I could have warned them. I had tried to warn them but it had come too late. Now I was a witness, possibly even a suspect. An officer had been hurt. No, I was kidding myself. An officer had died. Now they would try and find me. And even if I told them the truth they would never believe me.

And then they would lock me up.

SEVEN

The helicopter circled away behind me, scanning the streets and gardens. As I approached the row of shops near the tube station, the buildings got taller, keeping me from tracking the helicopter and, hopefully, preventing it from tracking me.

They would be using thermal imaging cameras and I was sweating from the long run. The cool night breeze against my wet clothes would chill me quickly once I stopped running but for now I would shine like a beacon for the camera.

I stepped into the alley alongside a shop, letting the darkness and the narrow gap conceal me while I caught my breath. I could still hear the angry buzz of the chopper echoing around the empty streets but I figured that turning up at the minicab office out of breath, looking like a man on the run while a helicopter searched the streets would be a dead giveaway. I straightened my coat and used a tissue from my coat pocket to wipe the sweat from my face. Leaning against the wall, I re-tied the laces of my boots in a respectable fashion and then stood, adjusting my trousers so they covered my bare ankles and straightening my coat.

It wouldn't take the police long to work out that I had evaded them. They would watch the tube stations and alert the taxi firms. They had taken a good look at me and would issue a description from that. If I was going to be able to get a cab without being recognised I needed to do it soon.

Then it occurred to me, I could change my appearance. I could walk right past them and they would never know it was me. All I needed was the will to do it. The glamour Blackbird had shown me in Trafalgar Square the previous morning might be the key to evading my pursuers.

I closed my eyes for a moment, imagining myself wearing my suit and tie, ready for a day's work, fixing the memory of it, convincing myself I was wearing my business attire. I felt a shift inside as darkness stirred within me. There was an answering tingle on my skin.

Looking down, I found my clothes shifting and blending, the cloth of my coat rippling like water as my attention wavered. I struggled to fix the image, my boots switching to shoes and back to boots as I watched. It was no good, I simply didn't have enough control to maintain it. I let the glamour slip and reverted back to my true appearance. I would have to take the chance they hadn't alerted everyone yet.

I stepped out of the alley, trying to look inconspicuous, walking steadily towards the road where the taxi company had their all-night offices. Taking a cab directly into central London would lead the police to look for me there. What I needed was somewhere where there were enough people to make it hard to find me amongst the crowds even at this time of day. I needed somewhere that I might reasonably want to hire a cab to get to early in the morning. Paradoxically it would be somewhere where the security was much tighter. I needed Heathrow Airport.

Buttoning my coat, I walked out of the alley, trying not to look hunted.

I kept close to the buildings as I turned in to the side-street where the minicab firm was based. As I turned the corner, I saw the tell-tale flash of blue lights. From the shadow of a doorway I saw a fire engine roar past the end of the road, lights blazing, siren silent until it reached a junction further on where its brief wail echoed back down the wet streets.

The Fire Service, aside from putting out fires, also dealt with biological contamination. They were treating the flat as a contaminated area. If they thought the mould was some kind of manufactured biological weapon then their efforts to find me would be on a different scale. It took all my reserves of will-power to walk into the radio-taxi office and appear calm.

I opened the door to the smell of hastily smothered cigarette. The bloke manning the radio was wearing thick glasses and peering at a newspaper crossword, apparently oblivious to the smoke still rising from the waste bin.

He looked up. "Yes, mate?"

"Good morning. Could I get a car to Heathrow, please?"

He considered this for a moment and I hesitated, wondering if a description had already been circulated. I was about to tell him not to bother and start running again when he spoke.

"It'll cost you fifteen quid at this time of day, mate."

"That'll be fine, but I need to get there quickly."

"Got an early flight, have you?"

"Well, you know how long it takes to get through all the security these days. Better to be early than to risk missing a flight, eh?" It wasn't a lie, but he would assume I was flying out. Maybe the police would make the same assumption when they questioned him, later.

"It'll be two minutes, guv. The cars are just coming on shift. Shouldn't take long. Have a seat."

He spoke in staccato sentences and indicated the vinyl covered chairs by the door. I sat down, while he spoke into the radio, summoning a car for me. I was painfully aware that if the police walked in now I would have no escape. I fidgeted in the seat then forced myself to stillness. The minutes passed with agonising slowness. When the man looked up from his crossword and spoke, I almost jumped in my seat.

"Car's just outside, guv," he said.

"Thanks," I said, trying to conceal my nervousness with enthusiasm.

I got up and went outside. There was a Ford Mondeo estate parked outside. The diesel engine sounded rough and harsh. As I approached, the passenger window slid down. I leaned down to speak with the driver.

"Where to?" he asked me.

"Heathrow, please?"

"Right you are."

I opened the door and slid into the back, pulling it shut behind me. He set off without waiting for me to buckle my seat belt.

"Which terminal?"

"Sorry?"

"Which terminal at the airport? Should be written on your ticket."

"Oh, terminal one, please. That'll be fine."

"Europe, is it?"

"I have some family business to clear up," I told him, avoiding the direct question. "Personal matters."

"Well, I hope you have better weather than we're having here."

I let the comment hang, not wanting to get into a detailed conversation when I would find it difficult to lie to him. Our route took us past the tube station and, as we drove by, I could see a police car had pulled up on the pavement near the entrance. The officers were talking to someone in a London Transport uniform. One of the officers watched our car go past. I turned away, hoping he hadn't spotted me.

"Boys in blue having a busy night," the driver commented as we passed.

"Really?" I responded.

"Yeah. Didn't you hear that helicopter earlier? I reckon someone's done over the pharmacy again. They never learn, do they?"

I wondered for a moment who they were, who never learned, but offered no encouragement for him to continue.

Fed up with holding a one-sided conversation, the driver turned sport radio on instead. The endless speculation as to the outcomes of the weekend's fixtures was a dull monologue in the back of the car. I did my best to ignore it.

I kept an eye out for blue lights approaching fast from behind us, but there was no sign. I figured the policeman at the tube station must not have seen me, the wet and dark working in my favour for once. I used the respite in the back of the car to think.

There was no doubt in my mind that the Untainted were hunting me. I was sure one of them had been in the flat and in the back garden. It sounded like it had gone for one of the police officers, the one called Jim, the rugby player. I wondered briefly whether he had family, someone waiting for him to come home. Suddenly filled with guilt, I veered away from the pain of others, distancing myself from responsibility and concentrating on my own problems.

It had only taken the Untainted a short while to find me. What had she said? I had to keep running? Where to? Besides, I'd only have to bump into someone like Fenlock and I would be just as dead. I really needed Blackbird's knowledge and advice. She was the only one I knew who didn't want to kill me, rob me or arrest me.

The problem was finding her. I felt I had offended her by probing too far into her secrets. It wasn't that I wanted to know everything about her, but part of me needed to know who I was dealing with. I didn't think it would make much difference to me if she turned out to be like Kareesh and have pale skin and rows of pointed teeth, she had shown me nothing but kindness. She was quick and canny and in charge of her own destiny which was more than I could claim.

Kareesh had said she was hiding without being specific about what she was hiding from, but my guess was that it was related to her true form. Why was that such a sensitive issue? I had seen Kareesh and, while she was a little unorthodox, I thought I could accept her for who she was.

With Blackbird I felt our friendship was tenuous at best, though I wanted it to be stronger. The trouble was that I needed her a lot more than she needed me. What could I offer her? I knew she felt responsible for me, but that was hardly the basis for an enduring friendship, was it? Still, if I was going to make it through the next few days I needed her help.

That sent me back to the problem of finding her. In the real world I knew how to find people. I could use the internet or phone directory enquiries and ask for a name, a number, or some other reference.

Blackbird was different, though. She didn't inhabit the world of computers and databases. I didn't know her name, only what she called herself, and I was pretty sure that if I phoned directory enquiries their first question would be "Is that a first name or a last name?"

I had no idea where she lived. She'd told me she had a flat, and a flatmate, but she had not told me where it was. I pondered for a moment what the flatmate might think of her. Was the flatmate Fey too? Did they live together? And how did Blackbird pay rent for a flat? I knew so little about her that finding her by conventional means was impossible.

She'd said she would find me, though she had refused to be drawn on when or where. Perhaps the first thing to do was to go somewhere I knew she could find me. Maybe that would be enough. If I could get back to

Trafalgar Square avoiding police attention, I should be fairly safe there.

What had she said? *"You'll never be safe again, get used to it."*

I spent the rest of the journey in silence, half listening to the inanity of the radio and considering Blackbird's advice.

When we reached Heathrow I had the driver drop me at Departures for Terminal One. I was sure the police would find the taxi firm and the guy in the office would remember me. If I gave the impression I was getting a flight somewhere then that would be something else they would have to check before they found my trail again. At this stage, the more hares I could set running for them to chase, the better.

I paid the driver and walked into Departures, I was going to take the escalator straight down to Arrivals, but I spotted a small shop selling socks and ties. I stopped and bought a two-pack of grey socks. They were overpriced and not really suitable for my boots, but they were better than nothing. I strode through the people waiting to check their luggage and into the public toilets. There was a long line of stalls and I went right to the end. I locked the door, hung my coat on the hook and sat on the seat, removing my boots. My feet were red where the boots had rubbed, but there was little I could do about it. I unwrapped the socks and put them on, relishing the feeling of clean cotton after the harsh abrasion of the boots.

I could hear other people flushing toilets and washing hands as they moved around outside while I slipped my feet back into my boots and laced them carefully.

There was a *bang* as the door to the toilets was pushed open hard.

"Police! Clear these toilets! Everyone outside, right now! Come on! Everyone out!"

There was muttering among the people outside. I froze. I was trapped and there was no way out. They were going to arrest me.

"Yes, you too, sir. Outside. Right now! Everyone out!"

I could hear people being ushered out. There was a bang from the end of the row of stall, then another. They were checking every stall. There was no way out of the toilets except past them and they knew what I looked like.

Or did they? I had tried using glamour to get past them before in the alley and failed. Now it was my only hope. It was a risk I would have to take. They were looking for a man in his mid-forties in chinos and a T-shirt. I would try to show them someone else.

Steeling myself to ignore the thumps of successive doors being kicked open, I stood up and focused on my image. I imagined a younger me, thinner, none of the wrinkles that had come with age and experience, my hair dark and thick, longer than I had worn it lately. I focused on the sharp black suit, white shirt, black shoes and blue tie I had worn to a friend's wedding long ago. I held the picture of it in my mind, making the image real, making it solid. Knowing it was me and that was how I would look. The feeling inside me grew, sending tendrils of power into my veins. My skin itched and tingled. I repeated the thought to myself. I was sure it was me. I made it real. I thought about how it would feel to wear the suit, how the shirt collar would rub and how the lined suit would sit on my shoulders. I opened my eyes.

They had reached my stall. Before they could kick the door in, I unlocked and opened it. Now was the proof. He was waiting for me, the sound of the door unlocking alerting him to my presence. I stepped out.

He took one look at me. "Didn't you hear me? I said everyone out!" He shouted.

"Sorry," I told him. "Flying always makes me nervous." I edged past him towards the other two officers. They all had batons held ready.

Then I remembered that my coat was still hanging on the back of the open door. He looked inside.

"Just a minute," he said.

I halted, turning slowly, my inner mantra affirming my appearance, believing I was that younger man. "Yes, officer. Is something wrong?"

"A man wearing a long coat, T-shirt and khaki slacks. Did you see him?"

"I was in the toilet," I told him, "with the door shut."

He paused and then said, "You'd better leave." He turned to his colleagues. "You two, check the Ladies on the other side. He's here somewhere. Move!"

The officers ran past me into the connecting passage, heading further down the short access corridor for the Ladies. I walked out, concentrating for all I was worth on being the young man in the suit.

As I walked across the concourse to the escalator down to the arrivals hall, I saw other police, both armed and regular officers. They were walking slowly through the people waiting to check in, searching the faces. My attempt to mislead them by mixing with the crowds at Heathrow had nearly been my undoing but now it worked to my advantage. The face they were looking for wasn't the one I was wearing.

I couldn't see how they had found me so quickly though. It was almost as if they knew where I was going to be. If they had found the taxi then they could have stopped me earlier, but they hadn't. They hadn't found me until I arrived at Heathrow. Something had given me away.

Two people who looked like flight crew walked past me, a woman and a man in airline uniform. As they approached me, a mobile phone rang and I patted my pockets for it before realising it was the woman's phone that was ringing, but with the same ringtone as mine. She smiled at me as she answered, understanding my mistake. I returned the smile as she walked past.

It left me with my phone in my hand and then I realised what must have happened. They knew where I was because of my phone. The police had traced my phone and got the network provider to watch for my signal. In the car it had been moving too quickly but as soon as I reached Heathrow they had known where I was.

I thumbed the button to switch it off and then hesitated. The network provider would know as soon as I turned it off and would realise I had discovered how they were tracking me. I wanted them to continue searching Heathrow and not to start wondering where I had gone next. I left it on, wondering how long I had before they could locate it again.

As I weaved my way through the people meandering around the check-in area, I noticed a large family, probably Spanish or Italian. They were spread out and I had little difficulty arranging to accidentally collide with the youngest, who was towing along a smaller toy version of the wheeled cases various other family members had. Amid the confusion and apologies I slipped the phone into the front pocket of the bag. I felt a momentary pang of guilt at the chaos that would ensue when the police found them.

Having ditched the phone, I took the escalator down to the arrivals hall. It was much less populated at this hour. It was too early for the flights coming into Heathrow, though even here there were police officers, watching the exits.

Enough people wandered around for me not to look conspicuous and I strolled through, trying to look nonchalant. I took the lift down to the Heathrow Express, the rapid transit train into central London. As I turned onto the access corridor, there were three more police officers checking everyone that went past them to the platforms. I walked past them with certainty that I was a young man in a sharp suit and not the man they were looking for. I waited for the train in the full view of the security cameras spaced along the platform. I kept focusing on my appearance, reinforcing my self-image of the man I had once been.

As the train pulled in, I watched for the carriage with the toilets and walked along the platform as the train slowed. The train halted, the doors opened and I moved to a seat at the back of the carriage, rehearsing my appearance like a mantra in my head. A businessman in a suit followed me inside and sat at the far end of the carriage. Apart from him I was alone. The train remained stationary on the platform. Periodically, an automated voice forecasted journey times or announced that, for security reasons, passengers were not to leave bags unattended.

I looked at my hands. They shivered momentarily. The texture of my skin aged twenty years in a second and then reverted back. It was getting harder to control now the immediate threat had gone. What had Blackbird said? *"Magic responds to need."* The glamour had worked while I had needed it, but now it was failing.

I shuffled sideways out of the seat and went down the narrow corridor to the toilets. Stepping inside, I locked the door behind me, finally releasing the image I had been holding. Looking up into the small mirror my face was my own, wrinkles and all. Now I just had to hope there were no police on the train.

My eyes were gritty from insufficient sleep and the rough stubble over my chin was like sandpaper. Running cold water over my hands in the sink, I scrubbed my face and then dried it with a hand towel as best I could. I felt the train lurch and breathed a sigh of relief. We were moving.

I left the toilet and went through the connecting door into the next carriage, taking an aisle seat and scanning constantly down the corridors for signs of a search taking place. No searchers appeared, though a train attendant came and relieved me of more of my cash. It was a small price to pay to get away from the search at Heathrow.

The train was clean and brightly lit and the day outside had yet to dawn. I sat nervously in the corner of the carriage with half an eye on the corridor and wondered what would become of me. I was sure Jim, the police officer in my back garden, had been killed. The memory of him screaming, "Get it off me! Get it off me!" would haunt me for the rest of my life. My warning had come too late. I should have tried earlier, even though it would have labelled me as a lunatic. Briefly I wondered what had happened to the Untainted in my garden. Would it attack the other officers? Blackbird said that sometimes they just relish the mayhem they could cause.

One thing was certain now, though. With the strange mould in the flat and at least one officer dead, the police would turn the city upside down looking for me. My only advantage was that they still thought I was somewhere out near Heathrow.

Would the police go to Katherine? If they did, she couldn't tell them very much. Only that her perfectly ordinary ex-husband was having a paranoid episode and thought someone was trying to kill him. I only hoped she had taken my advice and booked a trip away somewhere for her and Alex.

Where else would they look for me? If the police went to my office and started interviewing my work colleagues then Blackbird's concerns about my going back to work would be unfounded. I wouldn't have a job to go back to. My company would call it redundancy and I was sure I would receive a generous settlement in return for my silence, but the organisation traded on its reputation for honesty and integrity. With my sudden failure to turn up for work, one whiff of a police investigation and my career would flat-line.

I stared out of the window as the lights of West London whipped past and contemplated a life in tatters.

The train slowed as we reached Paddington and drew to a halt in a stately fashion. I waited until the doors had opened and took a long look down the platform. There were no policemen checking people coming off the train. They had placed their cordon at Heathrow and so did not expect me to arrive here.

I considered trying to use glamour to disguise my exit from the station. Even before the last terrorist attacks, London was one of the most monitored cities in the world and I was sure there would be closed-circuit television cameras. The trouble was that without some immediate threat to focus the magic I wasn't sure I could control my glamour. Having it fall apart on me in the middle of a public place would attract attention I badly wanted to avoid. I would just have to hope they weren't looking for me here.

I walked as calmly as I could down the platform and out onto the concourse. It was still too early for the mass of commuters and the people around me were either the last dregs of last night or the real diehard early-morning lot.

Getting a taxi was easy as there was a big queue of them waiting for the early rush-hour. I settled into the back of a black cab and asked him to take me to Waterloo Station. If the police ever traced the cab then they might believe I was getting a train south from there. The Eurostar service to Paris from Waterloo was one of the ways of getting out of the country without flying. I had no doubt if I were to present my passport to United Kingdom customs then my name would flash up in large red letters on the customs officer's screen. That meant the police would know I hadn't left that way, but Waterloo also had trains to Kent and I had grown up in Kent, so there was yet another trail to follow if they got that far – when they got that far.

We breezed through the streets unhampered, taking routes that would be choked with traffic in a few hours time. As we crossed the river at Westminster Bridge, I asked the driver to pull over and drop me off at the far side. I told him I needed the fresh air. I paid him, giving him an unremarkable tip, and he drove off.

I walked away from the bridge until the taxi was well out of sight, then turned back and returned to the steps that led down to the Thames embankment. I walked along the river bank past the giant wheel of the London Eye where it stood, silent and empty, waiting for the long queues of tourists who would ride its capsules around the wheel for a panoramic view of the city later in the day. From there I passed under the iron-braced railway bridge and climbed back up the steps and onto the footbridge back over the river to Embankment Station and Charing Cross.

As I crossed the dark flow of the Thames, I paused above the murky water as it swirled out towards the sea beneath me while the orange glow from the underside of the dense cloud layer faded to a sullen grey. There was no flaming dawn, but the sky in the east lightened. The broken sunshine of yesterday had been replaced by the half-light that represented the majority of autumn days.

As I crossed to the centre of the bridge I realised the clocks would soon be changing over to winter time, and the days would get shorter and shorter until we were all like Kareesh, living underground. I had all this to look forward to, assuming I lived that long.

And yet the threat over me lent the day a new flavour. I found myself standing over the river in the misty dawn tasting the drizzle that drifted on the breeze, feeling truly alive for the first time in months. It smelled of salt and ozone and I understood that this was an easterly wind, rather than the prevailing westerly, and that it brought a little of the sea with it.

Taking my time, I meandered to the far side and took the steps down to the roadway where I could make my way through the open ticket hall of Embankment Station and up the hill to the Strand, turning left past the front of Charing Cross station and along the pavement to Trafalgar Square. I walked up the hill, past the pale portico of St Martin-in-the-Fields to the tables where I had sat with Blackbird the previous day.

The coffee shop showed no sign of life and, after the brief elation at having made it this far, I found myself empty and hollow. I had reached my destination and there was no one there. The pavements were empty and the coffee shop was dark. I walked across towards the National Gallery and down into Trafalgar Square, taking the steps down into the open square. I found a dry spot on the wall of the fountain upwind of the spray carried by the fickle breeze and sat, lulled by the sound of the water and the peace there. A couple of speculative early pigeons came and pecked at the debris around me and I wondered whether Gramawl was foraging nearby, finding titbits for his mistress. Probably it was too light for him now.

As I sat there, the traffic built slowly and steadily to the everyday muted roar. The cars, buses and taxis intermingled until they became mere background noise, indistinguishable from the whole. That brief period in Trafalgar Square gave me the strength to continue. It wasn't that the stone lions inspired me, though they were very grand, or that I borrowed strength from Nelson, the tragic hero dying in the arms of his friend. I had no intention of dying, honourably or otherwise. What leant me strength was the peace I found there, amid the maelstrom. The traffic revolved around me but didn't stir me, the buses roared and the motorcycles barked, but to no effect. The pigeons came and went and the drizzle faded. I felt like I was standing in the eye of a storm.

If only I could stay there.

EIGHT

I sat for an hour or more before people started walking across the square, heading towards work or some other rendezvous, and it lost its privacy. I was getting chilled so I wandered back the way I had come to find the coffee shop had opened. I ordered black coffee and added sugar before taking it outside. I sat among the deserted tables in the damp air and waited for Blackbird. On the war memorial across the pavement from me I could read the words "Humanity" and "Sacrifice". I hoped it wasn't an omen.

Waiting for someone when you don't know whether they're going to turn up is like a first date, full of uncertainty and trepidation. You hope for the best, but at the same time you're thinking about what you're going to do if they don't show.

I wondered what I might say to Blackbird if she walked across the square. I could tell her about discovering my glow and my unwelcome visitor. I could explain about being picked up by the police and the tragic events that followed. I was sure she would know what I ought to have done.

But then I thought about what she might say when she found out the police were searching for me. I was sure she didn't want that kind of attention any more than I did. What could I say to her? "Hi, it's me, the person you didn't want to see; I have lots of new friends and they're all looking for me." It didn't sound very positive. Then again, the mould spreading across the door might be a vital clue to what I was dealing with. She would have to help me, wouldn't she?

After an hour, I celebrated the beginning of the second day of my new life with another coffee. It had been this time yesterday that I had first met Blackbird and heard about the Feyre. She had expressed doubts that I would last until this new day and, to be honest, there had been times when I had shared them, but here I was. All I had to do now was repeat my success on a daily basis and I could look forward to a long life. I sipped my coffee but I couldn't enjoy it. I didn't want more coffee, I wanted to go and find Blackbird.

I was getting twitchy. I didn't know how long it would be before the search at Heathrow extended out into the wider city and my description started to circulate. At the same time, the boredom of watching everyone else go about their daily life wore away at my aversion to risk. I was restless, even changing seats a couple of times to refresh the dampness of my trousers. Still there was no sign of her.

Finally I had to admit she wasn't coming and that I couldn't stay. It crossed my mind that perhaps she was in trouble. This was followed by the realisation that if she was, she would be far better off dealing with it without my assistance. I needed her help, she didn't need mine. I stood up and looked around. Action was better than sitting and waiting for something that wasn't going to happen and I needed to be doing something. I needed to find her.

I could retrace our steps but where would that lead me? It would take me back to Covent Garden and to the tunnels beneath the tube station. Would Kareesh know where she was? If she knew, would she tell me? I doubted it but she might be able to get a message to her and let her know I was still alive. That might be enough. At least if I walked that way I could check with Megan to see if she'd seen Blackbird, assuming she was at her usual spot.

I considered walking up to Covent Garden along the open streets rather than following the circuitous route from yesterday. Blackbird had thought I wasn't ready to take the straightforward route yet. I would follow her route, then.

I took a deep breath and let it out slowly, then walked away from Trafalgar Square into Lower St Martin's Lane, turning into a side-alley where my shoulders would touch both sides if I stood straight on. Halfway down there were doors open into the rear of a pub where the sound of a vacuum cleaner told me they were cleaning up, ready for the new day's business. Stepping back out into the street at the end, I followed the route Blackbird had led me through, taking odd turns into back alleys and walking around the rear of buildings. Blackbird had used her glamour to make sure we weren't noticed but I wasn't sure how to do that. Perhaps if I just exuded a general ambience of *I'm supposed to be here* then no one would notice me.

I bypassed a corporate reception, the girl behind the glass giving me a half-glance as I went along the side of the building. Maybe it was working. I turned around the back of the building and followed what looked like a fire evacuation route the wrong way past some metal stairs and down towards a black-painted gate.

"Excuse me?" The voice came from a side passage.

A burly looking guy with the buzz-cut hair of a soldier in a security guard's uniform moved quickly up behind me, forcing me to turn and meet him rather than slip through the gate.

"Where d'ya think you're going'?"

"Oh, if I go this way I can find my way again." I pointed the way I was going.

"You can't go down there, mate, that's private property, that is."

"I'm so sorry." All the time, I was thinking *Forget me! Turn away! You didn't see me!* But it wasn't working.

"Well I'm afraid you're going to have to come with me and explain yourself." The security guard indicated back the way he'd come.

There was no way I was going with him. I glanced back towards the gate and, as I did, he leaned forward and grabbed my arm. I pulled away, but he had a firm grip. I turned back to his grim-faced determination and tried to pull his hand from my arm.

"Now listen, mate, you're going to get into trouble if you don't come with me."

He pulled at my arm again, tugging me off balance so I staggered towards him. I had my hand on his where he gripped my arm as I tried to pull back. Reaching to the core within me I focused my will on the single instruction: *Forget me!*

A pulse of darkness jolted down my arm and he staggered back as if I had punched him. His face went blank. He placed his hand on the wall for support. His hands came up to his eyes and he rubbed them as if he couldn't believe what he was seeing. I rushed back to the gate and shot back the catch so I could push my way through. I slammed it shut behind me, glad to get something between us. He was still leaning against the wall, squinting towards the gate and blinking as if the light were too bright to bear. I left him there and hurried down the walkway, cutting around the back of another building and coming out behind a row of shops. Moving quickly along my route, I came to another alleyway where I ducked out of sight into the entrance.

Now I had time to think, I was worried about the guy. I had tried to push him off but he'd been determined to drag me back towards the building. When I had finally managed to focus enough to get my magic to work on him I had been trying to pull his hand away. Blackbird had said touch intensified some gifts and I wondered what the effect on him would be. Maybe he'd be OK now his mind had stopped trying to deny I was there.

I took a moment to try and compose myself and decide what sort of spell, if that was the right word, I should use. What I really wanted was to be invisible but if gates and doors started opening on their own then that was bound to attract attention. The idea of *I'm supposed to be here* was subtle enough but it didn't have the imperative that *Forget me* had. On the other hand, *Forget me* had been too strong – or was that because I had been touching him at the time? It still seemed harsh and crude.

After some thought I settled on *Ignore me*, since that was really what I wanted.

Once I had the thought clearly in my head that I wanted people to ignore me, I reached within myself, trying to connect my intention to the source of power inside myself. It pulsed once and then subsided. Was that it? Had it worked? Still wary against further encounters, I continued along the route.

Thankfully I met no one else before I came at last to the black door onto Covent Garden Piazza where we had emerged yesterday. I smiled to myself remembering Blackbird's remarks about the buttercups. Rolled in them, she'd said, not on them, but in them. I would have liked to see her then, though perhaps that wasn't such a good idea since I had got the distinct impression that she hadn't been alone. A snag of jealousy pricked me, which was irrational given that she was so much older than me. Why should I care about the antics of someone twenty or more years older than I was? She wasn't even human, but then neither was I, apparently.

I pushed the door open and strolled out into the open piazza surrounding Covent Garden Market. The space was welcome after the claustrophobia of the alleys and walkways. At this time of day the tourists were still doing museums and galleries, leaving the square sparsely used. Delivery trucks were parked in the open piazza and there was no sign yet of the street performers and entertainers who would show up later when the tourists gathered.

I walked across the cobbles and under the glass roof of the covered market. I didn't think I was doing too badly in the circumstances. I had managed to follow Blackbird's route around the alleys and so far nothing had tried to eat me.

Megan was setting up her stall, intent on setting out the small boxes in their ordered rows. I watched her for a moment, though she showed no sign of being aware of my presence. Then I remembered my *Ignore me* spell and focused for a moment on dispelling its effects.

Megan turned around to collect more stones from the crate behind her.

"Oh! Rabbit, you made me jump." She stepped backwards, alarmed by my sudden appearance, one hand grasping the edge of the table behind her for support.

"Sorry, I didn't mean to startle you. You were so absorbed."

"Hmmm. Yes, I suppose so. Is Blackbird with you?" She scanned the stalls nearby as if Blackbird might be lurking there.

"I was going to ask you if you'd seen her, actually. I wondered if she'd stopped by."

"Really?" She returned to setting out stones. There was a note of scepticism in her voice. Didn't she know I would have trouble lying to her?

"So have you seen her?" I asked.

She looked up from what she was doing, assessing me. Then she took a small cloth handbag from the floor behind the stall and came around to lean against the front of the stall. Taking a green and yellow tin from it, she opened it to extract a roll-up cigarette.

"Smoke?" she asked.

"No thanks. I don't."

"I shouldn't either," she said. "Filthy habit."

Nevertheless she took a plastic lighter and lit the end of the cigarette, taking a drag that made her eyelids crinkle and then blew the smoke sideways, away from me. "You haven't known her long, have you?" she said.

"Not long at all actually," I admitted.

"She'll be found when she's ready and not before."

"Well, if she calls by, I wondered if you'd let her know I was looking for her?"

"I will if I see her."

"Thanks."

"But I won't see her."

"Why not?"

"Not unless she wants to be seen," she told me, taking another drag.

I hesitated. Did that mean I was wasting my time trying to find her?

"Is there anywhere in particular that I could go... where I might find her? You've known her for some time, right?"

"I've known her for a fair while, but we're not exactly close."

"I only met her yesterday. She rescued me."

"She has a habit of doing that. That's how I first met her. I thought I was going mad. I'd put one of my pieces down and the next minute it'd be gone. The little sods were cleaning me out, taking all my best work. I couldn't afford to replace them, not on my pension."

"Your pension? Did you retire early?" She didn't look much older than me, and certainly not old enough to be retired.

She laughed. "No, I didn't retire early. I retired at sixty-four and bought the pitch for the stall then. I needed something that would generate an income and I had a little money put aside for a rainy day. I'd been making jewellery as a hobby for a long time and it was a good way of combining what I liked doing with making a living."

"I thought Blackbird said you two had known each other for a long time?" If she'd met Blackbird after she had retired then it can't have been that long ago, could it?

"Not that long really, at least in her terms. That was in seventy-two."

"Seventy-two? But that would mean you were... No way!"

"I can show you my pension card if you like." She smiled, but it was an ironic smile. "What did you think? I've been around a while. Blackbird says my Fey genes are keeping me young and I suppose she would know. It might explain a few other things too."

"What sort of things?"

"Little things. I smoke too much, drink too much, stay up too late and do far too many things that are bad for me, but I've never had a day sick since my teens. These things should be the death of me." She held up the cigarette and took a last puff before dropping it to the floor and grinding it out with the toe of her embroidered slipper.

"It sounds like you have it made," I told her. "I mean, it's what every woman wants, isn't it, to stay young-looking forever?"

"It has its drawbacks."

"Like what?"

"For one thing, it gets difficult when I go to collect my pension. I don't look like I'm about to get a telegram from the Queen congratulating me on my centenary, do I?"

"Does the Queen still send telegrams like that?"

"I don't know. I guess in a year or two I shall find out, shan't I?" she grinned.

"So how do you get your pension?"

"Usually I have to sign to say I'm my own daughter and I'm collecting it for my mother who's too old and frail to come and get it for herself, which is ironic, isn't it?"

"Why is that ironic?"

"Because I don't have a daughter, or any other children." The sudden bitterness in her voice was palpable.

"I'm sorry, I didn't realise." I hadn't meant to pry into personal matters.

"You may live a long time, Rabbit, but you had better get used to the idea that you'll never be a father."

"I'm already a father."

It just came out in response to her statement but I realised as soon as I said it that I probably shouldn't have mentioned it. It was just that I had felt the need to shake off Megan's dark prediction before it turned into a foretelling. I cautioned myself to be more careful in future about who I told about my daughter.

Megan, though, was startled. "You are?"

"I have a daughter," I admitted, finding it too late to retract the statement.

"A daughter?" she muttered to herself, momentarily lost in thought. "Are you sure she's yours?"

She looked up suddenly as if she'd just realised what she'd said.

"Sorry. I didn't mean to imply that... it's just it's very unusual. A daughter you say? And the mother is normal – human, I mean?"

"I think so. At least she's never shown any sign of being anything other than completely normal." Then again, until yesterday neither had I.

"How old is she?"

"A little younger than me, why?"

"No, silly. How old is your daughter?"

"Fourteen." There was no point in being coy about it now. Besides, she appeared fascinated, as if I had just done something truly magical.

"Fourteen. Nearly of an age, then. Has she shown any sign of being gifted?"

"She's quite good at maths and science and she has a good eye for art."

"No. I meant signs of being Fey. Any strangeness about her, shifts in appearance, odd affinities?"

"I don't think so, not that her mother has mentioned."

"You'll know if it happens. For her sake I hope she takes after her mother, no offence meant. I hope she has a normal life and has a bevy of beautiful babies. I hope her children grow up while she grows old and she turns into a wrinkled grandma with grandchildren to care for and great-grandchildren to come."

It sounded like a mixed blessing, but Megan clearly thought she was wishing the best for my daughter. Her words also brought to mind the conversation I'd had with Kareesh the day before, when we'd been bargaining. She'd offered to tell me whether I would be a grandfather and I had thought that what she was offering to me was the chance to know whether my daughter would survive to become a mother. Perhaps, though, it had been more than that. Perhaps the trade I had refused was to discover whether my daughter could become a mother. Either way, I had chosen to receive the vision instead.

"Look," I said. "I'd better go. If you see Blackbird, could you tell her I was looking for her?"

Megan stood up and tucked her cigarette tin into her bag. "Stick around and she'll find you," she said.

"What makes you say that?"

"Trust me. I know."

She wouldn't be drawn any further on the subject, so I bade her farewell and went back to the bakery to buy breakfast. The savoury pasty came hot in a paper bag and I was suddenly famished. It was all I could do to wait until it had cooled enough not to burn my tongue. Running around in the small hours of the morning had left me starving.

I walked through the arcade eating my pasty and then dropped the paper bag into a bin before walking out onto the cobbled road up to the Underground Station to see if I could leave a message for Blackbird with Kareesh.

As I crossed the junction with Floral Street I was shoved sideways.

"Betcha thought you wouldn't see me again too soon, didn't ya?"

I stumbled across the uneven cobbles and turned to face my assailant. The long black coat and overuse of eyeliner gave it away. It was Fenlock.

I backed slowly away from the tall black-garbed figure down the side-road, holding my hands up in a placatory gesture.

"Hello, Fenlock. Look, I'm sorry about yesterday. It was a misunderstanding."

"Misunderstanding is it?" he jeered, pushing me again with a suddenness that took me off guard. I stumbled backwards on the uneven footing.

"Sent me on a merry chase, didn't ya? I bet you and her were havin' a laugh at our expense, weren't ya?"

"That was Blackbird." I scanned the road behind him.

There were people walking past, but none of them noticed my predicament. I glanced backwards to see if anyone was there but at this time of day these side roads were deserted. An empty white van was parked a little way off and that was all the cover there was.

"Well, she's not here to protect ya now, is she, bumpkin?" He loomed forward, appearing to grow in size as he approached. I backed away. He leapt towards me and grabbed me by the throat, practically lifting me from my feet. I grabbed at the hand clamped around my throat, gargling as he squeezed at my windpipe. I battered at his arm, making wild swings for his face and kicking at his ankles. He was oblivious to my thrashing and steered me sideways into an alley.

He thrust me backwards down the alley and I staggered down the passage away from him. A glance behind told me this was a dead end. He was going to murder me.

I pulled my wallet from my pocket. "Look, you can have this. It's all I have." I held it out, warily.

He swatted it aside, and it ricocheted off the wall and bounced onto the ground.

"Too late for that," he announced. "Ya should have thought of that before, shouldn't ya?" He stepped over the wallet as I backed down the alley.

"I don't have anything else!" I protested.

He launched forward and scooped me up by the neck, swinging me around until I thumped into the wall. I swung a punch at his face and it connected with his nose, but he just laughed it off, his hand squeezing my windpipe.

With my screams strangling in my throat, I tore at his hand with my fingernails, gouging into his skin. His muscles felt like steel hawsers.

I felt my toes leave the pavement as I dangled from his hand. He scraped me upwards against the brickwork, then carelessly lifted me back off the wall and slammed me back against it, jangling my wits. I tried to kick him, thrashing wildly in his grip. He barely noticed.

"Shall we shake ya and see what falls out?" he chuckled and slammed me against the wall again.

Spots were appearing before my eyes. If he didn't let go of my throat soon, I would pass out. In a flash of inspiration I grabbed his hand with both of mine and wrenched at the core of power within me.

Forget me!

The jolt went down my arms but the command rolled off him like water off the back of a spoon.

"Feisty, eh? I like 'em feisty!" He lifted me back off the wall, shook me like a rag doll and slammed me back, leaving me disoriented and parched for air. He was going to kill me.

I was starting to black out. Lights played around the edge of my vision. Spots mingled in and the alley went dim. The light was fading around me. I clawed at his grip, drawing blood but not breaking his grip.

"Huh?" His voice came to me as an echo, far away.

The moment of distraction was what I needed. I reached deep inside, forging a connection with the darkness, desperate to do something, anything.

In response I felt a deepening, an opening to a cold empty core in my being. Hungry darkness emptied into me.

His scream echoed in my ears, piercing and anguished. Its harshness needling into my brain. Fenlock tried to wrench his hand away but my fingers were still clawed around his wrist, nails embedded in the flesh. As he staggered back, I scraped down the wall, my feet thumping against the ground, jarring me.

I opened my eyes to find everything dappled with moonlit shade.

My glow filled the alley.

Fenlock was trying to back away from me, his arm still clamped in my grip. Something had changed. Something had shifted. He was looking at his arm with astonishment, as if a harmless insect had stung him. No, more than that – wounded him. My hands were black against the pale of his skin and his veins stood out dark on his arms.

"You fu–" His eyes lifted to my face and he froze.

He registered shock and then something else I didn't recognise; a kind of fascinated horror. I felt a hot wire of energy coursing down his arm into mine, lighting up senses I hadn't known existed. It sparked an unrecognised hunger that sang to me. The darkness flooded into me like a tidal rush and I yielded to it.

Fenlock shrieked again, this time in abject terror. He thrashed, trying to free his arm, flailing wildly and screaming like a banshee. My fingers dug into the flesh, the grip tightening in reflex, sinking into the skin as the heat flowed down his arm into mine. He pushed at my face with his free hand but then snatched his hand back as if it had been burned. He yanked at his arm but the strength had gone out of him. Though he jerked wildly against my grip, the tide was inexorable. The blackness spread into his bloodstream following the arteries to his heart. His flesh hollowed, his muscles and sinews standing out on his frame like a starved man. His voice broke into a cracked wail, his skin went sallow and his cheeks sank into his face in front of me. Repelled by the horror of his affliction, I tried to release him, but my fingers were cramped into spasm around his wrist. With a will of their own they bit into his flesh, refusing to release him.

In the last moments, he slumped against me, his papery cheek pressed unwillingly next to mine, my own frame the only thing holding him erect. His form dissolved in my hands, his flesh desiccating to ash, his clothes collapsing into a pile of powdery rags and collapsing to the floor. I stood there, little understanding what had happened, staring at the dust falling through my fingers and trying to comprehend what I had just done.

NINE

I expected to be breathless, battered and bruised. Fenlock had beaten me, thrown me against the wall and half-choked the life from me. He'd been going to kill me, but now there was nothing, just dust and rags. My glow faded and daylight returned to the alley.

My hands were still covered in grey ash. I felt fine. I felt better than fine. I felt invigorated, full of life and ready to take on the world. It was unreal. Staring down at the heap that had been Fenlock, I denied to myself that I had killed him. It must have been his fault. He brought it on himself. He must have caused it. I looked around for some other reason, some clue as to what had happened there.

As I glanced up towards the opening at the end of the alley, there was a silhouette. It was Blackbird.

"Blackbird, it's me!" I raised a hand to attract her attention, but the silhouette moved away. I trotted towards the opening and then remembered my wallet. I skidded to a halt and went back for it, snatching it from the ground, stuffing it into my pocket and trotting back out of the alley. I glanced back at the heap of dusty clothes. The light breeze that flicked though the alley stirred the ash from the clothes into a dust devil, scattering the remains. I turned away.

When I reached the side-street, she wasn't there. I looked up and down and then spotted her on the cross-roads where the road met the side-street. She turned towards the tube station.

I ran down the street to the junction. "Blackbird! Wait!"

I reached the crossroads and stumbled into a pair of Japanese tourists who politely shrugged me off with re-peated apologies. Muttering excuses, I barged past them and ran headlong after Blackbird. I caught a glimpse of her coat, turning into the station entrance and I thought I knew where she was going.

I ran up to the tube station, panting and out of breath. I was so flustered that I slammed into the barrier and then had to search for my wallet under the watchful eye of an Underground attendant. My card registered with the barrier and I went through, smiling apologetically.

A lift was ready to descend and I rushed forward to press myself between the closing doors before they shut. The few other passengers in the lift gave me cold looks as I shoved my way into the car, the door juddering closed behind me. The car jolted, and I got my breath back as it descended.

At the bottom I had to wait until the other passengers filed away. I used the method I had used in the alley to make everyone ignore me and headed for the doorway between the corridors where we had gained access to Gramawl's domain. The door was slightly ajar.

I pushed it open to find the passage and stairway in darkness, the light from the corridor illuminating only the top of the stair. There was no sign of a light switch, nor could I remember seeing one anywhere in the Un-derground. The lights were probably operated from a control room somewhere. Still, I had my own light.

The door thudded closed behind me. Standing in the darkness I let the wish to be ignored drop away and concentrated on summoning my glow, feeling the temperature in the enclosed stairway drop suddenly as light spilled out onto the stairs. It was getting easier to do this. Was that practice, or was it getting stronger?

I stepped down the stairs slowly and cautiously, wondering why Blackbird hadn't waited for me. Hadn't she heard me? Then another thought occurred to me. Perhaps it wasn't really her, but merely the semblance of her meant to draw me here? If it wasn't Blackbird, was it Carris? Had she seen what happened in the alley? Could she make herself look like Blackbird to lure me down here and take her revenge?

I took the stairs slowly, the swaying light making it more difficult to judge my footing. At the base of the stairs the corridor led on into darkness. I took a hesitant step forward into the gloom, allowing my glow to swell and throw back the shadows in its shifting, dancing light.

"Gramawl? Are you there? It's me, Rabbit. I came with Blackbird yesterday, remember?"

My voice sounded hollow and empty in the darkened passage. There was no answer.

"Gramawl?"

I walked forward a pace or two, my arms spread to show peaceful intent. Still there was no sign of him. I walked a few paces more. The light moved with me and the stairs gradually faded into the dark until it was just me in a length of illuminated corridor. I made slow progress. The passage angled left then right, as before, but when I came to the place where the stairway went up to Kareesh's den, there was no trace of the stairs.

How could they not be there? We had climbed those steps. I was sure this was where they had been. I felt along the wall where I recalled the opening, looking for some clue. There was only a blank wall with a smooth expanse of tiles. I stood in the dark wondering whether Blackbird had somehow got inside and was even now laughing with Kareesh at my expense. Then a tiny sound came to me from further down the corridor, like a scuff or a stumble.

"Gramawl?" Was he lurking there?

I remembered him appearing without a sound, and figured that either he'd wanted me to hear him or it wasn't Gramawl that was moving down there. Perhaps Blackbird had not found a way into Kareesh's den after all.

A row of fluorescent lamps marked the roof of the tunnel, though none of them offered the least glimmer of light. As I sidled along the tunnel it sloped downwards. I found the passage to be much longer than I had initially thought. Once I heard the tumbling flow of water but couldn't identify where it was coming from. Several times there were distant rumblings, whether from passing tube trains or irritated trolls I couldn't say. At one point I stopped, half deciding to head back to Covent Garden. Then I heard a distant echo of footfalls ahead and moved quickly to pursue it, only to be greeted by the empty walkway. Nothing entered the pool of light around me and I met no other soul.

At one point I shouted down the corridor. "Blackbird! I've had enough of this wild goose chase. Show yourself!" There was no sound, no light, and no answer. The light swung and shifted around me, disturbed by a wind I couldn't feel, rippled by a hand that didn't show, leaving me alone in the half-light.

I began to feel she wasn't down here, that she'd tricked me into following the tunnel and locked the door behind me, sealing me in to pursue the endless passages until I expired. I began to imagine the tunnel had no end and that it would go on, featureless and unlit, until I wore myself out or turned back.

At such points I would hesitate and wait, and after a short pause a small sound, some token of presence, would echo from the tunnel ahead, telling me the person I followed went before me. Was it an illusion, meant to tempt me on? Was it really Blackbird or something darker and more sinister?

I continued on down the passage. Occasionally there were marks of some previous human presence, whether a piece of graffiti or a discarded paper, but mostly these were old and yellowed. Once I came upon a smear of oil, smelling of minerals and machinery, with no remnant of the machine it had come from. These reassured me that I wasn't walking in a circle. A little further on an empty mineral water bottle proclaimed some more recent occupation. The tunnel began to bend and angle from its course and I got the feeling it was coming to an end.

Finally I reached the base of a circular stairway, similar to the one I had started on. As I stepped onto it I heard a door *thump* shut above me. I was meant to follow upwards.

Setting a steady pace, I climbed the stairway, convinced now that whoever was ahead of me was waiting above. The stairway wound round and around until I reached a steel-clad door on a landing. I took hold of the handle, half expecting it to be locked. It yielded easily and the door swung open to daylight.

I released my glow and let it die, emerging into a passage. On each end of the corridor, heavy doors blocked the way, but steps led upwards in the other direction with faint daylight indicating the way out.

The heavy door swung shut behind me with a *thud*, echoing the earlier sound.

Ascending the steps, I climbed into a room stacked with chairs and tables. A row of windows opened out onto a daylight street outside and I realised as a bus passed by below eye level that I had climbed to a level above ground. I stepped up into the room and blinked in the strong light. At the same time a hand circled around from behind me. There was a flash of something bright and I felt a sharp point press hard under my chin.

"If you so much as blink I will ram this blade up through your brain." It pressed into the underside of my chin, the point digging into my skin.

"Mmm," was about as much as I dared say, nodding was out of the question but I could hear the truth of her intent.

"Step sideways slowly," the voice commanded.

I did as she asked. It sounded like Blackbird, but I was taking no chances. So far she hadn't killed me.

"Just so you know I'm serious, if I see a glimmer of gallowfyre, a darkening of the ambient light, if a cloud even crosses the sun, I am going to shove this knife up through your head so hard it will stick out of the top, understand?"

"Mmm," I acknowledged, not really understanding but complying, the knife pressing the point into the root of my throat, under my chin.

"Step backwards slowly, one small step at a time. There's a wall behind you." I edged backwards, the knife lifting me onto tiptoe. "Turn left and face the wall."

I turned around slowly and she moved around with me until I faced the wall.

"Kneel slowly, facing the wall." I did as she demanded and as I reached an uncomfortable half-kneeling position she moved the knife so it stuck into the back of my neck under the base of my skull. Her knee pressed into my back, pushing me forward.

"Now put your arms out and spread your fingers wide against the wall. If you move a fraction from there I will kill you instantly. Do you understand?"

"Yes". I pressed my face against the wall. All my senses were telling me her words were the absolute truth. She would kill me.

"I'm going to offer you a choice. It's not much of one, but it's all you're getting. You can tell me what I want to know and I will kill you cleanly and send you back where you came from. Or you can refuse and I will bind you to this body so when it dies, you will also. You can hear the truth in my words, yes?"

"Yes," I could hear the truth in them. She was going to kill me. "But–"

The knife pressed inwards. "Now. I am going to ask my questions and then you're going to die. My question is simple. Why are you here? What did you come for?"

"Blackbird..." I had to convince her it was me.

"No!" The knife stabbed inwards and I'm sure I felt a warm dribble run down my neck. "No names, not even that one. I'm giving you nothing, understand?"

"But it's me, Rabbit. We spent the day together, yesterday. You can tell it's me." I hated the whiny quality in my voice but I was desperate. She had to believe me.

"How can you lie to me without my being able to hear it? Is this some new wraithkin gift?" Her voice had a puzzled quality, as if she couldn't believe what she was hearing. "How are you doing that? Tell me and I'll despatch you quickly and painlessly."

"No, please, it really is me. How can I convince you?"

"Convince me? I saw you in the alley with Fenlock. I saw the gallowfyre. I know what you are. I don't need convincing, I just need an answer." There was anger in her voice that translated into pressure in her hand. I tried to slide up the wall from a kneeling position. I needed her to believe me. I needed a distraction. I needed something.

"What's gallowfyre? You mean my glow?"

"Your what? No, enough games! Tell me and I'll finish it."

"Please! It's me. It's Rabbit. You know it's me. I can't lie to you, can I?" I pleaded with her, knowing any second she could end my existence.

"That's what I don't understand. How can you say that when I know what you are? How are you deceiving me?"

"I'm not lying! I'm not! Please listen to me." She had to listen.

"You must be lying. Tell me how." Her voice had a harsh edge to it. I knew at any moment she would push the knife home.

"Just wait a moment. Wait, please." I closed my eyes but tears still ran unbidden down my face. I didn't want to die like this, not by her hand. Why was she doing this? "Please, Blackbird, don't kill me. I'm not lying, I'm not. I can't. You know I can't."

My every nerve tensed, waiting for the searing pain I knew would accompany the knife. The waiting extended from seconds into minutes. The moment came, and passed.

I couldn't keep up that level of tension indefinitely. I hesitantly opened my eyes, still pressed against the wall.

"Blackbird?"

"Shut up!"

"There must be a way I can–"

"I said quiet! I'm trying to think."

The knife-point stayed pressed into the back of my skull and the pressure of her knee into my back increased. My knees were painfully jammed against the wall on the bare floor. It was intensely uncomfortable.

"Blackbird, can I move just a little?"

An exasperated sigh came from behind me. "It would be easier for us both if I just killed you and had done with it."

I took that as a No and kept still. It would be a shame if she killed me now just for irritating her. She hadn't killed me yet, though. There was hope.

"Answer me more questions. What did you say to offend Gramawl?"

"I didn't do anything to offend him. It was him who used his magic on me." There was a further pause. "Was that the right answer?"

"Which stone did Kareesh like best?"

"I don't know, ask her! No, wait a minute, the red one. It was dark red. It felt odd, wrong somehow."

"Tell me about your daughter. I want her full name and date of birth, where she goes to school, everything."

"You said I wasn't to tell anyone. You said I had to stay away from her and not lead anyone to her."

"I changed my mind. Tell me."

"What for? You said it was dangerous." I still wasn't exactly sure who I was dealing with. Maybe this wasn't Blackbird after all? Now that I thought about it, she didn't even act like Blackbird and telling her the details might enable whoever it was to find Alex.

"Just tell me or we end this now!"

I took a deep breath. "No. I can't tell you that. Ask me something else."

"Tell me!"

"No."

It sounded such a small word to end a life, but I wouldn't give away my daughter. I scrunched my eyes together tight and waited for the knife. Instead the pressure of the point was removed and she stopped pushing me against the wall.

"You believe me?"

"Just don't move!"

"I'd really like to sit back now, if you could just refrain from stabbing me?" I was feeling a little more confident, now the knife had been withdrawn.

"You may sit back, but keep your hands on the wall where I can see them." She still sounded angry, or maybe just scared. I kept my hands pressed onto the cold surface but sat back on my heels, sighing at the relief as I was able to take some of my weight off my knees.

"Tell me about last night," she demanded, "after I left you at the tube station. Tell me all of it and try not to leave anything out. Don't make any sudden moves. I've still got the knife."

I didn't need reminding. A sticky trickle was running down my spine.

I started with the tube ride home and told her as much as I could remember. I told her about trying to blend in with the commuters, about clearing out the flat and putting my life into three padded envelopes. When I explained about waking in the night and discovering my glow and how excited I was, she laughed, but it was hollow.

I got ahead of myself about the thing in the hall and had to go back and explain about the squeaky stair that had brought me back to wakefulness. I explained how I had sealed the door to keep the creature from entering my bedroom. When I explained about the black spots, she hissed between her teeth, but then told me to continue.

I told her about climbing over the balcony and running away with my rucksack, then getting arrested and being taken back to the flat by the police.

"You went back? Willingly?"

"They weren't going to accept no for an answer. Besides, there wasn't much I could do."

"You wouldn't have got me back in there," she said.

"They went first. They checked every room with me coming after."

"That wouldn't bother her. She could have been in the flat all the time and they'd never have seen her until it was too late."

"Her?"

"The Fey that came after you was female, though the body she inhabited may just as easily have been male. A door wouldn't stop her normally but she was using a human body."

"Why wouldn't the door stop her? I sealed it with magic. It worked."

"You sealed the door shut, which was well done, but a shade isn't entirely corporeal. They can dissolve into things, entering through the tiniest crack. They're almost impossible to kill because you can't touch them. In darkness they can lurk in any shadow. She could have been in your flat all the time you were there and you'd never have known."

"She called me 'brother'. She said, 'Brother, open the door.' It was really creepy."

"You didn't tell me that before."

"I didn't remember. I was trying to climb out of a first floor window at the time. Why did she call me that?"

"I'll explain in a moment. So you went back inside?"

"The officers went in first. There was no sign of her in the flat but the walls and ceiling were covered in mould. The police wanted me to explain it, but what could I tell them?"

"It was darkspore."

"The mould?"

"That's how I knew the Fey that came for you was female. She used darkspore to weaken the door so she could go through it after you sealed it shut. That's a gift that only a shade can use."

"I think one of them found her. While we were upstairs in the flat, two of the policemen went around to the back garden. She was hiding in the hedge."

"She must have wanted them to find her. They would never have seen her if she didn't want them to."

"I think she used the mould on him. That, what did you call it, darkspore?"

"Darkspore spreads by touch. It will run over any surface until it reaches flesh."

"And then what?"

"It consumes wherever it touches."

Her words were cold and quiet and I thought about how close I had come to reaching out and testing that black stain with my fingertip. I shivered involuntarily, remembering the sound of strange manic laughter drifting up though my window over the screams of the policeman. I thought about the other officers and the firemen that had been called to the flat.

"There was a fire engine," I told her. "I think it was sent to my flat to deal with the darkspore. Will they be able to contain it?"

"The darkspore will revert to mould once she withdraws her power," she said, "and she wouldn't have stayed long. The news would be too important to delay for the sake of a little fun."

She had a strange idea of what constituted fun. I thought about my ruined door and my mould-stained walls. I wondered whether I would ever be able to return there now it was filled with the memories of spreading blackness and the sounds from the garden.

"When the screaming started, that's when I ran. I kept running until I couldn't run anymore."

"If she had really wanted you, she would have had you. Maybe she changed her mind about you once she saw the gallowfyre?" The question was more to herself than to me.

"You said that before. What's gallowfyre? Is that what my glow is called?"

"Will you show it to me?"

"What, now?"

"Call it forth, but stay down there where I can see you."

I closed my eyes and concentrated on reaching inwards. The darkness answered and the room chilled suddenly, a fickle breeze shifted in the room, drawn up the stairs from below. I heard Blackbird's sharply indrawn breath. When I opened my eyes the room was dim with the speckled light shifting in milky waves on the wall in front of me. My hands were black against the wall.

Blackbird's voice was soft behind me. "Dismiss it. Get rid of it, please." She sounded over-keen for me to stop when I had only just called it, but something in her tone told me it would be wise to indulge her. I released it and it died, the light in the room returning to normal.

"Do you remember I told you that the creature pursuing you was one of the Untainted?"

"Was that what came after me last night?"

"The Seventh Court of the Feyre are the Untainted. They are the one court that has never mingled its bloodlines with humans. They regard all the other courts as being tainted by the stain of humanity, a refuge for mongrels and half-breeds like you, and like me. We are the reason for their exile from this world."

"We are?"

"The Feyre were a dying race. They lost the ability to reproduce and their numbers were dwindling."

"What happened to them?"

"They were the victim of politics."

"What?"

"Politics led the Feyre into a selective breeding programme that spanned millennia, a side effect of which is that they have become infertile. Children among the Feyre are rare indeed. Their numbers plummeted until there were barely enough to survive extinction. Then they discovered that the union with humanity was fertile. It gave them new hope."

"So that's how I came to have a Fey ancestor?"

"In all likelihood, yes. The Seventh Court rebelled, though. They said that humanity would dilute Fey blood until all that remained were petty conjurers and snake-oil merchants. It caused a schism. In a desperate move, they tried to eliminate the half-breeds, all in one night. Fortunately the alarm was raised before they could complete their task. There was a bloody and brutal skirmish which the Untainted lost. They escaped to a world apart, exiled from their own kin. Now they return to complete the job they started, one mongrel at a time."

"What has this got to do with me?"

"As darkspore is a gift of the shades, Rabbit, gallowfyre is a gift of the wraiths. Only male wraithkin can summon it."

"I don't get it. If the only ones who can call gallowfyre are the wraithkin, and the wraithkin are the Untainted, then how did I inherit the ability to call it?"

"You shouldn't be able to, but we've seen you do it. One of your ancestors must have been wraithkin."

"I thought you said they don't breed with humans?"

"Until this day I would have said that with my hand over my heart."

"I still don't see how it could be, though. I mean, they must have, mustn't they? One of the Untainted must have... you know?"

"All I know, Rabbit, is you shouldn't be able to do that. You can rise now, if you wish."

"You're not going to kill me?"

"You summoned gallowfyre, Rabbit. When the Seventh Court rebelled, gallowfyre was used by the Untainted to drive a wedge into the armed ranks of the other courts. Those that didn't flee in terror had the life sucked out of them until their dried husks fell from the air. I took a grave risk letting you call it, but if you wanted to kill me, you could have done it then. You are who you say. Get up."

She didn't sound very pleased about it, but I settled for being able to stand up. I leant against the wall and stumbled to my feet. Cold from kneeling on the hard floor had seeped into my joints and I tried to rub some warmth back into them.

"The path I took you on yesterday was deliberately long," she continued. "After I left you at Leicester Square last night I retraced our steps and set wards along the path so I would know if you followed it again."

I suddenly realised why we had taken such a circuitous route the day before.

"You set me up."

"I set the Untainted up. If it retained some of your knowledge then it was possible it would try to follow the route back to Kareesh, seeking to kill her. She is one of the oldest and the opportunity to eliminate her would be a hard temptation to resist."

"You used me as bait."

"No one survives the Untainted, Rabbit, least of all someone as naive and inexperienced as you. I set the wards on the path to give myself time to be waiting for your body, should it return along the path."

"You were going to use me to lead it underground where you could kill it."

"Not you. I hadn't expected you to survive the night."

"You might have given me the benefit of the doubt."

"I did. When I saw you speak with Megan it set me wondering if perhaps by some chance you might have survived."

"You watched me talk to her? But if I had been taken by the Untainted then she was in terrible danger."

"Megan is small fry compared to Kareesh. I couldn't see the Untainted risking exposure just for her sake."

"And what about Fenlock? Did you set him up too?"

"He was an unexpected complication. Once he had you, though, there was little I could do to intervene. I knew what would happen once he got you into the alley."

"He damn near killed me."

"He confirmed what I'd already deduced. You used gallowfyre on Fenlock. He was so convinced you weren't a threat that he didn't understand what was happening until it was too late."

"I didn't mean to. It just happened. I was trying to get his hand from around my throat and I started blacking out. When I opened my eyes my glow was everywhere."

"Panic reaction. Your instinct brought it on, but you would still need to have intended to use it."

"I was trying to push him away with magic. I tried to get him to forget me."

"He was already using his magic on you, filling you with fear and panic."

"When I couldn't get free, I let it loose. It was the only other thing I could do." The memory of my hands clawed into his wrists returned to me. I felt vaguely nauseous.

"It's ironic really, he probably saved you. Your panic reaction sucked the life essence out of him, consuming the very thing that makes him exist. It's obscene."

I was shocked by the cold tone in her voice. "He was trying to kill me."

"Sure, and he would have, but your essence, your lifeblood and your magic would have spilled out, consuming your flesh and returning it to the earth, completing the cycle and at the same time, beginning it again."

"You believe in reincarnation?"

"Not in the sense of a soul reborn, but in the cycle of nature and magic, yes. All magic is given by the earth as life is given. It is eventually returned to the earth to become again. It is not a belief so much as an expression of the Feyre's existence. We live, we die and others will come after us, it is our nature."

"I was only defending myself."

She continued as if I hadn't spoken. "But that way, nothing comes after. The cycle is broken. It's what was originally thought to be the cause of Fey infertility. The wraithkin were slowly consuming us, one by one, until there was nothing left to come back. They were preventing us from beginning the cycle again."

"But you said it was selective breeding. Politics, you said."

"I still believe that, but I am one of the Gifted, a half-breed, and partly human. There are many of the Feyre who still believe the wraithkin are sucking us dry and that is the reason we cannot breed. They believe that by consuming life in its essence, the wraithkin are eating our future."

"Can't you explain it to them? Make them understand?"

"You're asking me to overturn a hundred millennia of belief with five minutes of science." Her expression said this was unlikely to work.

"So that leaves me as some kind of ghoulish parasite."

"It's not like that. The Feyre believe the world is in balance, that where there is true beauty there must be ugliness, where there is life, there must be death. The wraiths and the shades are our darkness, Rabbit, but they're not parasites, they're Fey."

"Either way, it doesn't leave me in a very good position, does it? The Untainted are already hunting me and as soon as the rest of them realise what I am, they will be too."

She laughed bitterly. "They're not going to hunt you. They will avoid you. The wraithkin are what the Feyre frighten their children with. And as for the Untainted, I have no idea what they'll do. As far as they are concerned, you can't exist. That must have been what saved you. She must have been as surprised as I was to find you could summon gallowfyre. I only wish I could have seen the expression on her face."

"Would you want to get that close?"

She was silent. I looked up and for a fleeting second there was something cold behind those grey eyes. She turned away, walking towards the street window, looking down onto the traffic and concealing her expression.

I worked my knees then gingerly walked forward towards the brightness of the windows, using the wall to steady me as my joints regained their mobility and joined her at the window, though not too close.

At the windows I stopped.

"Blackbird, that's it!"

"What is?"

"That building, the one with the roof covered in verdigris across the street, that's the building from the vision, the one Kareesh showed me."

"Why would she show you a vision of Australia House?"

I looked out at the distinctive green-stained roof of the building opposite.

"I honestly have no idea."

TEN

The building across the road was the one from my vision. It was suddenly sharp and clear in my mind. No wonder I had thought I recognised it. I must have been past it hundreds of times.

Blackbird stood at the window, looking across the street, but she wasn't focusing on the building. She was lost in thought. Whatever it was she was thinking about, it didn't lighten her mood.

"Are the visions always like this, so fragmented and disjointed?"

There was a pause while she returned to herself and then she spoke, looking out over the street rather than at me.

"The way Kareesh once explained it to me, the future is a warren of paths and junctions. She has shown you the main junctions you might pass through from your present. Which path you take, though, and where you end up is for you to choose."

I tried to imagine time as passages and tunnels criss-crossing into the future. It didn't help. I glanced at Blackbird, staring stiffly out of the window.

"What's wrong?" I asked her.

"It's nothing." She dismissed my question and

continued to watch the traffic, but I could hear the lie in that statement.

"Does finding out that my Fey ancestor was wraithkin make that much of a difference?"

She didn't answer my question.

"Look, I can't help who my ancestors were. If it makes you feel better, I just won't summon it again, OK?"

My words fell into her silence.

"If there's anything I can do…"

"You can't."

It was said in a flat quiet voice, without emotion or warmth. It wasn't a reprimand as much as a statement of cold fact. I turned and looked at the building again, unsure of what to say. I understood that there was a part of her that hurt, the part that showed in her eyes at odd times, like last night and now. I wanted to offer her simple comfort against that hurt but I knew if I faced her now, it would be raw in her eyes and she would turn away.

"I'm sorry," I offered.

"What for?"

"I don't know, but if it makes any difference, I am."

"You're sorry." She laughed without humour.

"Yes."

"It's not you that should be sorry."

"Why?"

"Because…" She stopped and then sighed. "Because I was going to kill you."

"You didn't know it was really me."

"I didn't know at first, but then I realised it was you and I was going to do it anyway."

I took a deep breath. "Can I ask why?"

"It's complicated."

"I don't understand."

"No, you don't. But a big part of me, a strong part of me, wanted to shove that knife in as far as it would go. I wanted to see your blood pool on the floor and watch you die." Her voice was brittle and she was more of a

163

stranger to me in that moment than at any time since we had met.

"But you didn't." I kept my voice calm, trying to steady her.

"I knew it was you and I still wanted to kill you."

She was trying to explain it to herself, as if her hand had been guided by some external force.

"The important thing is, you didn't."

"I was going to."

"But I'm still here. So it's OK."

"It's not OK. It'll never be OK."

And there it was, the dead end I encountered every time I tried to reach out to her. I stood watching the traffic, unable to cross the chasm between us. I was surprised when she spoke.

"When I was little, we lived in a house in a forest."

Her voice lost its edge and softened with memory. I had no idea where this conversation was going but I left her space to think about what she wanted to say and it was a while before she spoke again.

"The house was deep into the trees. At night, sometimes, I went to sleep with the wind roaring in the canopies around the house. It was elemental, and I loved it."

There was another long pause.

"My mother used to hold me up high and whirl me around and tell me I had wings and that one day I would fly..." Her voice broke and she stopped again. She fished in a pocket, pulling out a rumpled hanky.

"She used to leave me with my father for hours sometimes. She would kiss his cheek and tell him she'd be back soon. He would smile and busy himself outside. He loved the forest and would spend hours chopping logs or mending things. I would go up to my room and play, wondering where she went.

"There was a pitched roof below my window at the back of the house and, one time, I stepped out over the sill and slid down the slates to the soft earth. I sneaked around the house and followed my mother into the forest while my father was occupied. It didn't take long to catch up with her, she was in no hurry. She followed a path though the trees to a clearing.

"I nearly cried out when I saw what came out of the forest to meet her, but she ran towards it and threw herself into its arms and he picked her up and whirled her around above his head, the way she did for me. It was the first time I saw Gramawl."

She stiffened, steeling herself against whatever was coming.

"I never heard my mother and father fight. Then one night I woke to her screaming my name up the stairway, telling me to run and hide." Her voice solidified into ice. "I didn't know what to do. I wanted to go to her, but there were sounds downstairs, strange sounds, screams, crashing, my father yelling – it sounded like they were fighting. I didn't understand."

I could hear her, steadying herself with long slow breaths.

"I went to my window and opened it wide. It was a wild night and the wind was tearing leaves from the trees in the dark. Everywhere was moving, swaying in the moonlight and I stood at the window and thought how I would slide down the pitched roof and run and find my mother's friend in the forest and tell him to come and help. But I couldn't. I was scared. It was dark and wild, and I wanted her to come and get me. I wanted her to come and tell me everything was well.

"The noises downstairs ceased, quite suddenly, and I backed into the corner of my room and made myself as small as I could. I put my hands over my eyes and peeked through my fingers. I still wanted to see, do you understand? The moonlight came into my room, dancing across the ceiling with the wildness outside. I leaned over to look outside, but the moon wasn't shining in."

Her voice had gone quiet and small.

"I tucked myself back in the corner, just as the door was thrown open, and my instinct shouted in my mind 'I'm not here! I'm too small! You can't see me!' But I was only young and there was no magic in me to answer."

She took a long slow breath.

"The figure in the doorway was darkness. He was outlined in moonlight, but he was just dark. The light in the room swam with the trees outside as he entered the room. He went to the open window and looked out into the night. I could have touched his coat, I was so close. He turned back and went to the mirror hanging over the dresser, my faerie mirror, the one my mother had bought for me because it had tiny winged figures carved into the frame all around it. He placed his hand on it and the light from his hand entered it, turning it milky and then clear as the moonlight shone through it."

She glanced sideways at me, then looked back resolutely at the road.

"He said, 'They're dead, but the girl has run off into the forest.' For a moment I thought he was talking to me and I nearly said, 'No, I'm here,' but then a voice came from the mirror, distorted and slowed down.

"It said 'Find her.' That's all. Just two words: 'Find her.' It sounded so cold, so angry.

"The figure took his hand from the mirror and the light within it faded. He turned back to the window facing me, but there was no face, just blackness. The light swelled until a nimbus formed around him and I was sure he couldn't fail to see me squeezed into the corner. Then he took a step towards me and vanished.

"The room went dark, but it was a normal dark, a welcome dark. I stayed there, curled into the corner, too terrified to close my eyes in case he came back. The wind died down and the room faded into grey and I stayed pressed into the corner, sure the figure of darkness was waiting for me to give myself away.

"As the light grew steadier, there was a noise on the stairs, a creak as something heavy shifted. Gramawl, my mother's friend, unfolded from my doorway and filled my room. He didn't make a sound, but he opened his arms and I uncurled myself and ran to him, burying myself in his embrace."

She blew her nose noisily.

"There was no point in looking for her. The Feyre stand between life and power, holding the two in equilibrium, but when they die there's nothing to hold the power back. The magic consumes their flesh and bones in a last flare of power. We buried my father in the forest, Gramawl and I. It was the only thing to do. He loved the trees."

She tucked the hanky back into her pocket and straightened her coat.

"Afterwards, I went back up to my room and smashed the mirror. I couldn't bear the thought of his hand on it, calling the moonlight. Then Gramawl took me to Kareesh and she took me in, just like that. She didn't dwell on what had happened, and I grew up in the forest with her and Gramawl as foster-parents, though she is more like a grandmother to me. She told me what I was and who I was and taught me about the Feyre. They were both there for me when no one else was."

She pushed her hair back from her face, sniffed.

"When I was older, I asked her about that night and about what had happened. I asked her why the wraithkin hadn't seen me, though I must have been plainly visible. She told me she would tell me when I came into my power and that then I would understand. So I waited.

"And when the time came, she taught me what power was and how to wield it, tutoring me in the subtleties and nuances of it. She showed me what it means to be Fey. I thought she would tell me about that night, when I had learned enough, but she never raised it. She let me take my time until I was ready to ask again."

"When I finally did, she explained it to me." She turned to face me, finally, her eyes red-rimmed, skin puffy and blotchy. "You remember when I sent you to the moors with the wolves? That's one of the gifts I inherited from my mother. That's what my mother did to the wraithkin, but she couldn't bind him to it. Without his name, he could shrug it off any time he wanted to. So she made a world for him identical to the one he was in, except I wasn't in it. He couldn't see me because, for him, I wasn't there."

"She saved you," I said quietly.

"She saved me, but to do it she had to touch…" The tears welled in her eyes again and she fumbled for the hanky. "She had to put her hand on that blackness, defenceless against what he could do. He consumed her power, sucked the life out of her and discarded her, and she stood there and deceived him while he did it so that I…" The tears ran down her cheeks unheeded, the hanky wrung between her hands. "So I…" Her shoulder shook and she turned her back to me.

I stepped forward to offer some comfort.

"Don't!" She threw her hand back, warding me off. "Don't touch me."

"I'm sorry, I didn't think—"

"You can't help it. It's what you are."

Her shoulders shook.

"I can't change what I am."

"I know. But that's why I wanted to kill you. Part of me still wants to."

She stood apart and I watched her cry.

Sometimes Alex hates me. She rails against me and screams and shouts and stamps about as if she can't contain the fury within her. Then she cries and screams again and I try and stay calm and soothe her. And when her anger is spent, she won't let me touch her, won't let me hold her. So I wait. And when the storm has finally blown itself out and she's calm again, I open my arms and she'll come and press her head against my chest and accept comfort from me.

I waited until Blackbird had calmed herself and then

168

I opened my arms in that way to her, knowing that, being Fey, touch had other connotations to her than to my daughter but wanting to offer her that simple gesture against her pain. Her grief was wrapped about her like a veil and it was beyond me not to offer some comfort. She hesitated at this human gesture and I thought she would turn away from me again.

Instead, she shook her head. "No, I'm all right, really. It's just that I've never told anyone that before. Kareesh and Gramawl knew but I've never told anyone else. Only with you being…" She dried up.

"Yes." I dropped my hands back to my sides, awkwardly. At least I knew why she pulled away.

She blew her nose on the dishevelled hanky and stuffed it back into her pocket, looking up at me.

"So now what?" she lifted her chin, making a bold effort to put the weight of the past aside. Eyes still puffy, she was determined to move on, rather than dwell on what had been.

"I don't know. I was hoping you'd be able to tell me."

"The building over the way, there. You said it was the one in your vision. What about it?"

"I don't know. It was mixed up with a whole load of other stuff. I just know it's the one. In the vision there was a sign by the main door carved into the stone, that's all."

"What does it say?"

"I don't know. I couldn't see it clearly."

"We should go and look then."

"Are you sure you're up to this?"

"I'm fine." She broke into a half smile. "I thought I was over it, it was all such a long time ago, but when you summoned the gallowfyre… it brought it all back. I know it's wrong to blame you, but…"

"You still do."

"I don't blame you. I don't. It just feels like I should."

"Because of what I am?" I rubbed at where the point of the knife had pressed under my chin, feeling the break in the skin.

"The rational part of me knows you aren't him and could never have been him. It's just my feelings haven't caught up with the rest of me yet.

"I understand. Sort of."

"We should go and have a look at this building of yours. Maybe the writing on the doorway will tell us something."

I accepted her change of subject and she turned away from the window, straightening her coat, and took the stairway down to ground level. I tagged along, down and through the darkening passage to the heavy street door. Blackbird turned the catch, shot back the bolt and opened the door, spilling daylight into the corridor. We stepped out onto the pavement along the Strand, attracting only mildly curious stares from passers-by. Blackbird let me past and then stood at door, masking what she was doing with her body. It made a low *crunk* sound and when she tested it again, it was locked.

I stepped across the wide pavement and turned to look at where we had emerged. A sign along the base of the arched window above the street declared it to be the Strand Station of the Piccadilly Railway.

"I've never heard of a Strand Station," I told her. "In fact, I didn't know there was a tube station here at all."

"There isn't. The line was supposed to go through under the Thames but the extension was never built. This is as far as they managed."

She turned and walked brusquely off down the Strand with me trailing after her. Then she slowed, allowing me to catch up so we could walk alongside each other. It was a small concession, given what she'd told me.

We crossed the busy road when the traffic thinned momentarily and continued across the road down the side of Australia House. The building was roughly triangular in plan, being the easterly point at the end of the long crescent formed by Aldwych alongside the Strand. There were doors for the public set along the side of the building with notices about opening times for the issuing of visas and other documents. Posters of Ayer's Rock, Uhuru or whatever it was called, adorned the walls inside.

We followed the pavement past these until we came to the blunted point of the triangle where the Strand opened out into a wide thoroughfare. A church faced us across the broad paved area where the trees were shedding, the leaves whirling around in a fickle breeze. Turning back, the entrance to Australia House was impressive with tall stone pillars and heavy iron gates folded back against the wall inside the entrance porch. To either side of the doorway, stone statues graced the entrance, while high above the gates a bronze sculpture of heroic figures on untamed horses adorned the frontage. Inside the doorway there were letters picked out in gold, carved into the door pillar where I knew they would be. Blackbird leaned down to inspect the writing.

"What does it say?" I asked.

"It says the stone was laid in..." She translated the roman numerals. "1913. Does that mean anything to you?"

"No. Should it?"

"Are you sure? It must have some significance or you wouldn't have seen it in the vision."

"Well, perhaps it's not the building that's significant. Maybe we're supposed to meet someone here, or find something?"

I looked around at the roads, busy with passing traffic. No one approached us with a secret code word or a mysterious package. There was a distinct absence of things with clues written on them.

"Do you see anything else that looks familiar?" Blackbird asked.

"Not really. The sign is the right one, but it's just a carving showing when this was built."

I found myself conscious of the huge ornamental iron gates turned back against the wall on each side of the entrance. They were beautifully made and I couldn't help feeling there was something significant about them.

"I wonder what was here before this was built," she mused. "I don't remember anything particularly special."

"Even if there was something, it was demolished a hundred years ago to make way for this." I watched the gates, feeling that somehow they were also watching me.

"That isn't a very long time, really. I can't recall that there was anything particular here, though it was a pretty rough area. I'm sure I would remember."

"So, where does that leave us?"

"It leaves us asking why, I suppose." Blackbird scanned the surrounding buildings.

The gates definitely had my attention. Were they the thing I was supposed to find here? Were they the clue we were looking for? I found myself reaching out to touch the dark ironwork.

"Perhaps if we ask at th– NO!"

My hand touched the metalwork and a jolt went through me like a lightning bolt. I remember something slamming into my arm and the trees above me spinning, then crashing onto my back on the paving. My breath went out of me and the back of my skull banged against the concrete. For a moment, everything went black.

When I came to, Blackbird was leaning over me. She'd moved me onto my side and had her palm pressed against my forehead. Despite that, a dizzying nausea welled up in me and I threw up the remains of my pasty on the paving slabs. Blackbird leant back until the retching stopped and then handed me a practical hanky. It was still damp.

"Are you all right?"

I nodded weakly, wiping my mouth with it. At least I thought I was OK. I did a mental check for broken bones. My arm was numb where I had touched the gate and the nerves in my hand were jangling.

"Are you OK, mate?" The Australian twang in the question meant that although I couldn't see the questioner I knew we had attracted attention from the building.

"I'm not sure," Blackbird responded. "My friend got a shock off those gates just now."

There was a slight pause. "That's impossible. They're not electric or anything. He couldn't have done." A man in uniform, possibly a security guard, walked into my field of view. "Are you OK, sir?"

"I think I'll be OK in a minute. Can you help me sit up?"

"Do you think that's wise? I could get an ambulance for you, if you like?" The long "A" of ambulance was almost comical and I found myself smiling at his Australian accent, despite my aching head.

"Well, you've still got a sense of humour about you." He stepped back and let Blackbird help me to a sitting position. I sat on the cold paving with my head against my knees while the spinning sensation slowly subsided.

"I've never seen anything like it. You went up in the air like you were doing a backwards somersault. I saw it on the monitors." Clearly this was the most exciting thing that had happened all day and now he had established I wasn't dead he was determined to make the most of it.

"Well you should definitely have those gates checked," asserted Blackbird with all her authority. "They caused a nasty accident. Next time someone could be killed."

"I still don't see how," he commented, taking his peaked hat off and scratching his head. "Maybe some sort of static build-up?" He glanced back at the gates, inert inside the doorway. "What were you doing, anyway?"

"We were trying to work out how old the building is."

"1917," he said. "Well, what I mean is, they were able to move in by then. I don't think the building was fully finished until after the First World War."

The way the intonation in his accent lifted at the end made every sentence made it sound like a question, as if everything were uncertain and he was looking for constant confirmation of reality. Having banged my head on the paving, I knew how he felt.

"The decorations must have taken a while to complete," he continued. "It's very grand inside. We used to have open days so you could look around, though that had to stop after the 7/7 bombs. How's your friend?"

Blackbird stood up. "I think he'll recover but that could have been serious."

"We've never had any trouble before. I can't think why he would get a shock from there."

"Do you want to go and touch the gates, after that?" she asked him.

"No, I think we'll have the electricians in to check them out, first, eh?" he grinned.

"It might be wise. We were just trying to find out about the building. Do you know what was here before all this?" She gestured at the grand façade.

I was a little miffed that Blackbird was more intent on the security man than on my injuries, but it did present an opportunity to find out more. I sat on the ground and listened while she gently pressed him for more information.

"I've worked here for thirty years and I don't remember anyone mentioning anything before this. You'd be amazed at some of the enquiries we get, though, people wanting to emigrate and everything. We don't get many historical queries, though. Mind you, one of my colleagues trained as one of those guides, you know, an official London guide? He's got a certificate and everything. I could ask him if he knows anything."

"That would be very kind."

He turned and went back into the building, taking a careful look at the gates as he passed them. Blackbird turned back to me.

"What on earth did you think you were doing?" She kept her voice down, though her anger was evident.

"I thought the gates might be the reason we were here," I said defensively.

"They're made of iron!"

"What's so special about iron?" I asked.

"Iron is the antithesis of magic. All the Feyre react to iron. It's one of the things that marks us out."

"I didn't know."

"Couldn't you feel it? What on earth possessed you to touch them?"

"I told you, I thought they might be what we came for."

She probed the back of my head with her fingers. "Nine times idiot!" she hissed. "It's a good thing you weren't right inside the doorway or you'd have been flung back into the other gate. If your head had hit iron instead of concrete, you wouldn't be sitting here nursing a headache. Look up at me."

I lifted my head off my knees and looked up into her grey eyes, surprised by the concern that showed there.

"At least your pupils are the same size. How do you feel?"

"A bit nauseous, but the world has stopped spinning."

"I still can't believe you touched them. Didn't it feel wrong?"

"Yes, kind of, but at the same time it was compelling, almost alive."

"Let me see your hand."

I could feel the pulse throbbing in my palm and when I opened my hand I found my fingers had red wheals where the bars had touched. I looked up at Blackbird and she shook her head.

"You won't do that again in a hurry. Is it sore?"

"It's still numb."

"Is anywhere else numb?"

"My arm was completely numb, but it's just my forearm now."

"If the feeling doesn't come back in a little while, let me know."

She offered her hand and supported my uninjured arm as I got to my feet. I was a little unsteady, but once I was vertical I felt better.

"Are you up to coming and finding out what our antipodean friend has come up with?"

I nodded and then wished I'd spoken instead. My head pounded. I swallowed and steadied myself. Blackbird tucked herself under my arm and helped me towards the doorway. At that moment, the stone Megan had given me flared to warmth against my chest. It was odd that it had chosen this moment to become active again. Maybe it was reacting to my injury. Megan had said it had something to do with physical awareness.

Blackbird helped me through the entrance, carefully avoiding the black iron of the heavy gates. It was incongruous that the older of us was helping the younger, though she appeared unconscious of the irony. Inside there was a security desk with glass screens between us and our security man. He was holding the phone tucked onto his shoulder, meanwhile waving his other hand and making an expression that must have been intended as "Hang on a minute, I'm on the phone".

I leant with my back against the counter, observing that the inside of the doors was separated from the rest of the building by more security screening. One of those walk-through metal detectors you see at airports had been installed. Clearly they took the security seriously, as he'd said. What little I could see of the inside of the building indicated that it was decorated in the style of the kind of country house that had grand ballrooms.

We waited while the muffled sound of the guard's voice came through the glass.

"Wrong building?" He conversed with his hidden colleague. "You're sure about that?"

Blackbird tried to interrupt him to explain that it was this building we were interested in, but he held his hand up to pause her and asked his colleague to repeat his last sentence again. Finally, he thanked them and hung up, turning back to us and speaking through the screen.

"You've come to the wrong place."

"It was this building in particular we were interested in," Blackbird explained patiently.

"Yes, but you see, the history isn't here. It's at the Royal Courts of Justice across the way there." He pointed out of the glass doors at the street.

"But it was this building..." Blackbird repeated.

"Yes, I got you, ma'am, but the history of this building is over at the Royal Courts. My colleague trained as a guide, like I told you, and he says that this ground was paid for by something called a quick rent."

Blackbird, who had been looking at me with an expression of exasperation, suddenly focused back on the man.

"A quick rent? Do you mean a quit rent?"

"It could have been. Yes, that was it. I thought it sounded funny."

"Why would there be a quit rent?" she said to herself.

"He said the Ceremony of the Quit Rents is held every year at the Royal Courts across the road and if you wanted to know more about this building, you should be asking there. Apparently the ground for this building is owned by the British Crown and the Corporation of London pay a quit rent for it. They have information over at the Royal Courts and you should enquire there." He showed us a victorious smile, revealing uneven teeth stained by heavy smoking.

Blackbird thanked him for his help, while my attention was drawn to a bank of monitors set up on a side-bench. They were obviously used to monitor the security cameras and they depicted various views of the exterior of the building. One of them, though, had been adapted back to its original purpose and was showing a twenty-four hour news programme.

It had suddenly flashed up with a photo-fit picture of a middle-aged man with a scrolling caption underneath. The caption said this was a picture of a man police urgently wanted to interview in connection with the death of an officer in West London that morning.

It wasn't a good likeness. The hair was too dark and the forehead too high, but there was no mistaking the image.

It was me.

ELEVEN

The photo-fit picture on the television was unmistakably of me. I grabbed Blackbird's wrist.

"We need to go," I told her

"What's the matter?" she asked.

"Now." I let a note of urgency register in my voice.

She glanced at me and then thanked the security man again for his help.

"Will your friend be all right?" he called through the glass at our retreating backs.

"He'll be fine. Thanks for the information," Blackbird called back as we pushed outside.

Once out on the wide paving, she steered me away from the entrance and under the nearby trees, away from the security cameras.

"Are you unwell?"

"I've got a bit of a headache, but no, I'm OK."

"The nausea hasn't returned? You're not seeing spots or blurred vision?"

"No. It's something else." I told her about the picture on the television. "There was no mistake, they're broadcasting pictures of me. Anyone we meet may have seen the pictures and report me to the authorities. It's all getting out of hand."

"They're bound to be looking for you, in the circumstances."

"Maybe it would be for the best if I turned myself in. They must have figured out by now that I had nothing to do with the death of that officer. I was just an innocent bystander."

"And you think they'll just accept that, do you?"

"It's the truth."

"Yes, but it's not all of the truth, is it?"

"Well, I'm not going to tell them everything, obviously."

"So what are you going to say? You can't lie to them. Not convincingly."

"I just won't mention it."

"An officer was killed, Rabbit. Do you think they won't want every detail? These people are trained to take statements from witnesses and they won't stop until all their questions have answers. How long do you think it will be before you tell them about what was on your stairs? How long before you're trying to explain about dying on the Underground, the Feyre, the Untainted, and me."

"Oh, so you're just worried I'll drag you into it, is that it?"

"Don't be stupid. What can you tell them? You don't know enough to give me away."

"Yes, and you made sure of that, didn't you?"

She sighed, exasperated with me.

"Don't read into it more than there is, Rabbit. The police are the least of my worries. Yes, it would be inconvenient if I had to abandon my present life and start again, but I've disappeared before and I can do it again if need be."

"You'd just abandon me."

"You're the one who wants to give himself up."

"I have to. It's only a matter of time before someone recognises me. It's better to give myself up than to be caught running. Don't you see?"

She looked at me with pity. "Poor Rabbit. You still don't get it, do you?"

"Get what?"

"Even if you tell them everything, they're not going to believe you."

"They'll have to."

"You didn't believe me when I explained it to you, and you were the person it happened to."

"Then I'll show them. They can't deny the evidence of their own eyes."

She laughed. "Oh, that'll get their attention. Enough to convince them you are nowhere near as innocent as you protest."

"But if I show them. If I summon my glow – what did you call it, gallowfyre? –

then they'll have to believe me."

"They'll believe what they want to believe. You can show them gallowfyre and what you can do with it and that will do more than anything else to convince them you are a danger to yourself and others. They will do what they always do."

"Which is what?"

"They will protect the public from the danger as they perceive it and they will avenge the death of their own. They will lock you away."

"They can't do that. No jury in the land will convict me just for being there when it happened. I wasn't even in the garden."

"No jury will ever come to hear of it. An assessment will be made by experts. They will make a recommendation to the court. A court order will be served and you will never see the light of day again."

"You can't just imprison people without charges, not in this country. Not since the Magna Carta. What about *habeas corpus*?"

"You won't go to prison. You're not a criminal and you won't be charged with anything. You'll go to a hospital. A special hospital where the nurses wear iron keys round their necks, the doors have iron locks and the patients are kept constantly sedated for their own good. Is that how you want to spend the rest of your unnaturally long life, drugged up to the eyeballs?

"I don't think it will come to that."

"Don't you? An officer died. They are not going to be satisfied with vague answers and platitudes."

I thought about the scenario she had painted. Unfortunately, it sounded all too realistic.

"Do they really have hospitals like that?"

"Fey genes got mixed up with humanity's a long time ago. For the most part it results in people like Megan who never really get noticed. Occasionally, though, the genes come out strongly, as in your own case."

"There are others like me?"

"Of course there are. The genes pop up in every generation. It's pretty rare, so for the most part no one notices. If they are weak then it is usually explained away as something else; a talent for sailing in light winds or an ability to light fires maybe. Mostly people's gifts come out in puberty, but Fey genes can be fickle. They can express themselves at any time, in any circumstance. How do you think you would feel if you woke one night to find that when you looked in the mirror, it wasn't your face looking back? Or how about if your belongings started to take on strange and perverse properties? What if you started to see flashes of the possible futures of people you touched? Would you be able to keep it to yourself? Or would you start telling people not to take the last bus home or to stay away from blonde people? What do we call people like that, Rabbit? What do we call people who behave in ways we don't understand?"

"We call them psychics. Clairvoyants."

"No, they're the rational ones. They are the ones who learn to cope with it and find a way to live. What do we call the others; the ones who see things no one else sees, hear things no one else hears?"

"We call them crazy."

"And what do we do with the crazy people?"

"We keep them safe, away from everyone else."

I had answered my own question. Of course we had places like that. We had them because we needed them. Blackbird watched me as I thought it all through and realisation dawned.

"You're telling me I can't go back. Even if there were a job and a life to go back to, I couldn't return to it. If I try to explain what happened, they will treat me as if I'm insane."

"I'm trying to explain that things have changed. It's not all bad news. You're old life died when you did and a new life began. Now you just have to accept that your old life has gone and move forward."

"But what about my daughter?"

"That depends. It depends on you and it depends on her. For now, the best thing you can do is stay away from her."

"For how long?"

"At worst? Until you die or she does. But maybe only a few years."

"Years?" I thought about all the things I would be missing in the time before I could see my daughter again. She would be a grown woman by then. Would she even remember who I was?

"You should stay away from her until she either comes into her own power or until the authorities forget about you and assume you've left the country, died or simply disappeared."

"But years?"

"If that's what it takes, then yes. Remember, if you survive, you have many more years of life ahead of you."

"But she may not have."

"How much of your life would you trade for a glimpse of hers?"

"You don't understand what it means to me, Blackbird."

"Don't I? I understand a lot more than you realise, but I don't let it blind me to the obvious."

"And what's that?"

"That if you love her then you want what's best for her."

"And that means staying away from her."

"You will only lead the danger to her. You need to keep away from her for now."

"For now. But I won't abandon her, Blackbird. I can't."

She gave me a long look. I thought for a moment she was waiting for me to add something, but that wasn't it. It was as if she was trying to decide something about me, perhaps whether I meant it or not. I knew I meant it.

"If you are going to stay free, you're going to have to learn to use your gifts. You will need them to conceal yourself from the police and from others hunting you. The Untainted may have failed to kill you once, but they will not give up. They will come for you again and when they do, you had better be ready."

I took a deep breath. The image on the screen came back to me. How long before they had a proper photograph? Hours, I was guessing. I needed to concentrate on the thing in front of me and deal with it one step at a time.

"What do I need to do?"

"Come with me."

She walked away, weaving easily through the traffic flowing around Australia House, confident I would follow her. I watched her go for a moment and then followed. Where else could I go?

She walked across the road to the area in front of the pale stone church where someone had been sweeping the fallen leaves into neat piles. There was a bronze statue of Benjamin Disraeli on a stone plinth in front of the church. The steps around its base were drying in the thin sunshine.

"Here," she said, "this will do."

She sat down and indicated I should sit beside her. I joined her, finding the stone cold and still slightly damp.

"Now," she told me. "We need to find you a new face."

"Out here?" We were in the middle of the open area where anyone could see. Cars and buses rumbled by around us.

"Don't worry. No one will notice us."

"It's a little exposed," I pointed out.

"If anyone sees us they will think we are having a conversation or eating an early lunch, maybe. They will not look twice."

"How do you know?"

"What do you mean, how do I know?"

"How do you know what they are seeing or not seeing? Maybe they can see us perfectly well. How can you tell?"

"I can feel it. So can you, if you try."

Now she mentioned it, there was something. An elastic thickening of the air spread around us. I wafted my hand through it. I expected somehow it might pull and tear, but it stretched and reformed around my hand.

"Can you feel it now?"

"Are you doing that?"

"I am bending appearances, making us unremarkable so we can experiment. Now, I want you to change the way you look, like you did in the airport. Become the young man in the suit again."

"And no one will see?"

"People may see, but no one will notice. Only me."

I glanced hesitantly around and tried to assure myself we were not being watched. Then I closed my eyes and focused on the image of the young man I had once been. I formed the image in my mind and made it real.

The darkness inside awoke and a prickle of power crawled across my skin. I opened my eyes and looked at my hand. It shivered back and forth between younger and older as I watched. My appearance shifted uncertainly and I knew I had failed.

"This is what happened before. It was better when the police were searching for me."

"You anchored your glamour to your fear. As soon as you stopped being afraid, it unravelled."

"But I nearly have it." I watched my hand stabilise and forced it to stay young and smooth.

"It's taking all your concentration. Could you read a book like that? Or play a guitar?"

"I can't play a guitar when I'm not holding it."

"And you'll never learn if you have to focus your entire being just to maintain your glamour. Let it go and we'll try again."

My hand shifted back to its familiar form.

"Take a deep breath and let it out slowly. You will need a clear idea of how you wish to appear."

"The same as before?"

"Perhaps a wedding suit is not the most useful look unless you plan to spend the rest of your days trying to blend in at weddings? Besides, it's really too close to your own image. You might still be recognised. You need something different, a look that no one will associate directly with you."

"Should it be like someone I know?"

"Only if you're sure you will never meet them or anyone who would normally recognise them; unless you are pretending to be them, of course. But pretending to be someone else can get very complicated. Better to choose the features of people you know and interweave them. Take the hair from this person, eyes from that, a mouth and nose from another, the posture and movement from the next, you see? It's easier to choose things you like but it can be just as effective to choose things you hate. The important thing is that it is clear and memorable."

I rifled through my memories of friends and acquaintances, searching for aspects of people I liked. It was harder than it appeared and it was some minutes before I had built a mental image I thought I could work with.

"It doesn't have to be totally exhaustive. People will fill in the details for themselves if you give them enough clues. They will see what they expect to see."

"OK. I'm ready to try." I took a deep breath and closed my eyes.

"Don't close your eyes."

"You said it made it easier."

"Yes, but if you have to close your eyes every time you use magic, you are going to end up walking into a lamppost."

I acknowledged her point with a smile.

"Or get stabbed," she added.

The smile faded. "Do all you people go around stabbing each other?"

"It can be quicker, cleaner and faster than using power," she pointed out. "If it is a test of strength then you would use power and prove yourself. But if it is life or death, choose life by whatever means."

"Does using 'whatever means' include what I did to Fenlock?"

She hesitated, her lips forming a thin line. The pause was a long one. Then she nodded.

"I apologise," she said.

"For what?"

"For what I said about what you did to Fenlock. You did the right thing. You survived, he didn't."

"You said it was obscene," I reminded her.

"I was upset. It brought back a lot of things I thought I'd dealt with long ago. I have apologised."

She said it in such a way that told me she wasn't going to repeat it. She had formally accepted my apology when I had asked her if she were a witch. It occurred to me that, maybe amongst a people who settled disputes by stabbing each other, it was important to know whether your apology had been accepted or not.

"Thank you. I accept."

She nodded, soberly. "Time to try again," she said. "Watch me."

She shrugged and her appearance melted. Beside me sat a young woman. It wasn't the woman from the square but another, younger woman, much more casually dressed in a tight T-shirt and denim skirt. Her hair was ash blonde and straight down her back. She was long limbed and slightly built, with skin so pale it looked almost transparent and eyes that were the most startling lavender under her pale lashes. I found myself thinking how attractive she was, how she would stand out in a crowd. It was disturbing when I knew, or thought I knew, what lay underneath. I had to remind myself I still had no idea what Blackbird really looked like.

She shrugged and was Blackbird again.

"You see?"

I didn't really, but I took a deep breath to steady myself and tried again. I reaffirmed the mental image I had chosen and tried to imagine myself that way, believing it was my face, my image. It was very hard not to close my eyes. I lifted my palms to see them flicker, their appearance shifting as I tried to control it. I forced it to stabilise, hardening the image by force of will. The air chilled suddenly, the leaves whipped from their piles by a sudden gust of wind, to whirl around us in a miniature maelstrom.

"Gently," she urged. "You're encouraging a flower to bloom, not yanking a chain."

I concentrated on reinforcing the image. I had my hands steady, but now my clothes shifted. I let out a sigh of exasperation, releasing the image and letting my appearance slip back to normal. The leaves fluttered to the ground around us.

"I can't get it stable, it's too complex. You make it look so easy."

"You're going about it the wrong way. By trying to force it you are using far too much power and focusing all your attention on it. Just let it happen."

"If I let it happen then nothing happens."

She smiled encouragingly. "Once more. This time stop trying to will yourself different and just let it become."

I tried again.

"Nothing's happening."

"Give it a chance. Feel your skin. Feel the way it defines your sense of self. Recognise the weight and texture of your clothes and the way they fit. In a moment you're going to shift it, all at once, like trying on a new jacket, a new jacket that will fit so perfectly that you're going to keep it, wear it, and live in it. Now, shift."

The lull of her words helped. I stopped trying to force the change and let myself accept it. I felt it change, felt the weight of my clothes alter, the tightness of my belt easing. I discovered how unexpectedly comfortable it was, how easily it became real.

"There, that wasn't so hard, was it?"

I looked at my hands. They still looked like mine, though I now wore a ring that was my father's. I had borrowed a canvas jacket I liked from a friend and it rested across my shoulders with comfortable warmth. I was wearing jeans and trainers, where before I had been wearing trousers and boots. At this thought, the trainers flickered and became boots again. I fought to get them back, and as I did, the whole thing unravelled and I sat as before.

"Damn! I thought I had it then. I let myself think about my boots and it started to come apart."

"Stop trying to bludgeon it into submission and let it come. Once you have the image, let it become established. If you start thinking about how it was, the old image will start to reassert itself. It's only following your thoughts. Once more, you can do it."

I tried again, finding it easier to slip into the comfortable jacket and the jeans now I knew what they felt like. I steered my thoughts away from what had been, letting only the new image dwell in my imagination. I acknowledged small sensations, the way my ring had calloused my finger and how I needed to brush my longer hair back from my face.

"Just sit," she advised. "Let it settle."

I lifted my hand to my face, feeling the smoothness over my chin where stubble had been. A residual scratchiness appeared, reminding me not to think about what had been but to focus on how it was now. The smoothness returned.

"I could get used to this. I might never shave again," I grinned at Blackbird.

She took my comment seriously. "Don't be tempted to disregard the needs of the image you're wearing. If you would need to shave for that image, then shave. Otherwise you'll get lazy and people will start to notice. I still wear make-up sometimes, even though it's a pain, just to make sure it looks real. I can do make-up with glamour, but if I didn't remind myself regularly how it really looks, imperfections and all, then it could end up looking too perfect to be true."

I stood and turned around slowly in front of Blackbird. "How do I look?"

"Not bad," she encouraged. "Your own mother wouldn't recognise you."

"That was the idea."

"Your hair looks a bit black for someone with your skin colour."

"I could have dyed it," I pointed out.

"You could have, but men of your generation are not known for their familiarity with hair products. There, that's better. That's more of a dark brown."

"I didn't do anything."

"Your glamour adapted. I told you, it's like riding a bicycle. If you think about it, you'll fall off."

"If I don't think about it, will it revert?"

"Not now, I think. We'll walk slowly and let you get used to it."

She got up, brushing the back of her coat where she'd been sitting on the step. She walked gently around the base of the statue, looking up at the bronze and I fell in beside her. As we strolled, I took the opportunity to ask her about what the security guard had said.

"What did he mean about a quit rent? You were interested as soon as the security guy mentioned it."

"It's a form of payment from medieval times. A quit rent was paid, usually in goods or services, to be quit of an obligation. Let's say you were obliged to raise a levy of soldiers to fight for your baron. You could pay a quit rent of horses or fodder and be quit of the obligation to raise the levy. Do you see?"

"How do you know all this stuff?"

"I'm attached to Birkbeck College at the University of London. I lecture in medieval history there."

I suddenly recognised the manner. Should I be offended that while teaching me to use my glamour she'd been treating me like one of her recalcitrant students? We made our way slowly around the side of the church towards where the road narrowed again and a crossing led over to the entrance of the Royal Courts of Justice.

"Do you think the quit rent could have anything to do with the vision?"

"I don't know, but it's worth exploring. Kareesh said the vision would show you the way to find something that was lost, something of value that would be worth your joining in the courts. If the land on which Australia House stands is paid for by a quit rent, then that must go back to medieval times, perhaps dating back to whenever it was that the thing we are looking for was lost?"

"It's a bit of a long shot."

"Do you have any other ideas?"

"No."

"The things in your vision weren't random, I can tell you that much. They were there for a reason."

"Couldn't the vision have been a little more obvious?"

"Well, Rabbit, I don't think seeing into the future is either easy or straightforward, but if you know a better way of doing it then, by all means, feel free to volunteer your services."

"I asked for that really, didn't I?"

"Yes. I think so."

We gently strolled in silence for a moment. I walked along beside her and accepted her light rebuke without feeling she had pushed me away again. Perhaps the friendship I had hoped for was not impossible.

Across the road, I recognised the imposing entrance to the Royal Courts of Justice from the background of TV reports of high-profile cases and controversial High Court decisions on the evening news. The grand gothic architecture and arched stone doorway were obviously meant to impress anyone entering its portals seeking to engage or to avoid the forces of justice. The black iron railings flanking the doorway gave the entrance a new sense of menace, at least for me. Thankfully the gates were drawn back to the side.

We crossed the road and walked between the gates. I could feel the malevolent hum from the iron as we passed. I gingerly touched the marks on my fingers, invisible now beneath my glamour. Now the sensation in my hand was returning it felt like I had been burned.

Inside the arched doorway, we were faced with a new challenge. There was a well-staffed security post with guards, an X-ray machine for scanning bags and a walk-through body scanner. I halted Blackbird in the entrance porch. Two women stepped past us, talking as they handed their bags over to the guard to be scanned. I turned my back to the guards.

"Are they checking ID?" I asked Blackbird.

"No. Stop looking so furtive. They're just scanning everyone's belongings."

"OK. I'll wait here while you go and ask inside about the quit rent thing."

"You need to go and do this, Rabbit. If there's something there from your vision then I'm not going to be able to recognise it."

"You're the one that knows about quit rents. I'm not even sure what the question is."

"Just ask them if they have any information about the ceremony of the quit rents or about the land on which Australia House stands."

"We could both go?" I suggested.

"You need to do this. You need to prove to yourself that you can walk right past them. Think of it as a test."

"If it is a test, what happens if I fail?"

"You'll be fine. Go on."

"What if it's more historical stuff?"

"If you find there's something that really needs a historical background then I'll come in and we'll both talk to them."

"Why won't you come in with me?"

"You made the bargain, Rabbit. The vision Kareesh showed you was of a future in which you survive, but it's up to you whether you follow it or not. You never mentioned me in the vision. Just by being here I may be changing your future. If I start altering things then it may never come true."

It crossed my mind that I could tell her I had seen her in the vision, that we had been together, but I knew she would hear the lie in it straight away.

"Just walk though, right?"

"Straight past them," she confirmed.

"And you'll be here when I come out?" Her talk of changing my future had made me wonder whether she meant to ditch me again.

"I'll be here."

It was the answer I needed.

I gave her a nervous grin and turned hesitantly in through the inner doors to where the first of the security guards waited. He offered me a plastic tray and waited while I dumped the contents of my pockets into it so they could feed them through the scanner. I smiled briefly and he indicated I should step through the arch of the body scanner. The arch beeped and I had to stand while a burly security guard ran a black wand up the inside of my legs, down my back and over the inside and outside of my arms. The arch was obviously set to a high sensitivity since the only metallic thing I had left on me was my belt buckle.

He cleared me without comment and I collected my wallet and small change and breathed a silent sigh of relief as I made my way around to a reception desk where a middle-aged black lady was typing at a computer. I stood and waited until she'd finished whatever she was doing and turned to look up at me.

"Excuse me," I used my best business voice, "do you mind if I ask you a really unusual question?"

She lowered her nose so she could peer at me over the top of her spectacles.

"Honey," she replied, in a warm voice that spoke of limitless patience, "you ask away, 'cause I heard it all."

I smiled, disarmingly I hoped.

"I was talking to the people over at Australia House and they sent me over here to ask about the ceremony of the quit rents. Is this the right place?"

"Sure is, honey. Every year we have a ceremony going back hundreds of years. In fact it's due in the next few weeks. Do you want to attend?"

"You can come to it?"

"Sure you can. I don't know the date off hand, but I can find out for you?"

"That would be very kind."

"Just a moment then." She picked up the phone, looking heavenwards for a second while she remembered the number, then dialled a rapid sequence of digits. She smiled at me and waited while it rang. She paused then put the phone down again.

"It's going through to voicemail. I think she must be out at lunch, as I don't think they're in court today. If you come back after two, I can confirm those dates for you then?"

"That would be fine."

By this time, there was someone else waiting in line behind me, so I thanked her and moved to the side to let them take my place. She was just as helpful with them as she'd been with me.

I took the opportunity to take a brief look around for things I might recognise from the vision. The interior of the Royal Courts was as grand on this inside as it was on the outside, with high vaulted ceilings decorated with intricate patterns like tiny coats of arms supported on slim stone pillars. None of it matched the images from the vision, though. Were we still on the right trail? How would I know? I walked around and went back through the one-way exit back to the entryway

I was relieved to find Blackbird was waiting for me, just as she'd said.

"I found a receptionist who knows the person to ask about the ceremony. She rang them, but they're at lunch at the moment. She says we can come back at two o'clock and she'll try again for me."

"That's good."

"So we can find out about it then."

"I already know."

"Pardon?"

"I already know. You can buy a fact-sheet from the kiosk behind you in the annex there for a pound. It tells you all about it."

I looked behind me to find a tiny gift shop tucked into the side of the porch, selling postcards and mementos. I glanced back at Blackbird and she held up a laser-printed leaflet titled *The Royal Courts of Justice*.

I searched her expression. There wasn't even a hint of smugness.

"Did you know about this before I went inside?"

"I swear I saw it after you went in." Her expression held the ghost of a smile. She wasn't lying to me, but there was something fishy about that last statement.

She passed me the photocopied sheets and I turned through them. There was a complicated diagram on the second page showing the relationships between the various courts of the land.

"How does this help?" I glanced up at her.

"Here, at the back, it tells you all about the Quit Rents Ceremony. It's held every year about this time. Look it says here."

Blackbird took the leaflet back and leafed through it. She arrived at a page and quoted from it.

"The annual ceremony of the rendering of the quit rents by the Corporation of London to the Queen's Remembrancer on behalf of the Crown is an ancient, time-honoured and traditional ceremony that may be the oldest surviving ceremony next to the coronation itself."

"How does that help us?"

She held up a finger.

"It is feudal in origin and character since it represents the rendering of rents and services in respect of two pieces of land, one being a piece of wasteland called 'The Moors' at Bridgnorth in Shropshire and the other being a tenement called 'The Forge' in the Parish of St Clement Danes, probably on the land now occupied by..." She wagged her finger. "Yes, Australia House." She grinned at me, triumphantly. "Look, it says right here."

I wasn't looking at the paper. My mind's eye was scanning back through fragmented images.

"A forge?"

"Yes. What about it?"

"Do you remember I told you in the vision that I'd seen a dark hall filled with water? It had an island in the middle of the stream with a misshapen altar on it."

"Yes, I remember."

"That's what I've been trying to recall. The shape was peculiar but I couldn't put my finger on it before. It was quite distinctive, even under the flotsam clinging to it. It's not an altar."

"If it's not an altar, then what is it?"

"It's an anvil."

TWELVE

Blackbird handed me the leaflet, pointing out the relevant section. I scanned through it quickly, then went back to the beginning and read it through slowly.

> In respect of The Moors, the Quit Rent consists of the presentation of a blunt knife and a sharp knife. The qualities of these instruments are demonstrated by the Comptroller and Solicitor of the City of London, who will bend a hazel rod of a cubit's length, one year's growth, over the blunt knife and break it over the sharp.
>
> Hazel rods of this length were used as tallies, which is like a counting rod, to record payments made to the Court of Exchequer by notches made with a sharp knife along their length and after the last payment, split lengthways with a blunt and pliable-bladed knife, one half being given to the payer as his receipt and the other half being retained by the Courts to vouch its written record. This quit rent has been rendered for over 750 years, the earliest recorded notice being in the Shropshire Sergeantries in 1211, during the time of King John.

The Quit Rent in respect of the tenement called The Forge consists of six horseshoes and sixty-one nails, which the Comptroller and the City Solicitor count to demonstrate that the numbers are correct before rendering them to the Queen's Remembrancer on behalf of Her Majesty.

"Why would they still be doing this after seven hundred and fifty years? Surely the rent for Australia House can't still be some horseshoes and nails, can it?" If it was, then I was paying far too much for a flat in the suburbs.

"Maybe it can. Maybe they've been doing this for so long, they no longer wonder why. It's strange, though. I mean, here we have a ritual going back hundreds of years that involves the splitting of a hazel rod and an exchange of iron. Hazel has always been symbolic for the Feyre and iron – well you already know about iron. Maybe it means something?"

"Do you think the ceremony is what we came here for?"

"The anvil is what you saw in the vision, but the forge may be the connection between Australia House and the anvil."

"In the vision, there was a door, like a hatch, high up on the wall across from where the anvil stands." The image of it floated in my memory like a fragment from a bad dream.

"Then if we find the anvil, we find the door. Wait a moment, there was something else here." She flicked through the pages of the leaflet searching for something. "Here it is, on the back.

I read over her shoulder. "'There are in excess of a hundred and fifty Judges, Registrars and Masters in the Royal Courts of Justice.'"

"Not there. Here."

"'The River Fleet runs under the buildings.' Do you think that could be the underground river I saw in the vision?"

"It must be. It can't be a coincidence, surely? We just need to find a way down to it."

"OK, but you've seen the security in there. They're not going to let us wander around in the basement looking for a lost river."

"There will be external manholes, I expect, but they will be covered by cast iron. I think you've had enough iron for one day, don't you?"

"In the vision, I followed the flow back up from the outflow into the Thames, but it had a huge grating in the way. From the brief look I got at it, the grating looked pretty solid."

"Come on." She walked down the steps into the sunlight.

"Where are we going?"

"We're going to see if there's someone who knows how we get down to the underground river."

She turned and walked out into the daylight, tucking the leaflet inside her coat and leaving me to follow on behind. I trotted after her then slowed as I caught up to walk along beside her into Fleet Street. Reaching the entrance to a narrow alley between buildings, she caught my arm.

"Down here."

She ducked into the passage, which opened out into a side-street with Georgian doorways facing along one side. She approached a black door and lifted the brass knocker, letting it fall with a clatter.

I heard a faint voice from within. "Come."

Blackbird pushed open the door and we entered a dim hallway. The bare brickwork along its length was soot-stained, the mortar crumbling from the joints. The door swung shut behind us, leaving us in semi-darkness. There was a doorway to the side that shed an uncertain light on the wall opposite and Blackbird moved forward to stand in it, her shadow shifting and dancing on the wall behind.

"Greetings, Marshdock," she said. "I give you good day."

"And a good day to you too, Blackbird," came a deep voice. It had an oily tone to it, though, as if the welcome were not entirely heartfelt. "What have you brought for me today?"

Blackbird stepped inside and I moved to stand in the doorway behind her. A wide stone fireplace in the back wall held a bronze basket with a great log laid across the heap of ash beneath. Flames licked up the side of the log, casting a fitful light into the room and across the ceiling. The window to the street was barred by heavy shutters, the only light coming from the fire.

The room was dominated by an enormous desk, its surface inlaid with dark leather scattered with oddments like paper knives and inkwells. The figure behind the desk had pale brown skin with a worn creased texture to it. He looked rumpled, shrunken. He wore an old-fashioned coat that looked two sizes too big for him and I wondered if he had indeed once been larger. His eyes and nose were too big for the rest of his face and it gave him a childlike quality that was immediately dispelled by the hardness in his eyes.

"I have a question for you. Something I'm trying to locate," she told him.

He leaned back in his stud-backed chair, an expression of light distaste curling his thick lips, as he considered us both.

"You've come to the well too often to be dipping again without something to give, Blackbird."

"This is only a small thing. I need to tap into your formidable local knowledge."

"Even small things have value, girl, and once again you bring me nothing. Who's this?" He nodded towards me.

"He's the one who wants the answer to the question. I wouldn't ask for myself."

"Ask for whom you wish. It wouldn't matter to me if he were the High King of Auld Albion. The answer would be the same: you're wasting your time. You could be out there finding some useful snippets of information, something of value. Instead you're dawdling here, eating up the warmth from my fire."

"I want to know if there's an easy way down to the Fleet River where it runs under the Royal Courts of Justice. There must be a way down. I just want to know where it is. I'll owe you a small favour."

"You owe me a small favour already."

"I'll owe you another."

"I don't need another."

"Come on, Marshdock. This is a tuppenny question."

"It is until you don't know the answer," he smiled.

"Are you going to tell me?"

"Are you going to give me something in return?"

Blackbird paused. "Fenlock's dead," she announced.

"Half the market knows that, Blackbird. Carris is running around like mad cat, pulling her hair and shrieking about her lost love. I'm surprised you can't hear it from here."

"Is she swearing revenge?" Blackbird asked.

"Who wants to know?" he countered.

"I do." My voice interrupted their haggling. "I would like to know." If Carris wanted revenge for her partner's death then I thought I should be informed.

"And what's it to you?" he asked me.

"He killed him," Blackbird announced.

I glanced at Blackbird and she shrugged her shoulders. "You might as well show him the whole thing. I'll wait outside."

"What?" I asked her.

"Show me what?" asked Marshdock, leaning forward in the chair and putting his hands on the desk.

"Show him," she instructed. "Or you'll have Carris and half the market on your trail. Make it good."

She caught my arm and pulled me from the doorway further into the room, leaning momentarily close, whispering, "Show him some strength now and it'll save a lot of trouble later."

202

She slipped past me into the doorway. "Oh, and don't forget to ask him about the way down to the river." There was a short pause and I heard the door to the street thump shut.

"What is it you're going to show me?" asked Marshdock, suspicion entering his voice.

I wondered how to play this. Show some strength, she'd said. As I hesitated, Marshdock snatched the paper knife and vaulted spryly up onto the desk, holding the knife low, ready to strike.

I raised my hand to ward him off and there was a pulse of power as the darkness within me reacted. Fire whooshed out of the grate, scattering ashes across the floor and for a second it went pitch black. Then pale light rippled out across the walls, making the room swim in moonlight. Marshdock was caught, hand still raised ready to strike, balanced on the edge of the desk.

We stood, momentarily frozen, my own uncertainty mirrored by the sudden halt in his assault.

"F'shit, you're Untainted. I'm dead." His voice had lost all its arrogance.

Caught between launching at me with the knife and retreating back behind the desk, he wavered, the blade in his hand glinting in the milky light. I lifted my hand, meaning to warn him back. The action brought a pulse of brightness that rippled away from my fingers. He turned away, wincing in expectation.

His reaction helped me realise I had the upper hand. He thought I would kill him the same way I had killed Fenlock. I had no intention of killing anyone if I could help it, but it would give me the opening I needed.

"I did kill Fenlock, but he attacked me first," I told him. "I defended myself."

Marshdock backed slowly across onto the far side of the desk and climbed down, warily retreating and making a show of placing the knife back down where I could see it. "It was self-defence," he agreed, rather too readily.

"If he had not attacked me, I would not have harmed him."

"So you say. I'll be sure to mention that to Carris." He climbed down, moving around the back of the chair, putting its high back between him and me.

"Is she swearing revenge against me?"

"She's not dumb enough to ask a blood-price until she knows who killed him. I would imagine her desire for revenge will be dampened somewhat when I tell her what became of him. You'll let me explain that to her, will you?"

"Tell her she should not make the same mistake he did."

"I'll tell her, I will." The relief in his voice was tempered by the white knuckle hold he had on the back of the chair.

"And now I have given you something you didn't know before, perhaps you would tell me where the way down to the river is, the one that runs below the Royal Courts of Justice."

"Do you know where the Devereux is?"

"The what?"

"I'll draw you a map."

He edged forward until he could reach a scrap of paper and a pencil.

"Here look, this is the Strand, and these are the Inns of Court. Past the Devereux Inn, see?" He quickly scribbled a map onto a scrap of paper and slid it across the desk towards me.

I reached forward to collect the scrap and he snatched his hand back, retreating behind the chair again. The lines on the paper were unreadable in the wavering light. "Will Blackbird know where this is?"

"Sure, sure. Near that pool, look. It's a black door. You'll find it."

"Then I thank you for your help, Marshdock. You'll explain things to Carris?"

"I will, truly. Just as you said."

"Then I will take my leave."

I backed out into the passage, letting the gallowfyre dwindle and fade, turning to leave by the door to the street. Blackbird was waiting in the half-light of the corridor, her fingers pressed to her lips in an expression of secrecy. She opened the street door and we exited.

The door swung shut behind me with a heavy sound.

"You did very well," she told me.

Her comment was accompanied by the sound of bolts thudding home in the door behind me.

"He was much more cooperative once I'd summoned the gallowfyre."

"You'll have less trouble now they know what you are, and believe me, by sunset most of the country will know. That information will buy Marshdock favours from now until year's-end. You've done him a favour."

"Then he owes, me, doesn't he?"

She smiled up at me. "Yes," she said, "he owes you."

She took the scrap of paper from me and studied it.

"This shouldn't be too hard to find. It's not far." She led the way back through the passage and waited for me so we could walk back towards the Strand together.

"And what kind of Fey is Marshdock?" I asked her.

"He is of the luchorpán."

I stopped. "Did you just say leprechaun?"

She stopped and turned to face me. "No, I didn't. I said luchorpán, but that's where your word comes from. The luchorpán are makers. They have clever hands and a way of getting into the nature of a thing, giving them properties beyond the norm."

"I've just met a real leprechaun in the middle of London. Aren't they supposed to live in Ireland?"

"Don't get confused, Rabbit. Leprechauns are what you get in stories. The luchorpán are as dangerous as any of the Feyre and you should treat them with respect."

She stopped outside a hardware store. "Wait here a moment."

She went into the shop and emerged a few minutes later with two small metal torches and some batteries. She had me hold onto one torch while she put batteries in the other and then we swapped. Then she set off again at a pace, torch in hand.

I set my pace by hers and walked along beside her. "Why are you always so touchy when I ask what the Feyre are like?"

She didn't slow down at all, but I could tell she'd heard me. After a while she sighed as if letting go of a weight and drew to a halt.

"I am of the Fey'ree."

"You are?"

"That's the question you really want the answer to, isn't it? What am I? What do I look like? Am I an ogre with four-inch tusks or a nymph with green hair and suckers on the ends of my fingers? Are you happy now?"

"Alex had faeries, lots of them. Little figures dressed in gauze with flowers for hats and–"

"I said Fey'ree, not fairy."

"You have to admit it's pretty close. At one point Alex wouldn't leave the house without wearing her wings. This is bizarre."

"So you say."

I was detecting a measure of hostility.

"Blackbird, why is this such an issue for you? I'm just telling you what she did. She was in love with fairies, they were everywhere, in the posters on her wall, on her windowsill. You even said you had a fairy mirror yourself."

She crossed her arms. "I'm sorry I told you that now."

"Oh, Blackbird, please don't be offended. You know I don't know what a Fey'ree or a luchorpán looks like, so I'm not in a position to make the sort of judgements you seem to think I'm making. I just want to learn more about the people that I am newly part of. Is that so wrong?"

She sighed again. "It's just that the Feyre used to inspire humanity with feelings of wonder, or dread, or panic. Not cutesy images of mushroom houses, fishing rods and flower petal hats."

"You're worried I think you have a mushroom house and a petal hat."

"Yes. Well, not that exactly, but that kind of thing."

"Well I don't think that. I'm a little worried that I still don't know what you really look like, but that's more from uncertainty than the idea that you might live in a mushroom. I would like to know what you're really like, but I recognise that it's not my right to know and you'll show me as and when you wish to. I reserve the right to be shocked, inspired or terrified then."

It was a bald statement of truth, which I knew she would hear in my words, though it just came out like that. I had wanted to be honest, and now I was worried I had gone too far.

"Oh, Rabbit. You say the nicest things." She stepped forward and kissed my cheek and then walked off down the pavement, leaving me more baffled than ever.

I shrugged and followed, turning down a side alley that wound past the Devereux Inn and between the backs of buildings into an open courtyard with a fountain. When I caught up with her, she was standing at an inconspicuous doorway.

"Is this it?"

"According to Marshdock there should be a way down through here." She pressed her hand against the flaky paint on the heavy wooden door and pushed. The door swung open and there was a stairway down into darkness.

Blackbird led the way down and I followed. I turned on my torch as the door swung shut with a solid *thunk* behind us.

It was easier walking down the stairway in the torchlight than in my own flickering glow. It wasn't that the torchlight was better illumination, but it didn't shift and sway of its own accord. We descended a little way then turned back on ourselves, with the sound of water getting stronger as we went down. Another flight down we turned back again and I could clearly hear the water now.

We came out onto a walkway made of bricks that stretched out in either direction into darkness. In front of us was a weir with teeth of rusted metal sticking up out of the water, combing the larger detritus from the flow. It was about fifteen feet wide and the water falling the three feet to the next level almost drowned out our voices.

"Which way?" Blackbird shone her torch up and down the tunnel.

"Upstream, I guess. We want to go back towards where Australia House and the Royal Courts of Justice are."

She set off ahead, her torch swinging around the vaulted ceiling. I had a moment's thought for what would happen if there was a sudden downpour and then went after her.

The narrowness of the walkway meant it was easier to walk near the water, but it was also where the footing was slimier and I constantly found myself having to negotiate past nameless rubbish washed up in the last flood. We made our way slowly upstream, bending around away from the noise of the weir to find another weir in front of us. Bottles and rubbish were caught in the teeth for now, but that would soon change if it rained. I wondered where it washed out and then realised I knew. I had seen the iron grid of the outflow in my vision where it emptied out into the Thames.

We curved around again and the noise changed tone. It became deeper and reverberant. The tunnel ended suddenly and I knew where we were.

"Here. It's here," I called to her.

The space opened out into a vaulted cavern. At the far end from us was a waterfall, some eight or ten feet tall with ladders either side providing access to the upper level. There was a metal gantry over the waterfall. The ceiling went up straight fifteen feet or so from there then curved into a vaulted brick roof. I swung my torch around and dropped the beam so I could see the island. It was in the centre of the pool of water fed by the waterfall. Now I could inspect it I could see that it was man-made and brick-sided. The top was shelved with outward sloping layers and in the centre of it I could see what we had come to find.

I didn't need to see it to know it was there. It sang to me in a low discordant hum that set my teeth on edge and made my stomach sour. The anvil sat on its plinth, malevolent and dark, streamers of nameless filth caught on it. Nor did I need to touch it to know what it would do to me if I did.

"It's just like you said," shouted Blackbird over the constant thunder of water, she walked forward level with the island.

"There should be a door in the wall, over there." I swung the torch around across the wall on the other side, finding vaulted alcoves built into the walls. There was a darker outline, rectangular in the wall opposite. I couldn't see it clearly in the torchlight, but I knew it was there.

The only way I could see of getting across was to climb the waterfall and then cross the gantry down on to the other side.

"We'll go over at the gantry," I shouted to Blackbird and pointed my torch.

"No need," she shouted back. She took a step or two backward and then skipped forward and launched herself off the walkway ending up on the island, ten feet away, with an easy grace. She edged her way around the plinth with the anvil on it and readied herself to jump across to the far bank.

There was no way I was attempting that.

"I'm going the long way around," I shouted over to her. Apart from the difficulty of jumping across, I did not want to get that close to the anvil. I made my way to the gantry ladder. It was stained and smeared with slime, like everything else, but it looked sound enough. I could have done with some protective gloves, but I would just have to settle for washing my hands thoroughly when we got back to the surface.

I put my hand on a rung at chest level and rattled it, making sure it was secure. It held firm, so I tucked my torch in my pocket and put my foot on the rungs and started climbing. I reached the top without incident and hoisted myself up onto the gantry. This was above flood level, so although it wasn't pristine it wasn't smeared with slime like the ladder. I used the handrail to walk across, pulling my torch to take a look at the anvil from this higher viewpoint.

From this new perspective, it was clear what it was. The shape of it, with the horn sticking out at one end, was quite distinctive. It was only the streamers of flotsam and filth that disguised its true nature.

I switched off the torch and replaced it in my pocket so I could have both hands free for the climb down. I could see that Blackbird had leapt nimbly across to the other side and was investigating the wall. I knelt down, reversing towards the ladder and feeling with my feet for the rungs below me.

It was tricky to balance on the edge and move backwards onto the ladder. Concentrating on that, I didn't notice the light growing in the distance down the long tunnel in front of me until I had my hands on the rungs and was climbing down the ladder, about to drop below eye-level.

What caught my attention was not the way the arch of the tunnel was illuminated. It was the way the light flickered, sending shifting milky beams across the domed ceiling as if it was reflecting off the water.

Except it wasn't the water that was causing it to flicker.

THIRTEEN

I had to look twice before my brain caught up with my eyes. Then I looked at my hands and, no, it wasn't me creating that shifting luminescence. That meant only one thing.

My scramble down the ladder may have been ungainly and noisy, but the clatter was easily drowned out by the thundering waterfall, which also meant my attempts to attract Blackbird's attention went unheard. I had to make sure that the light from Blackbird's torch did not give us away.

I made it to the bottom and then had to fumble in my pocket for my torch. The ledge was narrow and it was still pitch dark. The torch tangled in my pocket and I wrenched at it to pull it free. My fingers were slimy from the ladder and as it came free it slipped out of my fingers and bounced on the bricks at my feet then skidded over the edge and vanished into the dark water below.

I swore.

There was no time to see where it had gone. I used my hands to feel my way along the clammy wall, stepping sideways towards Blackbird. I could see the glimmer now on the tunnel ceiling over the gantry. It was getting stronger.

I shuffled towards the place where Blackbird was examining the wall with her torch. I daren't go any faster for fear of losing my footing. I finally reached her and tugged at her coat.

"Blackbird, we have to get out of here!"

"What's the matter? Where's your torch?"

"I dropped it."

"Already?"

"Turn yours off. There's someone coming."

She turned off the torch. "Where did you drop it?"

"Never mind. Look." I pointed upwards to the glow building above the gantry.

"Why didn't you say?" She started shifting along the ledge.

"I was trying to. You were more interested in the torch." The light was growing over the gantry and starting to illuminate the vaulted ceiling.

"There's no time. In here." Blackbird dragged me into one of the alcoves created by the vaulting. The alcove was shallow and we crammed into the limited shadows created by the supporting pillar.

The light grew brighter and then spilled out over the water. I pressed in alongside Blackbird.

I leaned forward. There were two figures standing on the gantry. One of them was a blank silhouette against the dark, a wraithkin like me. I pressed myself in again.

"How many?" Blackbird whispered against my chest.

"There are two, a wraithkin and one other. The other looks normal enough."

"Can you see what they're doing?"

I leaned forward again slowly. Blackbird tugged at my sleeve. "Don't let them see you."

"I know. I won't."

I leaned out again to peak around the pillar. The two were still on the gantry with the normal-looking one making grand gestures towards the central island and the anvil. The conversation was quite animated, but we were too far away to overhear them.

"They're arguing."

"What about?"

"I don't know."

"Let me see." She leaned forward across me while I leaned back against the wall.

"They're coming down."

"Shit! Can we hide?"

"Not with magic. Your first use of it would give us away like a beacon."

"Then let's run for it."

"We'd never make it. If it comes to it, jump into the water and let the flow carry you downstream to the weir. Try and stay underwater for as long as you can."

"I can't swim."

"What?"

"I never learned."

She pulled back and the glint from her eyes in the dark told me she was looking at me. "Well it's never too late to start. Just try not to drown and let the water carry you."

"Can we fight them?"

"Can you? I can't. At least one of them is wraithkin and that doesn't bode well for the other."

"I don't know. What do I have to do?"

"If you don't know, it's too late to start teaching you now."

"I thought you said it was never–"

She pressed her free hand against my mouth, silencing me. As soon as she did I could hear the voices.

"...of inspection. We were simply asked to check it was intact." The first voice was bold and arrogant.

"Yes, and it is." The second voice dwelled on esses in a way that was hauntingly familiar.

"Well now we have seen it, can we go?"

"It was your choice, Raffmir, to come in your true form." The words were slow and slurred as if the speaker couldn't form the words properly.

"And yours, sister, to wear that sham you call a body."

"It serves a purpose, for now. I travel in my own form when the need arises."

I knew that second voice now. It had stood outside my bedroom door and called me brother.

As the wraithkin moved towards us, the shadows shrank and we were forced into the narrow space next to the pillar. I slid around to face the corner and Blackbird edged into the narrow space between me and the wall.

The wraithkin's back came into view and I pressed into Blackbird. Glancing sideways, I could clearly see the nimbus around his hand where his sleeve drew back as he gestured, only emptiness within. He looked like a hole in the world.

"Are you satisfied now, sister? Can we go?"

"The lock is untouched, the seals unbroken. And yet I sense a presence."

Blackbird's hand sought mine, her fingers squeezing readying me to jump into the water. Between us, the stone pendant around my neck pulsed into warmth. It found a rhythm, matching my heartbeat, each beat stronger than the last. My attention was split between Blackbird's pressure on my hand, the stone pulsing at my breastbone and the dark figure with his back to me.

Raffmir stepped backwards towards us, facing across the water to the anvil. "You can see it is undisturbed. Your senses are distorted by the barrier, my sister. Let us return and relate what we have found."

"It smells."

"Of course it smells. It's a sewer. What did you expect?" He gestured across to the island and the anvil, throwing his hands wide and narrowly missing my arm. "I'm surprised you can sense anything close to that. It's giving me a headache."

"The barrier persists."

"Not for much longer."

"You are sure it is failing?"

214

"Certain of it. There is a worm at the heart of the ritual and each time they repeat it the barrier becomes weaker. Once it fails we shall be free to come and go as we please."

"Then we shall feed." The glee in her voice was chilling.

I knew what she meant when she said feed. I remembered the chilling sounds from my back garden, the screams of "Get it off me!" before they were choked off.

"Come, let us go. I can feel this world giving me wrinkles."

"You are vain, Raffmir."

"Just because you don't get wrinkles, it doesn't mean the rest of us are vain"

"I wasn't talking about the others."

Raffmir stepped back along the ledge and retreated from us, the shadows lengthening. I let out a breath I had not realised I had been holding. We stayed pressed into the alcove while the source of the light climbed back onto the gantry.

We could no longer hear what was being said over the roaring water and the light finally faded down the tunnel. The darkness reasserted itself and was then replaced by the faintest luminescence from the brickwork. They were leaving,

Blackbird made to move out of the shadows, but I squeezed her hand hard and she stopped.

"What?"

"Can't you feel it?"

"What?"

"She's waiting up there."

"What for?"

"Us."

I leaned sideways very gently to peer around the pillar. The light was vanishing over the gantry, but in the shadow that remained there was a dark shape outlined. I eased back.

"She's on the gantry."

We stayed where we were and the light grew again. He was coming back. I wondered what it was I was sensing and whether she sensed it too. Should we throw ourselves in the water now, while they were furthest away, or wait and see what happened? I didn't fancy my chances in that dark water, not while there was a choice.

Light flickered across the vaulted ceiling and rolled out over the pool again as he joined her. I took a chance and looked around the pillar. He was addressing her back, but she was leaning on the rail over the gantry, as if she was listening for something.

"Does she know we're here?" Blackbird whispered close to my ear.

"I don't know. She knows something's here. Maybe she's spotted my torch."

"Where is it?"

"It fell in the water next to the waterfall. It was switched on. She may be able to see it from the gantry."

"Oh, Rabbit. If they come back down the ladder, we're going for the water."

"Can they catch us?"

"Raffmir may be able to reach us with gallowfyre. If he can, we're lost."

We stayed still, the strange shifting light exaggerated by the reflections from the roiling water. The warm heartbeat of the stone against my breastbone contrasted with the cold seeping from the bricks. The source of the light didn't move, but I began to wonder if that shambling figure wasn't using the light to climb back down the ladder and explore the recesses, searching for the source of her unease.

Blackbird had said that just a touch of the spreading rot would be enough. How would we see it spreading over the walls and roof in the shadows? Was it running across the bricks, even now? I sniffed the air, trying to detect the sharp, fetid odour that accompanied the darkspore. Against the background smell of the sewer, it was well masked. The prospect of the dark flows beneath us were more appealing by the second.

Finally I could stand it no more and I leaned out again to peek around the pillar. The two figures were still on the gantry. Then Raffmir stood and stretched, and the other figure pushed back from the rail and ambled past him, the walk not quite human, as if having a jointed limbed body was awkward and unfamiliar.

I watched as the light faded under the arched ceiling. Perhaps, finally, they had given up and gone.

"I think they've left."

"Are you sure?"

"I don't know. The stone's still pulsing."

"What stone?"

"The one Megan gave me. It's around my neck."

Blackbird pulled her hand from mine and the stone flared with heat and then slowly cooled.

"It's not the wraithkin that's doing that, it's me."

I looked down at her, still tucked into the corner in front of me,

"I don't understand."

She lifted her chin and there was something in her eyes, even in the darkness. It was a faint inner glow, like a green ember dying with a core of inner heat. Her eyes held something I didn't recognise, defiance maybe.

"What?" I asked her.

"We need to go, while we have the chance."

She was avoiding my question. What did it mean when the stone reacted like that? Next time I saw Megan, I would ask her. I leaned out again, searching for any sign of them. "I think they've really gone this time."

"Can you feel her?"

I listened to the inner sense. "I think she's gone. Come on, we'll go downstream."

"We have to get over to the other side. The exit is over there and there are no crossings further down."

"I am not going up on that gantry."

"I thought you said they'd gone?"

"Yes, but for how long?"

"Fine, then you'll have to jump across like me. It's not that hard."

"I can't get any nearer to the anvil. Can't you feel it? It's like sitting under a thunder cloud."

"You tell me then." Exasperation rang in her tone. "How are you going to get to the other ledge?"

"Perhaps I could climb across the weir, further down?"

"Perhaps you could fall in the water and demonstrate your swimming skills?"

I looked again at where the anvil sat humming in the dark. It had the same quality as the gates at Australia House, only much, much worse. There was a brooding malevolence about it and I knew if I went near it, spite would leap across the air and strike me down. I would not be able to cross via the island, even if I could make the leap.

"I'll cross at the gantry. Meet me on the other side."

"Before we go, we should take a quick look at the door in the wall."

I hesitated, but it was what we had come for. "Can I use your torch?"

"I'll shine it for you, butterfingers." I could hear the smile in her voice in the darkness.

We edged back along the ledge to where the dark rectangle showed in the brickwork. It was like an iron safe, set into the wall. The frame had rusted where the damp of the brickwork had leached at it, but the door itself was solid black iron. There was a small square keyhole in the centre.

"It looks pretty solid, doesn't it?" I commented to Blackbird.

"She said it was sealed and that the seals were intact. I wonder what she meant?"

The door was a mere echo of the malevolence of the anvil. Nevertheless, I didn't fancy touching it. "What do you think is inside?"

218

"Whatever it is, no Fey was meant to reach it."

There was no handle and no other hole I could see. If the square hole were a keyhole, I couldn't see how it turned.

"We should go," I insisted, "before they change their minds and come back for another look.

"I agree. Go and check the gantry is clear. I'll wait for you here and then jump across."

"Why can't you check the gantry?"

"You're the one who insists on using it. I prefer to use the island."

I looked towards the island and then the gantry, both obscure in the dark.

"Can I borrow your torch?"

"What, and lose the only light we have between us? I think it would be better if I looked after it, don't you?"

"I can make light."

"Yes, and that will bring back Raffmir and his sister back faster than anything else. Just get on with it, before they come back."

Reluctantly I sidled my way around to the gantry and then felt my way onto the slimy ladder. I climbed it looking upwards unable to tell whether anything lurked in the shadows above, waiting for me to poke my head over. Thankfully nothing was.

I crossed the gantry carefully, as swiftly as I could, and lowered myself down the ladder on the other side. My descent was more elegant this time and I soon joined the dimly lit figure of Blackbird who had skipped lightly and lithely across the gaps below, belying her pensioner's appearance.

I joined her in the ring of torchlight and we made our way back along the ledge downstream. Once we were clear of the anvil hall the noise of the water diminished.

"What did Raffmir mean about the barrier?" I asked Blackbird as she shifted our remaining torch between illuminating the path forward and making sure I didn't step on something slippery.

"I told you that the Untainted live in a world apart and they can cross into our world. You've seen that they can take over the body of someone gifted who is newly dead and also that they can also cross like Raffmir, as themselves. There was a time when they could only cross at certain times of the year, near the equinoxes or at a solstice, the times when things are balanced."

"And now they cross all the time?"

"Not all the time, but their crossings have become more frequent and over a longer period."

"He said the barrier was weakening," I reminded her.

"You know, it's strange. Kareesh taught me about the Feyre and about Fey history. It's not a written record like human history; it's wound up in stories of great deeds and terrible disasters the Feyre tell to their children and their grandchildren. She never mentioned a barrier against the Untainted, though. You'd think she would have done."

"A barrier would make sense. The Seventh Court take themselves off to their other world and the rest of the Feyre bolt the door after them."

"So where are the tales of this deed?" she asked. "Where are the names of those powerful enough to seal the gap between the worlds? It must have taken the combined efforts of more than one court, perhaps even all of them, to create a barrier that would withstand the Seventh Court. You'd think they would be proud of such an achievement."

She held the torch steady for me while I edged past the weir.

"Maybe it wasn't the Feyre that did it," I suggested. "You said hazel and iron were both symbolic for the Feyre. Maybe the Quit Rents Ceremony has something to do with it? Maybe it was humanity that sealed the barrier against the Seventh Court?"

"No, that's a human tradition. Humanity doesn't have any magic of its own, unless..."

"What?"

"They wouldn't have, would they?

"Wouldn't what?"

"What if the Six Courts cheated?"

"What do you mean?"

"What do the Six Courts have that the Seventh doesn't? What's the difference between them?"

"Humanity, I guess. The Seventh Court doesn't have anything to do with humans."

"Precisely!"

We reached the stairway up to the access door and began climbing the steps up to the surface. We emerged into daylight and walked down to the pool in the open courtyard so we could wash our hands. I dipped them into the chilly water and scrubbed them together to remove the slimy residue. A curious goldfish came to investigate the cloudy water, and then flicked its tail and vanished as soon as it came near the discoloured water from my hands.

"So the Six Courts have humans and the Seventh doesn't. So what?"

"The Six Courts knew any barrier made by them could eventually be undermined by the Seventh. A barrier made with Fey magic could be broken with Fey magic."

"So they got their humans to do it?"

"Perhaps initially, yes. They made the barrier, symbolised by hazel and iron and sealed it in an annual rite so it would be continually reinforced. Then they got humanity to carry out the ritual for them, so none of the Courts could break it."

"That works for the Feyre, but why would humanity take on such a duty? From their point of view, one lot of Feyre are as bad as another. Why would they take sides? Better to let them all kill each other."

"Hmm, you're right. What's in it for them? Still, if the barrier fails then we're all in trouble. You heard Raffmir's sister. Once the barrier comes down she and her friends intend to feed and I'm guessing it won't just be other Feyre they're preying on."

"Well, for the moment we have the advantage that we know what they're up to."

"That's just it, though. We don't, do we? All we know is that Raffmir said there is a worm at the heart of the ritual and the barrier will fail because of it. If the ritual is the Quit Rents Ceremony then what's wrong with it? You said they're still doing it, even after all this time. So where's the worm?"

"We have to speak to the Queen's Remembrancer. Maybe he will know what's wrong with it?" I glanced at my watch. "It's gone two o'clock. We could go back and talk to the nice receptionist. She was going to check the dates of the ceremony, so maybe we can turn that into an introduction?"

I shook the remaining water from my hands and Blackbird and I wound our way back through the alleys and courtyards to the Strand and the Royal Courts of Justice.

I was more confident about approaching the security station this time, now that I had managed to maintain my glamour for a while. Blackbird was right, after a time you got used to it and didn't give it a thought. I emptied my pockets into the trays for the scanner and went through the metal detectors.

"Let me handle this," I suggested to Blackbird.

She gave me a sceptical look, but conceded. I moved up to the reception desk where the same lady was typing at her computer. She looked up as I approached the desk.

"Hi, honey, did you want me to find out those dates for you now?"

"Actually, I was wondering whether it would be possible to have a chat with the Queen's Remembrancer."

"You want to make an appointment?" She reached for the telephone.

"Well, we were really just hoping for a quick word, if he or she is available."

"He's usually quite booked up, I'm afraid. The Remembrancer is only a ceremonial role and his other duties take up most of his time. Would you like me to talk to his clerk and see if he can slot you in later in the week?"

"Hmmm. Not really. It's kind of urgent, in a historical way. Is there any possibility you could have a word with his clerk and see if we could have five or ten minutes now? I would really appreciate it."

She peered at me over her glasses. "This is highly irregular, but I suppose there's no harm in asking. Who shall I say wants to see him?"

I realised I was going to have to give my name and we were still only ten feet from the security station where the guards were scanning the belongings of people returning from lunch. "It's Niall... Niall Dobson." I borrowed my ex-wife's surname in a moment of inspiration, "and this is my friend..." I ran out of steam as I realised the only name I had for my companion wouldn't do for this occasion either.

"Veronica." Blackbird stepped forwards. "Doctor Veronica Delemere. I'm with the University of London at Birkbeck."

I glanced sideways at Blackbird and then back to the receptionist, who gave me a look that said she wasn't impressed by University types. Nevertheless she picked up the phone and dialled a rapid sequence of digits.

"Claire? Claire, it's Marcie. I have a couple of visitors who would like to speak with the Queen's Remembrancer about his duties. One of them is from Birkbeck and the other is from...?" She looked up at me.

"I'm just an interested amateur," I demurred.

"He says he's an amateur, but he's very charming." She smiled at me in a conspiratorial way. "Yes, I know he's busy, but they only want fifteen minutes and they say it's urgent."

She paused to listen.

"I know, I know, but they just wondered if he would meet them. They claim it's about something historically interesting. Ten minutes would do? You know how he is about his history." There was a pause. "Sure, I'll wait."

She whispered to me. "She's just checking."

"We really are very grateful for your help."

"Oh, that's OK. He loves historical things, especially if there's a mystery. There is a mystery, isn't there?"

"Oh yes," I nodded. "It's a mystery all right." I glanced at Blackbird.

Marcie's attention was drawn back to the phone.

"That's great. I'll send them up." She put the phone back on the cradle. "She says you can go on up now. Just don't try and sell him something or you'll get me in a world of trouble. You see that balcony there and the archway below it? Go up the stairway and turn to your right at the top. Go down the corridor and Claire will be waiting for you. Don't get lost."

"We won't, and thanks."

"No trouble, honey. Turn to your right, remember. I hope you find what you're looking for."

"I hope so too."

I turned to follow her directions, Blackbird at my side.

"Charming, huh? It looks like you have a fan there," she suggested.

"Doctor Veronica Delemere of the University, eh?" I countered.

"Well I can hardly be called Doctor Blackbird at the University, can I?"

We went to the archway and found a stone stairway leading upwards. There were lots of signs directing you to one court or another, but we ignored these. The stone stairway had white stripes painted on the edge of each step and a dark wooden handrail. They were quite steep. We turned right, as instructed, walking down the corridor past the courtrooms.

Waiting there was a petite brunette with short straight hair. She didn't see us until we were quite close and I wondered whether she was seriously shortsighted. Her jacket and skirt were dark and sober and she looked all business. She thrust out her hand at me, rather aggressively.

"Claire Radisson. Pleased to meet you."

"Hello, I'm Niall Dobson and this is Veronica Delemere."

Claire shook our hands in short tight gestures.

"Perhaps you'd like to come through?"

She turned on her kitten heels and marched off down the corridor, plainly expecting to be followed. We hurried along behind.

"There are so many people who want His Lordship's time and only so many hours in the day. It would only be possible to give you a few moments, I am sure you understand." She implied that there was no room for compromise. There was something else here, though. Deception rang in her tone.

"Of course, we will be brief," Blackbird reassured her, glancing at me with a raised eyebrow.

She walked down the corridor and then turned off to the left, stepping past a doorway and ushering us into a neat ante-office with a desk and bookshelves. Small touches like a floral tissue box and the handbag placed on the cupboard behind the desk led me to believe that this was her space. There was a further set of double doors that remained closed. I figured that in order to gain access to the inner sanctum we would need to satisfy her that our business was worthy of his lordship's time.

"Perhaps you'd like to tell me what this is all about?" She moved around the desk, putting it between her and us.

"It's concerning the duties of the Queen's Remembrancer and the Quit Rents Ceremony. We would like to ask His Lordship a few questions, if that's possible."

"I'm afraid he has a full schedule. Can you be more specific?" Again, I was sure she wasn't telling us the truth. Perhaps she was just checking to see if we were wasting his time?

"We're interested in changes," Blackbird expanded, "the way the ceremony may have developed over time."

"And you've spoken to him about this earlier?"

"No, but you already know that, surely?"

She gave a brittle laugh. "I'm afraid that, as His Lordship's clerk, I only deal with his business affairs. Do you know him personally?"

There was a lot of dissembling going on here, but we needed to get past that and speak to the man himself.

"No, we've not met him before," I said. "So, would it be possible to have a few words with him, if he has a moment he could spare us?" I hoped I was being as charming as Marcie had made me out to be.

"I'm afraid that won't be possible." This time there was no deception.

"But Marcie said she was sure you would be able to find a slot for us. We only need a few minutes."

"You misunderstand me; you can't see him because he isn't here. He was at a late briefing last night until about ten o'clock. He left in good spirits at about half-past ten."

She looked from Blackbird to me.

"He hasn't been seen since."

FOURTEEN

Claire looked from one of us to the other. "I was hoping your 'urgent matter' might provide some explanation as to where he might be." Claire was gauging our reaction to the news that the Remembrancer was missing. Is that what the deception was all about? Did she think we were responsible?

"No, we were hoping to meet him to speak with him about the ceremony," I explained.

"Then I am afraid you will be disappointed. He's not here."

"When you say he's not here, you were expecting him, yes?" Blackbird suggested.

"He has appointments in his diary but he hasn't come in this morning. As I am sure you can imagine I have a hundred things to re-arrange, so if you wouldn't mind…?"

"Have you rung his home?" Blackbird asked.

"Look, I don't know what business it is of yours, but–"

The phone rang on her desk. She glanced down at the display and then picked it up.

"If you would excuse me for a moment?" She turned away, cradling the phone close to her shoulder.

"Hello, Elizabeth? No, there's been no word."

She paused.

"I've checked with the hospitals and there's no one matching his description. I'm sure if there'd been an accident we would have heard by now."

She listened to the caller.

"No, look I'm sure it's nothing. He'll turn up, just wait and see. I have some people with me at the minute but I'll call you the moment there's any word, I promise. Yes, straight away. Promise. Bye."

She turned back to us and put the phone down.

Blackbird turned to me. "He didn't get home then. That's not good."

"Do you think that's our worm?" I asked her.

"It could be, though from the way it was said I got the impression that the worm has been there for some time. It's not a recent thing."

"Would you mind," asked Claire, "continuing this conversation elsewhere? As I have already told you, the Remembrancer isn't here and as I am sure you can appreciate, I have a busy day ahead of me."

Blackbird asked Claire, "Has he had any strange visitors? Has anyone unusual come to call?"

"Look, the police will be here shortly. I am sure they're capable of sorting this out. Now if you wouldn't mind…"

"Anyone who appeared drunk? Or slow?" Blackbird persisted.

"No, now look, I really… What do you mean, drunk?"

"Someone that slurred their words and seemed uncoordinated, maybe?" I suggested.

"Anyone asking about the ceremony?" Blackbird added.

Claire looked between the two of us. We suddenly had her attention.

"There have been phone calls, just recently," she told us, "that sounded as if the person calling were drunk. I put them down as prank calls."

"Did the person sound is if they were calling internationally, over a long distance?" Blackbird asked.

"What do you know about this?" Claire demanded.

Blackbird ignored the question. "Did they ask about the ceremony?"

"Oh God, the ceremony." Claire ran her fingers back through her hair in an unconscious gesture. "Well, hopefully he'll have turned up by then. We can put it back a day or two, but–"

"But it must go ahead," Blackbird finished for her.

She gave Blackbird a very direct look but confirmed it. "The ceremony will have to go ahead, regardless. It's been a continuous unbroken sequence for centuries. Now I really am sorry, but that is as much time as I can spare you right now. If you'd like to come back when His Lordship is here then perhaps he will spare you the time to go through this with you, but in the circumstances I'm sure you can see that we have other priorities."

I suspected she knew more, but she had no reason to tell us anything..

"Marcie said that we might come to the ceremony. Is that still possible?"

"Yes, it was originally planned for next Tuesday but the date may change now, of course. If you contact reception at the beginning of next week, they should be able to confirm dates by then."

"Can you arrange another Remembrancer by then?" Blackbird queried.

"Hopefully we won't need to."

Blackbird looked at me and then at Claire. "I think you may need to arrange a substitute."

"I get the impression that you two know more about this than you're letting on." She gave Blackbird a steely stare, but Blackbird was a match for her.

"Likewise," she answered.

"Would it help," I offered, "if I said that we'll do anything we can to assist?"

"Thank you, but unless you know where His Lordship is, I don't think you can help."

229

We had reached stalemate. She wasn't going to budge, even though I was sure there was more she could tell us. Something had to shift, and it wasn't going to be her.

Blackbird turned to me. "I don't think there's any more we can do here. The ceremony will go ahead with or without the Remembrancer."

"But the worm?"

Blackbird shrugged. "Ms Raddison, the police aren't going to be able to help you. If you want to find your Remembrancer then you're going to have to trust us."

"I don't have to trust anyone," she said firmly.

"Very well," said Blackbird. "Come on Niall, we have things to do."

"But what about the worm?" I said.

"I can't make her help us. Come on."

She walked out of the office. I gave Claire a helpless look and followed. I caught up with her in the corridor.

"Where are we going? We need to know what's wrong with the ceremony."

"Don't worry," she said quietly. "She'll call us back by the time we reach the stairs."

We reached the stairs and looked back. There was no sign of Claire.

"Maybe we should go back?"

"Maybe that isn't your path," Blackbird said, and took the stairs down.

I followed her down into the vaulted hall below and we headed for the exit.

"Do you have a plan? Is there another way to find out?"

"We need to look for the next part of your vision. With that we can move forward."

"I don't even know which is the next part. It could be any of them."

"We're not getting anywhere with her. There must be another way." We went through the exit gate, back out through the high stone doorway into the sunshine.

"So where now?"

As we exited into the road, one of the security guards came through the entrance and called after us. "Excuse me? Sorry, were you with Miss Raddison a moment ago?"

We stopped. "We were," said Blackbird.

"She called down. She says you left something in her office."

"Did she? Then I guess we'd better come back for it." Blackbird smiled at me. "Told you."

"You weren't sure," I said to her, but she just smiled.

We repeated the ritual with the scanners and then made our way back up to Claire's office. She was waiting for us.

"Perhaps," she said, "we could try again?"

"That depends on whether you can help us," Blackbird said, "so that we can help you."

"If there's something you know, something that could help us find Jerry, I would like to know it."

"Let's go back to the phone calls," said Blackbird. "They have a hollow quality, as if the speaker is in a large room, or on speaker-phone, don't they?"

Claire's expression didn't change.

"The speaker's voice is strange and slurred, drunk even, and there's a delay, like on international long distance."

She still didn't say anything.

"There's something about them that doesn't sound like a phone call. The etiquette is all wrong. How am I doing?"

"Go on," she allowed.

"These aren't the normal enquiries – 'Would His Lordship be available for such and such a date or this or that event?' – these are odd calls, as if the caller isn't used to telephones."

Claire cleared her throat. "The first time it happened, it completely caught me out. It was Monday, I think, and we were dreadfully busy. I picked up the phone and said hello. It was an internal number, you see?" She glanced at the phone on her desk.

"The caller asked, 'What does the Remembrancer remember?' There was no greeting, just the question. I think I said 'I beg your pardon?' and the caller said, 'What does he want?' They slurred their esses and it was difficult to understand them. I said 'What does who want?' wondering whether they were drunk. The caller said, 'The Remembrancer, what does he want?' I asked them who was calling and they put the phone down. The thing was, right through the call, there was an engaged tone in the background as if the lines were crossed. I put it down to a fault on the line."

"But it happened again," Blackbird prompted.

"This time it was another voice, more confident and not slurred, but still odd. It was another internal call so I just picked up the phone and said 'Claire speaking' and the caller laughed, like it was funny."

I looked at Blackbird, but she was focused on Claire.

"The voice said 'The ceremony is cancelled this year, Claire.' I knew it was the same kind of thing because the engaged tone was in the background again, so I said 'Who is this?' The laughter started again and then something was wrong with the power because the lights went dim as if the voltage had dropped. I slammed the phone down."

"And the lights came back on?" Blackbird suggested. She nodded.

"That's just as well. What happened then?"

"I asked Marcie to trace the call. It was obviously somebody playing pranks, but I didn't think it was funny. All calls for the courts are logged and tracked, for departmental billing and for security."

"What did it show?"

"It came back with 'extension unregistered'. We had the phone people check into it, but they said it was some sort of external line fault, so we were no wiser."

"Have they called back again?"

"No, but the second call was only yesterday. How did you know what happened?"

"I saw it before," said Blackbird, "a long time ago." Her words made me think of a little girl, curled in a corner, watching a dark shape speak into a mirror.

"Would His Lordship have come back here last night? Could he have picked up a call?" I asked.

"He may have done. The calls go through to his office if I'm not here."

"Have you been in his office today?" asked Blackbird.

"Yes, several times."

"Can I take a look?"

"You can look, but he's not in there."

Blackbird went to the double doors and pushed one open, standing in the doorway to observe the room. Satisfied that it was indeed empty, she stepped through. I stood in the doorway behind her. She walked around the large desk with its dark, polished surface and green leather inlay, the walls stacked with row upon row of legal texts. She slowly circled the office, drawing her forefinger across the polished surfaces.

"Not here," she said.

"I told you he wasn't there," said Claire, from over my shoulder.

That wasn't what she meant. She meant he hadn't died there.

I stepped back into the ante-office and she came after me and pulled the door closed behind her.

"If you get another call like that, put the telephone down straight away. Don't speak to them, don't listen to them. Just put the phone down, OK?"

She nodded. "Do you have any idea what happened to him?"

"Perhaps. When did you speak to him last?"

"Yesterday. He had an evening engagement and I left him to it. He never went home. His wife is frantic with worry and calling here every ten minutes. I've already called all the hospitals and alerted the police, but there's no sign of him. I was sort of hoping your historical mystery might have something to do with it. He's a keen historian. It's possible he went off on some wild goose chase."

"Does he do that a lot?"

"No, nothing like this has happened before. That's what's so worrying. What if he's been kidnapped or something? We deal with all sorts here, organised criminals, gangs, murderers, everything. The police are coming in an hour or so to talk to me, but there have been no demands or ransom. In the absence of anything else, I think they're hoping he'll just turn up."

Blackbird glanced at me. It must have crossed her mind, as it had mine, that if one of the Seventh Court had been outside my door last night then they might have been in other places too.

"If you don't find him, the ceremony will still go ahead?" Blackbird asked her.

"It won't be the first time we've had to improvise to make sure it happens, but yes, it will go ahead."

"So the ceremony has changed?" I asked her.

"The ceremony has been conducted under the offices of the Queen's Remembrancer for almost eight hundred years and is virtually identical to how it was originally performed. Even the words are identical, if a little archaic. In every respect, the ceremony is legally identical to the ones carried out in the thirteenth century."

"But you said you'd had to improvise," I challenged. "You can't be using the same horseshoes that were used eight hundred years ago, surely?"

"Actually, the shoes are the originals and are the oldest horseshoes known to be in existence. There have been some minor changes, though, of course. Countless different people have been involved in performing the ceremony and some of the items have had to be renewed, but in every respect it is as identical as we can make it to the ceremonies performed in the reign of King John."

"Which of the items have had to be renewed?" asked Blackbird.

"Why are you so interested in this?"

"It's possible," Blackbird said, "that changes in the ceremony have something to do with your missing Remembrancer."

"Then you should inform the police. Anything that can help to find him…"

"The police aren't going to find him, Claire."

"Then you know what's happened to him? If you do…"

"No. But there are things here that the police can't deal with. We can try to help you but you have to help us too. There is a great deal at stake."

Claire looked from one of us to the other. "What do you want from me?" she asked.

"We need to know what has changed in the ceremony. I can't tell you when it changed because we don't know, but something changed at some point, maybe in the last hundred years or so and it may have a lot to do with why your boss didn't make it home last night."

She folded her arms, chewing her lip as she considered our request. "And this will help to find Jerry?"

"It may explain what has happened to him," Blackbird offered.

Claire weighed that. "Come through into the office. I'll bring you what I have."

She brushed past us and opened the doors to the Remembrancer's office. She brought two chairs forward from the wall and we were invited to sit across from the empty chair of the absent owner. Claire disappeared for a few moments, and then returned with a rectangular bundle wrapped in soft black cloth. She unfolded it on the desk, revealing a thick brown leather-bound book.

"This is the Journal of the Queen's Remembrancer, or at least the latest version of it. The earlier ones are in the restricted archives of the Public Record Office at Kew. This one is from about 1870 onwards." She smiled apologetically. "The duties of the Remembrancer were made largely ceremonial after the Queen's Remembrancer's Act of 1859."

She slid the book towards us. "Please be careful with it, it's quite delicate. There are some cotton gloves here," she glanced at me, "but they're probably too big for your hands." She passed them to Blackbird who was clearly a more suitable person, in her eyes, to be handling valuable documents.

The leather binding of the journal showed its age and use. Each hand that had held it over the years had added to the smoothness of the leather until there were two burnished patches, one on each side, where you might naturally hold it to lay it out to write.

Blackbird slipped the soft cotton gloves on and moved the book in front of her. I stood up and moved behind her so I could look over her shoulder.

The book was a little smaller than a standard letter size and creaked when it opened. She turned to a page indicated by a length of red ribbon sewn into the binding. There were rows of neat script. Each short entry described an event, the annual Trial of the Pyx being one, but there were others. Each had a date, written out in long-hand, the nature of the event and a list of those present. Some small details of the event were recorded and, occasionally comments were added about some aspect of the duties or roles performed.

On the previous page was the entry for the last year's Quit Rents Ceremony. It detailed the attendees, including the City of London's Comptroller and Solicitor and various representatives of the Corporation of London. Certain attendees were starred, though why they were picked out wasn't obvious. Blackbird leafed slowly backwards through the volume, finding almost identical entries for each year of the ceremony. After we had gone back about fifteen years, the hand changed to a more circular script, but the entries remained the same. Each year the knives were submitted and the horseshoes and nails counted. A response of good service for the knives or good number for the nails was given in return. The formalities of the ceremony were completed and the entry ended with some benign comment about an amusing address or ceremonial presentation.

Blackbird leafed back to 1945 and then slowed. I realised she was checking to see if the ceremony had been disrupted by the war, but there were the entries again, good service and good number for each year between 1939 and 1945. We went back again, stepping slowly back in time. I came to understand that the role of Remembrancer lasted between ten and twenty years, almost regardless of what happened in the world at the time. There was one script that lasted only three ceremonies and I could imagine some illness overtaking the person, particularly as the hand became more difficult to read until it was passed to a smaller, neater hand that wrote in precise rows of near identical characters that were more difficult to decipher than the hand that had preceded it.

The First World War was the same. There was no indication of the carnage going on in Flanders, just entries for each year, notes of visiting dignitaries and acknowledgement of the service and the number.

Claire stood up and went to the door. "I'll be just a moment," she said, unsure about leaving us alone with the book. "I have something else to show you."

She slipped out of the room, leaving Blackbird and I to leaf through the faded pages.

"It's like a heartbeat," I commented, more to myself than to Blackbird.

"This is it, Rabbit. This is the ritual. Don't you see?" Despite her calm outward appearance, I realised from her tone of voice that she was excited.

"The City of London isn't the same as London, the city. It has defined boundaries, its own Mayor, a corporation to manage its affairs and it is founded on the one thing humanity will protect to the end: wealth. What did the leaflet say? This is the oldest legal ceremony in England other than the coronation. Here you have the link between the kings of thirteenth century England and the legal system that preserved the existence of the monarchy into the present day."

"It's not perfect protection, though, is it?" I remarked. "The French overthrew their monarchy and founded a republic. We had periods where the position of the king or queen was very precarious. Anything could have happened."

"But it didn't, did it? Even Cromwell didn't succeed in removing the monarchy permanently. Maybe there was more than one reason for restoring the monarch to the throne."

"I don't think there's any way of…What's that?"

The hairs on the back of my neck prickled and before I realised it I was upright. Blackbird stood, her chin coming up, almost as if she was almost scenting the air. Tension built in the room like the moment before a lightning strike and I found myself backing away from the doorway.

"I thought you might like to see this. It's not really… Is something wrong?" Claire entered through the half open door carrying a small bundle. Wrapped in a soft black cloth, I could see heat-haze writhing off it like poisonous dark fumes. Blackbird backed away with an expression of tight distaste on her face. I couldn't get enough oxygen. The presence of the object was suffocating.

"What is it?" Blackbird asked.

"It's the Quick Knife," Claire said. "And I'm afraid it's broken."

FIFTEEN

Claire stepped forward and laid the broken Quick Knife on the desk and folded back the cloth.

It was difficult for me to see the knife clearly for the haze around it, but there were clearly two pieces to it. I backed further away and I could see Blackbird was having trouble maintaining her composure.

Claire looked up from the table at us, curious at first while a slow understanding grew in her eyes. She looked again at the knife and then back at us. There was a tense silence as she considered our reaction. I think Blackbird was trying to act normally, though she was failing. I wasn't even trying.

"You're from the other courts, aren't you?" Claire spoke quietly and it wasn't a question. She stepped back and pushed the door closed behind her. I wished she hadn't.

"Other courts?" Blackbird simply repeated the phrase.

"One minute. I need to get the box."

Claire opened the door again and stepped out, closing the door behind her, but leaving the knife unwrapped on the desk. I considered edging around the room and running out of the building. I glanced at Blackbird who clearly had the same thought.

The door opened and Claire entered carrying a dark wooden box. She placed it onto the table and opened it, then re-wrapped the knife in the soft dark cloth and placed it into the open box alongside a similar knife that gleamed with a dull sheen. As she closed the lid, the tension in the room evaporated. Blackbird and I visibly relaxed.

"Well, that was exciting, wasn't it?" Claire said in a slightly brittle manner, turning to lean on the edge of the desk, regarding each of us in turn.

Neither of us spoke. It was clear that Claire knew more about this than we had thought, but what she knew and why was still an open question.

"I think it would be a good idea if we had some tea, don't you? Yes, that's probably the thing. Please, make yourselves comfortable again. I apologise for the disturbance. It never crossed my mind." She went back to the door, turning back, almost as if she were checking we were still there. "Give me a few moments."

We were left alone again, though the door had been left ajar.

"What is that?" I asked Blackbird.

"She called it the Quick Knife. It may be a corruption of Quit Knife, for the ceremony, do you think?"

"I have no idea, and I don't really care. Are we leaving?"

"No, this is important. She clearly knows more about this than we imagined. If we leave now we may miss something."

"I won't miss the contents of that box. Did you see it?"

"I've never seen anything like it. It must be part of the ceremony. Didn't the leaflet mention a pair of knives?" She delved into her coat to retrieve the leaflet. "Here it is. 'Two knives, one blunt and one sharp.' Which one do you think that was?"

"I don't know, I couldn't see through the haze around it."

"Haze?"

"Like fumes, coming off it, distorting the air around it. You couldn't see them?"

"No, but I could feel them."

"It's dangerous, Blackbird. That's not a ceremonial blade. It's intended for something much darker."

"That's the point, though, isn't it? We're looking for something much darker."

The door pushed open and we both lapsed into silence as Claire entered with a tray loaded with a teapot, milk, sugar and even a plate of biscuits.

"Would you mind moving the journal, please? I must apologise for my thoughtlessness earlier. It never occurred to me that you were, well, like that."

"Like what?" Blackbird moved the journal across the desk away from the tea and the dark wooden box.

"From the other courts. I think 'Fey' is the proper term, is it not?" She put down the hot teapot and set about arranging cups and saucers, not meeting Blackbird's intense scrutiny.

"It is," I answered, winning a sharp look from Blackbird, but my curiosity at her use of that particular word was too strong to let it go. Besides, I wasn't telling her anything she didn't already know.

She gestured to Blackbird to take a seat, and we both looked at the box containing the knife.

"I could move it to the sideboard if you would be more comfortable?" she offered.

"It would make things easier," Blackbird responded.

She picked up the box and was then caught as she made to move towards me and I backed away. Just the thought of what was in the box was enough to make me stay clear of it. She smiled an apology and turned the other way to discover a worried look on Blackbird's face. She was made of sterner stuff, however, because she smiled a nervous acknowledgement and moved around towards the door, allowing Claire to get past and place the box on a small table near the leaded window where the dark wood of the box was set against the warmer tones of polished chestnut beneath it.

"There, that might be better. Shall we have tea now?" Her version of a disarming smile had a fragile quality to it and I wondered just how confident about this she really was.

"That would be kind," Blackbird agreed and we moved to sit around the desk, Claire at one end of the desk and Blackbird and I at the other. She poured out three measured cups and added milk in precise quantities, making me wonder how often she performed this small ritual.

"It would be helpful if you could show me some credentials?" she suggested, handing each of us a cup and placing the plate of rich tea biscuits near to us, so she could move the tray out of the way.

"What sort of credentials?" Blackbird countered.

"I am sure you understand that I need to make sure you are who I think you are, if you see what I mean?" The brittle smile returned.

"A demonstration?"

"If you wouldn't mind?"

"Give me your hand, then."

She demurred. "I'd rather not, if you'll forgive me. I was warned against direct contact. A simple change of appearance would suffice." She appeared ruffled by this exchange.

"Very well." Blackbird shifted slightly in her seat and then her form melted, reforming into the red-haired girl from the coffee shop in the square, except she wasn't dressed in quite the same style. This was simpler, with none of the polish or gloss that had been part of that persona, but a simple fresh beauty that left me wondering, yet again, who I was dealing with. She held it for a moment and then melted back into the Blackbird I knew. It was impressive, and disconcerting, and it was pure Fey.

Claire had acquired the look of a deer caught in the headlights, but she dissembled well. "That's, well, that's fine, and your colleague?"

Claire turned to me. I glanced at Blackbird and she shook her head slightly. "I'll vouch for my colleague."

"I'm afraid my instructions are quite specific. All parties are to identify themselves. I'm sure you understand the reasons."

"Something small then, please, Niall?" she suggested.

I guessed that she was trying to steer me away from summoning gallowfyre, as I had with Marshdock. I was somewhat at a loss to come up with an alternative, though. I didn't want to change my whole appearance as Blackbird had done as I was only just getting used to the face I was wearing. If I reverted to my real appearance then Claire might recognise me as the person the police were seeking, so that wouldn't do either.

I looked around and my gaze caught the reflection from an ornate mirror on the back wall. "Something small?" I nodded towards the mirror.

Blackbird glanced at the mirror and raised an eyebrow at me. There was a sense of challenge here.

I calmed myself for a moment and then reached out to the mirror, not with my hand, but with my will. I pulled at the surface of the mirror, reaching for what I knew was there. The mirror, though, felt like a dead thing with nothing that would give me any purchase.

Blackbird had said the other wraithkin had used the mirror, and I had drawn lines in the mirror's surface only last night. I knew it could be done. Last night had been different, though. It had been like drawing in a thick viscous liquid. Maybe I was mistaken to call to the reflective surface of the mirror. Maybe what I needed was within.

I focused again, clearing my mind, and reached out with my will, pulling at the silvery depth of it. I reached within and formed a connection. This time I could feel the tension there, the inertia of it. Power pulsed within me and the ambient light in the room dimmed as the mirror went milky white.

"Gently, Rabbit, gently," Blackbird encouraged.

I relaxed my hold on it a little and the light in the room returned, the mirror clearing, but I could feel the connection with the undercurrent in the mirror. A sound grew gently in the room. It had the ambience of a large busy space. The sound of people milling around gently entered the quiet room. Then an announcement reverberated through, confirming that the British Airways flight to Hamburg was now boarding at gate 14. The sound included little shuffles and scrapes, layered over the ambience and I knew that this was where Alex was. My unconscious mind, worried about her, had somehow located her though the mirror and brought me the sounds from where she was. In a way, it was comforting though it felt a little like eaves-dropping on someone else's conversation. Hadn't the announcement said Hamburg? Is that where they were going? Suddenly conscious of my audience, I released the mirror before the sounds gave away who it was we were listening to. There was a slight ripple as I let go, radiating out slowly across its surface like a stone dropped into a pool of slow silvery syrup.

Blackbird was smiling at me. "Is that sufficient?" she asked Claire.

Claire hesitated for a moment, taking a deep breath, and asked the question that was bothering her.

"How do I know you're not from the wrong court?"

"That's simple. They are only interested in wrecking the ceremony and making sure it doesn't happen. If we were from that court then you would be dead by now." Blackbird smiled, and it was not a comfortable smile. "Your turn," she prompted.

"What do you mean? I certainly can't do anything like that."

"No, but you said all parties must be identified. How do we know you are who you are supposed to be?"

"I'm the clerk to the Queen's Remembrancer."

"Suppose you tell us a little more, some background, just to reassure us."

"Very well. I already said that I am the clerk to the Queen's Remembrancer and you know I am the care-taker of both the current journal and of the knives. Perhaps I should say that I am the latest in a long line of clerks to this office, since the time of King James I, when certain very particular duties of the role were passed to the clerk when the king decreed that he would have no truck with witchcraft and neither would any of his officers.

"Actually, things became easier when the duties were passed to the clerks. Each clerk chooses their successor and so is able to instruct them in the duties to be per-formed, rather than being appointed by the monarch, which is the case with the Remembrancer. Being able to choose who will be clerk after us gives us a continuity that perhaps would otherwise have been lost. Of course, there's always the chance of accidents, so each clerk makes a bequest in their will of a journal, a little like this one, containing instructions on how to conduct the ceremony. It has references to certain texts, now mostly in the private archives of the Public Record Office, showing the line of succession from each clerk to the next, together with the original royal decree instructing the ceremony to be conducted for as long as there is a throne in England."

"Does the current Queen know you do this?" I asked.

"I've never met the monarch, as it was the Remem-brancer that was presented to her, so I have no way of knowing, but on balance I think not. After James I, the kings and queens took a deliberate disinterest in these matters, making it easier for them to deny all knowl-edge. I know from my predecessors that the Church was very determined to stamp out anything heretical or pagan. The ceremony survived, though. It was a matter of law, not faith, and therefore outside the Church's ju-risdiction. I am the latest in a long line of clerks going back to the time of King James. I serve the Remem-brancer and it is part of my duties to see that the ceremony is carried out annually and that the Remembrancer plays his part."

"And you know about the Feyre?" Blackbird gently steered her.

"There are notes in the journals. They make fascinating reading if you can decipher them. They're much less straightforward than the official journal you have there, though. There are entries concerning certain meetings; it isn't until fifteen hundred and something that the word 'Feyre' is actually mentioned. Before that they are referred to as 'The Others' or 'The Visitors'."

"Go on."

"Remember, a clerk can go through their entire term and not meet anyone from the other courts. It's quite a privilege, in a way, though there have been incidents."

"What sort of incidents."

"I'm not sure I should say."

"Claire, I promise no harm shall come to you by our hands this day. You have nothing to fear from either of us."

She deliberated for a moment. She must have known something about the Feyre and their inability to lie convincingly because she continued, "When I said we were warned against direct contact? That was after my predecessors demanded proof from one of your kind. From what she told me later, she was quite direct, shall we say."

"They took it the wrong way?" Blackbird suggested.

"I was called to a hospital out in the country in the Thames Valley, an asylum I suppose you might call it. She was screaming my name, crying that she needed me. When the doctors phoned me, I explained that I barely knew her. I had been interviewed by her on a civil service panel while at university and then she invited me to spend a week at the Royal Courts of Justice as work experience. I liked her, but you couldn't say we were friends. She was insistent that she needed to see me, though, and the doctors thought it might calm her.

"When I arrived, she was screaming about spiders crawling all over her, in her hair, her ears, her eyes. She was scratching herself with her nails and they had to sedate her. I sat with her and held her hand for a while, hoping it would be enough to calm her down. Quite suddenly she was lucid and recognised me. She told me I had been chosen for an extremely important job, a secret vocation. I thought she was raving, of course, but then she told me about the safe containing the knives and her journal. She told me to go to the Queen's Remembrancer for the key – that's Jerry. She said he would be expecting me and that it was more important than I could possibly realise. I was still half convinced it was some sort of delusion, but she was different, focused.

"I left her that afternoon only half convinced as to whether to follow it up. I was waiting on some interesting job offers and I wasn't sure I wanted to work in the Royal Courts. I waited a week before curiosity got the better of me and I rang the office and asked to speak to the Remembrancer. He invited me down to read the journal, and afterwards we talked. I've been with him ever since."

"Did your colleague ever recover?"

"I used to visit her regularly. Once, on one of her better days, she was able to explain some of what had happened. But she never really recovered, no."

"I'm sorry, Claire. Some of our kind can be touchy."

"She was warned, as was I. The journals are quite clear on some things."

Listening to Claire, I realised the Seventh Court had made a mistake. It looked like they had eliminated the Queen's Remembrancer, hoping to further undermine the ceremony. They had it wrong, though. It was the clerk that was important, not the Remembrancer.

"Tell us about the knife," Blackbird suggested.

"The Quick Knife? It was one of the two knives used for the Quit Rents Ceremony. The other is the Dead Knife, which is the other knife in the box. In 1933 the Quick Knife was dropped and it snapped in two. I can show you the entry in the journal. Everyone was very surprised when it broke and at the time it was taken as a bad omen. It was due to be used for the ceremony the next day and there was no time to make another. Luckily my predecessor had a friend with connections in the Tower of London and they arranged for another set of blades to be sent over. They're on permanent loan from the Royal Armouries and of a rather different style, but the ceremony carried on as before and the bad luck was averted."

"Can we see them?" Blackbird asked.

"I don't see why not. Just a moment and I'll fetch them. They're in the safe." She rose again and stepped out, leaving the door ajar.

"Is it wise to get more knives? What if they're like that one?" I nodded towards the dark-wood box.

Blackbird glanced at the knife box and shook her head. "Wait and see."

Claire returned with another bundle wrapped in black cloth. There was no sense of anything about it when she placed it on the table and unfolded it. Wrapped inside the cloth were two blades, or rather tools. One was a small neat hatchet and the other a kind of bill-hook with a broad flat blade. The blades were polished as if they were made of silver, or perhaps they were plated. They were clearly ceremonial.

She looked at us.

"May I?" I indicated the bill-hook.

"Of course."

I picked the bill-hook up from the cloth, finding the oddly shaped blade lighter than it looked. I tested the edge with my thumb and it was sharp. The broad, flat blade reflected distorted scenes from the room. If it came from the Tower armouries, then it probably had a distinguished and honourable history.

"It's unusual enough, but it's totally different to the original Quick Knife. It's just a blade."

"We brought an expert from the armouries in to see if the Quick Knife could be mended, but apparently it is the wrong sort of metal."

"Or the right sort," Blackbird added. "It's very likely to be made of some sort of iron. If it were pure then that would make it brittle. That's why steel replaced iron as the metal of choice, it's much more resilient. What's the other knife in the case made of?"

"Some sort of alloy, definitely not iron. Would you like to see it?"

"Maybe later." Neither of us wanted her to open the box with the Quick Knife in it. "The broken knife is the key. Once the Quick Knife was broken, the ritual was weakened. Each time the ceremony is performed with the wrong knives, it weakens a little more." She glanced at me. "A worm at the heart of the ceremony, do you see?"

"There's nothing in the records saying that the ceremony must be conducted with a particular set of knives," Claire commented. "It just says that two knives must be presented, one blunt and one sharp, and must be tested for their qualities."

"I'm sure you've carried out the ceremony according to the instructions you were given," said Blackbird, "but that in itself is not enough for the ritual to have power. I'm sure now that the knife is the reason the barrier is weakening and also the reason why your Remembrancer is missing. You know he's not coming back, don't you?"

"He's not dead," said Claire.

"That may not be the worst of it," said Blackbird. "It is in all our best interests to make sure the ceremony goes ahead with a new knife, and soon."

"You want me to change the ritual, just because you say so?"

"No, I'm not telling you to change it. I'm saying you have to put it back to the way it was, the way it was meant to be. If we don't then the consequences may go far beyond the fate of one Remembrancer and his clerk."

"I don't know..."

"Claire, we stand on the edge of something terrible. The breaking of the Quick Knife has changed things, weakened them. If things break down completely then the incidents you refer to could be the very least of it. We need to get the knife repaired or remade."

"It can't be welded or fixed in that way. We tried. The only way is to get a new one made."

"Can you do that?"

"I can't, but perhaps you may be able to."

"Us? Neither of us want to get anywhere near it."

"It mentions in the journals, when the nails became too rusty to use. Two of your kind came and took them away and got them re-forged."

"That's very unlikely, Claire."

"Oh, I don't mean they did it themselves. I mean they took them to a smith and he did it for them."

"Where would the Feyre get a smith from?"

"From the same place as always, the Highsmiths."

"The high smiths?"

"The Highsmith family, the people who rent the Moors in Shropshire. They are the smiths to the Six Courts. Surely you know this?"

It was our turn to admit we didn't know all of it. "I guess you are not the only ones to lose things," Black-bird conceded.

Claire acknowledged this with a nod. It relieved some of her tension that she was not the only one fumbling in the dark.

"The Highsmiths were the family that produced the new set of nails. All except for the sixty-first one."

"Why wasn't the sixty-first nail remade?"

"It didn't need to be. It's made of a different metal to the rest and it hadn't rusted. It's like the Dead Knife, rather than the dark metal of the others."

"I wondered about that when I read it in the leaflet,"

said Blackbird. "Ten nails for each horse-shoe and then another. I thought it must be a spare."

"No, the sixty-first nail is different from the rest, though I've no idea why. Shall I get it? It's in the safe with the others, ready for the ceremony next week."

"We'd like to see it, thanks."

Blackbird and I waited, both wrapped in our own thoughts, while Claire retrieved the nails. They were in a velvet case, a little like that used for jewellery, which she unrolled across the table. Each bundle of nails had a pocket and it was immediately clear to Blackbird and I that the nails were iron, though thankfully they didn't have the noxious aura of the Quick Knife.

The last nail in the roll had a pocket of its own, though. Claire extracted it and held it up so I could see it, unsure of my reaction. It was the same size and shape as the other nails, a square section about two or three inches long, narrowing sharply along its length to a fine point.

"Any ideas?" I asked Blackbird.

"No, I don't see why that one should be different from the others. It's not iron, or anything like it, is it? Is there nothing in the journals about it, Claire?" she asked.

"Nothing obvious, no. The nails were taken back to the Highsmiths about a hundred and fifty years ago, but the sixty-first was returned with the rest, unchanged."

"Well, the problem is with the knife, not the nails. Do you have an address for these Highsmiths?"

"I can get it for you."

She replaced the nail and rewrapped the bundle, taking them out again while Blackbird and I considered what we had learnt. For my part, the revelation that there had been regular, if infrequent, meetings between humanity and the Feyre was an eye-opener. It had never occurred to me that such things might be going on, but why would it? People didn't generally notice things they weren't looking for.

"Somebody knew this was going on," said Blackbird, her thoughts following the same lines as my own.

"Claire obviously does, and presumably the Remembrancer, if he's alive?"

"No, I mean the Feyre. I'm beginning to see another hand in this."

"What do you mean?"

"Do you remember I said yesterday that I wasn't following you, but it wasn't random chance that put me there either?"

"Yes, you said it was fortune."

"I chose my words carefully. I really wasn't following you, but I was waiting for you."

"For me?"

"Not for you specifically, but for someone or something. Kareesh sent me a message, which she does from time to time when she an errand to run or maybe a message to be delivered. She said: 'Be at the southern end of the Leicester Square tube station platform at the morning peak on Thursday and make yourself useful.' She didn't tell me what to do or why, but that's pretty standard for her. I waited there to see what would happen.

"And then I collapsed down the stairs onto the platform."

"I was waiting on the other platform, but it didn't take me long to realise what was going on."

"So did she mean for you to save me?"

"It's hard to tell with her. You, of all people, know what the visions are like. Did she know what would happen or did she just know I should be there?"

"As you say, it's hard to tell."

"But what if she did know? What if she knows what's going on better than we do?"

"Then why doesn't she just say?"

"I think they're ashamed, all of them."

"Ashamed of what?"

"Of doing dirty back-door deals with humanity. Of needing humans to make a barrier strong enough to hold back the Seventh Court. That's why there's no record, no stories. To keep the Seventh Court from stealing their babies and possessing their dead, they stooped low enough to strike a deal with humanity, and now they won't admit it."

"Why not? What's so terrible about wanting to protect your children?"

"The courts rule absolutely, Rabbit, but they rule by consent, not force. The Feyre agree to be bound to the courts for protection and survival. They agree to abide by court law for the good of all. But if someone like Marshdock was able to implicate the rulers of the courts in conspiring with humanity then it would show them up as weak, ineffectual and incapable of protecting anyone. The whole structure would be undermined. Knowledge like that could earn you a lifetime of favours, Rabbit. A Feyre lifetime, not a human one. If you were to share this with Marshdock, for instance, he could become very influential, able to grant favours to those he owed for his position and power. That makes such knowledge dangerous. Those in power would do almost anything to keep the information out of the hands of Marshdock and those like him. Eliminating a couple of half-breed Fey who were poking into things that were none of their business would be the least of it. When the stakes are that high there isn't much they wouldn't do."

"Nobody knows we know about it, though, do they?" I pointed out.

"Claire knows some of it, now. But she's in as much danger as we are."

"Then we have to make it clear to her that she's not to mention this to anyone."

"I don't think she would anyway. Secrecy is her default position."

"What about Kareesh?"

"She can't be certain and anyway, she started all this. I'm sure of it now. I'm just not sure what we're supposed to do about it."

"Can we leave it as it is, pretend we don't know?"

"And what about the consequences? What happens when the barrier falls and the Seventh Court come through to settle the score? And even if I choose to stand aside and let that happen, you can't. This is where your vision leads. You bargained for a gift, Rabbit. You gave her the stones and in return she showed you your future."

"There are many futures. You said so yourself."

"Yes, but in the one she showed you, you survive. You're able to see it because you survive. It wasn't some random sequence of images that she showed you. It was your own future. Who knows in how many other futures you are killed, or lost, or eaten."

"Eaten?"

"I don't think the Shade outside your bedroom door wanted to tuck you up and read you a story."

"So I have to carry on."

"You're taking a terrible risk if you don't."

"I'm taking a terrible risk if I do."

"But the vision tells us you survive."

"For now."

The discussion was put on hold as Claire returned with the address.

"This is where they lived about one hundred and fifty years ago." She offered Blackbird the slip of paper.

"A hundred and fifty years is a long time. Do you think they'll still be there?" Blackbird handed me the address. It was a farm near a village called Eardington in Shropshire.

"They farm the land paid for by the Quit Rent. That's why they're there. They've been there since twelve hundred and something, so I doubt they will have moved. If anyone knows how to fix the knife, it will be them."

"We're grateful for your help, Claire, but you mustn't tell anyone we've discussed this. Your life may depend on it," I told her.

"What do I tell the police? They'll be here in half an hour." The nervous edge was back in Claire's voice.

"Tell them about the calls. Tell them what you knew before we came, but don't mention anything about the Quit Rents ceremony unless they ask. As far as they're concerned it is just an official duty of the office."

"And what about Jerry?"

"The Remembrancer?"

She nodded.

"I'm sorry, Claire, but I think he's probably dead."

Her eyes filled and she turned away, fishing a rumpled tissue from her jacket pocket and removing her glasses to dab at her eyes. "We don't know," she said. "There's still hope."

"I suppose there is a chance that he's just delayed or something," Blackbird admitted, though the sour note in her voice told me she didn't believe this herself, "but you must prepare for the worst."

"I'll do what I must," she told us, replacing her glasses after her moment of weakness, squaring her shoulders.

"The bad news is that if the Seventh Court find out it's you and not the Remembrancer that ensures the continuity of the ceremony–"

She folded her arms as if a chill had suddenly taken her, looking from Blackbird to me. "Then I'll be next."

SIXTEEN

Claire stood in the office, her arms held tightly around her. Despite her years of service, the reality of her role was only just hitting home.

"We have to go, Claire," said Blackbird.

"What can I do?" she asked.

"Maybe you could stay with some friends until this blows over?"

"I can't leave the office. What about the police? What about Jerry?"

"I don't think he's coming back," she suggested gently.

"What if they come here, after me?"

"Don't be here. They don't know you're involved and we won't tell them, but if they figure it out or if they get it from Jerry..."

"He wouldn't tell them."

"He may not have a choice. He won't be able to lie to them."

"I can't leave."

"There's no one to be clerk for, Claire. Either he comes back from wherever it is he's gone to or..."

"Or what?"

"Or he doesn't. You have to make sure the ceremony

happens in either case. Otherwise things will get worse, not better."

"There are arrangements that will need to be made."

"Then make them. We'll be in touch when we know whether the knife can be fixed. In the meantime don't take strange phone calls and spend as little time alone as you can."

"I don't have anyone I can… That is…"

"Don't go where you're expected to go. Find somewhere else, someone else. Don't be alone."

"I don't have anyone…"

"Then find someone."

Blackbird's words came out harsh, but well meant. Claire's expression clearly said it wasn't as easy as Blackbird made it sound, but she simply nodded, accepting the principle.

"You need to take this with you." Claire retrieved the dark wooden box with the knives from the side table and passed it to Blackbird who accepted it reluctantly.

"Take care of yourself," Blackbird advised, slipping the box into her shoulder bag and zipping the bag closed so it wouldn't fall out.

"I'll try."

Blackbird ushered me through the outer office and into the corridor.

"Will she be OK?" I asked Blackbird.

She didn't answer my question, but marched ahead, out of Claire's earshot, leading the way down the steep stairway. She was down the steps and halfway across the entrance hall towards the exit before she spoke.

"Claire will be fine until the Seventh Court work out it's the clerk that's keeping the ceremony going, at which point she won't be fine."

We pushed through the exit gate across from the security station and stepped back through the entrance into the afternoon sunlight.

"We need to get the knife fixed before they work it out," she said. "At the moment they think they've won.

They've eliminated the Remembrancer and they think the barrier is breaking down."

"It is breaking down."

"If the ceremony is performed successfully with the proper knives then it will reinforce the barrier. Meanwhile, the Council will realise that we know what they've done."

"The Council?"

"The rulers of the courts form the High Council of the Feyre. It's where they resolve disputes between the courts and discuss issues that affect them all. It doesn't have any powers over the individual courts. But if they entered into an agreement with humanity then they did it together. No single court could speak for all of them."

"We still don't know for sure that's what they did."

"Yes we do."

"We know they needed humanity to make the barrier, but we still don't know what the deal was, do we? Let's say humanity agreed to perform the ritual and carried it out for eight or nine hundred years. Why? What's in it for them? They don't even know the Feyre exist. Even Claire only knows part of it."

"That's the point, isn't it?"

"What is?"

"That's the deal. Don't you see?"

"What are you talking about?"

"It's all around us. Humanity goes its own sweet way while the Feyre sit back and let them. That was the deal, coexistence in return for security, peace in return for maintaining the barrier."

"You're guessing."

"Only partly. I've sat and listened to Kareesh's tales of how it was before. I know that when they first encountered humans, the Feyre made sure they knew whose land they were in. They hunted them, kidnapped their children, terrified them and murdered them in their beds. By the time the Feyre had finished with them they were literally afraid of the dark. Something changed, though. I always thought it was because there were so many humans and the Feyre were dwindling. No matter how many humans the Feyre scared off there were always more. Now I know different. This is what changed. They made a deal and they will know we have found them out. They won't like that. We could make some very powerful enemies."

"But if we don't fix the knife–"

"Then the barrier will fall. The Seventh Court will break through and Raffmir's sister will get her wish."

"So we have to fix it. If we don't fix it then the Un-tainted will come for everyone; us, my daughter, my wife."

"Ex-wife," she reminded me.

"We can't let that happen, even if it means the Council turning against us. Kareesh said that if I found the thing that was lost then I would have a place in the courts, didn't she?"

"Something like that."

"That's what she said," I protested.

"She said it was the sight of something to secure your place in the courts. She didn't say you'd live to enjoy it."

"It's a better option than the certain knowledge of what the Seventh Court will do if the barrier falls."

"Perhaps."

"Who knows, maybe the Council will be grateful and reward us?"

"I can tell that you've never had any dealings with the courts."

That was true, but I knew from corporate experience that the gratitude of those further up the hierarchy was unreliable at best.

"Do you have a better idea?"

"I guess not," she sighed.

"Then we have to figure out where we can hire a car."

"A car? What do you want a car for?"

"To get to Shropshire. It's two hundred miles, near enough. How did you think we were going to get there? I don't think the Underground goes as far as Shrewsbury."

My sarcasm bounced off her. "I thought we would walk," she said.

"Walk? If we walk, the ceremony will have been and gone by the time we get back."

"That depends on which way we walk."

She led the way down the Strand onto Fleet Street. I caught up and walked alongside her.

"You're remarkably sanguine about this for someone who has just decided to take on the Untainted and the High Court."

"You wouldn't understand."

"Try me."

She carried on walking while she thought about it.

"I'm far older than you," she said.

"What's that got to do with it?"

"I've seen a lot of Fey; when they get older they become withdrawn. They hide themselves away from harm. They hold their lives closed so they won't die, horde them like treasure."

"And?"

"And they atrophy. They're still living but they might as well be dead for the all the difference it makes. I don't want to end up like that. I want to live before I die."

"So you'll spit in the eye of fate and see what happens."

"Maybe not spit, but I won't hide when fate intervenes. We were meant to discover this. They've been hiding it for centuries and now it's breaking down. If we hadn't discovered it then the barrier would fail and it would all go sour. Now we have a chance to fix it."

"And the consequences?"

"Let fate decide the consequences." She lifted her chin, determined.

"Fate isn't always kind, even to those she favours."

"That's true where I come from too. You see? We do have something in common."

As we walked down Fleet Street she appeared to be looking for something.

"So we walk to Shropshire?"

She gave me one of those cryptic smiles that meant she knew something I didn't, and she wasn't going to tell me what it was.

"A car is basically a metal box on wheels. You're not going to be comfortable sitting for hours in a steel box, are you?" She strolled along the pavement and then surprised me by stepping into a bookshop.

I followed her in. It was full of legal and history books, serving the local concentration of lawyers. The only fiction volumes were hardback best sellers, displayed on a stand by the door. Blackbird ignored these and went to the back of the shop where there was a display of maps.

"Ordnance Survey maps," she announced. "Perfect."

She began selecting maps and consulting the backs until she found the one she wanted. She fanned it out in front of her, resting it precariously on the shelf, and then took out the slip of paper Claire had given her and consulted the map with it.

"It should be here somewhere." Her finger circled the map around the area to the south of Bridgnorth.

The land on the map had been shaped by the same industry that had marked my own home county of Kent. I could see the places where the streams had been diverted, dammed and sluiced to power water wheels and where woods had been coppiced to provide charcoal for the furnaces. Iron making was engraved into the landscape like a signature. In the past, this wouldn't have bothered me, but now I wondered how I would react to the presence of all that iron. I rubbed the sore patch on my hand, conscious of the after-effects of my encounter with the iron gates at Australia House.

"There's the village." I pointed out the location on the map. "It can't be far from there."

"It looks like the right sort of place to find a family of smiths," she grinned.

She refolded the map and went to the counter to pay for it. I waited at the door and then we walked back along the way we had come, towards the Strand.

"Are you serious about walking to Shropshire?"

"Yes," she said. "And no." That teasing smile was back again.

We walked back past the Royal Courts of Justice and she led the way to the other side of the road and over to the church across the square from Australia House. We approached the door and she held up her hand.

"Wait a second. There's somebody in the hallway. We don't particularly want to be observed entering."

"Blackbird, we have a long way to travel, by whatever means. Now is not the time to be visiting churches."

"We need to visit this one."

We pushed through the glass-panelled door into a dim hallway before the main body of the church. I could hear someone in the open space beyond, moving what sounded like a heavy piece of furniture. We walked quickly around to the right, down a curving staircase and under an arch down into the crypt. You could hear the bass rumble of the traffic flowing around the church to either side.

The crypt was well lit around the white-plastered walls between the pillars. Gravestones and memorials were set into the plaster. The room was familiar to me, even though I had never visited the church before. The way the pews were arranged in ranks, the placement of the altar, even the arrangement of flowers. I had seen it before.

"This place was in my vision." I turned slowly around, trying to fit my visual perspective to the one in my head. "And I was over there." I pointed to the centre of the crypt and then walked over to a spot between the rows of wooden seats.

"You're sure?"

"I think so." I looked around, slightly disoriented by trying to overlay the fragments from the vision onto the reality, shifting position and feeling my balance return as the mental image and the visual image came into line.

"Can you feel it?" she asked.

"Feel what?"

"Listen."

I listened and heard the grumble of the traffic and the faint sounds of someone moving furniture upstairs.

"What am I listening for?"

"Under it all. Below sound, below hearing."

"How can I hear something below hearing?"

"You can't, so try."

I stopped and listened, standing between the rows of wooden chairs on the stone floor, and sure enough, there was something. When you subtracted the noise of the traffic and the hubbub of humanity, there was another sound that hummed beneath it. I cocked my head and it became more distinct.

"What is it?"

"You hear it now?"

"A sort of low rumble. What is it?"

"It's one of the Ways. It runs right under here. In fact it is why 'here' is here."

"A Way?"

"It's like a line of energy under the earth connecting places together."

"Like a ley line?"

"Ley lines are similar, but they're mixed up with other things like old roads and green lanes. But you know where there are Ways because you can feel them."

"Like here."

"Yes, like here. Do you trust me?"

Her question caught me out. It must have showed on my face because her eyes registered the doubt in mine. The truth was she had too many secrets.

"Do you trust me to show you something? Here and now."

"Yes."

Her hesitant smile acknowledged the gap between hope and expectation. Was my trust important to her? It shamed me, after all we had been through, that I was unable to offer my complete trust. Then again, she made it clear on a number of occasions that she had her own priorities and I had no idea how far they would press her. I wasn't ready to offer unqualified trust.

She walked around behind me, holding my shoulder to gently prevent me from turning with her.

"I'm going to ask you to follow my instructions. Where we're going I won't get chance to explain, so I want you to just do it and I'll explain afterwards, OK?"

"Why can't you explain now?"

"It'll make much more sense afterwards."

"So I have to trust you."

"Yes."

"You could just tell me."

"I could, but you've already found several disadvantages to being Fey. This is one of the advantages."

"Are you sure I'm going to like it?"

"Trust me," she whispered.

It was hard after the day I'd had. She hadn't led me wrong though. Perhaps I could trust her for this one thing.

She stood behind me, placing her hands on my shoulders, orientating me gently until I was facing the side wall of the underground chapel.

"After the first step, I want you to step aside and take a deep breath to steady yourself and then, when I step in after you, I want you to step back on the line of the Way and step again, straight away, understand. Don't say anything and try not to make a noise, OK?"

"What do you mean, steady myself?"

"You'll understand after the first step, I promise."

"Off the line and on again, don't make a noise. Got it." It was simple enough, but she was making a big deal about it.

"Remember what I said." She squeezed my shoulder and I nodded again. "Now, close your eyes."

I did as she asked, conscious of the pressure of her fingers on my shoulder.

"You remember how it was with the mirror in Claire's office, how you connected with it, called to it?"

"Yes."

"Feel below your feet. Feel the flow of energy there."

I reached down to the low vibration under the floor and tentatively felt towards it. Whereas the mirror had been still, like a windless pool, this was a torrent. It raged and crashed beneath our feet, surging along. I swayed slightly, unbalanced by its momentum.

"Steady. You're just trying to create a connection with it, not to hold it. Just recognise it. Say 'Hello' to it, acknowledge its power and accept it."

"It's very strong."

"Don't try and fight it, you'll lose. Just connect with it and let yourself be known."

I reached out into the torrent as you might dangle your hand into the water from a speedboat, feeling the buffeting from it and knowing its power.

"Now make a connection with it and take a step forwards, I'm right behind you."

"But—"

"I'm right behind you. Remember what I said."

Tentatively, I reached to the darkness inside. It was eager to connect with the torrent below. I showed it what I wanted and the darkness snaked down, faster than I had anticipated. I felt the torrent rise beneath me. I took a step forward and it crested up under me and surged, carrying me off with it while I screamed and yelled at the joy of it, forgetting everything she'd said about being quiet. It was like surfing and skydiving rolled into one.

My foot hit the floor and I stopped, staggering forward slightly. The echoes of my yell died around me. I opened my eyes and it was dark. I could still feel the river of power beneath me. I remembered Blackbird's instructions and stepped off the line just in time. A breeze turned out of nowhere and she melted into existence beside me.

"That was fantastic! Where are we?" I was excited and elated by it.

"Shhh." She pressed her hand over my mouth. "Hush."

Light spilled downwards, revealing a cellar space with a staircase leading upwards in front of us, the light spilling down the steps from a door opened above.

"Is there someone there?"

The voice had a querulous quality to it that led me to think it hoped that there wasn't. A light bulb clicked on to my right.

She whispered almost soundlessly, "Quick, before they get down here."

She pressed me to the line again and I stepped onto it, ready this time for the rush. The Way answered with enthusiasm and I was swept up on a tidal wave of power. I opened my eyes this time and I could see the sparkles and whirls of it, turning and running. I realised that unlike a river it didn't flow in one direction, but in all directions. My step landed and I was somewhere else.

I stepped off the line, further into the dusty shadows lined by the streaks of light, and Blackbird emerged after me, stepping from the breeze that whirled the dust up to streak the darkness with lines from above. I grinned at her in the dark.

"This time you follow me. There's more than one Way from here so I'll go first."

"How do you know which is the right Way?"

"I'm just choosing a direction, initially from the orientation of the church, and then after that it's all down to feel."

I watched as she stepped onto the line. A breeze sprang into life, swirling the dust up into the slivers of light from above and she was swept away. I stepped onto the line after her. I could feel the path of her presence, like a bed still warm.

I reached down into the stream of energy beneath me and welcomed it as it welled up underneath, carrying me into the depths across an emptiness filled with ribbons of light and dark, whorled and streaked, echoing with disembodied voices.

SEVENTEEN

I had thought all the stops on the Way would be in the crypts or basements, but our next step surprised me by depositing us in a woodland clearing. Crows lifted from the treetops and circled around us, cawing their alarm as we slipped into their domain in a cloud of falling leaves. The trees were at the crown of a hill. Between the trunks you could see miles of open countryside laid out below us.

"Where are we now?"

"Near Hereford, I think. We need to head north from here."

The subtle change in her voice should have alerted me that something had changed but I wasn't ready for the shift in Blackbird's appearance. She had switched to the girl in Claire's conference room. The dappled sunlight filtering through the rust-tinted canopy showed me a young woman rather than an old lady.

"What's with the change?"

Her hair still held the vivid corkscrew curls from the girl in Trafalgar Square, though the glamour and polish of that earlier persona had been replaced by a casual beauty. The short skirt from before was now a long flared cotton one in gypsy colours and her top was sleeveless, in bold blue. A pale blue woollen shawl wrapped around her shoulders and down around her arms. She twirled around amidst the drifting leaves.

"What do you think?" She smiled as she completed her turn.

"It's fine, Blackbird, but I think I prefer the older you."

"Do you?" she challenged. "Or do you just feel safer?"

"You haven't answered my question, why the change?"

"I think a man your age travelling with a younger woman causes less comment, don't you? Anyway, I told you, I'm tired of hiding."

There was something about that little addition that rang differently in her voice. Not a lie, but it made me look at her more closely. She had acquired a freshness, a sparkle that had nothing to do with the autumn sunshine filtering through the trees.

"We'll rest here a moment," she turned away from my scrutiny to look around the clearing. "How are you holding up?"

"I feel great. Travelling down the Way is fantastic."

"The Ways leave you elated and full of energy, but it will quickly wear off and leave you feeling tired and washed out. Too much of it and you can lose focus."

"What happens then?"

"You don't want to get lost on the Way."

I didn't feel tired or lost. I was buzzing. I had so many questions.

"What are the sounds you can hear on the Way?"

"The low rushing sound is the Way, itself."

"No, I meant the other noises, the ones that sound like the echoes of voices."

"I don't hear those."

"You don't?"

"No."

"I'm sure I heard them."

She hesitated.

"Is something wrong?" I asked her.

"No, nothing's wrong. At least I don't think so. It's just that there are gaps in my knowledge, Rabbit. I know it must seem like I know all about the Feyre, but the truth is that I only know the ones I've met, or seen, or heard about. You present me with things I've never come across before. Tell me, what do you see when you travel down the Way?"

"There are flashes of things, flying past. Spirals, eddies that twist and turn, lights that streak past like shooting stars in a sea of blue so deep, it's just… It's hard to make sense of it."

"When I travel, I see a river of fire streaked from blue through to yellow and orange. It's like riding on an explosion of flame."

"Why is it different?"

"I am Fey'ree, a creature of fire and air. When I call to the Way, it answers me in kind, bearing me on a river of fire and air. When you call to it, it answers according to your nature."

"What is it then that I'm seeing and hearing?"

"The Feyre believe in five elements. Each of the Feyre expresses those elements in their own way, which is what makes us different from each other. The greyne are of water and air, the trollen of earth and water, each an expression of its essence."

"I thought there were supposed to be four elements."

"Earth, air, fire, water, and the void."

"What's the void?"

"It is the space between things; the emptiness dividing one from another. It is everywhere, between everything. Without it there would be no you or me or anything else. It would all merge into a single mass. The void is the element for the wraithkin."

"Is that bad?"

"There is no good or bad in it, it just is. As I told you, I am a creature of fire and air and, as such, I can't be harmed with it. I could put my hand in a flame and it would be hot and it might hurt, but it wouldn't burn me."

"So what does it mean to be of the void?"

"I've no idea, I've never been in a position to ask anyone before."

I thought about that for a moment. How would she know? The wraithkin had taken themselves apart from the rest of the Feyre a long time ago and even in the best of times I got the impression that they were secretive.

"It didn't look like nothingness."

"Pardon?"

"The void. It didn't look like nothing."

"I didn't say it was nothing, I said it was between things. When we were in the conference room, back at the Courts of Justice, what made you choose the mirror?"

"Well, it was there on the wall, and you told me the wraithkin that came that night… you know?" A shadow crossed her eyes, but I pressed on. "Well, you said he spoke into the mirror, so I wondered if I could too."

"And you did."

"It worked quite well, didn't it?"

"That's why I have to be careful what I say to you. Before you called to the mirror I had no idea you could do that without touching it. Remember, the wraithkin on that night put his hand on the mirror?"

"Yes, but it felt like the same thing."

"And it was, but would you have tried if I had told you that you couldn't do it that way?"

"Probably not," I admitted.

"So by letting you follow your instinct, rather than filling you full of my preconceptions, you discovered something for yourself. Honestly, Rabbit, at the moment I am your worst enemy."

"No, Blackbird. You're my best friend."

I had expected a smile for that, but instead her expression changed to something more guarded and neutral.

"You place too much trust in me."

"Do I?"

"You know you do. You admitted as much when we were in the crypt." She avoided eye contact, wading slowly through the leaves around her ankles.

"You've helped me enormously. You must know how grateful I am?"

There was a long pause. She was focused on the distant farms visible through the trees.

"I did not think you would survive last night."

"I know. You explained that at the underground station."

"It doesn't make a very good friend, though, does it?"

It was my turn to pause.

"You are meant to be here," I told her.

"Pardon?"

"I was tempted before to tell you before that you were in the vision, so you would come with me, but the truth is I didn't see you."

"You can't lie to me like that, Rabbit."

"I know, and I didn't try, but I was tempted."

"So what makes you say I am meant to be here?"

"Because I knew the crypt from my vision as soon as I saw it, but if you hadn't been there I would never have known it existed. Why would I? I didn't know about the Way or where to find it, but you did. Therefore you had to be there with me." I gave her a hesitant smile.

"Someone else could have told you."

"Who? No one else will speak to me after what happened with Fenlock, you said that much yourself. No, you may not have appeared in the vision, but you're meant to be here, I'm certain of that."

She turned away again, staring across the fields as the breeze rustled in the branches overhead.

I changed the subject. "How come we're not in a crypt or something?"

She paused, then waded back though the leaves towards me. "The Ways were here long before the churches were built. There used to be temples and shrines on some of the node points and when Christianity arrived, the sites became churches. What better way to ensure a set of followers than to incorporate the old religions into the new?"

"So was there something here, on this hill?"

"Who knows? Sometimes the nodes are just places, like any other. Sometimes they are the sites for grand structures. You never know."

"What happens if you crash into someone's funeral in a church or something?"

"I generally take the precaution of using glamour to divert attention away but you can't do that entirely. Sometimes you just have to keep going until you find somewhere empty. There a knack to it, like treading stepping stones, you just hop from one to another."

She mimicked a hopping, jumping step across the clearing.

"If you appear and disappear in a moment, people don't believe what they've seen. They rationalise it as a reflection or a trick of the light. At worst, a place gets the reputation for being haunted. Are you ready to go again?"

I nodded my assent and she stepped over to where the line was. She glanced back at me and then the leaves whirled up around her and she was gone. One moment I was sure she was there, the next moment there were just a vortex of falling leaves in an echo of the vision I had received from Kareesh. Well, at least I knew I was still on the right path, even if it was a strange one.

I stepped onto the line, feeling the echoes of her passage and felt the breeze spring up. There was a whirl of leaves and the glade was far away.

I followed, emerging into another darkened cellar, filled with dusty woodwork. Blackbird had her torch out and was opening the map. She folded and unfolded it until she had the place she wanted.

"Once more, I think," she whispered.

She folded the map and tucked it into her bag and switched off the torch.

"Are you OK?"

"I'm fine."

"You'll sleep well tonight, I think."

"I was supposed to sleep well last night. Then look what happened."

She caught my hand and squeezed it in the dark. "Ready?"

"Yes, I'm ready."

She was right about the ways. Once the adrenaline wore off you were left feeling slightly disconnected from the world and very, very weary. Or maybe that was being woken at four in the morning by somebody trying to eat you. Either way, I was reaching the end of my endurance.

I felt the air twist around me as she left. I stepped onto the line, forcing myself to focus on the sense of her passing.

The Way swept me up once more, the disembodied voices sounding strangely familiar. The words were just out of hearing, and I thought that if I listened more closely maybe I could make out what they were saying. I felt the void twist and bend around me and I realised with a sinking feeling that I had missed Blackbird's trail. I twisted around, causing the way to eddy and swirl around me. It condensed and cleared leaving me hanging suspended, with no frame of reference with which to orientate myself.

I bathed in the lightless depths of it. Pale fire crept onto my fingertips and streamed into the empty dark. I tried to focus on Blackbird, to force the way to take me to her. I felt it veer and eddy as I curled and spun aimlessly. The voices wailed distantly, and I began to fear they were the voices of past travellers who had lost their way in the void. Fear sharpened my senses and I pulled at the fabric of the emptiness, bending it to my will, calling to it, forcing it to take me to her.

The emptiness answered my summons. I lit up with a nimbus of ghostly fire. I was inside and outside myself, a reflection of myself as witness. It pulled at my hands and feet and wound around me like a tentacle, exploring me, tasting me. I think I shouted her name. The way tensed and bunched, compressing me while I accelerated madly. I screamed and shot forward.

I remember flying, the sensation of the air rushing past my ears. I thumped and bounced in a jarring impact and rolled along the ground. Finally I lay on my back, breathing hard. When I opened my eyes, Blackbird was leaning over me.

"What did you do?"

"What? Sorry?"

She tucked her skirt underneath her and sat on the grass beside me while I got my breath back. A few feet away, an ancient gravestone started with "HERE LIES…"

My heart was still thumping in my chest and memories of how the void had twisted around me distorted my grip on reality, making me faintly nauseous.

"What did you do?" she repeated.

"I don't know. I got distracted by the voices and lost you. I thought I was stuck and I panicked."

She leaned over me, looking into my eyes, possibly for signs of concussion. The late slanted sunlight filtered through her curls and I was struck again by how beautiful she was. Her lips curved in a way that gave you a sense that she was always on the edge of a smile and her eyelashes were incredibly long.

"What?" she whispered.

"Nothing, I was… nothing." I closed my eyes, but that was worse because it made my head thump. I swallowed and opened my eyes again.

"Are you OK?"

"I just need a minute."

"I thought I'd lost you." She looked down at me, concern gradually replaced by another expression I couldn't interpret.

"I thought I'd lost myself," I admitted.

"I heard my name. You *called* for me."

"I got stuck, sort of."

"You called my name," she repeated.

"I was lost. I couldn't find you."

She paused, that strange expression in her eyes again.

"Are you always this..." She faltered.

"This what?"

She leaned across me, resting her hand on the grass on the other side of me and lowered her face and kissed me, pressing her warm soft lips to mine. Her eyes were open, watching my reaction. I was so surprised, I lay there numb for a moment, unable to react. The stone around my neck pulsed into warmth at her touch, reminding me of its presence. She lifted her lips slowly from mine and then brushed her nose against mine, watching me all the while.

"Dense," she said.

"Pardon?"

"Dense. Are you always this dense?"

"What do you mean?"

"You have no idea, do you?"

"About what?"

"See what I mean?"

She leaned down and kissed me again, fully this time, pressing herself down on me so the warmth of her weighed on me. The stone against my chest flared with heat, her body pressing it between us as instinct took over and I kissed her back. Her lips were soft and firm and she tasted of sunshine. My senses swam with the scent of her and I found my fingers brushing back her hair of their own volition.

She lifted herself, head on one side as if she was waiting for me to say something.

"What was that for?" I asked her.

She paused, considering the question.

"Dense," she said, nodding, "definitely dense."

She pushed herself back and lifted herself to her feet, brushing the threads of grass from her skirt. She squinted into the sunshine and then collected her bag and the map from the grass a short distance away. She wandered back over and dropped the items in an unceremonious heap.

"What was that about?" I asked, shading my eyes against the sun behind her.

"Well, I stepped off the line and waited for you and instead of following me, you didn't. I stood around for a while and was wondering whether I should travel back down the way and try to find you when I heard my name. You were calling for me but I couldn't see you anywhere. Then the air sort of bent around itself and you came hurtling out and crash-landed on the grass."

"No, after that."

"After that? After that I wondered if you'd broken your neck, but it's OK because I think you landed on your head."

"After that."

"After that I kissed you."

She stepped across me using both hands to tuck her skirt between her knees and then knelt down, one knee either side of my stomach. The light was still behind her, but she leaned over me putting her hands on either side of my head so her shade sheltered my face.

"Would you like me to do it again?"

Her voice was softer and had an edge of huskiness to it. She lowered her face so her hair fell around us and I could see those fabulous green eyes glinting at me. I was acutely conscious of her weight resting low across my stomach.

"Blackbird, I thought we were…" I stopped and started again. "I thought you were…"

She sat up, her weight suddenly heavy on my stomach, her arms folded. The sunlight was full on my face again, but I could see the spark of anger in her eyes.

"What did you think, Niall? That I'm too old for you? What is it with you and age? I was born in 1642. Work it out if it matters so much to you."

"I thought we were friends."

She put her hand on my chest and pushed herself up, standing over me, looking down. I pushed myself back up onto my elbows.

"Friends? Is that what we are? Really?"

She turned, collected her things from the ground and walked up the slope, shoulders square and head up. In a moment she had vanished around the corner of the low stone church. I shook my head, trying to clear it, wondering if the fall had knocked the wits out of me. None of this made any sense. I knew she was angry with me, but now I couldn't figure out what I'd done wrong.

I pushed myself to my feet and brushed the dry grass stalks from my clothes, finding myself largely unscathed, despite the bad landing. I stood up and looked around. I was in a graveyard behind a church, the ground sloping steeply down to a little stream hidden in the thickets at the bottom. The church was surrounded by ancient yew trees and it took me a moment to orientate myself. I struggled up the slope between the graves and found the gravel path around the church.

I caught sight of her sitting on the wooden bench in the lych-gate. She was sat in the long shadow of the surrounding trees as if nothing had happened. I shook my head again, wondering whether anything had happened or whether I was suffering the after-effects of a bump on the head.

I walked down the path and through the gates to stand in front of her.

She looked at me, head on one side in that characteristic pose. She took in the dishevelled appearance, the bits of grass still caught in my hair. Deprived of sleep, chased, threatened and almost killed several times, I wasn't sure I understood anything anymore.

She got to her feet, shaking her head and chuckling to herself, and walked off down the lane. I trudged after her, more confused than ever. Had the fall addled my wits completely? Had she really kissed me or was I hallucinating? No, she had definitely kissed me. But then she stomped off in a huff and then laughed at me.

She paused, waiting for me to catch up and then walked alongside me. I felt confused and resentful at being made fun of, but she didn't say anything and after a while I subsided into a circular thought pattern leaving me no wiser.

We walked down a twisted lane, sunken between hedges as the light faded into twilight. There were glimpses of farmhouses and outbuildings through the hedge and the occasional distant tractor. A single car passed us, slowing as it drew level and then accelerating away once it was past. We crossed a bridge over a brook and started the climb up the hill on the other side. Real blackbirds scolded their alarm at our passing and there were occasional rustlings from the hedge beside the road that might, I suppose, have been a rabbit. She didn't speak and I had no idea what to say, so I stayed silent, mulling over what had happened.

My relationships with women had always been fraught. Even my marriage to Katherine had been difficult. We had been brought together by friends who thought we were made for each other, and at first that had been true. We wined and dined, and went to the theatre and talked of culture and art and politics. We were affectionate and even passionate. We stayed up late and spoke about history and philosophy and our jobs and even our friends, but never about us.

Our relationship was something we never discussed. I liked her a lot, but in the end it had been she who had seduced me. It was she who pushed our relationship from an intellectual exchange to a physical consummation.

Quite suddenly the relationship changed. I found the physical aspect of our relationship overwhelming. I was obsessed with her. I couldn't wait to see her and be with her. But she wanted something beyond the moment, beyond the enjoyment of each other.

We broke up on a Friday. I was looking forward to a weekend of Katherine. I thought everything was fine until she called me and told me it was over. When I asked her why, she told me she wanted more than just sex and when I said that I thought we had more than sex, she laughed and said that was the problem. I told her I didn't understand and she told me she thought that was true.

That was why I asked her to marry me. Not immediately, not then, but later. I found I couldn't bear the thought of living day to day without her. It wasn't until much later that I realised I couldn't live with her constant suspicion and innate mistrust. By then we had Alex, and everything had changed.

"You're quiet." Blackbird brought me back to the present.

"Hmmm?"

"We've walked about two miles and you haven't said a word."

"I was thinking."

"What about?"

"Nothing."

"Two miles of nothing?"

"Old stuff, stuff that's gone; things long passed."

"Want to talk about it?"

"No. It's history."

We walked on, rounding a bend and walking past a farmyard where a tractor was left running unattended, the driver presumably engaged in one of the buildings.

"Blackbird, why aren't we friends?"

"Aren't we?" She looked sideways at me. "I thought we were."

"But you said–"

"Back there? I don't know if we were friends then, but we are now, if you want to be."

"Would you do something, for me?" I asked her.

"What's that?"

"Stick with me, stay friends with me."

I waited while she considered my request. She didn't just say "OK", and I valued that. She treated my proposal seriously. Friendship wasn't something I offered lightly or trivially. It was a commitment to a way of being. It cheered me that she considered it carefully.

She skipped forward and turned in front of me, leaving me no choice but to stop or step around her. I stopped and she rested her hands on my chest.

"Do you know what you're asking?"

"Yes. No. Is it so terrible to be my friend? Does it mean something else to the Feyre?"

"No, it's not terrible and friendship amongst the Feyre has all the usual connotations. But do you know what it means when a guy says to a girl, let's just be friends?"

"Oh, I see. I didn't mean that. I meant be my friend as well, alongside anything else you can be, that you want to be."

"And what do you want, Niall?" Her eyes were sharp and focused.

"Honestly? Right now I want a good night's sleep somewhere where no one is trying to kill me and the comfort of knowing I have a friend in the world. Beyond that, I am prepared to see what tomorrow brings."

"A true answer and a fair one." She turned and continued walking, leaving me once more to catch up.

"So is that a yes, or a no?" I asked her.

She looked back over her shoulder. "It's not a no."

I caught up with her and settled back into her gentle pace.

"It wasn't exactly a yes, either," I pointed out.

"No, it wasn't, was it?"

And I had to settle for that. I figured that I had offended her earlier when she thought I was rejecting her attentions. Now she was more reserved.

"As your friend, Niall..."

"Yes."

"Would you confide in me? Would you tell me your secrets?"

"As your friend, I might, assuming I had any secrets."

"Hmm. So if you liked someone, would it be a secret?"

"Not a secret exactly, but it might be difficult to talk about."

"Why would that be?"

"She might be very complicated. I might not know where I was with her, even if I did like her quite a lot actually."

"She might be older than you?"

"She might, but that wouldn't necessarily be a problem."

"Then why would she be complicated?"

I sighed, wrestling with the theoretical realities. "Because she might have a lot of secrets of her own; because she might change in the wink of an eye and be someone different, someone I didn't know or someone else that I did, if I ever knew her at all. How would I know who she was?"

"How do any of us know? We only show the parts we want others to see. We might not be able to cloak it in magic or switch in a moment, but we can all be different people, if we choose."

"That's true I suppose, but it's hard to trust someone when you don't know who they are." And trust, as I had learned too late with Katherine, is where friendship and even love are founded.

There was a long pause while we walked along, side by side, in silence.

"You could get to know her," she suggested.

"Yes," I agreed, "I might just try that."

We walked along and after a few more yards, her hand slipped into mine and we walked along companionably. We could have been out for an evening walk if it weren't for the dark box in Blackbird's bag.

"Glamour has a kind of side effect," she said, apropos nothing in particular.

"It does? What kind of side effect?" I had visions of all my hair falling out or my teeth going green.

"It becomes second nature."

"How is that a side effect?"

"You use it all the time and it becomes the norm. It becomes part of you."

"Why is that a problem?"

She stopped and I halted, waiting for her to carry on. Instead she looked pensive, worried even.

"What's the matter?"

"Niall, do you like the way I look?"

"Is it important? I mean you look lovely, but looks aren't everything."

"Do you? Because I can change it if you don't."

"What would you change it to?"

"Anything. Anything at all. Blonde, brunette, buxom, boyish, fat, thin, pink, green."

"No, no. You don't need to change the way you look for me. You just need to look like yourself."

"That's the thing." She hesitated. "I don't know what I look like. I've had glamour since I was fifteen and I've looked however I've wanted ever since. You want me to look like I am, but I choose how I am. I don't know how not to choose."

"What happens if you just relax and let go?"

"Nothing happens. I stay like I am. I've been doing this for so long I can do it in my sleep, literally."

"What do you want me to say?" I was bemused and rather at a loss for words.

"I just wanted you to know. It seemed important to you and I felt I should explain."

She walked along beside me again, but her hand didn't return to mine. I felt as if I should apologise again, but I wasn't sure what for. Because I had assumed that she looked like a retired lady and not a young woman or because she didn't know what she looked like any better than I did? It was hollow and I was sure if I said anything, it would sound it.

We walked down a gentle hill with a big brick farmhouse on our left. The hedges had recently been flail-cut

283

and torn pieces of sticks and leaves were strewn across the roadway. It reminded me of my life.

As we walked down the hill things began to register with me. It was like a seeing a cloud that suddenly looks like a dragon or realising the vase you were looking at is really the silhouette of two faces.

I stopped and she came to a halt with me.

"Do you know where we are?" I asked her.

"We can't be too far away now. We must have walked a couple of miles and it's only about five to the village." She extracted the map from her bag and started unfolding it.

I walked past her a few paces, watching images come into line and visions fulfil themselves.

"You don't need the map. It's here."

"We can't be at the village yet, it's another mile or so at least."

"Come and look."

She refolded the map and came and stood beside me, looking down a short access track at a pair of ornate iron gates attached to brick pillars with a large old brick farmhouse set out in a courtyard beyond them. The farm looked neat and well cared for.

"Are you sure?"

"Look at the name."

The sign was for Forge Farm with a neat anvil depicted in the centre of the cast-iron oval sign.

"There could be more than one. There were no end of forges and foundries in this area a hundred years ago."

"Look at the roof."

Along the line of the roof were three iron doves, black and outlined against the darkening skyline. One was pecking while the other two were artfully engaged in each other. At the other end of the apex an iron cat stalked along the cap-tiles, ready to pounce on them. It was the cat from my vision. As soon as I had seen it from the road I had been certain.

"Sure?"

I nodded.

"We'd better go and introduce ourselves then.

"Blackbird, before we do. I have another request, if you'll allow it?" I spoke gently, aware that the wrong word at this moment would lead to a rift between us, just when I thought we were getting closer.

"What?" Her answer was curt, but not harsh.

"Would you stay like you are now, just for a while, until I get used to it? I rather like you like that."

She didn't say anything, but as we walked down the track towards the farm her hand curled into mine again. It was such a small thing, but it lifted my heart and I couldn't help the smile that came unbidden to my lips.

EIGHTEEN

The gates to the farm were a challenge. They were wide enough so you could drive a combine harvester through them easily. They were at least ten feet high at the outside, sloping down through an elegant curve to about seven feet in the middle. The foundations for the pillars must have been put in specially because they were cold forged iron and neither Blackbird nor I were going to touch them.

There was no bell or knocker. We could see there were lights on in the house but we were a good distance away so it was doubtful anyone would hear us if we called out. In America there would have been an intercom so you could get the gates opened electrically. This was Shropshire.

The problem was solved by a couple of dogs. They tore out of one of the barns as soon as we came close to the gates, baying and barking fit to wake anyone within a quarter mile. They were great big things with huge ugly heads, tusk-like lower teeth and coats the colour of burnt toffee, possibly some kind of mastiff. Their brakes weren't too good as they skidded and collided with the gates at the end of their run in a race to be first to bark at the visitors. The gates didn't even rattle.

"Well, that should get us some attention," remarked Blackbird.

The dogs barked on for a good couple of minutes but no one came. They growled and ran up and down the gates, intimating that, if they could only get out, we would be dog-meat.

"OK, maybe not. Still, we don't have to put up with this racket." She turned to the dogs.

I don't know what she did, because it only lasted a second and I had my eye on the dogs. I caught a glimpse of something out of the corner of my eye as she shifted shape momentarily. The effect was instant and dramatic. Both dogs backed away from the gate, one turning and running back towards the farmhouse with its tail between its legs, the other backing off about ten yards, still barking, but with all the hackles raised down its back. Its back legs were down and braced. The bark had changed too, becoming darker, more urgent.

"Brave dog," she remarked, nodding towards the one still barking.

"Doesn't help us get past the gates, though does it?"

"Hello?" A figure emerged from the house, the other dog close on her heels. She'd obviously been cooking because she was dusting flour from her fingers.

"Hello!" I answered.

She walked across the yard towards us, having trouble because the dog stayed close to her legs, putting itself between her and us.

"Stupid animal." She pushed it away, but it was not budging from her. "Can I help you?"

"We're looking for Mr Highsmith," I called to her.

"Yes?" She looked at the dog, still growling and barking, well back from the gate. "Topaz! Heel!"

The dog glanced at her and then continued its barking.

"Topaz! Come here!"

The dog backed slowly towards her, never taking its eyes from us, still growling deeply.

"Is this the right place?" It was difficult to have a conversation through the gates and across the yard, but she showed no sign of wanting to open the gates with the dogs acting so strangely.

"This is Highsmiths' farm, yes," she admitted, still watching the dog.

"Could we speak to Mr Highsmith?" I asked, across the divide.

"What about?" She made no move towards us.

"We need to speak with him about an urgent matter, something we would like him to do."

"And what sort of thing would that be?" Suspicion tinted her tone.

"We need him to do some ironwork," Blackbird added.

"I'm afraid you've wasted your time."

"Have we come to the wrong place then?" I asked.

"No, He's here. But he doesn't do commissions any more. He's getting on, you see."

"He'll do this one," Blackbird asserted.

Another figure appeared from one of the sheds around the courtyard. This one had the universal blue coveralls farmers wear. His were dark with grease and he had the look of a man that had been in the middle of fixing something and had been interrupted.

"What's the matter with the dogs, Meg?" He walked over to her, wiping his hands down his thighs.

"They rucked up when these people came calling and then Tasha here came bursting into the kitchen and hid under the table, growling at the door, silly dog." Nevertheless she reached down and stroked the dog's ears, reassuring her.

"Topaz, heel!" The larger dog turned and trotted back to his master, then stood by his legs, still rumbling at us.

He walked forward. "Can I help you with something?"

"We've come to see Mr Highsmith, about some ironwork," I repeated.

"I don't do ironwork no more, and my Dad's getting too old to take on work. Maybe I can recommend someone to you?"

"No, I'm afraid it's you we need to do it. It's specialist work."

"As I say I don't do ironwork anymore. There's no money in it."

"This isn't for money, although I dare say there'll be payment," said Blackbird. "This is about two knives, one blunt and one sharp."

That clearly hit a chord, because his manner changed.

"Meg, go and get Dad, will you? And take the dog with you. Lock her in the back kitchen."

"But Jeff–"

"Just go and get him, would you, please?"

She walked off, clearly not happy with the situation, but following his instructions.

He walked a little closer, setting the dog barking again until he hushed it with a word.

"What kind of work is it you're wanting?"

"It's one of the knives. It's broken in two. Someone dropped it a while ago and no one's been able to fix it."

"Cold iron, is it?"

"We're not sure. We don't get too close to it."

That brought a grim smile to his lips.

"You'd better come in, but I'll lock the dog up first."

"Don't worry, he won't bite us. We'll be fine," Blackbird assured him.

"I was thinking of the dog."

He walked the dog back to the house, leaving us standing outside the gate. He was only inside for a minute or two and then he walked back out accompanied by another man. They were from the same mould, these two, the same shoulders, the same wide set walk so that they ambled rather than strode. Even though the older man was now thin-haired and grey, you could see the muscles that still burdened his frame.

The younger man lowered his head and explained something to him quietly as they walked across the yard in the gathering dusk, becoming silent as they came within earshot. He came forward and walked to the gate, drawing back a long bolt so the gate could swing open wide enough to admit us.

"You'd better come in." He was reluctant to admit us, but he did it anyway. We stepped through, wary of the iron on either side of us.

"This is my dad, Ben Highsmith. I'm Jeff."

"I am called Blackbird, and this is Rabbit." The animal names sounded strange in the context of an introduction, but the old man just nodded as if he expected something like that.

They didn't offer to shake hands or make any other welcome, but led the way to the farmhouse. I followed after Blackbird until we reached the door of the kitchen. Blackbird halted at the door.

"Come in. I'll put the kettle on and we can talk business." The old man's voice was like his son's but hoarser, lived in.

"Sorry, would you mind?" She nodded towards the beam over the doorway.

Hanging there was a huge iron horse shoe with its open end down, like a magnet. Even from behind Blackbird I could feel the waves coming off it. He picked it off the nail and took it inside. We followed to watch him carefully balance it on the beam over the door from the kitchen into the rest of the house.

He turned to see us watching him. "No offence meant."

"None taken," Blackbird responded.

He opened the door and yelled through the gap. "Meg, get James down here, will you?"

"He's on PlayStation." The reply came from up the stairs beyond the door.

"Tell him to come down."

"He's on PlayStation." She repeated it as if that explained why he wasn't coming.

"One minute," he remarked, and went through the door, closing it behind him.

The kitchen was well fitted out with modern appliances and a big range cooker at one end, all lit by modern spotlights over the work surfaces. Jeff filled the kettle and set it on one of the rings to boil. He indicated the big kitchen table and we took a seat at one end. One of the dogs barked behind another door, presumably a utility room of some sort.

There was something about the house that made me uncomfortable. The kitchen was modern and well equipped without being at odds with the age of the house. It all looked very cosy and tasteful, but I felt I couldn't rest there. There was something about it that jangled my nerves and set my teeth on edge.

The door to the house re-opened and a sullen teenager in a black T-shirt illustrated with paint-splashed writing came through, followed by the old man.

"This is my grandson, James. James, this is Blackbird and that's Rabbit."

"Funny names," the boy remarked.

"Mind your manners, especially with their kind."

The lad muttered something under his breath and went to sit down at the other end of the table.

"James here is a modern lad. He sees no use in spending time at the forge and learning how to make iron turn to his will. He likes computers, don't you, James?" This was clearly a long-standing dispute.

"Dad, let the boy be," the father interrupted in a tired voice.

"Show him." The old man's request was directed at Blackbird.

"You want us to show him the knife?" Blackbird asked.

"No. I want you to show him why the Highsmiths have been the High Smiths to the Seven Courts for nigh on a thousand years. Things have changed, I know, and the boy needs to go his own way." He nodded an acceptance to his own son. "But I want him to learn the ways of iron first and for him to know why he must learn them. I want him to have something to tell his grandchildren. Come to that…" He went back to the door. "Just wait a second, will you?"

He opened the door and yelled through. "Meg? Lisa? Come into the kitchen. There's something you've got to see."

"Dad, I don't want the girls involved," Jeff insisted.

"Don't you? Lisa's spent more time in the forge with me than James ever did. You say I've got to let the boy have his way? Well that's fine, but someone's got to carry on the line."

"The women have never been part of it, Dad. You know that."

"Not true. They just haven't been part of it for a very long time, but you keep telling me times have changed and we have to adapt. Well, I'm adaptin'." He folded his arms across his broad chest.

The woman from the yard appeared in the doorway. Behind her was a girl about the same age as my own daughter, with fair hair tinted honey-blonde in a way that made you think it was the outdoors that had bleached it, not chemicals. She had a rangy quality you see in long distance runners. Against her mother's plumpness she looked lean.

Now they were together I could see that the boy took after his mother. He had the same down-turned mouth and thickness of hair. The girl took after her father and grandfather. She would be tall, lean and fair, though probably without the thickness of muscle.

"What's this all about, Ben? These people upset the dogs and yet you bring them in and set them at my kitchen table and then you pull us all in here. No offence meant, but I tell it like it is." This last was addressed to us.

"I apologise for interrupting your evening, Mrs

Highsmith," Blackbird responded. "And we're grateful for your hospitality, but our need is urgent."

She acknowledged Blackbird's apology with a nod but then focused back on her father-in-law. "Well, Ben?"

"The Highsmiths have been on this land for almost a thousand years, Meg. You joined the family fifteen year ago, and you've been a daughter to me, you know that. But there are secrets in this family that have been kept for all of that time."

"What's he talking about, Jeff?"

The son looked helplessly at his wife and then his father, caught between secrets unshared and the events we had brought into the house. "I'm sorry, Meg. It's about the land, the forge, the farm, all of it. You know the rent on this place is a pittance. Well there's another part to it. These people are from the landlords and they've come to collect the rest of the rent."

"What do you mean, the rest of it?" Her voice was rising in pitch with her anger.

"I mean they want us to make things for them. Iron things."

She looked from one man to the other and neither of them would meet her gaze.

Ben turned to Blackbird. "You'd best show them. They won't believe you otherwise."

Blackbird nodded. "Rabbit, perhaps you could show them what you showed me in the Underground station this morning?"

"What, here?"

"Here, please, and now," she insisted.

"Do you mind telling me what this is about? Jeff? What's going on?" Meg's voice was getting more edgy by the second.

"They're not 'uman, Meg, not like us." He shook his head, unable to meet her questioning stare.

She looked at us, pulling her daughter to her, as if she was unprepared to believe what she was hearing but unwilling to risk that it might be true.

"What do you mean, not human?" she asked him.

I had done this before, but not for an audience and I wanted it to look good. Yet as soon as I started to focus I realised something was different. Something about how it felt reminded me of the moment out on the Way when I had become lost in the void. I had called it and it had answered. Now when I called, it answered as if I had never broken that connection. It was right there waiting for me, always present. The image flashed into my mind of being haloed in cold white fire, hanging in space, and I felt something tense inside me, something huge.

The lights in the room dimmed as I drew on it and at the same time the dogs in the next room started baying in long mournful howls. Everything went still. The hum of the fridge, the background noise of a TV in another room, everything just stopped, leaving the sound of the dogs isolated in the stillness. The electric lights flickered and died and gallowfyre flooded into the room.

"Shit! Shit!" The boy stood up at the end of the table and backed away, knocking the chair over in the process.

Just as in the vision Kareesh had showed me, a piece of mistletoe hanging over the door of the room with the dogs in it flickered into life, glowing green in the half-light in response to the magic building up like a thunderhead in the room. Cold white fox-fire danced into being on the worktops, bouncing like playful stars along the edges until the entire room sparked with it.

"Jeff?" Meg shepherded her daughter away from us towards the end of the kitchen where the old man and his son watched us with grim faces. "Jeff, make him stop?"

"It's what they are, Meg. They're Fey. They won't hurt us. They need us." His face looked grim in the swimming light.

I barely heard him. The void sang in my veins like a heavy chorus. I felt the hunger of it building. I felt its need swelling within me. The room burned with cold flickering fire and that fire knew me, sang to me.

A voice came though the swell of it.

"Rabbit? Can you hear me, Rabbit? Let it go. Let go of it now." Blackbird coaxed me down like a policemen talking a jumper down from the ledge of a tall building.

I released it, pushing it back, and it flickered and died. Regret accompanied that release. I knew I couldn't hold it forever, but part of me wanted to, wanted to revel in it and bathe in that ethereal glow.

The lights came on and the fridge juddered into life. The background noise re-established itself. Blackbird's hand rested on mine for a moment.

"Are you well enough?" she asked.

I nodded, shaken by the intensity of it.

"What have you done?" Meg asked the question of the two men, glancing at us as if we might leap out of our seats and bite her.

"It was done a very long time ago, Meg. We just carry the burden, as will they." The old man indicated the children. "We're not just Highsmiths, we are the High Smiths of the Seven Courts of the Feyre. We have the land and the house and all that goes with it. In return we work iron for those that can't abide it. I didn't know if they would come in my lifetime, but they're here and we must pay."

"What happens if we don't pay? What happens?" The question was initially to the men, but then redirected to us.

"Mrs Highsmith, we haven't come here to threaten you or your family, but to seek your help. If no one will help us then there may be worse times ahead for all of us, human and Fey alike."

Her appeal was interrupted by a mobile phone ringing. Everyone jumped at the sound and then listened to it ring until the boy, James, pulled it from his pocket and answered it.

"Hullo?"

He listened for a moment and then continued.

"Yeah, the power's been down here as well. It must have been some sort of problem with the supply."

He glanced at his father and then at me and then mouthed a single word to his mother, presumably the name of the caller.

"It's fine now and we're all OK," he said. "Yeah, thanks. Did it? Yeah, me too. I'll talk to you later. Bye."

He looked at his mother. "That was Jaz. The power was off in the village and for miles around. Her mum wanted to know if it was off up here too." He looked over at me again. "I think she was just ringing to see if we were all right."

"You mustn't speak of this James," his mother instructed him. "Tell no one, understand. You too Lisa, not even your best friends, OK?" They both nodded solemnly.

"What do you want from us?" She addressed Blackbird and I directly.

"We need to get something remade." She unzipped her bag and pulled out the wooden box, placing it on the table and sliding it towards the far end within their reach. "It's been broken for some time, but we've only just found out."

The old man stepped forwards and unclipped the catch. He lifted the lid of the box and the wrongness spilled out of it. Blackbird hissed between her teeth.

"Snapped clean through," the old man commented professionally, holding up the handle end. He showed it to his son who took it from him and examined it. "It shouldn't break like that. Any idea what happened to it?" he asked us.

I was grinding my teeth together at the jarring dissonance it created in the room. It was Blackbird who answered for us.

"We think it was dropped." Her expression of distaste echoed my own.

"Still, it shouldn't break like that. What do you think Jeff?"

Jeff held it up to the light. "I think it was cooled too quickly. Look at the way the discoloration's taken here." He scratched his nail on the flat of the blade near the break.

Their love of the dark metal was a reflection of our own distaste. It came to me that it was what was wrong with the house. It was nicely fitted-out, but it was steeped in iron. When you looked, there were nails hammered flat into the beams, an iron trivet sat on the worktop next to the stove. Everywhere, little bits of it were incorporated into the fabric of the house.

"Can you fix it?" Blackbird's question was straight to the point. We wanted to spend as little time near the knife as possible.

"No, once broken is broken. You can't weld it or even re-forge it. The iron's too pure to work it after it's cooled. We can make you another though. We've got the metal, haven't we, Jeff," the old man offered.

"That would be excellent. When can you do it?"

"We can do it tomorrow. It'll take about a day to make."

"You'll have it in the morning," Meg Highsmith interrupted, "even if they have to work all night."

They both looked at her, then at each other. Then the old man nodded.

"Tomorrow then, but late morning," he agreed. "Lisa, go light the forge, will you?"

The girl nodded seriously to her grandfather and went around the room the long way around the table to avoid us, slipping out into the yard and the last of the daylight.

The old man dipped into the box again and pulled out the other knife.

"This must be the Dead Knife. I've never seen either, though I was told about them, of course. This one is something different, though." His voice had a tone of respect in it. He passed it to his son, who gave him back the broken Quick Knife to replace in the box. Once the broken parts were seated in the recess made for them, he closed the lid and Blackbird and I could relax. He smiled at our obvious relief at the closure of the box.

"It was never meant for your kind, that knife. Cold iron, it is, and hard as it could be made, though brittle with it. That's why it broke. The tiniest fault would be enough. This is a different matter, though."

He took the Dead Knife back from his son.

"This was made by the High Maker of the Six Courts. Fey metal, it's near enough unbreakable." His voice was filled with respect as he examined the leaf-shaped blade, then put the point on the surface of the table and flexed the end of the blade, the tip bending so it formed an elegant curve. He let it go and it sprang back, ringing lightly with a clean clear note.

"Here, it was made for hands like yours." He passed it across, holding the back of the blade so I could take the handle.

The wooden handle was smooth with use. It had a metal core that spiralled back around the handle end so that it formed part of the handle. As soon as my hand touched the metal, the blade shivered and went black. It didn't just darken, it went completely black. I turned it and it moved without reflection, giving it an odd hollow aspect.

"It was made to respond to the Feyre, just as the Quick Knife was made for human hands," Ben added.

I put it on the table and slid it towards Blackbird. As soon as my hand left it, it returned to the dull metal it had been. She hesitated and then tapped her forefinger on it, lightly, to test it. Nothing happened, so she picked it off the table and it flickered to life. The blade changed colour, turning ruddy grey and then glowed a dull red.

"It's not hot," she said, but was then startled as the blade burst into flame, long licks of flame travelling up the blade away from her hand.

"Wicked!" That was the boy, James. It was pretty impressive.

She turned the blade in her hand, the fire rippling up the blade like a burning brand. "What happens if you–"

The fire along the blade turned blue and intense, the tip turning slowly white, spreading down the blade. I realised that I could now feel the heat coming off it, though Blackbird was unaware of it. She placed the blade back onto the wooden table and then picked it up quickly as she realised it had scorched the surface of the bleached pine. The dark outline of the blade was there, scorched into the surface of the wood.

"I'm terribly sorry..." she apologised, glancing at Meg. The blade returned to yellow flickering flames again.

She turned it this way and that, looking for somewhere heat-proof to place the burning knife.

"Here," I said, "give it to me."

She hesitated, then passed it to me and for a second both our hands touched the knife, my open palm and her fingers on the handle. The flames went black, like the reverse of fire. They still rippled off the blade, but they were flames of shadow, not light.

I glanced up and met Blackbird's look. She felt it too; a meeting in the metal, a mingling of her magic and mine. Her eyes widened and she snatched her hand back. I had felt her warmth. What had she felt that made her snatch her hand away like that?

The blade went black in my hand. It was cool, cold even, and I was about to place it back on the table when I changed my mind.

"What did you do to make it hot?" I asked her.

"I just focused on it, like you do with the Ways," she answered, clearly as mystified by the knife as I was.

I focused my will gently on the knife and tried to connect with it. It was as if it answered but there was only vast emptiness. I reached further into it and it appeared the same, like a bottomless well. It didn't react to me the way it had to her. I shrugged and was about to put it down when I had another thought.

I reached within and let the darkness inside me connect to it, then pour into it.

The room vanished.

NINETEEN

When I poured the darkness into the knife it took me aside, slipping between the cracks of the world. We're so used to describing geometry in terms of up and down, in and out, that the vocabulary to describe it is inadequate. There were places all around me at impossible angles, intersecting with each other, passing through each other. My eyes refused to register the complexity of it all.

I floated through them, sampling each one as if flicking through the pages of a paperback. In some it was night-time and others not. Some were searing cold or unbearably humid. It was like a dish with too many flavours, or an orchestra with every instrument playing a different tune in different time, I was overwhelmed by it.

It wasn't like being lost on the Way. I wasn't lost, I was just disoriented. I knew where I was because I was there. I could be anywhere though. I could be in the farmhouse in Shropshire.

There was a shriek.

"Oh God! You made me jump."

Meg Highsmith had her hand across her chest as she calmed herself. Blackbird burst through the doorway from the yard.

"Are you all right? Where have you been? Are you OK?"

"I'm fine," I admitted under the barrage of questions. "Where did everyone go?"

"They're readying the forge. You've been gone over two hours."

"Have I?" I looked at the knife in my hand and then placed it carefully on the table. It faded to grey. "Two hours?" I glanced at my watch, confirming what she was saying, but still finding it hard to accept.

"Where were you?"

"I'm not sure. I think I was in lots of places, all at once. They all overlapped, it was confusing. Some of them were different, really different."

Jeff Highsmith burst into the door behind Blackbird. "What happened? Are you OK?" He looked to his wife.

"I'm fine," she echoed my remark. "He just made me jump. One second he wasn't there and the next he was."

"You've been gone for hours," Blackbird repeated, coming close and looking up into my face. "I didn't know what had happened to you. You just vanished."

"I was floating." I tried to conjure up a mental picture of the myriad of places jumbled up together but it just made my eyes ache. I tried again. "There were facets of places, like slivers." I shook my head, trying to clear the fogginess shrouding my thoughts.

Meg Highsmith was practical. "Do you want tea? Tea is supposed to be good for shock."

Blackbird declined her offer. "No thank you, Mrs. Highsmith. I think we should go. We've prevailed on your hospitality too much as it is. Is there anywhere nearby where we could stay the night?"

"I'd offer you a bed here, but..." Jeff trailed off, looking at his wife. She didn't say anything, but her answer was written on her face.

"That's OK, we understand."

We could see they were not going to be comfortable with us in the house, given what they'd seen, and neither would we be comfortable there. There was too much iron in the place.

"Let me phone down to the village for you," she suggested.

She went through the door into the rest of the house. Jeff stayed with us, unwilling to leave us unsupervised, but with nothing to say.

"Would you put the knife back in the box for me, Jeff?" I nodded towards the Dead Knife resting inert, its shadow burnt into the tabletop beside it. I didn't want to touch it again and find myself somewhere else.

He nodded and there was a brief moment of discomfort as he opened the box and slipped the Dead Knife in next to the broken one.

"What time should we return to collect the new knife tomorrow?" I asked him, taking the box from him and passing it back to Blackbird to stow in her bag.

"If you come late morning, we'll have it finished."

"Thank you. I appreciate that we've just appeared and asked you to drop everything to do this."

"That's the agreement, isn't it?" he shrugged.

"Yes, I suppose it is. Is there anything we can do to help?"

"Not unless you can hold a pair of tongs over a hot forge?" He smiled at our expressions. "No, I thought not."

Meg returned. "The nearest hotel is in Bridgnorth, but there's a pub in the village called The Chequers that would put you up for the night. They don't take guests normally, so it might be a bit rough and ready, but it's clean. They do nice food."

"That's great," Blackbird thanked her.

"Do you want a lift down to the village, Jeff will take you?" She was obviously feeling guilty now about turning us out.

"No thanks, Mrs. Highsmith. I think the walk would do Rabbit some good. The night air might clear his head."

"We'll see you tomorrow, then," she said.

There was an awkward moment when we would have shaken hands, but Jeff rescued us from it.

"Come on then, I'll have to open the gate for you."

He escorted us out into the yard. It was full dark now and clouds had appeared to dapple the sky, backlit by a low moon. There was a slice of missing time I couldn't account for that left me feeling slightly at odds with the world.

"The village is about fifteen minutes' walk down the lane. Are you sure you don't want a lift?"

"No thanks. We'll be fine making our own way."

"Yes. I suppose you will. The Chequers is on the main road through the village, on the right. You can't miss it. See you tomorrow then."

I wished him a good night as we slipped carefully through the gate and into the lane, walking into the darkness a little apart.

"I was worried about you," Blackbird said, after a few minutes. "You just vanished. I had no idea whether you were coming back." There was a note of accusation in her voice.

"I'm sorry. I didn't know it was so long."

"Where did you go?"

"Everywhere, and nowhere. I must have lost track of time. It wasn't anywhere but it was close to a lot of places. You said your elements were fire and air, and when you held the knife, that's what appeared. The same must have happened with me and the void. I think I was between things, in the space that separates. Does that make sense?"

Blackbird considered this. We were walking along separately and I couldn't help thinking back to when we had both touched the knife. I had felt her presence then, a kind of warmth running through the contact, and I

304

was pretty sure she had felt my presence too. The question was, what had she felt?

The void was there all the time now, not as an intrusion but rather like a thought mulling away at the back of my head, unresolved. Just thinking about it reinforced the connection with it, calling it forward. So when the flames on the knife held between us had turned black, had she touched that aching emptiness, felt the endlessness of it?

At first I had been frightened by the void but then I began to understand that it knew me, welcomed me, that it was home for me. Blackbird didn't have that connection. She was something else, a creature of fire and air. Did that mean it felt different for her? Did it frighten her. Repel her? I wanted to ask her, but it was too close to other questions I was avoiding. I had seen Blackbird embrace a monster, shaggy with hair and with tusks for teeth. But the Feyre didn't tell stories of trolls to frighten their children. The Feyre had a different idea of what constituted a monster. They frightened their children with the wraithkin.

Walking along the lane, the hedges silhouetted against the moonlight, I wondered. Was my future to become like Raffmir and his sister?

"How are you feeling?"

She hadn't raised her voice but it sounded loud in the stillness broken only by the rhythmic trudge of our feet. How was I feeling? In the context of my thoughts it was not such an innocent question.

"OK, I guess. Tired."

"It's been a long day for you."

"And a strange one. Full of surprises." I glanced sideways at her, seeing only her outline.

"Yes, for me as well."

A car came out of the dark towards us and I dropped back behind her to allow it to pass more easily. It rolled down the lane, coasting past us, its lights bright then gone as it faded into the lanes. I increased my pace to catch up with her, feeling even that small effort draw on my depleted reserves.

"Not far now," she encouraged.

We came to the first streetlight of the village and passed beneath it. Houses bunched along the road and a few windows still had curtains drawn back showing families clustered around the bluish light of the TV. A man walked a dog towards us, the dog pulling at the lead to investigate the strangers and then trailing behind to sniff at our passing. At least it didn't start howling.

The Chequers was an island of brightness in the village, the car park half-full and the noise of rock music emanating from the bar. It was a large two-storey building with a high peaked roof and tall bay windows with mock-Tudor beams painted black against the white of the walls. We followed the signs to the lounge bar where it was quieter. It was still brash after the quiet intimacy of the darkened lane. There were a few couples sitting at tables and a group of friends, drinking and laughing at the far end of the bar.

"A very good evening to you both. What can I get you?" The landlord was a stocky man, with a neatly trimmed beard and bushy eyebrows. The welcome was warm considering that he must have known we weren't local.

"Mrs Highsmith phoned for us earlier, about accommodation?" Blackbird explained.

"Ah, yes. I spoke to her myself. It's for the one night, is it?"

"Yes please."

I leaned against a bar-stool.

"And it's just the one room, or is it two?"

"One," she said.

"Two, please," I said at exactly the same time.

She turned and looked up at me, and there was something in her eyes I hadn't expected. She looked hurt.

"One," I said to the landlord.

"Two," she said at the same time.

She laughed and the hurt vanished, replaced by amusement.

She lifted a hand and pressed her forefinger against my lips, hushing me with a touch.

"We'll have one room please," she clarified, glancing sideways at the landlord.

"You're sure? It's a double, but we charge the same for two singles." The landlord was amused at our confusion.

"Quite sure," she confirmed. Her eyes gleamed up at me and she lifted her finger away slowly, daring me to contradict her.

"Right you are then. The missus is just airing the room for you now, but it'll be a few minutes yet. Would you like a drink while you wait? The kitchen will be closing soon, so if you want food, you'd best order straight away."

My stomach rumbled in answer to that. "Food would be great," I told him.

He passed a menu from along the bar. It offered pub-grub standards like lasagne and fried scampi in breadcrumbs. Everything came with chips.

Blackbird quickly settled on a shepherd's pie and I chose steak. We ordered the local brew and the landlord pulled us two pints of fragrant dark beer before taking our food order through to the kitchen. We took our drinks to a table away from the noise of the other customers.

The foam of the beer made a moustache across my upper lip, which amused Blackbird. I felt a little awkward after the discussion about the room. Did that mean we were spending the night together or was it that she didn't trust me to spend a night alone without getting into some sort of trouble? We were safe here, weren't we? No one but the Highsmiths knew we were here.

"A pigeon for your thoughts," she offered.

"It's a penny, a penny for your thoughts."

"Not where I come from," she grinned.

I smiled in response and shook my head. "I don't think I'm thinking clearly enough to translate my thoughts into anything worthy of a pigeon."

"It's certainly been a full day," she admitted, resting back against the padding of the bench seat. "I'm glad we came here, rather than trying to stay at the farm."

"I think Mrs Highsmith would have found that difficult. They are a lot like the people from where I grew up, in Kent. It's the same sort of countryside, similar background. The people keep to themselves, not trusting outsiders."

"The Highsmiths are good people."

"Yes, Jeff will have some explaining to do when this is over, don't you think?"

"That might be a conversation to stay clear of. Do you think they'll be able to do it, in one night?"

"We have to trust them to do their part. I don't know anyone else who can do this for us, do you?"

"No."

"Then we just have to assume they can and they will. We won't know until tomorrow in any case."

We lapsed into silence, the boisterous noise from the group of friends filling the room.

"So tell me what it was like, growing up in Kent?" she asked.

It was a neutral topic, away from the trials that tomorrow might bring, so I told her about the village in Kent where people from ten miles away were considered foreigners and everyone knew everyone else's business. She was a good listener and I found myself talking about favourite pets, long departed, and running wild across the countryside with a gang of similarly unkempt children. I told her about making arrows from bamboo sticks filched from the potting shed and bows from willow branches and how we had shot the arrows as far as they would go, just for the fun of running after them and seeing where they landed.

"It wasn't a safe childhood," I told her, "but it was adventurous. I went weir riding, just the once. The kids that I hung out with had all done it and they dared me. They would get a fertilizer bag and hang off the bridge on the upstream side and then drop and ride the mill-race down into the pool at the bottom."

"I thought you said you couldn't swim."

"I can't. And after that I didn't want to. I had this idea that I could grab the bridge on the other side as I passed and climb up. The mill-race was covered in slippery weed and when the moment came I couldn't reach and it swept me down into the roiling water at the bottom. I was pulled under, into the churning river, deep into the hole carved out by the tumbling water, turning and twisting. My lungs burned while I thrashed about, unable to tell which way was up."

"How did you get out?"

"My friend Rich jumped in after me. I nearly drowned him as well, but he fought me off and caught hold of my shirt and dragged me to the bank. I owe him my life for that, I would have drowned. I still don't like water, even now."

"Are you still in contact with him?"

"No, I lost touch with him when I went to university and he went to work on his father's farm."

"You should send him a postcard or something," she suggested.

"Dear Rich, still out of my depth here in the land of 'you wouldn't believe'. Having a lovely time. Wish you were here."

Her smile vanished at my words.

"I'm sorry, that sounded bitter and I didn't mean it to."

"That's fine. You're entitled to a bit of cynicism from time to time."

"Am I?"

I was rescued by the food arriving. We tucked into it and there was silence for a while, punctuated by appreciative grunts from me as I found the steak both large and juicy and the chips freshly cooked. We were both taxed by the day, but the combination of good food and decent beer helped us to recover both physically and emotionally.

I finished my steak while Blackbird was still eating, so I told her about my job and projects I had worked on. I ordered another pint while she finished her food and then she told me about life in the university. She described her students, the hopefuls and the wastrels, the ones she knew would pass and the ones that would certainly fail. She parodied her academic colleagues with their pet theories and rivalry, their affairs and indiscretions.

Eventually the bar was all but empty.

"Your room is ready any time you are," the landlord hinted gently.

We thanked him and he cleared up the glasses while we got ourselves together.

"Do you need help with your bags?" he asked.

"No, thanks," I told him. "We're travelling light."

That raised an eyebrow, but he made no comment and led us behind the bar and up a back stairway. From there we were taken past living rooms to another stairway and a door that opened into a converted loft-space.

"This was originally going to be our bedroom, but by the time it was finished my son had gone to college and there's only me and the missus. It's used as a guest room, now. There's an en-suite through that door, there. There are toiletries that you're welcome to use and plenty of hot water, just help yourselves. Breakfast is any time after eight. Anything else I can get you?"

"No, thank you," said Blackbird. "It's great, really."

"I'll leave you to your rest then." He turned and left, closing the door after him and we heard his steps as he retreated down the wooden stairway.

"Heads or tails for first shower," she asked me.

I sat down on the edge of the bed, suddenly feeling the effects of the beer.

"You have it."

"Sure?"

I nodded and she slipped into the bathroom, followed not long after by the sound of running water.

I sat on the edge of the bed, finding it pleasantly firm. I took my trainers off, then lay back on the bed and waited for Blackbird to finish in the shower. It crossed my mind that I could have phoned Katherine as the pub would have a public telephone, but it was too late to do that now. Then it occurred to me that I didn't need a phone, I could find her through the mirror over the dresser if I wanted to. That would be like spying on her, though, and besides it would involve moving from the bed.

A second later, Blackbird was shaking me. "Are you going to sleep like that or are you getting a shower first?"

I groaned, realising I had been dozing, forced myself into an upright position and sat, rubbing my eyes. Blackbird was wrapped in a large bath towel, pink-skinned and combing her fingers through her hair.

"Shower?" she prompted me.

I stumbled to my feet and went into the bathroom. It had no windows, just an extractor fan high up on the wall. One corner was given over to a shower enclosure. I stripped off my clothes, hung them on the back of the door and climbed into the cubicle.

The water was initially cool, but warmed quickly so I had to turn it down. How hot had she had it? It reached a comfortable temperature and I stood under the shower head letting the water run down over my eyes, my face and down my body. I was dog-tired, but the shower was a good idea. I used the soap provided and scrubbed myself from head to toe.

Once out of the shower, I wrapped my damp towel around my waist and looked at my reflection. It didn't look like me, but that was OK. My glamour had held and I had become accustomed to my new face. Is that

311

what she'd meant by the side-effects?

Taking her advice about maintaining my image, I took advantage of a disposable razor to scrape the dark shadow from my chin. I was conscious of the woman in the room next door and I felt I should at least be presentable. I had no idea what she was expecting, but having a chin like sandpaper wasn't going to impress.

I splashed my face with cold water and dried it on the hand towel. Looking up in the mirror I looked tired but scrubbed, which was probably as good as I was going to get. I considered putting my underwear back on, but then rejected it having just got myself clean. Instead, towel secured around my waist, I took my clothes back into the bedroom.

Blackbird was sitting propped up on the pillows, her bare shoulders showing above the duvet. Her hair was dry.

"Where's the hair dryer?" I asked her.

"There isn't one."

"How did you dry your hair?"

"It dries itself."

That didn't really help me.

"Where are you going?"

"I'm going to try and dry my hair with a towel."

I went into the bathroom accompanied by a light chuckling from the bed. When I emerged a few seconds later she was grinning.

"What?"

"Nothing."

"Something is amusing you."

She tried for a straight face and failed, using the duvet to hide her grin.

I did my best to ignore her, hanging my clothes over the chair. To be honest I was unsettled. She was unlike any woman I had ever encountered.

"Are you coming to bed?" she asked.

I walked around to the free side of the bed, lifting the edge of the duvet and the sheet beneath it to sit on the edge of the bed, so I could slide in next to her and slip the towel aside.

"Is there something you've forgotten?"

I twisted around to look at her,

"Lights?" she prompted.

I grabbed the towel again, wrapping it back around my waist, and padded around to the light switch next to the door and back again in the dark, trying to avoid tripping over random pieces of furniture in the unfamiliar room.

I slipped into bed beside her accompanied by her suppressed mirth.

"Do you always laugh at men you're about to sleep with?" I lay on my back while she moved the additional pillow onto the floor and lay back beside me.

"Only the ones that amuse me."

"And I amuse you?"

"You come across as so rugged and then you're so demure."

I didn't have an answer to that, so I lay in the dark looking up at the ceiling where the dim light from the night sky showed around the edges of the blinds drawn over the angled loft-windows. After a moment she moved across and nudged my arm so I would lift it and she could duck her head under and lay alongside me, her head resting on my shoulder and the naked warmth of her along my right side. Her hand draped across my chest. She hugged me around the middle then relaxed.

"Don't be hurt," she whispered.

"I'm not." I stroked down her arm, feeling the minute imperfections in her skin. She gave a long sigh and relaxed into me, her breath ruffling the hair on my chest.

"Niall."

"What? What is it?"

"You were snoring."

"Was I? I'm so sorry. I'm just so tired and–"

She lifted herself up and leaned over me, pressing her soft lips to mine. My body stirred in answer, but she drew away.

"Sleep, Niall. You need to rest. We have time."

She kissed my forehead and then untangled herself from my arm and settled down beside me under the quilt. I murmured something that was meant to be "Good night, Blackbird" and sank back into sleep, exhaustion finally claiming me.

Sleep was like a black well holding me inert and for a long while that was all I knew. It was only later that I began to dream.

I was walking down a path, my bare feet brushing through grass stiff with frost. Dark evergreens enclosed my way. As I walked, the path opened out into a circular glade, the sky speckled with stars that didn't sparkle; cold, hard shards of light against the blue-black sky. The clearing was about twenty yards across and at first it was unoccupied. I moved to the centre and turned around, trying to find a familiar constellation and orientate myself. As I turned, I saw the figure at the edge.

She was tall, her hair falling in long waves down over her shoulders and over the bust of her gown. It shadowed her face, leaving only the tip of her nose and the sensual curve of her mouth un-shadowed. She was grey, or maybe that was the starlight, because everything about her, even her face, caught the sallow pallor from the pale light.

"You came," she told me.

Her voice was soft and intimate with a satisfied smugness in its tone. I didn't answer; I wasn't even sure I could speak.

"They told me I had dreamed you, so dream you I have," she smiled.

I looked around for the path where I had entered the clearing but, in the way of dreams, it had gone. I turned back and she was a few steps closer.

"What do you want?" I found my voice.

"They told me I was getting old and that my wits aren't what they used to be, but you're here."

"Where is here? Who are you?"

"Do you not know me, little brother? Are we not of the same flesh, you and I?"

"I don't have a sister." I looked around desperately for an exit, backing away from her. The word "brother" triggered a memory and I looked back at her to find her a step closer.

"The question is, little brother, who are you? Where are you that you have become so lost?"

"I'm not lost."

"Are you not? Then where are you, little brother? Where do I find you?"

"You're a dream," I accused her. "You can't hurt me."

"Why should I hurt you? I just want you to come home." Her voice was quiet, close, gentle.

"I don't want to come with you. I have a home."

"And where's that, lost brother? Who have you been telling our secrets to?"

I didn't answer, just twisted around, finding all behind me a tangle of snag-thorn brambles, eager to catch and tear. When I looked back she was two steps closer.

"I don't have to tell you anything."

"But you have been telling, haven't you, lost brother? Come, little lost one, tell your sister what you've been doing? Tell me where you are."

"I'm not telling you anything. Leave me alone!" I was getting desperate. I could hear my own heartbeat thumping in my chest.

"Do you not have a kiss for your long-lost sister? Am I not welcome in your arms?"

She lifted her arms in welcome, holding them out to me imploringly. At first I thought it was a trick of the shadows, but her hands slowly started to dissolve, floating on an infinitesimal breeze towards me. Her forearms slowly expanded into specks of dust, spreading gently outwards to either side of me, forming a crescent with her at the centre.

She appeared to grow and fade at the same time, becoming translucent, even in that dim light.

I began to hyperventilate as my heart raced to find an escape. A cold welled up though the soles of my feet and leeched up my ankles, a cold that ached and pierced, stilling any feeling but bone-chilling numbness.

"Come," she said, drifting slowly towards me. "Embrace me, brother."

TWENTY

"Rabbit! Wake up! Wake up, damn you!"

Blackbird was shaking me by the shoulders, but it was like trying to climb out of the dark well of dream that had claimed me. I was so cold, my teeth were chattering and my whole body was shaking with it. My breath was coming in short gasps. I couldn't breathe. My eyes were open, but everything was clouded in misty grey.

"You think you've won," I heard her say through gritted teeth, "but I haven't even started."

She threw back the duvet and tore the white sheet back from the bed. Sliding across my legs, she straddled me, hip to hip, skin to skin. She took a deep breath, lifting her right arm high, her fingers stretched wide. Warm light filled her palm, spreading down the veins in her arm like molten gold.

Then she slammed the palm of her hand hard onto my chest.

"He's *mine!*" she shouted to the ceiling.

Heat poured into my chest like opening a furnace door. The tightness binding my ribs relaxed and I pulled a huge breath into my lungs. My body flooded with tidal warmth. I felt the cold shrink and recede until it nestled like a tiny shard of ice in the stone which still hung around my neck.

Her hand slipped under the thong and grasped the stone, giving it a sharp tug, so it came away in her hand. She held it up, above and between us, an expression of regret in her eyes. Her eyes closed, her hand opened and dust fell from it, drifting down onto my bare skin.

At that moment, dawn broke, bathing her in soft pink. Copper curls haloed around her head, catching the first light of day. Her breasts were pale, full and perfect, nipples dark and erect. The curve of her waist only emphasised the swell of her hips. As the light turned slowly golden, she slid her hands down onto my shoulders and leant over me. Her eyes had a corona of emerald around the black of her pupils, giving them a luminous quality. She had an unearthly beauty.

She spoke one word greedily, possessively: "Mine."

She kissed me hungrily and my body responded, wanting her, needing her. She kissed me harder, catching my bottom lip momentarily between her teeth, then moved back down my body, planting kisses in a line from my neck down to my nipples. Heat welled into me. Sensuous warmth radiated out from her kisses as she wriggled slowly backwards until my hardness pressed against her. She moved up and then down and I shivered as I slipped inside her.

Biting her bottom lip, she pushed herself upright, back straight, eyes closed in concentration as she began a rhythmic oscillation. She lifted her arms, slowly from her sides, each motion bringing them a little higher until they were outstretched, palms upward. Her chin lifted and she looked balanced, poised.

Behind her, great wings unfolded, delicate and pale, changing colour like oil on water as they unfurled until they were full and transparent, like dragonfly wings. She opened her eyes and the wings blurred into invisibility. The room whirled into motion, paper tumbling about as the draught caught it from the dresser and the sheet billowed out behind her, rippling in the vibrant air.

She raised herself in one long slow movement, her tongue pink against the dark of her lips, her eyes glowing with green fire in their depths.

"Mine!" she declared, and thrust downwards, pushing me over so I cried out, and my body arched in answer to hers.

I slowly regained myself, breathing into her hair in the dark with her draped over me, nuzzling into my neck. The darkness had returned as if the dawn had reversed itself. I realised that the light I had thought was coming through the blinds had been inside the room. She had summoned the dawn to dispel my dream.

She'd said she was a creature of fire and air and I had believed her, but I hadn't understood what that meant. It didn't tell the half of it. She was elemental, scary and incredibly beautiful. My arms were tight around her waist, my fingers interlocked behind her back and I hugged her to me, pressing her skin to mine.

She mumbled something.

"Huh?" I answered breathlessly.

She turned her head slightly and nibbled my ear and then whispered softly: "Mine."

"Am I still dreaming?" I asked her.

There was a huffing sound against my throat, that I interpreted as more laughter.

In answer she nibbled down my neck and then slowly, taking her time and with infinite care, she proved to me she was real.

I woke bathed in true sunlight in a snapshot from Kareesh's vision. The sheet was strewn across the floor, striped by yellow bars of light and the quilt was mounded in a heap at the bottom of the bed. The angle of the sunlight told me it was late morning and I sat up in bed, stretching to ease muscles that I hadn't used in too long.

I rose and went into the bathroom to splash my face with cold water. The shock of it woke me further, but still left me with a dream-like quality I couldn't shake. I looked up in the mirror, seeing a face that looked almost familiar. I had changed. In some indefinable way my glamour had altered, something was different.

My eye caught sight of the reflection of my shoulder, showing a semi-circle of teeth marks. I traced it with my finger. "Mine," she'd said. She had marked me as her territory.

I thought about that in the shower. I wasn't sure I was ready to be possessed in that way, but she had pre-empted that and claimed me for her own. If I didn't like it then why couldn't I stop smiling? That troubled me in a way I couldn't articulate all the way through dressing. I thought about it as I put the room into a semblance of order and then made my way down through the house.

She was in the lounge bar where we had been the night before, wearing a white silk shirt, which she tied at her waist, along with a long full dark green skirt. She was sitting at the table holding a mug of coffee over a plate of sausage, bacon and egg.

She put the coffee down carefully on the saucer. "Good morning, sleepy head."

Just the warmth of her voice brought back echoes of last night, inducing a low tightness in me. I sat down opposite her, covering my reaction, disconcerted by the influence a few innocuous words could have on me. She grinned as if she knew exactly what she was doing.

I noticed little changes in her too, or was it simply that I was seeing things differently? Her hair had a copper highlight I hadn't noticed before and her lips were stained as if she'd been eating raspberries. She looked up from her bacon and caught me staring.

"Did you sleep well?" she enquired politely, as if we had somehow slept separately and she was unaware of my nocturnal state.

"Like a baby," I admitted. I felt rested, restored.

"Excellent." She put a piece of bacon into her mouth and chewed thoughtfully.

"You?" I enquired in the same polite tone.

She swallowed. "Me? I was restless, up and down all night." Her eyes were wide with innocence.

"I'm sorry to hear that."

"Don't be. I slept till late."

"You're eating well," I commented on the full breakfast she was half-way though consuming.

"Restlessness makes me hungry."

The landlord appeared, whistling merrily and carrying a plate of toast for Blackbird. "Good morning. Can I get you some breakfast?"

"I'll have the same, please." I indicated Blackbird's plate.

"No problem. It'll be five minutes." He walked back to the kitchen, whistling the tune "She Moved Through the Fair".

"He's cheerful," I commented to Blackbird.

"Overspill." She grinned over a sip of her coffee.

"Overspill?"

"Our room is above theirs. I think they woke up in middle of the night and neither of them felt like going back to sleep." She grinned mischievously.

I coloured at what she implied. "You mean–"

"It's like when we were walking around the backs of Covent Garden. Some of my magic spilled over onto you, concealing us both. It's the same here, only it's stronger when there are two."

"Oh."

"Don't be embarrassed. It's a nice thing."

I remained slightly pink at the impact we had had on our hosts, watching her eat breakfast.

"You look different," I commented. "Nice. Fresh."

"Hmm. It's amazing what rampant sex does for a girl." She grinned impishly while I looked over my shoulder to see if we were overheard.

"No, I just meant you look..."

321

"Contented?" she suggested. "Satiated?" She speared a sausage with her fork and bit the end off, making me wince.

"No, I meant that you looked happy."

"I am happy. It's good for a girl to get what she wants, once in a while. You're mine, now."

Her use of the possessive pronoun echoed her words from the night before, disturbing me slightly.

"You don't own me, Blackbird." The words came out sharper than I intended and her brow creased into a frown. "Sorry, I didn't mean that to sound as harsh as it did, but you can't own people. They belong to themselves."

She shrugged off the apology. "I should have explained it before, but there was never a good moment." She dipped a piece of bacon into the yolk of her egg and popped it into her mouth.

"Explained what?"

"You haven't lived long among the Feyre, so you don't know, but they're different."

"In what way? I mean, I know they're different, but in what respect?"

"Their customs and practices are different. These days when humans choose a mate they sort of come to a mutual agreement about it between themselves, after a lot of dating and negotiating and promises and things. It's so muddled. No wonder so many relationships fail." She talked about it like it was an academic exercise, something she'd heard about, observed even, but never participated in. "The Feyre, on the other hand, are much more straight-forward and uncomplicated. The males make themselves available and the females choose who they like. It's easy. I chose you, and you're mine." She was very matter of fact about it.

"I'm only half-Fey," I pointed out, pouring myself the remaining half cup of coffee from the jug. "And so are you."

"In this respect, that's the half that matters," she explained reasonably.

"What if I don't want to be chosen?" I was getting upset, but she remained calm.

"I told you, the males don't get any say in the matter. It's a female prerogative and that's the end of it."

I folded my arms, feeling defensive.

"You were OK about it last night," she commented.

"That was different."

"That's what I mean about humans complicating everything. It's not different to me. It's the same." There was a spark of anger in her tone now.

"That's not what I meant."

"Look, Niall. You're getting all worked up about nothing. You're only complaining because you're not the one doing the choosing. Tell me one thing, are my attentions unwanted?"

"Well, no," I admitted.

"Did I force you into something you don't want? I mean, I could understand that the first time I might have caught you off-guard, but the second, the third?" She raised a sceptical eyebrow.

Whistling announced the return of the landlord with my breakfast, saving me from answering. I was still blushing when he placed the plate in front of me and asked me whether I would like any toast. If he noticed, he didn't say anything. I refused politely but asked him if we might have more coffee. He took our empty coffee jug and went off to make some fresh.

"I don't know why you're getting so upset. Fey males can wait a long time before they're chosen as a mate. You should be flattered, it's a great compliment to be chosen so young."

"I'm not young."

"You don't even have your first half-century. By Feyre standards that makes you a stripling."

"I don't judge myself by Feyre standards, and by my own standards I am a middle-aged man and used to making my own decisions."

The smell of grilled bacon was making my mouth

water and my stomach grumble, so I started on the plate in front of me.

"You haven't noticed then?"

"Noticed what?"

"How much younger you're looking?"

"Am I?" I looked around for a mirror, then stood up and went to the bar, staring at my reflection in the glass behind the bottles. She was right. That was what had been nudging at my subconscious in the bathroom, earlier. It still looked like the face I had adopted, but I had lost about five years, overnight.

I walked slowly back to our table, glancing back to make sure it wasn't an illusion. "What's happening?" I asked her.

"It's hard to tell. Your body could be changing because of the magic I awoke within you. On the other hand, you could just be adjusting your glamour to suit your mood. Are we feeling particularly pleased with ourselves this morning, by any chance?" she probed.

I grinned, shaking my head. She was impossible. As much as I tried to be offended that she had unilaterally determined the direction of our relationship, I couldn't stay angry with her. She was moody, fickle, scary, soft, warm.

I pulled myself back to reality and tried to focus on the food. But when I glanced upwards she was watching me, waiting for me to try and deny the truth.

"What am I going to do with you?" I shook my head again.

She picked up her coffee cup and looked at me through the vapour. "The same thing as last night, I sincerely hope."

I mistimed my swallow and the piece of sausage I was chewing went down the wrong way, leaving me coughing and spluttering. The landlord helpfully appeared and patted me on the back while she sat and chuckled at me from the other side of the table.

"Sorry," I apologised to him.

"Are you all right now?"

I nodded and he replaced the chrome flask of coffee. "Is there anything else I can get you before I go and do the cellars?"

"No, thanks. We're fine, really."

"There's no rush, take your time," he reassured me and then went about his tasks.

I took a slurp of coffee to help the food go down.

"Are we?" she asked me.

"Are we what?"

"Fine?" She put her elbows on the table and rested her chin on her knuckles, waiting for an answer.

I put down my knife and fork for a moment. I was willing to let the issue go and see how it went, but she wanted an answer.

"You'd better tell me what the position of concubine to Blackbird of the Fey'ree involves."

"Very well. It's not marriage, if that's what you're thinking; the Feyre don't marry."

I nodded.

"Well, you get to stay with me and bring me presents every day, pamper me and bring me my meals, and every second Thursday you take me to my bed and then you– " She was grinning at me now.

"Enough, enough. I'm serious."

"There are no proscribed tasks, Niall. It's not supposed to be a duty." She looked thoughtful for a moment, as if she thought perhaps she could introduce some. "You have to understand that the Feyre have been having problems with fertility for centuries. During that time the practice has evolved of letting the females choose the males they believe are most likely to get them with child."

"You're not!"

"I might be." She watched an expression of mild panic cross my face. "That's what it's for, Niall, don't be so naive."

"But I already have a daughter, and I am definitely not ready to start another family. What about–"

"Niall, calm down. It's very unlikely I'd be pregnant this soon."

My thoughts tried to go in fifteen directions at once.

"Just stop it. You just have to treat it as one of those things. If it happens, it happens. Fortune will decide." She was philosophical about it.

"But I'm not ready. I mean, I've only known you for a couple of days and I didn't realise what the consequences might be."

"Niall, you know where babies come from. You have one child already."

"No, of course I know where they come from, it's just that I hadn't thought it through. I just assumed—"

"You assumed I would take precautions to prevent a child."

"Well, yes. This is the modern world, after all."

She leant forwards, her face full of something raw. "Why would I do that, Niall? Why would I prevent something as wonderful as a new life?"

I suddenly understood what I had said and how much I was hurting her. It was not the same for the Feyre, or even the half-Feyre. She was over three hundred years old and it had never crossed my mind that in all that time she'd never had a child, but I could see in her face it was true. I was a father before I was thirty and it had all happened so naturally that I took it for granted, never giving it a second thought.

"I'm sorry, Blackbird. You took me by surprise. I was thinking of how I would manage to provide for such a child; who would look after it, care for it."

"I would care for it." She lifted her chin and dared me to contradict her. In that moment I knew that if anyone tried to harm a child of hers she would tear them limb from limb without a second thought, and I was in no doubt she was capable.

Since the break-up of my marriage I had drifted into occasional relationships, but they always ended bitterly when my erstwhile partner wanted more from me than

I was prepared to give. The ties of my daughter and my ex-wife were just too strong, too tangled, to set me free. Blackbird hadn't asked me for more, but she'd taken what she needed and she was prepared to fight to keep it.

"I'm sorry," I said. "I wasn't thinking."

"I'm not offended," she said.

"It's just that you took me by surprise."

She grinned at me again.

"Not like that." She showed no sign of repentance. "I mean, you surprised me by saying that you might be pregnant."

"If I am, then I am. If not, well then there's nothing to discuss, is there?" She looked defiant again.

I met her gaze and there was a challenge there, a challenge to say more, to be more to her. I knew the words, but they wouldn't come. I looked away. She let me fiddle with my breakfast until I gave in and set my cutlery down.

"Have faith, Niall, and all will be well."

I deliberately took her comment in the wider sense. "I can't help feeling it won't be that easy. In the dream, Raffmir's sister was looking for me"

She allowed the change of subject. "What do you remember?"

"It seemed more real then. There was a clearing in a forest of evergreens. It was unnaturally cold, frost on the ground with a crystal sky. She was waiting for me in the clearing, ringed around with thorns. She said something. What was it?" I cupped my face in my hands, trying to recall her words. "She called me Little Brother. That was it. 'They told me I had dreamed you.' That's what she said."

"Did she say any more?"

"She kept asking me where I was, who I was with, who I was talking to."

"Did you tell her?"

"No. I don't think so. She started fading, dissolving. I thought she was vanishing, but she didn't. She drifted in towards me and I was so cold."

"She was feeding off your life-energy."

"She can do that?"

"The older ones can. They can feed off the dreams of unguarded sleepers. That's how they survive."

"Can she do it again?"

"Maybe. It's harder for her now you have a connection with me. That's the other reason to be mine. If you're mine then no other can have you, and you don't want to be hers."

The memory of the dream soured my stomach and killed my appetite and I put the knife and fork down, unable to finish the plateful.

"Are you going to eat that sausage?"

"No, I've had enough."

She swiped it from my plate and devoured it.

"After all, I could be eating for two. Kidding, kidding." She laughed at my distraught expression, but underneath her laughter was an edge of mischief that said it really, truly might be true.

"Will you know if you are pregnant?" I asked her, brushing her teasing aside.

"After a while, of course. But I don't expect it will happen straight away, so you're quite safe really, though perhaps…"

"What?"

"You remember the stone Megan gave you?"

"Yes? What happened to it?"

"I think she thought we were together then, when you first met her. It's curious really. Do you remember it warmed when I touched you?"

"It did until last night, when it went cold."

"It responds to fertility. It was telling you there was the potential for life, that we are compatible."

"What do you mean, compatible."

"Fey fertility is complicated. Not all the Feyre are compatible with each other and only some combinations produce children. Not always the ones you expect, either."

"So what happened to the stone? Does that mean you're…"

"Quite the opposite. I had to get you back from her. Once she'd got her hooks into you I'd never get you free. I made a sacrifice. The stone helped to focus it."

"What kind of sacrifice?"

"The potential for one life in return for another," she stated, challenging me to criticise her decision.

"You gave her a life? You sacrificed an unborn child?"

"All sex is life, Niall. I gave her the potential for new life to distract her from you long enough get you free. Otherwise you'd still be lying up there, shivering and dying."

"At what price?" I asked her. I was grateful that she'd freed me from that dark glade, but the price was unthinkable.

"It wasn't a life, only the raw potential for one. I wouldn't give her a new life, even if it meant losing yours."

I wasn't sure whether I was reassured by that or not. What had we sacrificed? What price had we paid? Did she know? I didn't know what to say. I was torn between gratitude for getting me away from that chilling embrace and the shock and revulsion at how it had been achieved.

"Why did it have to be that? Isn't there another way?"

"A life for a life, Niall; nothing else is strong enough. The only way was to tempt her away with something stronger, something sweeter, and I was betting she hadn't been laid in a long, long time. It looks like I was right."

"So it wasn't a child? We hadn't, you know, conceived."

"I told you. It's very unlikely I would be pregnant this soon, no matter what happened. If it was that easy for us to have children, there would be a lot more of us."

"And you're not pregnant then. Not if the sacrifice worked."

"I only gave her the first time, Niall, to get you back. The second and third times were for me, and for us. I didn't want it to be for her alone. I want you for me. I want our child."

There was a raw need there, coupled with a desire that scared me a little, while at the same time making my trousers too tight. It was flattering to be wanted that much, but her determination made me wonder whether it was me she wanted, or the child I could give her.

Her words rang true, though, and I knew she meant them. Setting aside her desire for a child, she wanted me and was prepared to fight to keep me. And I wanted her. She was unlike any women I had ever met, and not just because she was part Fey. Her wry humour, her resourcefulness, her warmth, all had me thinking about words I hadn't used in a long time, words that had been poisoned for me by the break-down of my marriage.

"I want you too," I said, which was less than I could have said, but the unspoken words were still too hard, too loaded with other feelings, to let free.

Hesitantly, she smiled, perhaps understanding.

"I could do with a shower before we leave," she suggested as she licked the grease from her fingertips. "I didn't want to wake you, before. And then we have an appointment to keep."

We went back up to the room together. I put our things ready on the bed while she showered and was sat waiting to go, but then she emerged clean, naked and smelling delicious and it was another three-quarters of an hour before we were both dressed again.

She waited at the door to the stairs while I collected the bag and then kissed me warmly at the door.

"Mine," she repeated.

"I wish you'd stop saying that," I told her.

"'Tis truth."

She skipped lightly down, leaving me to negotiate the narrow stairway. When I reached the lounge bar she was waiting for me and talking to the landlord while he set up the pub for lunchtime opening.

"I hope you've enjoyed your stay. As I say, we don't normally do guests."

"Very much," Blackbird assured him. "It's a fine place you run here. I would recommend it."

I settled our account with some of my remaining cash, thanking him for his hospitality. Then we stepped out into the breezy sunshine to walk back down the lane.

As we came to the edge of the village, there was a payphone next to a children's playing field that I hadn't noticed in the dark. I asked Blackbird for a moment of privacy and she nodded and left me to make my call, taking herself to the middle of the field and lying on the mown grass, looking up at the clouds.

I fed coins into the machine and then dialled Katherine's mobile number. The number rang for four or five times and then picked up.

"Hello?" It was Katherine's voice.

"Hi Kath, it's Niall."

"Yes?"

"Are you both OK?"

"Who is this?"

"I told you, it's Niall."

The phone went dead and returned to the dialling tone. I kicked myself for not remembering our code-phrase and re-dialled.

"Hello?" Katherine answered more cautiously

"Katherine, how is the dog?"

"Niall, it is you. Why didn't you say?"

"I'm sorry, I forgot. You did the right thing, though, to put the phone down."

"We're being very cautious. We had a strange call yesterday and I've been screening them ever since."

"What do you mean, strange?"

"It was on Alex's mobile. She had it with her even though it wasn't enabled for international. She knew she wouldn't be able to call anyone, but she was hoping to be able to text her friends."

"Who called her?"

"We don't know. It was this strange hollow voice. Alex answered it and spoke to them. She said they told her they had news of a gift she was going to receive and they wanted to bring it to her. She told them she was away on holiday, but they insisted they would bring it to her wherever she was. Niall? Are you there?"

"Yes. I'm here." If they had found a way to reach Alex then things were worse than I thought. "Did she tell them where you were?"

"No. She thought it was one of those competitions that are always ringing up trying to make you call expensive numbers. She just told them she didn't want anything and hung up."

"Thank goodness for that. Did they ring back?"

"Not so far. She's had it switched off, though, as she can't text her friends and it was just wasting the battery."

"Don't let her switch it back on. In fact, take it off her."

"I can't do that, Niall. It's her phone. She saved up for it."

"Well, tell her not to turn it on until I tell her it's safe. Make her promise."

"I can tell her, but you know what she's like. She can't be out of touch for five minutes without getting withdrawal symptoms."

"Tell her it's important. No. Better still, I'll tell her. Put her on, would you?"

"I will, in a moment. She wants to speak to you anyway. Are you all right?"

I was touched by the concern in her voice. "I'm fine. Did you get away OK? No problems?"

"What's happening, Niall? What's going on?"

"It's complicated, but we're sorting it out. I think it will be OK. Just bear with me."

"Niall, this better not be some sort of joke."

"It isn't, really. You're somewhere out of the country, yes?"

"Yes. We need to be back for Monday morning, though."

"Not unless I call you first, to let you know it's safe, OK?"

"I have to get her back for school, Niall. We can't stay here."

"No. You stay where you are until I let you know it's clear. I don't care about school or anything else. Just trust me, OK?" There was silence on the other end of the line. "Katherine?"

"OK, but you'll call me as soon as you can. You won't just leave me hanging here?"

"As soon as it's clear. I promise."

"Don't do anything stupid."

Normally that admonition would have sparked a harsh come-back, but I could hear the worry in her voice. "I won't. Take care of yourselves."

"We will. I'll put her on now."

There was some background noise as the phone was passed across.

"Dad?"

"I'm here."

"Dad, are you all right?"

"Yes, I'm OK. I'm fine."

"Mum said you were in some sort of trouble."

"It's nothing I can't handle, I just don't want you and your mum dragged into it, that's all."

"She said someone was trying to hurt you."

"They tried, babe, but I'm ahead of them. Listen to me, now. I want you to keep your phone switched off while you're there, OK? It doesn't work abroad, anyway."

"But it's working. It rang."

"That's why you have to switch it off, sweetheart."

"But, Dad?"

"Alex, please. This is important. I don't want anyone to know where you've gone until I've sorted things out and they might use the phone to find you, understand? You have to do this for me."

"OK, I'll switch it off."

"Give the battery to your mum for safe keeping and then it won't switch on by mistake, OK."

"It won't. It doesn't do that."

"If you give the battery to your mum, I'll buy you some credits for it when you get home. How about that?" Bribery would usually succeed where parental authority failed.

"Well, OK, I suppose."

"Thanks, babe."

"Dad, when can we come home?"

"Soon. I'll call you."

"What do we do if you don't call?"

"Your mum will know what to do, sweetheart. I'll call you. Until then, I want you to stick with your mum. She'll look after you."

"It's not me I'm worried about." She suddenly sounded like her mother.

"It'll be OK. I promise. Go and give your mum a hug and I'll call you in a day or so when this is all sorted out, all right?"

"OK."

"You take care now."

"No. You take care."

"I will."

"Bye."

I waited to see if Katherine would come back onto the line, but it beeped at me and dropped the call, leaving me looking at the phone and wishing I had some way to explain.

I put the handset back on the cradle and the phone disgorged leftover coins into the change tray with a chunking sound. I collected them and pushed out of the phone box, walking over to where Blackbird lay looking at the clouds. I sat down beside her.

"Are they safe?"

"Yes, but they had a phone call like Claire's on Alex's phone. How did they know the number?"

"Maybe they called directory enquiries?"

"I made sure it's not listed. They're not supposed to give out the number."

She rolled over so that she could lean on her elbow and look at me. "Where are they?"

"I don't know, away somewhere."

"That's probably best," she remarked. "They should be safe once the ceremony is performed with the proper knives again. It will reinforce the barrier and stop them crossing so easily."

"Will we ever be safe again?" I asked her.

She shook her head. "Never. Better get used to it."

It struck me how different she was from Katherine, how much more independent. But then Katherine was looking after our daughter, which rather put a dampener on the independence thing.

Something had changed, though. Usually when I spoke with Katherine there was a bitterness from things unsaid or things that should never have been said that our separation hadn't salved. Like an open wound, it festered between us and leaked poison into my relationship with my daughter. But this morning had been different. I found myself worrying about Katherine and Alex, their safety and welfare still forward in my thoughts, but I wasn't left with the feeling that I had failed to meet even the basic standards of fatherhood. I didn't feel bitter about what she'd said, or not said. I was just worried, scared even.

I realised I loved them both. I loved Alex, of course, she was my daughter and the centre of my world, but it was a shock to realise I still loved Katherine. I had thought all of that had been burned up in the conflagration that was our divorce. Instead I found I still cared for her and it still mattered to me that she was safe, and if possible, happy. It was like putting down a burden I hadn't realised I been carrying. Perhaps I had finally begun to heal.

I had been daydreaming and came back to myself looking down into dark green eyes full of sky. She was watching me.

"You were miles away," she said.

"I was thinking."

"What about?"

"About how a woman I've known for a little over forty-eight hours could turn my life upside down and hand it back to me."

She shoved me playfully in the chest and, unbalanced, I rolled backwards. She scrabbled to her feet and leapt on top of me landing on my stomach. Catching hold of my wrists she pinned them to the grass with unexpected strength and then pressed her lips to mine until I stopped struggling and started cooperating.

She rubbed the end of her nose against mine. Shadowed by her hair, I looked up into her eyes seeing the green spark in them rekindled.

"You're insatiable," I told her.

"Impossible," she agreed, nodding slowly and brushing my nose with hers. That look of proprietary possessiveness came back into her eyes.

"Don't say it," I told her.

She leapt to her feet and grabbed her bag in one fluid movement and was walking off across the field while I was still getting to my feet.

"You'd better get used to it," she called over her shoulder.

I trailed after her, shaking my head and wondering what on earth I had got myself into.

The lane to the farm was bright with sunshine and filled with wildlife. A fox trotted casually across our path and we saw clouds of starlings circling overhead until they wheeled away. Kestrels hovered overhead searching for tiny prey in the grass, ignored by the sheep grazing in the fields beyond the wire fences. Blackbird curled her hand in mine and I was able to pretend for a while that we were simply walking.

As we approached the farm, though, the mood became more sober. The air downwind of the farm was tainted by the smell of charcoal and the hint of iron on the air had my breath catching in the back of my throat and so I avoided breathing in the smoke that was turned, twisted and swept away by the fickle breeze.

The dogs announced our arrival with a frenzy of barking; the smaller bitch would come nowhere near us but barked from the safety of the kitchen door. Jeff Highsmith came down to the gates for us, looking tired and smudged with charcoal and soot from his labours.

"It's almost done," he told us. "Dad's just finishing grinding off the edge."

He took us across the courtyard and into the kitchen, where his wife was waiting and then left us with her to go and see how the work progressed. Meg Highsmith greeted us formally but politely in a way that made me wonder what her husband had said to her. She offered us lunch but we declined on the basis that we had so recently had breakfast.

"A cup of coffee would be most welcome, though," Blackbird suggested.

Blackbird and I sat at the kitchen table as she busied herself around the kitchen preparing lunch for her family and coffee for us.

After a few minutes Jeff, his father, and his daughter filed in.

"There," he said. "Done." He placed the newly finished knife in the centre of the table with a flourish.

Blackbird and I looked at each other. The knife sat there, inert, innocuous, unremarkable.

"Something's wrong," we said in unison.

TWENTY-ONE

We sat around the table in the kitchen, Ben, Jeff, Lisa and James opposite Blackbird and I, while Meg fussed around us.

"I still don't see the difference," Ben Highsmith repeated, scratching his head.

"Believe me," I told him, "We would not be sitting here talking like this if it was remotely like the Quick Knife."

"But we made it the same," he protested.

"And it's definitely iron," Blackbird said. "But not like the Quick Knife. Rabbit is right; we would be able to tell straight away if it was the same. We would know as soon as you brought it anywhere near us, either of us."

Our hopes of restoring the knife to this year's ceremony and reinforcing the barrier against the Seventh Court were melting away.

"Do you know anyone else, anyone you could recommend?" I hated to ask, but it was all I could think of.

Ben Highsmith blustered, but it was his son who answered.

"There's no one else does the kind of work you need. That's why we've kept the skills alive all these generations. And there's none alive that's better with iron than

Dad. Dad, sit down, he's only asking what you'd ask in his place."

Ben had stood up ready to defend his honour, but then sighed and slumped back into his seat, resting his chin in his hands. "I s'pose," he admitted.

"Are you sure there's no way of mending the old one? I mean, it's potent enough, it's just not in one piece," Blackbird asked him.

Ben answered. "No, No. It won't take a weld and it can't be braised. Melting down the metal will return it to solid iron, but not in the way you want. Broken is broken with cold iron."

We lapsed into silence again.

"Can I see the broken one?" Lisa asked.

She hadn't said a word until now, sitting close to her grandfather as if she dwelt in his shadow. He was as startled as we were that she'd spoken.

"Fetch it out for her, will you?" he asked me.

Blackbird unzipped her bag and extracted the box with the knives in it, sliding it across the table towards them. "If you don't mind, Rabbit and I will go and stand in the yard while you look at it."

They waited while we stood and trooped outside into the yard. Even then, the prickling sensation down my spine, the ache in my bones, told me the moment the box was opened.

"What are we going to do now?" I asked Blackbird.

"I don't know what we can do. Get them to make another? Is there any reason it would be better than the one they've already made? Maybe they've lost the art, in which case we can only ask them to experiment and try and regain it. Whatever happens it will be too late for this year, maybe too late for all of us. If the barrier collapses..." She let the words trail away and kicked a stone across the yard. It bounced unevenly across the concrete.

I felt the dull ache subside and knew they had finished examining the knife before Ben Highsmith emerged, his granddaughter trailing behind him, her father following her out to stand watch behind them.

"This Quick Knife is useless, right?" He questioned Blackbird, brandishing the box.

"The broken knife can't be used for the ceremony," she confirmed, "unless it can be repaired well enough to cut a hazel rod?"

"Nah, but Lisa spotted something neither Jeff nor I had seen. I'd show you but…"

"We'll take your word for it," I told him.

"The blade of the knife has been hammered after it cooled. You can see it if you hold it up to the light. Jeff and I didn't believe her at first. We didn't even look for hammer marks, but sharp-eyes here spotted it." He smiled down at her and ruffled her hair affectionately. She grinned up at him, basking in his praise.

"So why don't you hammer the new one?"

"It looks like the original has been hammered cold and we know that if you hammer cold iron, it shatters. The metal's too brittle to take it. That's why we weren't looking for hammer marks."

"Then how could it have been hammered in the first place?"

"That's what Lisa wants me to try. She wants to see if the old knife can be hammered. If it can, then that might explain the difference between the knives. Or it could just shatter."

I looked at Blackbird. She nodded. "Do it," she told him.

We followed them to the back of the farm being careful to avoid the plume of smoke being whipped off the top of the chimney by the stiffening breeze. The forge was there, the bed of coals still burning from their night's work.

"Unlike copper, iron isn't usually hammered cold," Ben told us. "The knife we made for you was heated in the forge until the iron became ductile and then it was hammered into shape. Keeping it hot and hammering it drives out the impurities so you end up with something you can work with. That's wrought iron."

He went through the low arch into the forge. Neither Blackbird nor I made any move to follow him. He raised his voice and moved about in the dimness within, donning a leather apron and collecting things together while he continued explaining, raising his voice to be heard through the open doorway of the forge.

"Cold iron is harder to make," he called out to us. "A very particular ore is put though an ancient process to produce a lump of coarse iron called a bloom. The bloom is reheated and then hammered to drive out the impurities. It has to be cooled slowly enough to allow the crystals to form, but hammered enough to drive out the impurities. Hammer it too much and it'll shatter, too little and the impurities will make it brittle and it won't take the shape. Cool it too fast and it'll develop fracture lines, too slow and it'll be soft and never take an edge. It's all in the making."

He picked a hammer from a rack and hefted it, standing in the shade of the doorway. "You'd better stand back in case it shatters," he told us, picking a safety visor from a hook.

Jeff pulled his daughter away behind him, standing at an angle to the doorway. Blackbird and I moved well back behind a stone wall, well aware of what flying fragments of cold iron would do to either of us. From our position we couldn't see into the forge, but we knew when he took the broken blade of the Quick Knife from the box.

There was a long pause and then a characteristic sound

'Tink… tink… tink… tink… Thonk!'

Then a pause.

'Tink… tink… tink… tink… Thonk!'

Every time he hit the knife it made a jarring note that accented the wrongness in the metal. It was like scraping fingers down a blackboard, but a hundred times worse. By the time he was ready to stop I had a thumping headache and Blackbird looked no happier.

Jeff and his daughter crowded back into the forge to view the results. Blackbird and I had no wish to get closer to the knife or the forge, so we stayed outside. The headache had intensified and I was seeing vague images, like brief mirages, in the periphery of my vision.

I felt Blackbird's hand on my arm. "Are you well?"

I nodded, sending needles of pain through my forehead making me grimace.

"It's done now. They've finished," she reassured me.

There was an animated discussion going on between Jeff and the old man. They were arguing technicalities and sparking off each other. The argument died as quickly as it started. They put the knife back into its box and brought it back to us.

"It's still whole," Ben told us, "though the metal has started to crack. If I had continued it would have broken again."

"So is that a yes or a no?" Blackbird asked him.

"I think the lass has the right of it: it was hammered cold. Remember though, simply dropping it onto a hard floor was enough to break it in the first place."

"That was a fault in the metal," Jeff interrupted.

"Regardless, if we cold-hammered the new knife then it would crack and break."

"Not if we had the right tools," Jeff interrupted again.

"Jeff, we've been over this. The anvil would need to be enormous and specifically made for the job and the hammer would have to be tuned to the metal. Even then..." His frustration at his son evaporated as he watched the expressions on our faces change. "What?" he said.

"This anvil? How enormous would it need to be?" Blackbird asked him.

"Big. Bigger than anything we've got."

"About this long, so high?" She hopped around, miming the distances, unable to spread her arms wide enough to encompass it.

He looked askance at her theatrics, but nodded.

"We saw it," I told him. "It's in London, hidden." I described the anvil sitting on the island amid the dark water of the underground river.

"It sounds right, but without a hammer that's tuned to it, it only solves half the problem."

There was a pause while we thought it through.

"You wouldn't want to separate the hammer from the anvil, would you?" Blackbird suggested.

"No," I agreed, "But you wouldn't leave it lying around either, not where someone could appropriate it for some other purpose. It might get lost."

"Or stolen," she added. "You'd lock it away."

"Somewhere close by," I agreed.

"Somewhere safe."

"But we can't open it. It's sealed, remember?"

"Would the two of you mind telling me what on earth you're talking about?" the old man interrupted.

We described the square iron door in the wall, neither of us mentioning the two visitors that had come to inspect it while we had been there.

"But it's locked and we don't know how to unlock it," I told him.

"And you reckon there's a hammer in this lock-box?"

"Where else would you put it? It has to be there."

He scratched at his unshaven chin. "You might be able to break into it, but it sounds like you'd need heavy cutting equipment. Any idea how thick the door is?"

We both shook our heads. "The door is flush to the wall and not easy to get at. It's set in the wall above head-height over a thin ledge where it would be almost impossible to set a ladder, let alone apply any leverage once you had climbed it."

It was his turn to shake his head. "Even if there is a hammer in there, it doesn't sound like you'll be able to get at it without unlocking it."

"There must be a key." Frustration rang in Blackbird's tone.

"Are you sure the key's not with the anvil?" Jeff suggested.

"No, there's nowhere to leave it where it would be safe. Besides, why leave the key with the safe? There'd be no point in locking it if the key is with it. Are you certain you don't have a key here, handed down through generations, a family heirloom perhaps?"

"We can look," Jeff volunteered.

We followed Jeff back into the kitchen and he started pulling out drawers looking for keys.

"Jeff, I'm trying to put lunch together. Do you mind?" Meg Highsmith protested as Jeff started turning drawers out onto the kitchen table.

"It's urgent," was all he said and continued pulling things out.

Ben went into the room with the dogs, amid much snuffling and a low growl from the big dog at us. Ben emerged with a wooden box filled with bits of rusty broken tools, orphaned cutlery and old keys. He spilled the lot out onto the table. Meg folded her arms and sighed as they began sorting through the oddments.

"If you tell me what you're looking for I might be able to help," she offered.

They carried on sorting, but explained the dilemma of the missing key. There was a growing pile of old keys in the centre of the table, but none looked likely.

"It has to be quite large," I told her, picking up an ornate brass key. "The keyhole is square and about a quarter of an inch on each side. The thing is, it didn't look as if the lock turned."

"No, it didn't did it?" agreed Blackbird. "How do you turn a square key in a square hole?"

"Maybe it's a round key that goes in a square hole?" remarked Jeff.

"Maybe, but then where do the 'key' bits go; the bits that trip the levers?"

James Highsmith had watched all this from the far end of the kitchen table, but now he stood up and

344

started talking in low tones to his mother.

"I don't know, James. Ask them," she told him.

He turned to us, glancing at his father. "There's this PlayStation game…" he started.

"James, not now!" The disappointment in Jeff's voice at the change of subject to his son's passion was palpable.

"Jeff. Hear him out." Meg Highsmith stood behind her son. This was clearly a point of friction between the man and the teenager and it looked like Meg had had to stand between them more than once.

James hesitated, but at a nudge from his mother he started speaking again.

"In the game you collect an ornate dagger, early on in the game. I thought it must be a magic one; you know, effective against certain types of monster? But after a while, you stop using it because it's useless. It's much more effective to use the bigger weapons."

Jeff sighed, but subsided at a look from Meg.

"Then, when you get into the later levels there are people that try and buy it off you, or steal it, or trade it for something. It got so I kept it just because everyone wanted it. Anyway, you get to the big castle at the end and the drawbridge is up, the gates are locked, but you need to get inside to fight the big boss."

He paused, but found only blank faces. I don't think any of us had ever played on a PlayStation.

"The thing is, there's a little gate which you can get to by climbing around, but when you get there it's locked. The keyhole is a funny shape, like a thin diamond. The only way of opening the gate is to put the dagger into the keyhole. Then you're in."

"And?" said his father.

"I think what James is telling us is that while we are all looking for something shaped like a key, that may not be what we need," said Blackbird.

"You said the keyhole didn't turn," James pointed out. "Maybe it doesn't need to, if you have the proper-shaped thing to put into it?"

"So we're looking for something that could push into a square hole about so big." Blackbird held her thumb and forefinger apart to show them the size.

Everyone looked blank.

"That makes it worse," I said. "We were looking for a needle in a haystack. Now we don't even know if it's a needle." James looked crestfallen so I added, "But James may be right. A literal key may not be what we're searching for." That brought back a hesitant smile.

Jeff and his father started putting things back into the drawers and boxes they had come from, much to the relief of Meg. They cleared away the mess and James wiped the table and began laying out cutlery for lunch.

James looked at his mother and she turned to us. "Will you stay for some lunch after all?" she offered.

It was rather unfair to change our minds two minutes before it was served, so we made excuses and said we would go and sit in the sunshine while they had their meal. We walked around the back of the farm, past where the forge still smoked, and sat upwind on a low wall looking out across the fields.

"It could be anywhere," I said to her.

"Actually, I don't think it could."

She glanced sideways at me.

"I think the hammer was locked away to prevent the Seventh Court from hiding or damaging it, but there would be no point in keeping it safe if you couldn't get to it when it was needed, and no one knew when that might happen. If you think about it, everything has been left in place if you knew where to look."

"What about the anvil? That was pretty well hidden."

"But you knew where it was because of the vision. And I knew where to find you because Kareesh sent me her message."

"So you still think Kareesh is behind all this."

"Yes. She is the link that ties it all together. I still don't know why she didn't just tell us what to do, but I'm sure she has her reasons."

"Well, there's nothing in the vision to tell us where the key might be. There's nothing small enough to fit. And I've found all the pieces now, even if they're not quite right in my head. I know where to find the silhouette of the cat. We've found the anvil in the hall of water and we've been to Australia House. The vaulted roof is the crypt of the church where the Way started and the green twig is the mistletoe on Meg Highsmith's kitchen wall. The whirling leaves were on the way where we stopped in the copse, and the closing door was in the tunnels under Covent Garden. The only missing piece was the wrecked bedroom, striped in sunlight, and I woke to that this morning."

She shuffled along the wall slightly so she was next to me and she could slip her arm through mine. "It was a bit wrecked, wasn't it?" she reminded me.

"Yes, it was." I clasped her hand into mine and we watched the changing light over the fields as the clouds rolled across the sky, comfortable in silence.

My mind drifted with the clouds, sifting through the memories of the last few days. It amazed me how quickly I had adjusted to all of the changes in my life, but with Blackbird leaning against my side I had the inescapable feeling that it would be OK. We would find a way.

"If you are right," I said to her, "then Kareesh has given us all that we need. We have the anvil and the knives. We think we know where the hammer is. We have a smith who can work the metal and enough time to finish the job. We just need the key. James had the right of it when he said it might not literally be a key, but we're thinking about this in the wrong way. We're thinking of all the things that could potentially be keys when actually we only need to look at what we've been given."

"We haven't been given a key," she pointed out.

"We know it would have to be kept somewhere safe from the Seventh Court. We know the Seventh Court doesn't have any humans. If you didn't want the Seventh Court to have the key, but you did want the other courts to be able to access it, where would you put it?"

As I talked ,I realised where the key was and how we would get it.

"You would hide it somewhere only a human would find it or give it to a human who was protected in some way?" she speculated.

"But the Feyre don't regard humanity as reliable. Humans don't have long enough memories and they don't live long enough. So what do you do?" I was leading her through my logic now, to see if it was flawed.

"They've already solved that problem, by embedding the knives in a legal ceremony that will survive the death of any one individual."

"So what do we end up with that we haven't already found a purpose for? What is the thing that stands out like a loose end with no purpose we have yet discovered."

She thought for a moment. "The horse shoes? The nails? The sixty-first nail! That's it!" She jumped down from the wall. "The sixty-first nail is different from all the rest. It's made from the same metal as the Dead Knife. It's just the right size and the right shape."

"And it's kept with sixty iron nails and six huge iron horseshoes, one for each court, to ward off unwanted hands." I smiled down at her.

She reached up around my neck and pulled me down for a breathless kiss, then danced away. "Come on! We've got to tell the Highsmiths."

I slipped down from the wall and followed after her. When I reached the kitchen she was explaining to the Highsmiths that we knew who had the key.

"When will you be able to get hold of it?" asked Jeff, sipping from a steaming mug of tea.

"As soon as we can get in touch with the person who has care of it," she told him. "Except we don't have her number and today is Saturday. The Royal

Courts of Justice will be closed." She looked crestfallen at me.

"Why don't you call her mobile?" suggested James, over a mouthful of pasta.

"We don't have her mobile number," Blackbird explained. "I don't even know if she has a mobile."

"Everyone has a mobile," he told us, "even Dad." This got a wry grin from Jeff.

"Directory enquiries might have the number, but all I have is her name," Blackbird shrugged. "It's not enough to get a number."

We were stumped again. Then I had an idea.

"Mrs Highsmith. I wonder if I might borrow your mirror for a few moments?" I indicated the big mirror over the kitchen sideboard.

"Help yourself."

I went to the mirror, glancing back at Blackbird. I think she knew what I meant to do, but I recognised the expression of challenge I had seen in the meeting with Claire when I had used the mirror in the Remembrancer's office. I stepped over to the mirror behind Lisa and James, who turned their chairs to watch me.

"I thought you were going to look in it," Meg Highsmith said.

"I am," I told her.

I felt for the mirror, dipping below its surface to the grey realm beneath. It was like the other one, still and calm.

I reached within to the well of darkness inside and formed a connection. The mirror turned milky white and the light in the room dimmed. I remembered Claire's face, her neat hair and clipped manner.

"Claire?"

The mirror stayed tense but inert. Then a faint sound emerged, like a stereo that's been left on with nothing playing.

"Claire?" My own voice sounded hollow to me, reverberating in the stillness.

The sound continued. I could feel the connection there, but there was nothing. It was like an empty line.

"Maybe she really doesn't have a mobile phone?" Blackbird murmured into the hollow silence.

I reached over and pressed my palm against the glass. The mirror around my hand took on a pale light spreading outward until the whole mirror pulsed slowly with milky luminescence. Condensation formed on the surface as I pulled at the depths. The light in the room dimmed, the fridge juddered to a stuttering halt and the room temperature dropped about four degrees.

"Claire? Are you there?"

There was hissing, followed by a whine that rose in pitch as if something somewhere were being wound tightly. It twanged like tiny electrical threads were snapping. There was a ticking starting slowly and getting faster and faster until it was a constant buzz and then, suddenly, a ringing tone. The ringing tone was a positive sign, but there was something wrong, I could feel it in the mirror. It felt as if I was over-extended, unbalanced. Cold drops of sweat coalesced on my forehead while the phone rang and rang.

There was a click and a voice echoed around the room. "Hello? Who is this?"

Behind me, I heard James whispering, "Neat."

"Claire? Is that Claire?"

"Yes. This is Claire? Who is this?"

"Claire, it's Niall. We met yesterday. I need to speak to you."

"I don't know," Claire said, her echoing voice answering a faint voice in the background. "I thought it was switched off."

There was a pause. "Claire?" Holding the line open was telling on me. I could feel the chill creeping into my hand, numbing my fingers.

"I can't," I heard her say. "It won't. Hang on, let me past and I'll take it outside."

"Claire, can you hear me?" What was she doing?

There was a sound of movement, doors opening and overheard fragments of conversation. I held onto the line, not sure if I would have the strength to reach for her again if the connection failed.

"Hello?"

"Claire. Is that you?"

"This is Claire. Who is this?"

"It's Niall, from yesterday. We met in your office, remember?"

"Oh, Christ. Niall, what are you doing? How are you doing this?"

"I needed to speak with you urgently."

"Niall. I'm at the hospital. Jerry is here in a private ward. How did you call me? The phone was switched off because of the hospital and now it won't respond."

That explained why it was so hard. "Can you switch it on?"

"I can't do anything with it. What have you done to it?"

"I'll call back in a moment. Switch it on, can you?"

"It won't do anything."

"Give it a sec. I'll call you back." I released my hold on the mirror and took my hand away. It shivered as I released it, leaving my handprint outlined with condensation. We watched cold droplets of water run down the glass and coalesce on the edge of the frame. I waited for half a minute and then put my hand back on the mirror. "Claire?"

This time it rang immediately. Compared to the previous time the connection was effortless.

"Hello?"

"It's Niall."

"Yes. How did you do that?"

"It's… difficult to explain. Can you talk?"

"Hang on. Let me close the door. I'm in the rest room and you're not supposed to have mobiles on, even in here."

There was a short pause. "Go ahead."

"Is the Remembrancer OK?"

"He's in some sort of coma. They found him after you'd gone, down near the river. He was barely conscious and he hasn't come round since. His wife and daughter are here with him."

"Do they expect him to recover?"

"They don't know what's wrong with him. They say he muttered something about shadows coming to life when they put him in the ambulance but that was probably just delirium. He's had tests and things and as far as they can tell it's something to do with his heart, but they can't pin it down."

"What are they treating him with?"

"They don't want to give him anything until they know what they're dealing with. He appeared better after they'd got him to hospital, but then he got worse again overnight. It's like he's just wasting away."

I glanced at Blackbird, but she just shrugged.

"Listen, Claire, the reason I called you is that we need to get access to the nails for the ceremony? Can you get them for us?"

"I could, but I don't want to leave Jerry."

"You may have to if we're going to prevent a lot worse happening. Can you get to the nails?"

"If need be. But I don't like leaving him."

"Don't worry, we'll come to you. Which hospital is it?" If Blackbird could fix my heart, maybe she could do the same for the Remembrancer.

Claire gave me the name of a private hospital that I had last heard reported on the news when one of the royals was ill.

"We'll come to you," I repeated. "Maybe we can help."

"There's security. They're treating it as suspicious, though suspicion of what, I'm not sure."

"What kind of security?"

"The police are guarding all the entrances. I think it's mainly to keep the press out."

"OK, look, I'm not sure how long it will take us to reach you, but wait for us there."

"I'm not going anywhere. And Niall?"

"Yes."

"Next time, just leave me a message, OK?"

The connection closed.

TWENTY-TWO

I took my hand from the mirror, the outline of it still clear in the misty smudge of condensation.

James said, "Well, that beats directory enquiries."

There was a grumble of laughter from his father and the tension in the room eased a little.

I turned to Blackbird. "Do you think you could help the Remembrancer?"

"That depends on what happened to him."

"Without him it's going to be difficult for the ceremony to go ahead," I pointed out.

"That may be true, but it doesn't change anything. He may be dying naturally."

"You heard what Claire said: shadows that come to life?"

"I heard her. But if they've terrified him into heart failure then the damage may already be done."

"You helped me," I pointed out.

"That was different, Niall. I was there when it happened." There was an edge of impatience to her voice. "Maybe when we get there I'll take a look but I can't promise anything. In the meantime we need to finish the knife." She turned to the Highsmiths, seated around the table.

"What do you want us to do?" Jeff Highsmith spoke for them.

"We need you to complete the new Quick Knife. We'll have the key by tomorrow, one way or another. I think we can get the hammer. We need a smith."

"You'll have one," Ben Highsmith volunteered.

"Dad, it's a long way. It should be me," said Jeff.

"No, son. You stay here with your family and keep them safe. This could turn nasty, and if the worst comes to the worst then I'm at peace with it. I had all those years with your mum. I won't let you throw away the years you have to come."

Meg reached over and grasped Ben's hand.

"But Dad!" Jeff suddenly sounded like his son, James.

"How dangerous is it?" Meg Highsmith's voice cut across them both.

Blackbird answered. "If we manage to do it before anyone realises what we're doing, then the danger is minimal. He might slip and fall into the Fleet, which wouldn't be too pleasant, but that's about the limit."

"And if they realise?"

"Then there are those who will try and prevent the re-forging of the knife. They have already tried to kill Niall and you heard the state of the other person they found. I won't lie to you; I doubt we can win if it comes to a fight. Our best hope is getting the knife re-forged before anyone notices."

He shrugged his shoulders in a very matter of fact way. "I may be old, but I've been a smith all my life and I'm not weak. Anyone who tries to do me a mischief will get cold iron up his arse."

Meg forced a smile and Jeff squeezed his father's shoulder, though they must both have known it was bravado. Lisa pressed herself under her grandfather's arm, less willing to accept the bluster at face value.

"It may take us a little while to get the nail, but we should be able to meet you at midday tomorrow outside the Royal Courts of Justice. Bring the new knife and any tools you think you might need to finish it. The roads shouldn't be busy. It is Sunday, after all," Blackbird said.

"Aye. I'll be there."

She smiled and thanked him.

"It's the nature of the deal," he told us. "Besides, how many men can say they've worked metal for the Courts of the Feyre in their lives? Not many, I bet."

"Not many," she agreed.

"We need to get moving if we're going to be any help at the hospital." Blackbird was gathering our things together. "We have a long walk ahead of us, so we'd better get going."

"Can we give you a lift somewhere?" Jeff offered.

"Actually, I don't think we need one," I told him. "Ben, would you mind keeping the old Quick Knife here? It's broken anyway and it's probably more use to you than it is to us."

"I can do."

"Then would you pass me the Dead Knife from the case?"

He lifted the lid of the case, releasing the miasma that hung around the Quick Knife, and then closed it again after removing its dull grey twin.

"What are you intending to do?" asked Blackbird.

"I think there might be a quicker way back, and if it doesn't work, then our walk will still be waiting for us. It shouldn't take long."

Jeff slid the knife across the table within reach and I picked it up. As the metal made contact with my skin, it shimmered momentarily and then fell into perfect black, a broad leaf of darkness.

"Take hold of my hand."

"Are you sure you know what you're doing?" she asked.

"No, but you did say I should trust my instincts. I don't think it'll do any harm and it could save us the journey. Do you want me to try it on my own first?"

"No," she said. "I'll go where you're going. Then at least we won't get separated again." She reached out tentatively and grasped my hand. The knife stayed light-less but inert.

"Ready?" I asked her.

"Thank you, Jeff and Meg, for your hospitality," she said. "Ben, we will see you outside the Royal Courts of Justice at midday tomorrow."

"I'll be there."

"Now I'm ready," she told me.

I lifted the knife in my hand and focused on it. Then I called to the emptiness within me. It welled upwards into the knife and the world slid into neither up nor down. Everything interleaved without touching, over-laid and underlapped in a kaleidoscopic dizziness. We were close to everywhere without being anywhere. I kept a firm grip on the warm hand clasped in mine as we slid between places, finding the gaps where we could pass, tasting but not touching.

It occurred to me that we didn't have to go to London. I had the knife and was no longer bound by concerns of distance. We could go anywhere, be anywhere. The world would spin without us, if we dared let go. I only needed to choose somewhere calm and peaceful and we could find respite, just for a while.

The possibilities were arrayed about me, tempting me with all the variations of existence. Each one was a world in a bubble, independent and isolated from those around it. All I had to do was choose.

But if I chose a different world, then everything would change. The smith would arrive at the ren-dezvous alone and the knife would never be re-forged. The barrier would fall and Raffmir and his sister would come and go as they pleased, feeding on humanity. The world would slip into chaos.

I could not let that happen, if only for the sake of my daughter, for they would surely seek her out and do to her what they had failed to do to me. I refocused, aware now that the drifting thought pattern was part of the interstitial space we traversed. Something here set the mind adrift so that thoughts wandered and all sense of space and time were lost. I began to understand how it was that I had lost two hours when I was here before.

I forced myself to recall the image of the room above the abandoned underground station with the arched window looking out over the Strand. I formed the thought that we could be there.

And we were.

Blackbird staggered, unbalanced slightly by the sudden return of gravity and space. She looked around, recognising where we were. We could see through the window that it had fallen dark outside.

She let out a held breath. "How much time did we lose?"

I turned back, noting the change in her voice, realising that she had reverted to her older appearance, the one I had first encountered.

"Is something wrong?" she asked me.

"No. It's just I thought… never mind." I tried to hide my disappointment that she'd chosen to change back.

"If we're going to meet Claire, it has to be as someone she will recognise," she pointed out, reasonably.

"I know. I understand." It made logical sense, but I wasn't any happier about it.

She approached me and lifted her mottled hand under my chin. It felt strange, as if her hands weren't hers somehow. It was an effort not to pull away.

"It's still me, Niall."

"I know, but it's strange. I know it's you, still…"

"How much time do you think we lost?"

"I'm not sure. It couldn't have been long." It had still been light in Shropshire, but we were further east here, so had we travelled into the dusk? Was that why it was so dark?

She grabbed my hand and started pulling me towards

the stairs. "Niall, you have no idea about time there, do you?"

"What do you mean? It's not late."

"Not late? My watch says eleven o'clock. Which day is it?"

"What do you mean, which day?"

"I mean we left on Saturday. What day is it now?"

"It's still Saturday, isn't it?"

Blackbird pulled me down the stairs down to the corridor that led towards the street door. "I shouldn't have let you do that."

"But we're here, quicker than we would have been. Travelling on the Ways would have taken longer and been much more exhausting."

"You don't even know what day it is. What if we've missed the smith?"

"We can't have, can we?" I followed her along the darkened corridor to the heavy door leading to the street. I felt a tingling sensation as her power swept out around us so we could exit the door unnoticed.

She pulled back the bolt and twisted the lock, pulling open the heavy door and letting me past before she followed me out onto the pavement. We stepped outside into the street and I waited while she locked the door behind us. Once the door was secure, she let the magic surrounding us dwindle away.

Cars were still rumbling down the Strand, though it was less busy than it had been when we were here before. A pale-skinned guy in a duffel-coat, marking him out as a student, was walking towards us. Blackbird stepped into his path.

"Excuse me, do you know the time, please?"

He paused in his path and glanced at his wrist. "It's just before eleven." His accent marked him as a West Coast American.

"And it is Saturday, is it?" she asked him.

"Sure," he said. "It has been all day. Are you OK?"

"We're fine. Just making sure," she told him.

He stepped past and walked on, glancing back with a puzzled expression and then shrugged as if to acknowledge the strange eccentricities of the English.

"We're in time," she acknowledged.

"You see. I told you."

"Niall, tell me truthfully, before I asked that man, were you sure what day it was? Really?"

I couldn't lie to her. "No. I suppose not."

"I shouldn't have assumed you knew what you were doing. We could have missed the whole thing."

"It would have taken us almost as long to travel back on the Ways, especially if you take the walk into account."

"Yes, but we could just as easily have ended up at next Tuesday and missed the ceremony."

"We didn't, though, did we?" It was what she would have said to me in the same circumstances.

Blackbird turned to me, exasperation on her face. "Do you know where the hospital is?"

"I have the name of the hospital. I think it's somewhere near Marylebone."

"Then perhaps we should get a taxi. A cab driver should know where it is."

"Won't that be uncomfortable?"

"We're not going very far and it's safer than other ways."

She stepped to the edge of the Strand and hailed a passing black cab. It pulled across the traffic and drew up alongside us. I named the hospital to the driver and he gave us a curt nod, so we piled into the back.

The journey to the hospital took us down the deserted shopping streets, the lights still bright in the windows. As we came closer to our destination the shops gave out to offices and residential buildings. The cab turned left into a side street and pulled up by the kerb.

"Here ya go, mate." The driver announced our arrival.

I paid him out of my diminishing cash and he rumbled away down the street.

"There. That wasn't so terrible, was it?"

"No, but I'm going to need more money soon."

Trying to get more cash to bolster my diminishing reserves would be an interesting experiment, since I was sure if I used my cash card the police would know both where and when I had used it within minutes. They had already tried to track my phone, so the bank account would be the next logical step.

"We'll cross that bridge when we come to it," she said.

It was an acknowledgement that if we could get to the ceremony then we would need to start thinking about the longer term. It brought home to me how little I had left. My life was in tatters and I was hunted by both the Untainted and the police. Still, if the re-forging of the knife went badly then there wouldn't be any future for me to worry about. I needed to focus on the task in front of me and set the consequences aside for later in the hope that there would be a later.

"Claire said there was security at the hospital." I eyed the unguarded doorway as we approached, wondering what form that security might take.

"If they are on the alert for unexplained visitors and strange faces then we may have some difficulty reaching Claire, even allowing for the fact that I can make us less noticeable. We will need to know where they are in the hospital, though.

"What do you suggest?"

"Why don't you go in and use your charm. It worked at the Royal Courts of Justice."

"Will you wait here?"

"Come back out here when you find out what's going on," she called after me.

I walked across and up the steps through the front entrance into the well-lit reception. There were closed doors leading off to left and right at the back and a desk in the centre.

"Can I help you?" The middle aged lady sat behind the desk would look more at home in a corporate reception than a hospital.

"Yes, I hope so. I'm hoping to meet up with one of the visitors here. Her name is Claire Radisson. She's the clerk to the Queen's Remembrancer? I believe he's been admitted here and she's here with him. Would it be possible to see her?"

"I am afraid his visitors are restricted," she told me.

"I'm actually here to see the clerk, rather than the patient himself, but it's quite difficult to contact her while her mobile is switched off in the hospital," I explained. "I need to collect some things and I understand she's been here since he was admitted. It's quite urgent." I stressed the urgent part.

"What name is it, please?"

I used the name I had used when visiting the Royal Courts. "It's Dobson, Niall Dobson."

She consulted a list in front of her. "Is there anyone with you, Mr Dobson?"

"I have a friend with me. She's waiting outside."

"And her name is?" she prompted.

"Delemere. Veronica Delemere."

"Ah yes, Ms Radisson had left instructions that she was to be informed when you arrived. I'll let her know you're here. If you would care to wait for a moment."

She picked up the phone and indicated the chairs to either side of the reception area.

I thanked her, but went back past the chairs and out to where Blackbird waited. Walking from the well-lit reception out into the dusk, it was hard to locate her. I jumped when she tapped me on the shoulder.

"Don't do that."

There was a prickling of the skin as the delicate threads of Blackbird's magic wrapped around us while she drew me out of the light and into the shadows beside the doorway.

"Is something wrong?" I asked her.

"Maybe, maybe not. If that receptionist is expecting us then maybe others are too."

"How did you know she was…?" Then I realised what she'd done. "You were in there with me."

"I followed you in unobtrusively. I wanted to see what happened."

"You could have told me."

"If I had told you then you would have looked for me. You might have given me away."

"I wouldn't have."

"You wouldn't be able to help yourself. As it was, you acted normally and I was able to take a quick peek at her notepad while she was dealing with you."

"You were behind her?"

"They are up on the fourth floor. There's a note for her to call suite four fifty-two when we arrive. That must be where they are."

"Then let's go and find them."

"I don't like going where I am expected."

"You think it could be a trap? I don't think Claire would be involved in anything like that."

"She may not be running things. If the police are involved then who knows what may be waiting for us. Come on." She walked away down the street.

"Where are we going?"

"To find another entrance."

We walked around the side of the building and onto a side street. About three quarters of the way down the street there was an access ramp, big enough for the hospital laundry trucks. It led down into an area under the hospital which was blocked by a metal grid that rolled down from above. During the day when they were expecting deliveries it was probably rolled up, but now it sealed the ramp from the outside world.

There was a box on the wall with a circular grill and button to speak to a remote station. The entrance had two cameras monitoring it, one pointing at the box and another scanning back and forth along the entry ramp in an automated cycle.

Blackbird paused and then walked towards the shutter. The prickling of her magic intensified.

"Stick close to me."

We approached the wall box and she placed her hand upon it. There was a grinding squeak and the barrier began to rise.

"Don't you just love technology?" she smiled. "Years ago I would have had to get someone to come and let us in. Now we can do everything remotely."

"Won't the security people see us on the cameras?"

"They won't be looking this way. No one will see anything."

The barrier rolled down again behind us as we walked down the ramp. It opened out into a delivery bay with various doors into the hospital and three big roll-down shutters on loading ramps. They were all closed up and presumably locked. There was a bell-push next to one of the doors marked "Deliveries – Please Ring."

"What now?" I asked her. It looked to me as if we had just trapped ourselves down here, but that was probably just my inexperience.

"Well, we could go through one of these doors, but we don't know which way to go when we get inside."

"So what do we do?"

"We ring the bell."

She walked over to the button and pushed it.

"I thought we didn't want anyone to know we were here."

"No, we just don't want the people who are expecting us to know we're here."

"I don't see–"

The door opened and a bemused looking porter stood in the doorway. He looked Mediterranean in origin, Portuguese maybe.

"What are you doing out here? There is not supposed to be anyone out here at this time of day."

Blackbird turned to him.

"Ah, I'm so sorry. We're new here. I'm Veronica."

She stuck out her hand and smiled and the bemused man accepted it into his. As soon as she touched him his face went blank. Then he blinked and looked at us again.

"We don't usually have inspections on a Saturday night. Is there a problem?" he said.

"No, there's no problem. You know how it is, you get behind and you end up working all hours to catch up."

"Tell me about it. You'd better come through, then. Bring your colleague."

I followed Blackbird through the door and we waited while the man locked it again.

"We're going to the fourth floor today," she told him.

"Yes? You'd better use the service lift then. It's just down there on the right. You'll need a key."

"May we borrow yours?"

"Sure. I can come with you if you like?"

"No, it's OK. We'll be fine." He pulled a ring of keys from his belt and eased off one with a yellow tag attached to it, handing it to Blackbird.

"Thank you. We appreciate it."

"No problem. Let me know if you need anything."

He walked away down the corridor, unconcerned that he'd just let two complete strangers into the hospital and given them his lift key. We walked in the opposite direction, finding a service lift with wide doors.

"Is that what you did to me, in Trafalgar Square, that first morning?"

"Same gift, different application."

"What does he think he's doing?" I asked her.

"I'm really not sure, he was just being helpful. You'd have to ask him for the details. I created a reality for him where we were a normal part of his routine. I created just enough so he would believe it and then let him fill in the gaps. It's much more convincing if you let people do the hard work for themselves."

"So he thinks we come here every day?"

"Or often enough to make it unremarkable. He'll remember it in the same way he remembers what he had for lunch or what time he got into work. Not enough to make it stand out."

We came to the service lift and Blackbird pressed the button to summon the lift. A red light indicated that it was coming.

"So, in theory, I could still be having coffee with you in Trafalgar Square. All this could be a reality you created for me. Is that right?"

"In theory, yes, though if you start down that road then you'll never figure out what's real."

The lift doors juddered apart making a grinding noise that did not inspire confidence. Blackbird stepped inside and inserted the key, turning it to the priority setting. I followed her in and she pressed the button for the fourth floor. The door stuttered closed behind me.

"But this could be all in my head, like a dream." The lift jerked into motion.

"Your world is always in your head, Niall. It's the only world you will ever know. If you start to question everything you see then you are undermining your own foundations."

"But you can make me believe whatever you want."

"The further it gets from reality, the harder it becomes. Small changes are easy. That is what glamour does. It alters the perceptions of those around us to make them see us differently. It makes them perceive us as we want to be perceived. What I do is an extension to that, but it is fundamentally the same."

"So how do I know I'm not dreaming?"

"You don't. None of us ever do. All that we see or seem—"

"Shakespeare?"

"He knew what he was talking about. Everyone creates their own reality, Niall. It's just that the Feyre are better at it."

The lift jerked and shook and then halted, the doors sliding open on a hallway.

She strolled out, her power sweeping before her, making us unremarkable. It was late and all the visitors were gone for the night, but the nurses and medical staff didn't look at us twice. There were porters with trolleys and cleaners polishing the floors. None of them gave us a second glance.

At a hallway junction, a lone police officer watched where the three corridors converged. Blackbird smiled at him as we passed and he nodded distractedly in acknowledgment. The way he casually glanced away told me he wouldn't have any recollection of our passing.

The hospital had helpfully numbered all of the rooms, so finding suite four fifty-two was just a matter of following the sequence until we reached our goal. When the numbers came close it was obvious we had found it, because of the two policemen hanging around the nursing station at the junction where the corridor to the private suites branched off from the main walkway. They were engaged in casual conversation with the medical staff, but instead of facing the people they were talking to, they watched the corridors.

These officers were more vigilant, since the one facing us was taking notice of our approach. As we came nearer, though, a breeze sprang out of nowhere, flipping papers from the desk and strewing them around. The officer went to hold down a pile of sheets next to him only to have them whirl up around him. In a moment, they were all engaged in trying to hold down the flying sheets. We walked on past and I waited for one of them to call us back, but no one did.

"You could get anywhere like that," I told her. "You could steal the crown jewels or raid the Bank of England."

"And why," she asked me, "would I want to do that?"

"But you could have anything you wanted."

She turned in front of me and brought me to a halt, her hand resting on my chest. The numbers on the doors showed we were close, now.

She looked up into my face. "I have what I need, Niall, and I don't want for much more than that. The things I do want, though, can't be bought or stolen. They must be given freely."

For a moment there was something in her eyes that reminded me of the conversation we'd had over breakfast that morning and, for once, it was she who looked away.

"Blackbird?" I asked. "What are we going to do?"

She chose to interpret my question in the immediate, rather than the general sense.

"We're going to find the Remembrancer and see if we can help. What else can we do?"

She turned back to the doors and counted down the numbers towards room four fifty-two.

When I realised she wasn't going to wait for me, I followed.

TWENTY-THREE

Blackbird led the way down the corridor towards the suite that held the Queen's Remembrancer. She stopped at a door half-glazed with frosted glass.

"Here it is."

She turned the knob and eased the door open, peeking around the jamb, and then opened it more fully to allow us both into the room.

There was a white-framed hospital bed, head against one wall. A heart monitor sat silent on the far side, a jagged green line tracing the pulse of the man on the bed. He looked sallow, eyes closed, the lines on his face etched into the skin. Beside the bed, a thin young woman with tied back auburn hair looked as if she'd been startled awake by our entrance. She pushed loose strands of hair back from her face in an unconscious gesture. Another woman, sitting with her back to us, much older than the first, turned to us, her worried expression turning to mistrust when she realised we were not medical staff.

She stood up. "Can I help you?" She glanced from Blackbird to me.

Her hair was grey, but her fair skin and the way she brushed her hair from her cheek spoke of the close relationship between her and the younger woman. They had the same thin-boned frame that left the tendons stark on the backs of their hands, the same carved cheekbones leaving no doubt that they were mother and daughter. She had the determined look of a woman who would do something, if only she knew what to do.

"We're looking for Claire," said Blackbird.

"She's just stepped out for a moment. She went to meet someone."

"She was expecting us," Blackbird confirmed. "Do you mind if we wait for her?"

The hardening of her mouth and the slight stiffening of the shoulders said she did.

"There's a rest room across the hall," she said. "You can wait there."

"Has there been any change?" Blackbird asked.

"My husband is seriously ill." She emphasised the word "husband", confirming her place at his side and our place away from it.

Blackbird started to move towards the bed, but she stepped in front of her. "I think you had better wait outside," she said firmly.

Voices from the corridor distracted them both and there was movement outside. I stepped sideways, out of the way of the door, as vague outlines appeared on the other side of the glass.

Claire's voice was clear, speaking to a companion.

"...doesn't work like that. They'll come when they're ready and not before," a male voice replied in low tones as she pushed the door open, still looking back at the person in the corridor.

"They're not that sort of people–" She came to a halt at the sight of us standing in the room.

"What's the matter?" The male voice in the corridor was joined by a face over Claire's shoulder. The ruffled sandy hair over grey eyes regarded us with suspicion. "Who the hell are you?"

Claire pushed into the room, followed by the man.

"How did you get in here?" he asked, looking at Blackbird and me, then glancing back towards the corridor. "Elizabeth, are you OK?" he asked the woman standing in front of the bed. She nodded.

"They said they were friends of yours," she said to Claire.

"How did you…?" Claire trailed off, glancing back at the man in the doorway. Then she stepped sideways, taking his sleeve and drawing him into the room so she could push the door closed behind him.

Blackbird and I moved away from the door to give them some room. It was getting crowded.

"Claire? Who are these people?" Elizabeth wanted an explanation.

"And how did they get in here?" the man asked.

Claire took a deep breath. "These are the people I told you about, the ones we were to meet downstairs."

"There are two men at the end of the corridor that are supposed to be turning visitors away," he said. "What? They just walked past them?"

"It's not their fault," said Claire.

"Of course it's their fault," he blustered. "They'll get their ears bent for this, I can tell you."

"We came to see if we could help," Blackbird said quietly.

"The doctors are already doing everything possible," Elizabeth told her. "There's nothing anyone can do except wait."

The younger woman, who had been watching this exchange, took the limp hand of the man on the bed in hers, watching her mother.

"Perhaps I could take a look at him?" Blackbird suggested.

"As I said," Elizabeth spoke more firmly, "the doctors are doing everything possible."

"Perhaps if Veronica were to take a look?" Claire suggested. "She might see something the doctors have missed?"

"The tests were very thorough, Claire." Elizabeth glanced towards the bed. "It's down to him now."

"Not necessarily," said Blackbird.

"I think Mrs Checkland would like you to leave now," the man said.

"Very well," said Blackbird. "Claire, we need the nails. It's what we came for. Can you get them for us?"

"Please help him," Claire said. "You can see how he is. I can't leave him like this."

"You must," Blackbird said. "You must, because if you don't, there will be more of this and worse besides. You know it and we know it. Soon enough, they'll all know it unless we get the nails and you find another Remembrancer, someone alive enough to carry out the ceremony."

At her words, Elizabeth's expression hardened, her lips blanching to a fine line. Her hand lifted to cover her mouth.

"Oh that was uncalled for," said the man. "How insensitive can you get?"

"It's the truth," Blackbird stated. "Let me see, how does it go? His breathing is shallow, but there's nothing wrong with his lungs. His heartbeat is weak, and yet there is no trace of cardiac problems. He has no indication of disease; in fact his body temperature is low, not high as you would expect with an infection. He appears to be asleep, but he's not."

Elizabeth nodded. "They did a brain scan. They said it could be a shallow coma; he could wake up any time."

"He won't wake up," Blackbird told her. "I'm sorry for your husband, Mrs. Checkland, but he won't wake up because he isn't asleep. He's lost."

"What do you mean, 'lost'?" said the man.

"Can you help him?" Claire asked, cutting across the question.

"There may be a price to pay," Blackbird told her.

"We have money," Elizabeth said. "We can afford the best." The sliver of hope was enough to push back the tears from her eyes.

"I wasn't talking about money. There are higher prices than money can afford."

"What are you suggesting?" Elizabeth said.

"Let me see if I can help him first. Then we can discuss what it may cost you."

"Does anyone else here see that she's talking nonsense?" protested the man. "She's just exploiting your worst fears and taking advantage of your vulnerability at a bad time. It's the oldest con-trick in the book."

I edged closer to the door, intending to seal it if he tried to raise the alarm at our presence. Claire noticed my movement and held up her hand to me, her mute expression asking me to pause a moment.

"Sam, I asked you here to help. I know you think you're protecting us, but Veronica is possibly the only person who can help us. Don't ask me how I know this because I could never tell you, but I do know it. There have been plenty of times when you've been on assignment that you couldn't talk about and you've told me I just had to trust you. Now I'm asking you to trust me."

"But this is ridiculous," he protested.

"Is it? You have this place wrapped up tight yet they walked in without a soul seeing them. How do you explain that?"

"I'm about to ask that question myself."

"Please don't. I'll do my best to explain later, but you have to accept there are things I can't tell you. You're used to secrets in your job. It shouldn't be too hard to accept that I have them too."

Something in her words stung him. His face registered shock and surprise.

"If you'll allow them to help Jerry," she continued, "then I'll try and explain later. In the meantime I need you to accept this. In fact I need you to do your best to conceal the fact that these people were ever here at all. Sam, I need your help. You have to trust me on this."

"This is crazy, you must see that."

"Please, Sam?"

For a moment, he was debating within himself, then his shoulders fell. "OK," he lifted his hands in a gesture of uselessness. "I just hope you know what you're doing."

"Elizabeth?" she asked, turning to the woman standing between us and the bed.

"What are you intending to do?" she asked.

"Initially I just want to see how bad it is," Blackbird told her. "If I can't help him then I'll tell you. I won't lie to you."

"It won't hurt him, will it?"

"Not this part. Bringing him back, though, may not be as easy."

She stood aside. "You can take a look."

Blackbird walked around the side of the bed, looking across at Sam, standing with his arms folded in challenge.

She paused. "What do they call you, Sam-who-keeps-secrets?" Blackbird asked him.

"Veldon. Sam Veldon." He looked at Claire's crest-fallen expression. "What?"

Blackbird smiled. "Are you a policeman?"

"No," he said, the lie in his tone apparent immediately to me as it must have been to Blackbird.

"Something similar?" she asked.

"What's it to you?" he challenged.

"Will you have to write a report of this?"

"That depends what you do," he said.

"Claire said you know how to keep secrets. Is she right?"

"I have kept secrets, yes."

"You must promise me," she said to him quietly and evenly, "you will tell no one outside this room what transpires here, by whatever means. Are you willing to make that promise?"

"I don't have to promise you anything." His stance was rigid, arms crossed, feet square.

"Then I must ask you to leave," she said.

"On whose say-so?" he challenged.

"She's right, Sam. You have to promise," Claire insisted. "This must never be spoken of."

"What are you?" he asked Blackbird. "Some kind of *witch*?"

The intake of breath through my teeth drew everyone's attention, rather than Blackbird, so they missed seeing Blackbirds eyes narrow and her chin come up at the use of that word. The temperature in the room dropped and I could feel the magic prickling across my skin as she directed her anger back at Sam.

"Use that word again, Sam Veldon, and you will regret it for the rest of your short little life." She was moving slowly around the bed, stalking towards him, each tread increasing the pent-up tension building in the room.

Claire bustled past me and pulled the door open, bustling him out of the room and pushing him out into the corridor. "No," she insisted. "It's for your own good. Go and wait in the rest-room; have a cup of coffee, start smoking again, anything. Just don't say anything. At all. Do you understand? Nothing."

He looked into her face, frustration written across his features and then made a noise between a grunt and a sigh, turned suddenly and stalked away, leaving her standing in the doorway. She retreated and closed the door again.

"I'm sorry, Veronica, he can be so stubborn. He won't tell anyone, though. It's not in his nature."

Blackbird appeared unconcerned now that the object of her anger had left, dismissing it with a wave of her hand as the sudden cold dispersed.

"What's his given name?" she asked, looking at the figure on the bed.

Claire shot another warning glance to Elizabeth.

Blackbird spoke gently to Claire. "If I'm going to help him, I will need his name."

She looked uncomfortable and then said, "I know," earning a puzzled look from Elizabeth.

"It's Jerome David Checkland. Jerry for short," Elizabeth said.

Blackbird moved back around the bed, bypassing Elizabeth and focusing instead on the young woman beside the bed.

"And you are his daughter, yes?" she asked.

The young woman nodded. "Deborah Checkland," she confirmed.

"May I? I need to hold his hand."

Blackbird moved to sit on the edge of the bed and Deborah released her father's hand. Blackbird lifted it from the covers, cradling it in her own. She closed her eyes and the room warmed, taking on the heaviness that comes on long languid days. For a moment, the air over the bed shimmered like heat haze.

"Jerry?" Her voice sounded muffled, suppressed by the heavy air. "Jerome David Checkland, can you hear me?"

The silence deepened, so the background noise of the hospital faded, replaced by a summer day's laden stillness. The figure on the bed lost some of his pinched expression. His face relaxed and the lines smoothed on his forehead.

"Jerome David Checkland, I summon you to me. Be called."

The heaviness deepened and then relaxed. Blackbird opened her eyes again.

"Well, that would have been too easy, wouldn't it?" she told us.

"What's wrong with him?" asked Deborah.

"He's trying to return, but he is either being prevented or he doesn't know the way. I suspect he is being held against his will. If he is to break free then he will need our help."

"What can we do?" asked Elizabeth.

"I can bring him here, but only for a few moments. If we are to release him then we must persuade the one who holds him to let go, and they have every reason to keep him." She stood again.

"What will persuade them?" Elizabeth said.

"We need to offer them something sweeter, something to tempt them."

"Like what?"

"Like your daughter."

Deborah looked at Blackbird, and then at her mother, who was standing with her mouth open.

"No!" Elizabeth said. "I am already losing my husband. I will not lose my daughter as well. Deborah doesn't need to be involved in this," Elizabeth said firmly, walking around to join her and finding Blackbird positioned between them.

"On the contrary," Blackbird replied. "She may be just the lever we need."

"I'll do whatever needs to be done," said Deborah.

"Wait, child, until you know what the price may be," Blackbird told her.

Deborah stood up and it became suddenly apparent how tall she was. She stood a head-height above Blackbird. "I am not a child and I won't be treated like one. I'm twenty-two and quite capable of making my own decisions, thank you."

"Stay out of this, Deborah," said her mother.

"He's my father," she told them.

"Unfortunately, she has the right of it," said Blackbird, "and I called you child, not because you are childish but because you are his child and his bloodline. Blood calls to blood, and the ties of marriage mean that you are not of his bloodline, are you, Elizabeth?"

"No, well, obviously not," Elizabeth admitted, stepping forward to take Deborah's arm. She shrugged free of it, turning away to stand alone with her back to the wall. Elizabeth looked hurt by the snub but stayed by the bed.

"I am not suggesting we trade one for the other. Your daughter's presence will tempt her away from your husband. Blood calls to blood, as I told you. At the moment when that becomes apparent, I will have the opportunity to distract her and we should be able to pull them both back without getting caught."

"Who do you mean 'her'?" Claire asked.

"Niall knows of whom I speak." I had been standing in the corner unnoticed, but now they all focused on me. "Niall has stood where your husband now stands."

"Have you?" Claire asked.

I realised, then, what Blackbird meant when she said Jerry was lost. I knew where he was. He was standing in the cold glade, bare feet prickled by pine needles, surrounded by a ring of thorns. He was listening to a voice as dry as dust, trapped there by a woman dressed all in grey, arms held open in a chilling embrace.

"She won't let him go," I told them. "She'll leech the warmth from his bones until nothing remains."

"I'll do it," said Deborah.

"You will not!" Elizabeth snapped.

"It's my choice. Isn't it?" she said to Blackbird.

"Understand what you risk," Blackbird said to her. "If she touches you she can bind you there and we will have lost both of you."

Elizabeth moved to stand next to her daughter. "I couldn't bear to lose both of you. I simply couldn't."

"There's no one else, is there?" said Deborah. "If I can't bring him back, then no one can. He would do the same for me, whatever the risk. You know he would."

Elizabeth shook her head, staring up into her daughter's face as if she couldn't believe the words were coming from her mouth. Then she turned away, still shaking her head. Claire stepped forwards, drawing Elizabeth away from the bed.

"It's better than sitting here watching him waste away," Deborah said to her mother's back.

"When I call him back," Blackbird explained to Deborah, "the one holding him will know it. She won't release him without a fight, so she will come to claim him back. She won't be able to materialise fully so she should be weak. When she appears, you distract her, make her see you. She will understand the tie of blood, and hopefully that will be enough for her to try and take you both. When she does, the ties on your father will be weak enough to break. If we can close the circle while her hold on him is weakened then we can break her hold on him before she can get her claws into you. Once her hold is broken, there's nothing to anchor her here. She won't be able to stay.

"What if she doesn't want me?"

"She's old, arrogant and greedy. Don't worry, she'll want you. Just don't let her touch you, understand?"

Elizabeth stepped forward again. "Don't let her do this. Let me do it. I'm his wife. That should count for something."

"It does, but it's not the same. If you do it then there's every chance she will go for your daughter anyway. Blood calls to blood. It always has and always will."

"I must be able to do something."

"Stick to the plan and we'll be fine. Distract your daughter at the wrong moment and you could lose your husband and your daughter forever." She turned to me. "Niall, can you pull the bed out from the wall a little?"

I nodded and took the brakes off the bed so that it would wheel forward. Blackbird pulled the flowers unceremoniously from the vase on the side table and dumped them on the floor in the corner. Then she walked in a slow circle, dribbling water from the vase onto the floor but leaving a gap at the end of the bed.

"This is the gap we have to close, once he's free. Stay in the circle. Don't let her tempt you out of it."

"Do we have to be in the circle too?" Elizabeth indicated herself, Claire and I.

"She won't notice you as long as you don't make any noise or touch any of us. You should be fine." She completed the partial circle and returned to stand next to Deborah.

"Are you ready?" she asked her.

Deborah looked at her mother and then back at Blackbird. "I'm ready."

Blackbird dipped into her bag and produced a long thin spike of yellow bone. "Give me your hand."

Deborah looked warily at the spike and then hesitantly offered her hand. Blackbird took it by the fleshy part at the base of the thumb and stabbed the point of the bone into the flesh of her thumb, eliciting a gasp of pain and a corresponding flinch from her mother. Blackbird screwed the bone into the thumb.

"Shit!" Deborah hissed, trying to pull back the thumb, but Blackbird held it. She waited until the pain was livid on her face and then released her. She lifted Jerry's hand and pricked his thumb with the point, squeezing the thumb until the blood welled in a ruby drop.

"There, now mix your blood with his so she won't fail to see the connection."

Blood welled freely from Deborah's thumb, leaving a thin trail of drops across the cover as she reached to smear her own blood into that of her father's.

This done, Blackbird took hold of Deborah's shoulders and steered her around to stand with her back to the doorway. Deborah stood there, sucking her thumb.

Blackbird moved Elizabeth and Claire into the far corner of the room, away from her daughter. "Stay in the corners and keep calm and you'll get him back. Niall, the same applies to you. Don't attract her attention, understand?"

I nodded, manoeuvring back into the other corner, away from the circle.

"OK," she said, "are we all ready?" We all nodded in turn.

Blackbird took the hand of the man on the bed and used the tip of her finger to wipe the welling blood from his thumb. She held up the finger and then slowly licked the blood from the tip.

As soon as her tongue touched the blood, something changed. The lights began to flicker and buzz, filling the room with an uncertain green cast. Expectancy built in the air. I could taste copper in my mouth as if it had been me that licked the finger.

Blackbird spoke, and the words sounded thick, as if the metallic taste of blood on her tongue made the words difficult to form.

"By his blood I bind him,
By his seed I summon him,
By his flesh I find him,
She who holds him,
Accept the price of blood and pain,
And let him find his way home."

After each phrase, the temperature dropped until the room was as chill as an autumn dawn. The lights blinked, emitting greenish pulses that only served to deepen the shadows in the corners of the room. That last word – "home" – hung in the air, heavy with anticipation. It weighed in the room like a still pendulum, and then stirred. The sound of an indrawn breath brought everyone's attention to the figure on the bed. His chest rose and his eyes opened.

"Jerry?" Elizabeth's voice held sudden hope and she tried to go to him, but Claire held her back. Blackbird's sudden shake of the head was filled with warning.

"Beth?" His voice was hoarse after his long silence. It was as if he could hear her but not see her. His head moved and his eyes scanned across without seeing the figures around him.

At the sound of his voice, all the hairs on the back of my neck stood on end. Another presence had entered the room. The lights dimmed further as a tall figure paled into visibility in front of us at the end of the bed, just beyond the opening in the circle.

Swathed in grey, she stood, arms lifted wide apart. Her long hair shadowed her face, falling over the shoulders in a silver-grey mantle. The pleats in her gown fell to the floor so her dress draped the ground. Her head was bowed, as if in contemplation, her insubstantial form rippled in a breeze we did not feel. The room became still; not the heavy torpor that Blackbird had summoned but the brittle stiffness of hoarfrost under a starlit sky.

Elizabeth backed into the corner, feeling, as I did, the chill waves coming from the figure, her expression showing sudden realisation at the cold force we had summoned. My hand found its way, unwittingly to the handle of the knife under my coat. There was a light crackling sound and I saw the water on the floor around the bed had frozen, forming a ring of milky frozen droplets.

"Deborah?" Blackbird's voice was a whisper across the bed. "Let a little of your blood fall upon the floor inside the circle."

Deborah was transfixed by the woman. Slowly she drew her thumb from her mouth with a tiny sound, like a kiss. At the noise, the head of the ghostly woman lifted, scenting her. Deborah looked towards Blackbird, who nodded encouragement.

She held out her thumb and the jagged gouge welled visibly again with blood. A single fat droplet fell and spattered on the tiles.

The figure's head jerked across to focus on Deborah, who stepped back under the intensity of that gaze. The figure strengthened, coalescing, becoming more solid by the second. She allowed her arms to fall and the rustling of her gown gave her more substance. She stepped forwards towards the circle and, as she did, I saw that Blackbird had the vase held high, ready to dash it on the floor at the feet of the grey figure to seal the circle ahead of her.

At the same moment, a shadow crossed the frosted glass of the door. Like the grey figure it became more solid until the bulky shape of Sam was outlined in the glass. He pushed the door open and leaned in.

"There's something up with the power. They have an emergency generator, but– What the hell?"

Deborah twisted around to warn him back but the words never reached her lips. The grey figure swept around the bed and grabbed her hair, jerking upwards so she cried out. Without thinking, I pulled the Dead Knife from my belt and launched myself forward, and stabbed it into the grey woman's back.

There was a yell as Deborah was thrown backwards into the wall, bouncing off with a force that shook the room. Her feet skidded on the thin-crusted ice and she sprawled onto the floor. The grey figure whirled around, the force of it jerking the knife from my grasp and sending it skittering loose across the floor.

"You!" The tall grey woman turned her attention to me, apparently unharmed by the knife. She reached towards me and I backed away, trying to evade her grasping fingers as she reached to catch hold of my jacket. She advanced, backing me into the corner.

I slid down the wall trying to evade her. In the shadows of her hair I could see the feral gleam of her eyes and the white of her teeth as she realised she had me cornered.

"Nowhere to run, little brother." Her voice was soft, her tone sure. She reached slowly down to my face as if to caress my cheek with her clawed nails.

There was a crash from behind her. For a moment her smile stayed and then faltered. She whipped around to see the shards of the vase, the water from it sealing the circle behind her. Immediately, she started to fade. She knotted her hands in front of her face and let out an anguished cry, the scream of a predator denied the prey. It hung in the room as her form lost substance and dissolved. Sprawled in the corner, I watched the very last glimpse of her fade away. The room held its breath, waiting to see if she would return. The lights flickered and buzzed and the room blinked back to hospital brightness.

"Beth?"

The man on the bed was trying to sit up, weak but conscious and aware of those around him.

Elizabeth went to rush forward and was held back once more by Claire, who looked to Blackbird for the all-clear. Blackbird nodded and she released her. She rushed around the bed to where Deborah was lifting herself stiffly from the floor. As she pulled herself to her feet, her mother reached her.

"Are you hurt?"

"I don't think so. Nothing's broken." Her voice sounded shaky and thin.

"Deborah?" The man's voice was scratchy from disuse. "What are you doing under the bed? And what have you done to your hair?"

"My hair?" Unconsciously, her hand went to the back of her head where her hair had been grabbed. It was drained of all colour, white as cotton and brittle as hay. As her hand pushed through it, the white fell away like ash, leaving only ragged tufts close to her head. She looked at the grey smudges on her fingers where her hair was powdering. Her hand began to shake.

Elizabeth pulled her close, whispering, "It doesn't matter. You're safe, now." Deborah stared at the fine grey smudges on her hands. Elizabeth addressed Blackbird. "She is safe now, isn't she?"

Blackbird nodded, releasing a long breath.

In the doorway, Sam stepped fully into the room. "What happened? Where…?" He looked around the room, trying to make sense of what he'd seen.

Blackbird walked around the splintered pottery and helped me up from the floor.

"Did she touch you?" she asked.

I shook my head, accepting her help.

"I thought I told you not to attract her attention."

"She was here, in this room. You said she would be weak."

"Yes, I did say that, didn't I? It looks like the barrier's even closer to collapse than we thought."

"Did anyone else see a woman in here?" Sam asked.

384

Blackbird turned slowly towards him and then looked around the room with exaggerated care.

"I think you'll find, Sam-who-keeps-secrets, that no one saw anything."

He looked at Elizabeth, who was hugging her daughter while she tried to stop trembling. She shook her head. He looked at me and I shrugged. He turned to Claire.

"Don't ask me, Sam. You won't like the answer." She looked at him levelly, daring him to push it.

"What the hell happened in here?" he demanded. "The electricity was all over the place, she's lost half a head of hair, there's ice on the floor; look, it's still melting. What happened?"

"I broke a vase," said Blackbird. "You'd better get a dustpan and brush before someone hurts themselves."

I walked over to where Elizabeth was hugging Deborah and collected the knife from the floor, being careful to keep my body between the knife and Sam so he wouldn't see the blade darken at my touch, and I concealed it in my belt once more.

"Is she going to be OK?" I asked Elizabeth.

"Thanks to you. If you hadn't, well, I hate to think what might have happened."

"What's the matter with you people? Can't you see this is all some sort of scam?" he demanded.

"Make up your mind, Sam," said Blackbird, "Either it's a scam and nothing happened or there was something and you missed it. Which is it to be?"

"You think you're clever, don't you?" He pointed his finger at Blackbird. Claire tried to get between them but he resisted her. "You think you can pull a fast one, but I know you're hiding something. I can smell it."

"You're too smart for me," Blackbird confirmed. "You're right, we are hiding something. But even if it ran up behind you and bit you in the behind, you wouldn't recognise it for what it is. Go home, Sam."

"Don't tell me what to do."

"Sam, please?" Claire was trying to calm him down, but it only made him more angry.

"I thought you wanted my help, Claire. I thought you wanted me here. Instead you're conspiring with this charlatan. What am I supposed to think?"

"You're not supposed to think anything," she told him, "and I'm sorry now I even asked you here. Knowing the kind of work you do I thought you would understand, but you don't, do you? It's OK for you to have secrets but you can't bear it when anyone else does. It didn't work before, Sam, and I thought that was because you always put your work before me. But that's not it, is it? It's not your work. It's you."

He stood there, shaking his head. "I thought I knew you."

"No, Sam. You never tried to know me. Do as she says. Go home."

He looked from one of us to the next, searching for some clue, ending finally back with Claire.

"If I leave, I'm not coming back."

"That's right, Sam. You're not."

"Fine. If that's the way you want it." He turned back to the door, wrenched it open and stormed out, slamming it behind him so hard it made the glass rattle in the frame. In the silence that followed we could hear his footsteps fading down the corridor.

Claire turned back to us, her stern expression fading, become hurt and vulnerable with the shock of what she'd done.

Elizabeth stood. "Claire, I'm so sorry. This is all because of us."

"No. It was over a long time ago between us. I just didn't have the guts to admit it." Her eyes watered, but she brushed away the tears with the back of her hand and straightened her jacket, turning to Jerry who was still looking gaunt and pale on the bed. She smiled weakly.

"Will Jerry be all right now? Will that woman come back?" She addressed the question to Blackbird.

"Thanks to Deborah, Jerry is safe for the moment. Get a good meal inside him and a night's rest and he'll be fine. He'll need his strength for the ceremony on Tuesday."

"I don't need sleep," he said. "I feel like I've slept for a week already."

"I'm not sure the doctor will discharge him by then," said Elizabeth. "They'll probably want to do some more tests."

"He doesn't need tests. There's nothing wrong with him that food and rest won't remedy. But without the ceremony to reinforce the barrier, the woman who was here will be able to come and go as she pleases and there will be little any of us can do to prevent her. The way she sees it, she was denied what was rightfully hers and without the barrier, she will surely return to claim her prize. You saw how she came right into the room? That means the barrier is close to collapse."

"What can we do?" Elizabeth asked.

"We need the sixty-first nail. With that we can restore the Quick Knife to the ceremony and reinforce the barrier. If Jerry doesn't perform the ceremony this year, with the re-forged knife, then the barrier will fail."

She looked at each of them in turn.

"And now you know what happens if it does."

TWENTY·FOUR

We tidied up the room as best we could, replacing the bed against the wall and pushing the pieces of the broken vase into a pile before informing the medical staff that Jerry was awake. Deborah told the nurse that her father had smashed the vase when he had woke suddenly and she'd cut her thumb trying to remove a fragment from his. This explanation was received with a degree of scepticism and the nurse kept trying not to look at Deborah's hair, but in the absence of any other explanation she simply dressed both cuts.

She took Jerry's blood pressure and measured his temperature, concluding that he'd awoken from a shallow coma and told us she would have one of the doctors come and give him a full examination.

While the nurse assessed the patient and arranged for the debris to be cleaned up, Claire, Blackbird and I moved into the empty rest-room across the hall.

"We are to meet the smith at the Royal Courts of Justice at noon tomorrow," Blackbird told Claire. "We are going to need the sixty-first nail, the one that's different from the others. Can you get it for us?"

"The Courts are closed on the weekends and they don't encourage visitors for all sorts of reasons."

"We need it tomorrow. Without it the Seventh Court will be able to come when they want, how they want. What they did to Jerry will be the least of it. We need the nail."

"I should be able to get it for you in the morning. They're used to me coming in at weekends to do things for Jerry. I can go into the office and collect it then. You'll still have time to meet the smith at noon."

"That will do."

"Are you going to stay with Jerry until then?" Claire asked.

"Jerry will be OK for now. Her hold on him is broken. I think he'll be safe enough. It's you I'm worried about."

"Me?"

"Without you we can't get the nail and without the nail all the rest is for nothing. If the worst came to the worst we could get someone else to play Remembrancer, but you don't have a successor, do you, Claire?"

"I didn't think I needed one until recently."

"There'll be time to think about that later. For now, we need to keep you safe."

"Will it be OK to go back to my flat?" She looked worried now.

"Probably, though it might be best if Niall and I checked it out first."

"Very well. What will you do then? Do you want to stay the night?"

"Are you sure you don't mind us being in your home?"

"I'd rather you and Niall were with me than I was on my own, given what you've said. It's only a sofa bed, but it's comfortable enough for a night."

"Then we will stay the night with you. Thank you."

"Give me two minutes to call for a cab and let Elizabeth know where we're going." She turned away, then paused. "You are OK with a cab, aren't you?"

"Yes. That's how we got here."

She smiled. "Of course."

We waited while Claire took her leave of the people across the corridor. A glance through the open door showed Jerry sitting up, his daughter perched on the bed beside him, pale but smiling. When Claire came back, Elizabeth was with her.

"I wanted to thank you, both of you, for what you did for us," she said.

"You're welcome."

"You said there would be a price to pay?" She sounded hesitant, as if she was unsure what form that price might take.

"I did, and if it hadn't have been for Niall's quick thinking the price would be a sight higher. We were lucky."

"I think I know that now. Who would have believed? Well, anyway." She shook her head.

"If your husband is at the ceremony on Tuesday, then I will take the debt as paid," Blackbird told her.

"He'll be there. I don't think you could prevent him. Still, I feel I owe you."

"Don't offer more than you are asked for, Elizabeth," Blackbird told her. "There are those that will take all you have and more besides, if you let them."

"Well, thanks then, from all of us."

We said our goodbye and followed Claire down to reception. While Claire handed in her security badge we slipped easily past the receptionist and waited outside for her to follow. She joined us on the pavement and after a few moments a minicab pulled up alongside the kerb. Claire sat in the front with the driver while we took the back seat. We were driven through the darkened streets without speaking, each wrapped in our own thoughts. After a while, Blackbird's hand sought mine and I held it. It was easier in the dark when I couldn't see how old and wrinkled it was.

When we got to the flat, Blackbird went inside first. She walked around , trailing her fingers on the surfaces and walking softly as if listening for something. She vanished into the other rooms while we waited in the hallway.

When she reappeared she nodded. "They have not been here."

Claire pushed the door closed behind us, locking it and bolting it.

"There, that should hold them." She looked at me. "It will hold them, won't it?"

"Here, let me." I placed my hand on the door. It was more solid than the internal door to my bedroom, but I sealed it in the same way, imagining nails driven deep into the wall around it, sealing it shut. "That will give us some time if they come tonight."

"Time for what?" she asked.

"To run," I told her. "Is there another way out?"

"There's a fire door at the back of the kitchen with stairs down."

"Then we'd better seal that too. A way out is a way in."

"What if they come to both doors at once?"

"Then we have a problem. Try not to worry about it."

Claire gave me a wan smile and then busied herself putting away her things and getting towels and bedding for us. I sat on the sofa, politely refusing offers of hot chocolate and cheese sandwiches while Blackbird followed her around, collecting guest towels and sheets. I would not have thought it possible for someone to fall asleep amid such a commotion, but I must have nodded off. When I opened my eyes, Blackbird was sitting quietly on the floor next to the sofa that I had been sleeping on, watching me. Someone had put a quilt over me at some point and it was tangled around my legs.

"Hello," I said, blearily.

"Hello." Her voice was soft and almost inaudible.

"Have you been there long?" I asked her.

She looked comfortable enough, cross-legged on the rug, her elbows resting on her knees, chin on her hands.

"A little while."

I stretched the muscles that had tightened from sleeping in an awkward position, sticking my bare feet out from under the quilt.

"Are you OK? Did I steal the bed? You should have woken me.

"You looked so peaceful there. I thought I'd let you sleep."

"Have you had any sleep?"

"Not really. I napped for a while."

"What time is it?"

"It's nearly ten o'clock. If you hadn't stirred soon I would have woken you."

"I don't remember falling asleep."

"I went into the kitchen with Claire and when I came back you were snoring."

"Oh. Sorry."

"Don't be, you needed it."

Having woken up a bit more, I took another look at her. It was the older Blackbird but she looked different. She certainly didn't look as tired as I would have done after only a couple of hours sleep.

"Are you OK?" I repeated. "You look different."

"It's my glamour. It's changed a little."

"It looks fine," I reassured her.

"Too fine. I've lost about ten years."

That was what was different. She definitely looked younger. I remembered it had taken me a while to notice a similar change in myself yesterday.

"Why?"

"I'm having difficulty maintaining it. I keep slipping back into habits I lost long ago, things I thought I'd left behind. I haven't lost control of it since I was a child, but I'm definitely having problems now."

"Why?"

"I don't know." It wasn't quite the truth.

I pushed myself upright, scrubbing my hands through my hair, trying to clear my head.

"It's about time Veronica had an accident," she told me.

"What?"

"Or perhaps she should get an offer from an obscure American university to go and teach history there."

"I don't understand. You're leaving?" I couldn't believe she was saying this to me.

"No, silly. I'm not leaving. I'm just changing."

"But why?"

"Well, for one thing I can't carry on as Veronica with a boyfriend who looks thirty years younger than me without causing a bit of a scandal, can I?"

"I suppose not." At least she wasn't leaving.

"And then there's my glamour. If I can't reliably maintain it then my options are limited, at least as far as mixing in with society is concerned."

"But why wouldn't you be able to maintain it? You always have before."

"I'm not sure." Again, there was the half-truth.

"Blackbird, what are you not telling me?" It was going to be easier to just ask outright.

She was silent for a long while and I began to think she wasn't going to answer. I pushed my fingers through my hair, trying to gather my wits together.

"It can happen," she said. "I've been hiding, as Kareesh calls it, posing as Veronica for forty or more years now. Before that there was another lady, just as acceptable and unremarkable. There was lots of confusion after the Second World War, so it wasn't difficult to appear with few records and no papers. When she got too old to work, I swapped her for Veronica. The original Veronica died of a drug overdose in the Sixties. She was bright enough to be university material and alone enough so that she wouldn't be missed. It was easy to bring her life down to London and carry it on."

"But she's too old now?"

"Sometimes when things change, it's better to go with them rather than fight against them," she explained quietly.

"I don't know what you mean. What are you saying?"

"I'm not sure," she said again.

"Help me out here, Blackbird. I know I'm never at my best when I've just woken up, but I'm just not getting it. What are you not telling me?"

"I'll get you some coffee," she offered and stood up smoothly, padding out of the room towards the kitchen.

I untangled myself from the quilt and pulled my trousers on. I had obviously been so deeply asleep that I hadn't noticed someone had taken them off. I hoped it was Blackbird rather than Claire. I buckled my belt and followed Blackbird into the kitchen. She was busily making coffee.

"Blackbird, please talk to me."

She stopped and turned to me. She looked pensive.

"What is it?" I asked again.

"Sometimes the Feyre lose control of their glamour when they feel very strongly about something, or someone. It's a little like I told you on the first morning. If you feel fear, or lust, or envy."

"You feel envious?"

"No, but there are other feelings besides lust and envy."

"Oh." I wasn't sure how to react to that. I felt very strongly about Blackbird too, but was I ready to hang a name on those feelings?

"Or," she added, "they can lose control of their magic when their bodies change in response to other things." She turned back to the coffee.

"What kind of other things?"

She muttered something into the coffee pot.

"Sorry?"

"I said, it can happen during pregnancy." She turned around with a look of terrible uncertainty on her face.

"But you said it was too early, that you weren't even fertile." I was struggling to deal with the implications of this news.

"I said I didn't know when I was fertile and that it was too early to know. I'm still not sure."

"We only did it once." I was trying to get my thoughts straight in my head.

"Actually, from a biological perspective we did it four times, Niall. But I don't think biology was keeping score."

"So how do you feel?"

"I told you, I'm fine, I just feel different."

"Do you want to sit down?"

"No. No I don't want to sit down. Nor do I want to have my back rubbed. If I am pregnant then I am only just so. It could be weeks before anyone can actually see a difference."

"Of course. I knew that."

"Only, when we discussed this," she continued, "you said you weren't ready to be a father again and I just wanted you to know. You don't have to stay."

"What?"

"You don't have to be with me, just because I'm pregnant."

"Blackbird, of course I'll stay with you. Why would I leave?"

"I release you from that commitment. Things are different now."

"Yes, they are, but not in that way."

"You said you weren't ready to start another family and you didn't think about the consequences."

"Whoa. You just took me by surprise, that's all. I'd barely gotten used to the idea that you wanted to, well, you know. I just wasn't prepared."

"And because of that I won't hold you to it. You can leave."

"Don't you want me to stay?"

"If you want to, Niall, but only if you want to."

"I want to. I don't want to leave you, especially like this."

"Really? Think about this and all it means before you decide. Your daughter would have a half-brother or sister. The child will probably be Fey, while your daughter's genes may never express themselves and she may die human, long before you do. This baby may not even look human, particularly to her. Bringing up a Fey child will be different and is bound to split your attention away from your daughter. Is that what you want?"

I thought about it, treating her questions with the seriousness and consideration they deserved, but no matter what else I thought about it, I could not see myself walking away from her and a child that was ours.

I thought about my daughter, fourteen years old and almost a young woman. How would she cope with a younger half-brother or sister? What did Blackbird mean when she said it wouldn't look human? What did Fey babies look like? All of these questions assailed me, but they didn't change how I felt. If she was pregnant then I would stay with Blackbird and see our baby into the world. My daughter could learn to live with a half-sibling if she had to. Other children did.

"I'm staying. If you'll have me?"

"You're sure."

"Of course I'm sure. What did you think I would say?"

"I didn't know, Niall, truly. And I may not be pregnant after all, but I wanted you to have the choice."

"Why? Is it so terrible to have a Fey child?"

"Well, there's the mewling, screaming bundle that cries when it's not sleeping. You feed one end and wipe the other and if you're lucky you might get a full night's sleep once a month." She smiled at me. Some of the uncertainty had gone from her eyes and was replaced by something warmer, something that made me want to hold her.

I held out my arms and she curled herself inside them so I could rest my chin on the top of her head. We were standing there holding each other quietly when Claire came in.

"Oh," she said. "I'm sorry. I didn't realise you were..."

She stopped and looked at us, as if taking in what we were doing.

"I'm sorry. I'm interrupting."

She turned away, but Blackbird called her back.

"It's your kitchen, Claire." She untangled herself from me. "I was trying to make coffee. Would you like coffee?"

Claire turned back and paused in the doorway, there not being room for three of us. "Yes," she said in a distracted manner. "Yes, that would be nice."

Blackbird pottered around, boiling water and putting coffee into a cafetière she'd found in a cupboard.

"I hope you don't mind us making ourselves at home like this," she said to Claire.

"Not at all, I was..."

Blackbird shimmered and shifted where she stood, her image blending and shifting between Veronica, the younger Blackbird and various other women I'd never seen. It shifted back to Veronica and held.

She turned to me. "You see?"

"What was... What did...?" Claire stepped back slightly as if it might be infectious. "What just happened?"

"It's OK," I reassured her. "No harm done," I said to Blackbird.

Her form shimmered again and melted into the young Blackbird.

"This might be easier, in the circumstances," Blackbird muttered through tight lips.

She carried on making coffee as if nothing had changed. Claire looked as if she expected Blackbird to leap over and bite her. I slipped past Blackbird.

"She's not having a good day," I told Claire. "Lack of sleep after last night probably isn't helping. Give her a moment or two and a cup of coffee and she'll be fine."

"The coffee is for you," Blackbird called after me as I shepherded Claire back into the living room. "I don't want any this morning, it tastes acrid."

I stopped. Claire looked at me. "It's the only coffee I have," she explained.

"No, sorry. The coffee's fine, really. It's just Bla– Veronica! She's having one of her moods."

"She has moods?" Claire asked, warily.

"She'll be fine. I promise."

Claire moved over to the windows and let in the day- light. She opened the window, letting in city noises and fresh air. Then she went to a vacant armchair, perched on the lip of the seat and looked uncomfortable.

"I'm very grateful for what you did last night," she began.

"But you would rather we went sooner than later," I finished for her

She looked crestfallen at what I had said, then grateful and relieved.

"It's not that I don't trust you." She looked embar- rassed as she realised I would be able to hear the truth of that statement.

"All right," she admitted. "I am really grateful you stayed last night. If I had come back here alone after what happened yesterday, I don't think I could have slept a wink. It really helped. It's just that with you being what you are, I feel nervous around you."

"That's OK. We all have to go soon anyway to get the nail and we are grateful for your hospitality. We just need a little while to get ourselves together, that's all."

Blackbird appeared through the doorway, handed a mug of coffee to me. "Here, you had better have this back." She passed me the Dead Knife, holding it gingerly by the wood of the handle so her skin didn't touch the blade. I took it from her, watching the blade shimmer and fall into blackness.

"May I use your shower?" she said to Claire.

Claire was distracted by the black blade. "Of course. Help yourself."

"Thanks." She went towards the bathroom.

There was a pause while Claire waited for the bathroom door to close.

"You found the Highsmiths, then?" Claire commented, nodding towards the knife.

"We did. That's why we need you to get the nail."

"I see. You don't have to tell me, of course, but does it bother you when she's a pensioner one minute and a girl the next?"

"I'm getting used to it," I replied. "You don't have anything I could wrap this in, do you?" I indicated the knife.

Claire stood and went into the hallway. She returned a moment later with a towelling cloth. "It's an old one, too big for a flannel and too small for a towel." She passed it to me.

I carefully wrapped the blade in the towel.

"I didn't know it did that," she said, watching the knife shift back to dull grey.

"Neither did I. You should see it when Veronica holds it."

"Perhaps not," she demurred.

I let the subject of the knife drop and concentrated on getting ready to leave. An hour later we were all dressed and ready to go. I cancelled the seals on the doors and we left.

"I'm sorry if I was touchy earlier," Blackbird said to Claire as she locked the front door behind her.

"I didn't notice," said Claire. Curiously, that didn't sound untrue, as if she had willed it to be so.

"We're grateful for you putting us up and for coming with us to get the nail."

"And I'm grateful for what you did for Jerry. He would have died if you hadn't helped, wouldn't he?"

"Eventually," Blackbird confirmed.

Claire had called a taxi and a black cab was waiting for us when we got downstairs. We all got into the back and Claire gave the driver crisp instructions to take us to the Strand. I sat on the jockey seat while the two women sat on either side at the back while we rumbled through the streets.

Blackbird had gone back to the appearance she had in Shropshire, the one I had said I liked. She had a gypsy skirt and a loose cotton top in an emerald green that brought out the sparkle in her eyes. Her hair formed a cloud of gold and copper around her head and against Claire's sombre outfit of low heels, dark blue skirt and matching blouse, she looked exotic.

The cab driver dropped us near the church of St Mary-le-Strand and I paid him. We walked with Claire down the Strand and across the wide road until we were outside the Royal Courts of Justice.

"I won't be long," Claire told us.

"You're not going in alone," Blackbird told her. "We'll come with you."

"It's OK. The building is closed on a Sunday but they're used to me going in at odd times. I'll get the nail and bring it straight back."

"Don't imagine they've given up, Claire. They're just waiting for the right opportunity. You're not safe until the knife is re-forged and the ceremony has been performed. We're coming in with you."

She looked as if she were about to argue and then changed her mind. "All right then, if you think so."

We went to a side gate where a security guard was on duty. I felt a tingle as Blackbird's magic encompassed her and me. Claire nodded and smiled at him; we followed after. Claire pulled a pass from her handbag and the guard looked at it and nodded. He barely glanced at either Blackbird or me as we walked past behind her. Claire spoke to him for a moment and then joined us.

"Keith says it was quiet over the weekend and security haven't reported any problems."

"That doesn't mean anything. You saw how easy it is for us to get inside. The smallest distraction would be enough."

We walked through a side entrance and across the main hall over to the stone stairs up to the first floor. Claire's shoes echoed on the tiled floor as we followed her towards the office. As we approached she slowed down and then halted.

"What's the matter?" asked Blackbird.

"Nothing. It's just that, well, isn't it the other way?"

"Isn't what the other way?" asked Blackbird.

"The office. I know it used to be this way but now I'm not sure."

"What are you talking about."

"The office. Didn't we move offices?" She looked bemused as if her memory was failing her.

"Claire, we met you in your offices last week. It was at the end of this corridor. Unless you moved after we went on Friday then it's still there."

"Yes, of course. You're right. How silly of me." She still didn't sound convinced.

"Well go on then," Blackbird urged.

Claire looked confused for a moment and then carried on. As we moved down the corridor towards the door to the office I could feel the hackles on the back of my neck rise. Claire stopped again.

"Can you feel that?" I asked Blackbird.

Claire answered, "They're in there, aren't they?"

Blackbird moved around to stand beside Claire. "Who is, Claire? Who's in there?"

"I don't know. The people you're hiding from, the ones that will try and stop us."

"If they were in there then you wouldn't know it until it was too late. They're just trying to frighten you. Feel the fear and understand it. It's false. You have no reason to be afraid. It's your office and there's nothing there."

"But they're in there. I can feel it."

"It's an old trick, Claire. Confuse the path and then leave a non-specific fear for those who get through. Let it latch onto uncertainties and exploit inner fears."

"They were here, weren't they?"

"Yes, they've been here. They've gone, though."

"How do you know they're not still in there?" She glanced nervously towards the door.

"Because if they were, you wouldn't know about it until it was too late."

"It could be a double bluff. They could be in there waiting for us."

"Then why leave the warding?"

"To turn away casual intruders?" I suggested.

"You're not helping," said Blackbird.

"Claire could be right, though. What if they're in there waiting for us."

"Oh, don't you start. Listen to your heart. Feel the warding there and know it as I know it. Hold the fear up and examine it under a cold light. Greet it like an old friend. Can you do that?"

I tried to do as she said.

"Now, does it change? Does it switch to something else and wriggle into another crack in your confidence? Does it slither into deeper uncertainties, looking for darker fears to latch onto?"

"No. It's just that one thing. They're here and waiting for us."

"That's because there's no one driving it. It is what it is and that's all it can be. If they were here then it would feel different; as if it had a life of its own."

It made sense in a strange kind of way. The fear, once faced, was just that. It lost its power and became something small and irrelevant.

"I still don't think I can go in there," said Claire.

"I can," said Blackbird. She turned and swept towards the doors, throwing them open.

At the moment she opened the doors, the fear vanished. Beyond the doors, though, we could see the office was wrecked. Claire's desk had been upturned onto the floor with one steel leg bent out at an awkward angle. Bookcases filled with legal works had been pulled down and the books scattered around the floor. Handfuls of pages from books had been ripped from their bindings and strewn around the room, drawers were pulled open and their contents dumped onto the floor.

"Oh no," said Claire. "Look at the mess."

With the fear dispelled, Claire walked forward and stood in the doorway, surveying the damage.

The double doors into the Remembrancer's office had been flung open, the bookshelves pulled over and pictures pulled from the walls and smashed on the floor. It looked like someone had jumped up and down on them, buckling the frames and tearing the canvasses.

"I don't understand. How could this happen? We're supposed to have security."

"Not against intruders like these," said Blackbird.

"I need to call them. They're supposed to check these offices overnight."

"Don't blame them," I told her. "Can you imagine what walking down that corridor would have been like in the dark on your own?"

"But why didn't they raise the alarm?"

"For what reason?" Blackbird asked her. "Because they were scared? Because one particular corridor was triggering an irrational fear of the dark? Security guards are supposed to be immune from that sort of thing. I can't see anyone admitting they wouldn't check certain offices just because it was making the hairs on the back of their neck stand on end."

"Still, they ought to have done something."

"It's probably just as well they didn't. Can you imagine what would have happened if someone had disturbed the people that did this? At least all you have to do is clear up from the vandalism. There aren't any corpses."

"You have a point. I'd better let security know, though. They'll need to notify the police."

"Before you call in the police, we need the nail. If it's still here?"

"It should be in the safe at the back there." She began edging around the broken desk to get to the cupboard at the back of the office.

"Stop."

The words were out of my mouth before I was even conscious of the prickling sensation down my spine.

Claire paused. "Is something wrong?"

"Don't you feel it?" I glanced at Blackbird who raised her eyebrows.

"I don't feel anything. What is it?"

"There's something here."

"Are you sure it's not just the remnants of the fear warding? It can take a while to dissipate?"

"No. It got stronger as Claire went towards the cupboard with the safe in it. It's not the same. Claire, can you retrace your steps back to us?"

"I think so. I can't see anything odd, though. It all looks fine."

"Just do as I say. Call it intuition," I told her.

She negotiated her way back to us and then looked faintly bemused when nothing happened. "It looked fine to me," she repeated.

I followed the route she'd taken, taking each step slowly and carefully, looking for the telltale prickling that had alerted me. Something in the room was causing the sensation and I was trying to trace the source. As I came to the desk and began to edge around the bent leg, the unpleasant tingling returned, but as Claire had said, there was no sign of any barrier.

I was about to place my hand on the leg of the up-turned desk so I could slip past it when a jolt in my hand stopped me.

My hand was almost touching the metal, and where I had been about to grasp there was a tiny movement. A small cluster of tiny lightless spots were migrating across the surface to where my hand would be. The movement was slow and it was only the prickling sensation that alerted me to it. I snatched my hand away and the spots immediately halted. Then they spread out, slowly edging away from each other, until they formed a perfect ring across the corner of the metal surface.

The last time I had seen spots like that, they were in my flat. They had run across the walls and ceiling and then eaten through the wood of my bedroom door until it was rotted through.

It was darkspore.

TWENTY-FIVE

The vandalised office was not as randomly wrecked as I had thought.

Reaching sideways I lifted a torn leaf of paper from a ripped volume left on the top of a filing cabinet and held it between finger and thumb. I edged it forward until it just touched the edge of the black circle on the leg of the upturned desk. As soon as it touched the surface, the black spread onto the paper, running along it like a flame. Immediately I let go and it fell towards the floor, covered by the infecting mould.

I edged back from the desk to where Blackbird and Claire were waiting.

"It's darkspore. She's left spots of it in the office. I thought the vandalism was random. I thought they had taken out their frustrations on the office and left the room in this state as a warning, a kind of symbol as to what was to come. I was wrong. It's a trap. She was expecting us to come here and she left it so anyone who touched the furniture would be infected with darkspore."

"What's darkspore?" asked Claire.

"Never mind," I told her. "Just don't get any of it on you."

"It's more than a trap," said Blackbird. "The darkspore isn't her creature. It's her. It has her sense, her feeling. It can't see or hear but what it knows, she knows. If it had got onto one of us then she would know it, wherever she is."

"It could be everywhere," I told her. "It could be on any surface anywhere in this room; outside even."

"No. Like all Fey gifts it has its limits. The more of herself she left here, the more she is weakened. In time it will die without her. She spreads herself thinly to do this and it's a sign of desperation. It will only be in the places she thinks are important, the places she doesn't want us to reach."

"The safe containing the nail is behind there," confirmed Claire, "inside the cupboard on the floor."

"Could she have taken the nail already?" I asked.

"It's a very old safe; they keep offering to replace it with a new one, but it only contains a few documents, some petty cash and the items for the ceremony. The locking mechanism is partly iron, though. We keep it as a guard against, well, against your kind."

"So the nail should still be there."

"That makes sense," said Blackbird. "If she couldn't reach it then she would make sure we couldn't either. Hence the darkspore. We can't let her win, Niall."

"I know. How do I get into the safe? Is it a combination?"

"You'll need this key," said Claire holding out a long, double-sided brass key, the complex pattern of teeth attesting to the security of the safe.

I took it from her and considered my options. I could drag the desk aside and pick my way through the detritus scattered on the floor, but it would be like walking through a minefield. The thought of making the slightest contact with the darkspore made my insides turn cold. The noises from my garden were still haunting me.

"You said it's still part of her?" I asked Blackbird.

"Yes. She'll know if it touches you. If even the tiniest speck—"

"Good. Take Claire out into the corridor."

"Why, what are you planning?"

"Why do I have to go outside?" said Claire.

"Just do what I ask. I don't know how much I can control it."

"Niall, the last time you tried something like this we nearly ended up in next week."

"This is different. We're going to fight fire with fire."

"You can't do that here. It's not exactly subtle. People are going to notice." She glanced at Claire, none too subtly.

"What will I notice?" said Claire.

"Do you have another idea?" I asked Blackbird.

"Maybe I could use the knife, burn it out," she said.

"And burn the building down with it? With all these books and paper? The fire would almost certainly spread and if you miss a speck, just a tiny mote, then it's all for nothing. At least my way we get all of it in one go."

"It's her, Niall. She's going to feel it as if she were here. And you can't reach all of her, only the parts she left behind. She'll know you were here and she will hate you with a vengeance."

"You forget, I was in that glade with her. I stood there helpless, with my teeth chattering, while she helped herself. She thought she was being clever, leaving traces of herself, but now the tables are turned. So she'll know it was me? Good, I want her to."

Claire interrupted us. "Will you two stop talking in riddles? What's going on?"

"We need to be outside," Blackbird told her, guiding her by the shoulder out into the corridor.

"What's he going to do?" She looked back, trying to figure out what was about to happen.

"You have to trust us. I don't know what you've been told or what's in those journals of yours, but you have to trust us."

408

"What's the matter? What's he doing in there?"

Blackbird pulled the double doors closed behind her leaving me alone in the infected room. Even through the door I could hear Claire's persistent questions and Blackbird's reassurances.

I let it fade into the background.

When I fought Fenlock, I had used my talent unconsciously. Panic and instinct had brought it on and given me the break I needed, but then I had used it. It had sung its hungry song in my veins and I had listened and been seduced by it, consuming Fenlock utterly until only dust remained. I had felt sick afterwards, repulsed by what I had done and felt sure I would never use it like that again.

Now, though, I had a different reason. Now I had a chance to strike back, to make my presence felt and show my hunters I had teeth.

I closed my eyes and reached inward. The temperature dropped and all the little noises that accumulate unnoticed into the background died, leaving a potent hush. I opened my eyes and found the room swimming in moonlight. The dappled light rippled over the debris, making it insubstantial and bringing a faint sense of vertigo.

A noise filtering through the door distracted me for a moment. It was Claire. She was insisting there was something wrong, that the lights were behaving like they did with the strange phone calls. I heard her telling Blackbird they had returned and that I would need her help.

The door handle rattled behind me. I heard Blackbird's voice.

"He's fine, Claire. Come away from the door."

"It's them, I tell you. They've returned."

"No. It's Niall. He's doing this."

"Niall? How is Niall doing it?!" The rattling became more urgent. "We've got to stop him. He's one of them, isn't he? He's from the Seventh Court. He tricked us. He tricked me into giving him the key. Now he can get the nail. You have to stop him."

"No, Claire. Let him be."

The rattling intensified, but then halted suddenly, followed by a crumpled thump. Blackbird had dealt with the problem in her own way.

I turned my attention back to the room.

When Fenlock attacked me, I hadn't needed to call gallowfyre. My defence had been instinctive and once it had him I couldn't let go. This was different. The room was filled with dappled light but the gallowfyre wasn't active. It was merely there, an outward expression of my connection to the void. There was no enemy trying to throttle me or shake my teeth loose. Somehow I had to bend it to my will and make it do my bidding.

I pictured it in my head, rolling through the room, consuming everything. It swam uncertainly.

Stretching out my hand, I expected it to stream forth. It remained the same.

I concentrated on making it flood out, like a river or a stream. Nothing happened.

My hands fell back to my sides. So much for my ability to handle this. I had claimed I knew what to do, convinced that my instincts would come to my aid.

Blackbird had said I had to convince myself it was true, that I had to know and trust my instincts. Well I did know, but it wasn't enough. It needed something else. I was almost on the point of turning back to the door behind me and asking Blackbird for some helpful hints when it came to me.

Trying to wield gallowfyre like a sword or a club wasn't working. I been thinking of it as a weapon with which I could strike out. I was wrong. It wasn't a weapon. It was part of me.

Closing my eyes, I felt the cool dim light as it swam around me. I told myself it responded to me because it was me. I looked inwards, following the dappled light to its source deep inside, feeling it become stronger, harsher, burning like a molten core within me. In the centre of that core was nothing.

I had found the opening.

In my mind's eye it was both absence and presence, a duality at the centre of my being. It was a hole within me left gaping to the void, opening out into endless nothing and allowing endless nothing back in. I smiled inwardly, understanding it was a mirror and a gateway. I carried it with me. It would allow me to reach into the void anytime I wanted to. At the same time, it allowed the void to reach into me.

Now I understood.

I opened the gateway.

It rolled into me like a seething flood. I heard my own sharp breath and felt my spine arch as it hit me, flooding down my nerves with icy power. My muscles went rigid, my eyes shot open. My nerves shrieked as the floodgates opened and it boiled out of me, a swirling nimbus of ravenous shadows. The flickering moonlight showed the shadows of tentacles, unseen except for the darkness they cast in the light of the gallowfyre, they licked the walls and swept across the surfaces. The tiny motes left hiding there were consumed almost incidentally as the flood of dark power swept through the debris, the dark-spore sparking tiny flares in the roiling darkness as it was consumed. In those flares, I heard the echoes of distant screams as they boiled away.

It made me smile.

The void sang though me, its dark harmonies humming through my veins, the heavy bass of hunger rumbling around like echoes of thunder. It rolled like a restless flood around the room, searching for anything to fill that gaping emptiness. I held my breath. For one terrible second I thought it would turn back on me so I would end up like Fenlock, a withered husk. It calmed, though, pooling around me, sending curious tendrils into the debris, searching for morsels like a curious medusa.

"Niall! Niall, can you hear me? You might want to do something."

I turned to the door behind me. It had found the crack under the door and was coiling into the crevice. Panic filled me and, in response, it wriggled back and wound around me, curling around my legs protectively.

I found myself unwilling to pull it back within me. It was connected with me in a way that was profound. I knew I should send it back to the dark well within me but part of me wanted to unleash it and let it feed itself.

For the first time, I understood. This was what the Untainted wanted; to unleash their power on the world and let it sing its hungry song. This was what they were fighting for; the right to be true to themselves. The thought sobered me and I steeled myself, turning the coils inwards, calling the darkness to slip back into the well where it sank back into the core. My gaze turned inwards for a moment, marvelling at the thing within me. It was tiny yet filled with endless emptiness, a minute black sun shining inside me.

Blackbird had said in the room above the abandoned tube station, "We stand between life and power," not as a statement of belief but as an acknowledgement of fact. Here it was. This core of power was in me now, as much part of me as my heart or my mind. It would be there for as long as I lived and finally, when I died, it would turn on me and consume me.

Strangely, there was peace in that.

Blackbird started when I opened the door. She was standing close as if she'd been listening for something, but not so close as to touch the door.

"Are you well?" she asked.

"I'm fine."

She must have heard the uncertainty in my voice because she arched an eyebrow at me.

"I'm good. Just a little spaced," I reassured her.

She smiled. "The first time is like that. It's like opening a door in your heart."

"Or a well in your soul."

"Did you succeed?"

"I touched everything. If there were a trace left, I would know it." I looked down at the slumped form at Blackbird's feet. Claire's eyes were open, but she wasn't seeing me. "Is she going to be all right?"

"Get me a chair, would you? She'll be better if she's upright."

I turned back into the office and found an upturned chair which I placed against the wall. Blackbird dragged Claire inside and pushed the door closed with her feet. Between us we manhandled Claire into the chair.

I went to retrieve her handbag from the floor outside where it had fallen before anyone noticed what was going on, though I could feel Blackbird's influence around us, turning curious eyes away.

When I re-entered, Claire was sat forward with her face in her hands.

"Never," she said, "never do that again."

Blackbird stood out of arms reach. "You left me no choice. If you had broken into the room when Niall was calling gallowfyre then you would be dead."

"I should be dead." She looked up at me. "Gallowfyre. That's in the journals. Only the Seventh Court have gallowfyre, isn't that right?"

"Apparently," I admitted.

"I don't understand. If you're from the Seventh Court, why are you here?"

"He's not from the Seventh Court, though how that can happen, neither of us knows right now."

"So what does that make you?" she asked me.

"I wish I knew, Claire."

"Do you have the nail?"

"Not yet."

"I don't suppose there's anything I can do to prevent you taking it, though, is there? You have my key already."

"You need us to have the nail, Claire," said Blackbird. "I know you have doubts but we are your only hope."

413

"Hope of what?" she asked.

"Of preserving the world you live in. Of keeping the Seventh Court from entering your world whenever they wish and using it as they will."

"I suppose I believe you."

"You know I can't lie."

"I know you don't always tell the truth either. Very well, take it. Use it."

"Thank you."

I took the brass key and, despite being sure that no trace of the darkspore could remain, I picked my way carefully to the cupboard with the safe in it. The door was ajar and I kicked it open with my foot. Filling the bottom of the cupboard was an old safe with enamelled green paint and brass handles. The key fitted easily and turned with oiled precision. The handle turned down and I felt the solid clunk as the bolts retracted into the door. It swung open, revealing shelves of papers together with the soft black leather pouch containing the nails. I collected the bundle and closed the safe, locking it again to remove the key. The iron in the pouch weighed heavy in my hand, its jarring vibration making my nerves jangle.

I returned the key to her and handed her the nails. "It would be easier if you removed it."

"Still reluctant to touch the others?"

"I could tip them all out onto the floor and pick out the one I want, but that would be rude."

She considered this for a moment and then nodded, unrolling the case on her lap.

"If you wanted it badly enough, you could have taken it any time." She held up the sixty-first nail for me to take.

As I touched it, the metal fell into blackness.

Claire snatched her hand away. "Gracious, that's cold." She rubbed her hand. "Oh, it's like the knife, isn't it?" she said, catching on.

"Something else for your journal," said Blackbird. "If what we are intending works out, we will bring the new

Quick Knife to you later so it can be incorporated into the ceremony on Tuesday. Will you be here?"

"Yes. I have to get all this cleared up and there are all the preparations for the ceremony. There's still a lot to do. I'm going to be here until midnight at this rate."

"Don't take unnecessary risks. If you can, have someone stay close to you. If we're not back by nightfall, go to the Highsmiths in Shropshire. Take the Remembrancer and his family with you," Blackbird suggested.

"Will you meet me there?"

"No, but they have a house full of iron. You may be safe there for a while."

"A while?"

"It depends what happens when the barrier comes down. I think they will come here first. This is where it's weakest."

"What will they do?"

"Whatever it is, they've waited eight hundred years to do it, so I don't think it will be pretty."

"Should I warn someone? The authorities? The army?"

"No one is going to believe you, even if you tell them. And if they did, what are they going to do? Shoot people who look a bit strange? Evacuate London?"

"Bring the knife, I'll get Jerry to the Courts on Tuesday."

"That would be best," Blackbird agreed.

I slipped the nail into my trouser pocket, making sure it wouldn't fall out, and then Claire escorted us down to the security gate, her weak smile as we parted a testament to her uncertainty.

Out on the Strand, it had clouded over and fat drops of rain were starting to patter onto the pavement. It was just as well that we weren't there long. After only a few moments a huge white van pulled up alongside the pavement and the window wound down to reveal Ben.

"Jump in," he shouted over to us. "I'll get a ticket if I stop here." The police standing guard at the gates for the Royal Courts of Justice were already eyeing him warily.

We scrambled over and jumped up onto the bench seat of the van. Ben moved off and there was a brief fumbling followed by a short argument as I made Blackbird wear the only seatbelt. The other one was wedged under the seat somewhere.

"I've been driving round for about a quarter of an hour, waiting for you to show. We're not going far," Ben told us. "I just need to find somewhere to park this thing. It won't go into a multi-storey. It's too tall."

"What have you got in here?" I asked him.

"It's almost empty, but Jeff wanted the car and, anyway, this is a diesel." He said this as if it explained everything.

We drove down Fleet Street and turned down towards the river, making another right to circle down around the Embankment. Ben eventually found a metered parking spot around by Temple tube station. He fished into his overalls for change.

"How long do you think we'll be?" he asked us.

"That depends how long you need to finish the knife," Blackbird answered.

"If we get four hours, that should be enough shouldn't it? It costs the earth to park round here."

"It is a bit more expensive than Shropshire," I agreed.

He jogged through the raindrops and fed coins into the parking meter, returning with a ticket, which he peeled and stuck to the inside of the window. Then he opened the back of the van. He took out a blue metal toolbox, rusted in places where the paint had peeled away, and a short three-section ladder.

"I won't be easy to get that down through the passages," I told him.

"It's small enough to get into most places," he reassured me. "And we can use it to get to the keyhole. I can't scramble around like you young things. My legs aren't what they used to be."

I nodded, accepting his wisdom. It had been a good thought.

I carried the ladder for him and we walked quickly back up through the Inns of Court to get to the door leading down to the river. Blackbird knew where she was going, so she took the lead and I followed on after, putting Ben in the middle where we could keep an eye on him. Along the way I felt the tingle of Blackbird's magic gently encompass us, lest the strange procession of a young woman with a torch, an old man with a tool-box and another man with a ladder, walking in line through Temple on a Sunday, attract unwanted attention. I shook my head at the strange world I now inhabited.

We reached the doorway and Blackbird pushed it open, listening in the opening for any disturbance below. There was nothing to hear above the faint stir as the water fell over the weir below us. She produced the torch she had bought earlier and clicked it on. Ben found a larger torch in his toolbox. Mine was still at the bottom of the river, but I could make light if I had to. Anyway, it would take both hands to carry the ladder.

She led again and I followed with Ben bringing up the rear while he held his light for me as I manoeuvred the ladder around the tight corners of the stairway. He was right; it was a good size for tight places.

We reached the ledge along the edge of the river. The foam from the weir sloughed off and drifted luminously downstream. The river was higher and louder than it had been when we had been here before, the new rain swelling the flow.

With Ben holding one end of the ladder and me holding the other, we made our way slowly along the slimy walkway, scraping against the bricks as we edged our way along. With the ladder to carry, it took longer to reach the anvil, though I could feel the brooding presence ahead in the dark, waiting for us.

We knew we had arrived when the muted roar of the waterfall meant that we had to shout to each other. Blackbird flicked her torch around the arches and the gantry, shining it into nooks and crannies as Ben and I carried the ladder along the bank.

"We're on our own," she shouted to me. "There's no sign that anyone's been here and the iron door looks untouched."

It was good news. Part of me had been expecting Raffmir and his friend to be waiting for us, guarding the iron door. Perhaps we could get away with finishing this before anyone found out what we were doing.

Blackbird climbed up onto the gantry while Ben and I manhandled the ladder and the toolbox up behind her. Then we crossed over the gantry above the underground river and Ben climbed down so I could pass things down to him. I followed them down and we clustered around the place where the iron door was mounted high in the wall. Blackbird held the torch while I extracted the nail from where it was safely stored in my pocket.

"How does this work then?" Ben asked.

"I don't know. Why don't you try it first? I'd rather not touch the door if I can possibly help it." The memory of my chance contact with the iron gates at Australia House was still sharp in my mind. I had no wish to be thrown backwards into the churning water under the falls.

I carefully dropped the nail into the middle of his palm.

"Which way round does it go?"

"We don't know. Try it head end first. If it won't go in that way then try it the other way."

He reached up high and pressed the square end of the head into the lock. It went in a short way and stopped. He tried twisting it but nothing happened. The hole was just the right size for the head, though, making me think we were on the right track.

"Try the other way around," I told him.

He pulled out the nail and turned it point first. It slipped into the lock almost up to the head.

"There's some sort of spring mechanism." He showed me, pressing the nail in so the end of the head was flush with the door. As he relaxed his finger the nail sprang out again. The door stayed resolutely shut.

"It fits perfect," said Ben, "But nothing's happening."

"I think it needs a Fey hand," Blackbird said. "It would make sense as a fail-safe. The nail was entrusted to humanity, but humans wouldn't be allowed to open the door without one of the Feyre present."

"Well, I'd better do it then."

I was taller than Ben and I could reach unaided. Just in case, though, I fished into my pocket and extracted the Dead Knife. It was still wrapped in the towelling Claire had given me. If I was thrown backwards it wouldn't do to lose one knife while trying to replace the other. I gave it to Blackbird for safe keeping and she slipped it into her bag.

She stepped back and Ben made room for me. I steeled myself and reached up. Ben had left the nail in the lock and the head protruded about half an inch from the surface of the door. I put my forefinger on the end of the nail and it shimmered into blackness. I pushed it slowly in towards the door, being as careful as I could not to touch the surface of the iron. A hair's breadth away, there was still some give in the spring. I had to take a chance and touch the door.

I pressed the nail home. As my finger touched the surface of the door, the surface shimmered in the centre. A disk about the size of a large coin fell into blackness. The disk pushed inwards. There was a heavy clunk in the door and it stopped.

I carefully pulled out my finger and there was a further clunk as the crack around the door grew darker. I pulled the nail free from the lock and the heavy door swung open slowly. Moving backwards out of the way, I could see it opened into a deep cavity set into the wall. I couldn't see much inside despite Ben's attempt to shine his torch up into it, but I could feel the dark emanations coming from whatever was inside. Ben reached up and put his arm into the space.

"There's something here. Hang on a sec."

He got closer to the wall and reached up again, this time grasping something, stepping up on tiptoe to reach. I took the opportunity to step back and slip the nail back into my trouser pocket, keeping it safe.

"Whoever put it up here was a taller man than me or he had steps to climb on," said Ben.

"Shall I get the ladders?" I asked him.

"It's fine. I can manage."

He dragged the toolbox over and stood on it to give him the height he needed. Neither Blackbird nor I offering to help since we could both feel the vibrations from whatever was contained there. It had the same malevolent nature as the anvil and although that was a promising sign given what we were looking for, it didn't make it any easier for us to bear.

There was a scraping noise, audible even over the rushing water, and Ben used both hands to draw down a huge hammer. Blackbird and I both stepped back from it.

"It's a big 'un, isn't it?" Ben said, hefting it down to the floor. "It's much bigger than I'd have thought it needed to be. Are you sure it's the right one?"

"Oh yes." Blackbird was standing back, hand braced against the wall. I backed away towards the ladder up to the gantry. The cloying rankness of it pressed against me, like a weight on my chest.

"I might need a hand getting it over onto the island." He scanned the darkness between him and the island.

"We're not going to be much help to you there, I'm afraid, Ben. I don't really want to be any nearer to it than this and I think Rabbit's too close already."

I turned and scrambled back to the gantry ladder just to get away from the thing. Ben had said it would be tuned, but if it was then it was tuned to a note so sour, so off, it made my spine cringe to hear it.

I heard Ben behind me, asking Blackbird how he was supposed to get the hammer over to the anvil.

As I reached the top of the ladder I could see that getting the hammer across was going to be the least of our problems. Far down the tunnel above the falls a familiar flickering light was dancing across the vaulted roof.

"We have company!" I shouted down to them. "They're coming down the tunnels. Use the ladders and get over to the island. I don't think they'll be able to touch you near the anvil."

"Who is it?" he shouted.

"Not friends, that's for certain. Just get there as fast as you can. Blackbird and I will try to delay them, but start work on the knife as soon as you can."

"It's not quick work," he called up to me.

"Never mind. The hammer and the anvil will hold them off. They won't be able to touch you." I hoped it was the truth but uncertainty rankled in my throat as I said it.

He grabbed the ladders and began sliding them out to make a walkway across to the island.

Blackbird climbed up to the gantry after me. I stepped over to offer her a hand up.

"They've come," I told her. "They're coming down the tunnels. I can see the light of the gallowfyre reflecting off the walls."

We watched the growing light and the outlines of two dark figures making their way swiftly along the ledge at the side of the dark water.

"Shit!" she said. "I did wonder when they spoke before of the seals being intact on the door whether they had placed a warding on the door to warn them if anyone opened it. They must know we have the hammer."

"If Ben can finish the knife then maybe they'll just leave?" I suggested. I tried to keep the note of hopeless optimism out of my voice.

"They're not going to let him leave these tunnels, Niall. They came to stop us."

"He has the hammer and the knife. Maybe he can use them to protect himself?"

"While he stays on the island, he's probably as safe as he can be, but they won't leave him there. They don't have to do anything. He's so exposed and he can't stay there forever. There are two of them and they're very good at waiting."

"Can we hold them off?"

"We'll have to. It's too late to leave now anyway." The light was starting to flicker on the walls behind me as they approached.

"Blackbird..." Suddenly there were things I needed to say, things that stuck in my throat, not because they were lies but because they were true.

"You can tell me later." She lifted her chin, the determination showing in her eyes.

I nodded once and turned to the growing light in the tunnel.

TWENTY-SIX

Blackbird and I stood together, waiting for the Untainted to reach us.

We were at the only crossing place, the gantry between one side of the dark flowing water and the other, our backs to the thundering waterfall. To get to where the smith was re-forging the knife they had to face us. If I'd had more confidence in our ability to hold them off, I might have felt better about it.

Ben had crossed the river to the island below the falls, drawing the ladder across behind him. He had immediately started his preparations to work on the knife, spurred on by the arrival of the intruders. If he could finish the work then we might stand a chance of getting away.

As we turned our attention to the flickering light approaching down the long tunnel upstream there was a terrible sound. The clang of the hammer on the anvil was a sweet dissonance. It built in a steady *tonk... tonk... tonk... tonk...* until I thought it would jangle my nerves apart, but what came after was unspeakable. When the hammer hit the knife it was a jolt of agony.

THANG!

Vibrations jarred into the core of me. Everything sang in a fraction of a second of pure torment. It was like having something jab into the nerves of your teeth.

I shook myself, trying to shed the dying echoes and concentrate on the approaching threat.

Two figures were picking their way carefully along the walkway on the left-hand side of the tunnel. They were approaching rapidly without seeming to hurry. I recognised the first from the long Edwardian coat he had worn as he had thrown his arms wide while Blackbird and I pressed ourselves into the shadows behind him when we had been hiding in the shadows of the vaulting below. His features were a mere outline, silhouetted against the dappled light spilling up onto the archway of the tunnel. His gawky stature and the finicky way he picked his way past the more noisome debris on the walkway identified him without needing to hear the rolling baritone of his voice. It was Raffmir.

I also recognised the figure following him.

Unlike Raffmir who was moving quickly but carefully along the walkway, she moved easily. The long flowing pleats of her skirt rippled over the uneven surface without catching on the broken edges. She was tall, dressed in a long grey dress that only served to bring back the memory of a circular glade under a crystal sky. I realised now what I should have known all along. The slurring shambling figure that entered my flat and lay hidden in my garden, the one who we had encountered here in the tunnels and who had sensed our presence despite the dank smell and the thunder of the waterfall was the same woman who had drawn me to the frozen glade. It was Raffmir's sister who had called me lost brother and cornered me at the hospital. It was her darkspore I had burned away with gallowfyre. Except that this was neither a dream nor a walking corpse. This time she'd come in person.

Tonk... tonk... tonk... THANG!

The sound rang again down the tunnel, reverberating in the confined space. I cringed as pain jabbed into the back of my brain, echoing the hammer blow. The tunnel around Raffmir dimmed and faltered as the sound reached him, and he halted, uncertain of his footing in the onslaught of sound. Then he recovered and continued towards us.

They had come to prevent the re-forging of the knife and we were the only thing in their way. I glanced at Blackbird who was standing proud and ready. I squared my shoulder and reached within to the molten core of emptiness there. I opened myself to its call and let the darkness spill through me and out over the water, my own rippling light echoing that of Raffmir.

Tonk… tonk… tonk… THANG!

Again the hammer strike rang through me. The link with my inner core faltered momentarily as the sound of the hammer rang out. The glow from Raffmir faltered and for a second we were in darkness, surrounded only by the dying echoes and the thundering of the water over the falls behind us.

As Raffmir approached the gantry, his glow returned, as did my own. Fingers of shadow spilled out from each of us, worming out across the light between us as he reached. Gallowfyre tentacles swelled out and seemed to grapple, playing out the conflict in shadowed shifting moonlight between us.

Each of us tested the defences of the other. Where it touched there was a pressure, a sense of other, defining the boundary between us. At the boundary, a shimmering light flared into being, a purple so dark it was almost invisible. It hung like an ultraviolet curtain across the water ahead of us, defining the border between two powers, the wall of light flexing and bending like a dark aurora where we tested each other's strength.

It was Raffmir who called to us. "Greetings from the Seventh Court. We wish to parley."

Blackbird answered for us. "What is there to speak of?"

As she called out, Ben started hammering again.

Tonk... tonk... tonk... THANG!

The light faltered and the pressure between us dissolved. I struggled to regain my connection with the void. Raffmir was a split second faster and he took a bold step forward as his light spilled out over the water. I found my link and my own light flowed out again, the darkness I called from within buffeting against his.

"You know we have come to prevent the knife being re-forged," he called out. "You stand between us and our goal."

"And?" said Blackbird.

"First of all I would request you to ask your smith to pause in his labours so we may have a rational discussion. Otherwise this could quickly come to a ruinous conclusion. Let us try and resolve this in a civilised fashion, if that is possible." His tone reminded me of an English gentleman, forced into an unpleasant situation but prepared to discharge his duty nonetheless. Despite having to call over the muted thunder of the water, his tone was relaxed and warm, though there was an underlying menace to his smooth words.

"He's finishing the knife," Blackbird assured him.

"Then a moment or two of rest while we speak will allow him to approach his task with renewed vigour, will it not?"

"If I ask him to pause, you and your companion will do us no harm in the meantime? You will not move any further forward or take any advantage?"

"You stand between us and him. What can we do?" he asked, stretching his arms wide.

As he finished his sentence, the sound of the hammer began again.

Tonk... tonk... tonk... THANG!

Again, my link with the void faltered and once more he was faster than I was. He took another step forward, his sister edging up behind him.

"We can talk," said Blackbird, a little too eagerly. She turned to the rail behind us. "Smith! Hold your work.

We have a situation up here." She was careful not to name him, giving them no advantage they did not already have.

Ben paused, shouting back up to us. "You mean it?"

"Yes. But if anything happens to us, just finish it. Agreed?"

"Right you are." The tapping prelude to the strike of the hammer ceased and Blackbird stepped back to my side. Even though the hammering on the anvil was necessary to our task, it was a relief that it had paused.

"If your companion will stand down, then I will do likewise," Raffmir offered.

Blackbird looked towards me and then nodded.

I eased my hold on his defences and, as I did, he recalled his gallowfyre. It wound back towards him like a great tentacled beast slipping beneath the surface. I recalled my own and had to smile as the image repeated itself.

"Now, we can talk. Yes?" Raffmir spoke smoothly, unexcited.

"The smith has stopped work, but he'll continue if anything happens to us," Blackbird told him. "What do you want?"

"I would have thought that was obvious." The voice floated across the black oily water. "I want the barrier to fail and the world to return to the way it was, the way it should be," he explained.

"It can't," I interjected. "Too much has changed. The world belongs to people now, human people. You can't turn the clock back," I told him.

"Oh, I don't want to turn it back. Humanity has its uses after all, but I'm afraid that the balance of power will have to change. Humanity must learn some respect." He laughed in a warm rich tone at his own joke.

"And how do you propose to teach them that respect?" I asked him.

"Ah, well. That is where the old ways are the best, don't you agree?"

"No, not really."

"And there you have it. You have a mixed background and it clouds your judgement."

"They will not give up their hold on this world easily. They have developed considerably while you've been elsewhere."

"I know. My sister and I have watched them. They have come far, but they still have nothing to rival the power of the Feyre. Speaking of power, that's an unusual talent you have there."

"Talent?"

"Summoning gallowfyre is not a talent usually displayed among those you refer to as the Gifted. Do I have the term right?"

"That is what we call ourselves, as you call yourselves Untainted," answered Blackbird.

"Quite so. You see, my sister was sent to kill your companion and she failed. She came back with a story about a human summoning gallowfyre and no one would believe her, certainly not those that set her the task. But it seems she was neither dreaming nor hallucinating?"

"It appears so," I admitted.

"And do you know how you came to inherit such a gift?"

"Do you think I would tell you if I did?"

"I suppose not, but there's little harm in asking," he shrugged. "You do realise you cannot stand against us?"

"We won't know until we try, will we?" said Blackbird.

"Your companion hasn't yet the control to match my own and my sister hasn't even begun to use her considerable talents. You will die here if you defy us."

"Then why are we even having this conversation?" she asked.

"I am giving you the opportunity to withdraw. There is no need for us to come into conflict over this. We are of the same blood, are we not?" The taint of falsehood hung over that last sentence.

"And you'll just let us walk away, will you?" Blackbird asked.

"Of course. There will be time later to engage in the settling of old scores."

"And the smith?"

"The smith stays," he stated in a cold voice, but then warmed again. "Surely we are not going to come into conflict over one measly human life?"

"You forget," said Blackbird. "We are each part human ourselves. Human lives mean more to us than they do to you."

"Your own lives should mean more. Leave now and we'll spare you, this once."

"We are not leaving," Blackbird told him.

"Come now, he knows he cannot best me and you are no match for my sister. We already know which of us is the stronger."

He was right, but I had remembered something else.

"It is true that you bested me in our first contest. But that was before I knew you. That was before I could name you, Raffmir."

There was a momentary pause. Then he erupted into laughter, a chocolate sound, completely at odds with the situation. "Oh, that's rich." He laughed. "I won't ask how you came by that name because you wouldn't tell me."

"Your sister told me."

I dropped it into the dark pool of his laughter and it faltered.

"I did not!" Her denial was filled with spite.

He could hear the truth in my words so he would know she had indeed told me, though not the circumstances. I blessed Blackbird for showing me that trick in dealing with Fenlock and Carris. The name might give me the edge I needed.

He turned to her and spoke in low tones for a moment.

"Never!" she screeched. "He's lying, I tell you."

429

"It's almost as if she doesn't know what she's saying any more." I used the same oily tone he'd adopted with us.

"Shut up!" she spat. "Half-breed mongrel scum."

"Peace, sister. I would love to know how he came to know that name, but it matters not." He addressed himself back to me. "Will you bargain with me, then? We both want something, do we not?"

"I don't want anything from you," I told him.

"That remains to be seen. Come, there must be something I can be tempt you with?"

"You have nothing I want."

"On the contrary, I can offer you the one thing no one else will. I can offer you a place for you and for your daughter. I spoke to her, you know?"

"She wouldn't speak to you." Now I knew who had called her mobile.

"You left her number on the phone-pad in your flat. It said 'Alex new mobile'. Unusual to give a boy's name to a girl. Initially I used the telephone but it said she was out of the area. I could still reach her, though."

I kicked myself mentally. I had been through the flat three times and I had still missed the numbers written on the phone pad in plain sight.

"There is nothing you could possibly offer us."

"Has your companion not explained to you how things are yet? How interesting." He paused, letting the words sink in. "Has she not told you that you will never be accepted into the courts of the Tainted? The Six Courts are very fine, and they accept humans, mongrels and pure Fey almost without discrimination." He laced his words with sarcasm. "But they will never accept one of the wraithkin."

"Why not?"

"You would have to ask them that, of course, but I believe they are repelled by our kind. We are uncanny to them and they will not allow us that close. Instead, you and your daughter would be orphans, renegades, unprotected and vulnerable to anyone that's prepared to set a price on your heart."

"I can look after myself," I told him, putting faith behind that assertion.

"And your daughter? If she shows her Fey genes then she will be as my sister. You see, my friend, our kind have a choice. We can be shunned and spurned as abominations, labelled as feeders on life and harbingers of doom. Or we can be respected and feared. But only the Seventh Court can offer you legitimacy and security. The others will not have you. Ask her."

This last was directed at Blackbird who stood beside me. I half-turned, so I could keep an eye on him and still see Blackbird's face.

"Is it true?" I asked her quietly.

"There's never been a need to," Blackbird protested. "The wraithkin don't join other courts."

"But Kareesh said we would have a place in the courts."

"What she actually said was 'the sight of something to help you secure your place in the courts'. I won't mislead you; these things can be tricky. She meant exactly what she said and nothing more."

"So she could have meant the Seventh Court."

"I don't know. Perhaps the Six Courts would make an exception. Your case is unique."

"You see how it is." Raffmir spoke again. "They will not have you. Only we can offer you a home."

It was a blow to realise that the sanctuary promised in Kareesh's vision was not as sure as I had thought. If the other courts wouldn't offer their protection then where did that leave Alex and me? His words set me thinking. My prime reason for being here was to gain some security for my daughter and for myself, to allow us to live unmolested. If we were part of the Seventh Court then they would stop hunting us and let us be, wouldn't they? He'd managed to hit on the one thing that might tempt me.

Then again, once the barrier broke down, the Seventh Court would be able to move freely into this world and everything would change. My friends, my work colleagues, even my enemies would all become fair game for the wraithkin. I didn't think I could live with that on my conscience and remain sane.

There was another factor he did not know about. If Blackbird truly was pregnant then there was another life to weigh in the balance. No world of Raffmir's making would be a safe haven for either child, for they would both be half-breeds.

Raffmir had stayed quiet, letting me consider. In the end it was time which weighed against him. It gave me the chance to consider what he had actually offered. Precisely nothing.

"It is an interesting offer, Raffmir. But I wonder if you are empowered to make such a bargain? Can you guarantee our safety within the Seventh Court? Can you even guarantee we will be accepted?"

"In life, there are few things guaranteed, my friend, but I will be your sponsor to the court and I will do my utmost to ensure that you and your daughter are accepted into it." His words twisted like worms. It was as close to a promise as he could come without actually answering my question.

"Then you are not empowered to offer the sanctuary of which you speak, but only to champion it."

"That is the same for all of the courts. The final decision always rests with the lord or lady that rules there."

"So I am to place my fate and that of my daughter in the hands of someone who has systematically organised the execution of every half-breed and mongrel they could find, along with those harbouring them? You take me for a fool, Raffmir."

"You are consigning yourself to a life on the run, my friend, maybe worse. Think of your daughter."

"I am thinking of her. You have nothing I want, Raffmir."

"If you do not withdraw then you will die. What of your daughter then?"

"You said you were the stronger, Raffmir, but that was before you mentioned Alex. I will not lose this battle to you, for to lose would be to consign my daughter to your hands and I will not let that happen if it means my life. I will fight you to the death. Yours."

"Then die!" Gallowfyre rolled out across the water, tentacles of black shadow coiling out.

My own dark twisting coils met his in a flare of indigo. We wrested like entangled sea monsters, searching for a weakness.

Beside me, Blackbird shouted down to Ben, "Smith! Finish the knife. Your life depends on it," then she turned back to the fray.

Across the water, Raffmir's sister appeared to fade slightly, then she stepped lightly up and floated across the full width of the water to the other bank, forcing us to divide our attention between the two opposite sides of the stream.

Blackbird was muttering into her cupped hands. She lifted them to her lips while keeping her eyes on Raffmir's sister. She blew into her hands and a warm glow kindled there. Suddenly she threw her hands wide and a hot buzzing swarm emptied from her palms. Huge hornets erupted in an angry vortex around her. She pointed at Raffmir's sister and they veered in a mass out across the water, swirling around the grey figure.

She laughed. "You cannot hurt me like that. You cannot sting what you cannot touch." She became less substantial, drifting into a pale shadow hanging in the air while the hornets formed a vortex around her.

Tonk... tonk... tonk... THANG!

The sound of the hammer on the anvil echoed around us. My struggle with Raffmir faltered as we both lost hold of our power. Raffmir's sister seemed to coalesce, while the swarm of hornets evaporated into a swirl of mist.

As the sound faded, the focus of the conflict returned. Raffmir took advantage of the lull and took two bold steps along the bank, reducing the distance between us. Once again he was faster to recover and I found myself racing to reach the darkness within me before I was overwhelmed by him.

"I will not fail, Raffmir!" I called out.

At his naming, my darkness found fractures where there had been none before. My gallowfyre slipped through his grasp so he was forced to take a step back, then another. He regained his footing and fought back against me with renewed intent.

"My turn," Raffmir's sister declared.

She pressed her faded hand to the wall and from it seeped a smooth blackness that covered the walls and ate the meagre light. Even the dappled glow and violet shimmer that Raffmir and I created found no reflection there. It spread outwards running over the brickwork, the antithesis of quicksilver, streaming down the walls and onto the walkway, spreading onto the gantry where Blackbird and I stood.

Blackbird pointed at the gantry, sweeping her hand across the walkway, drawing a line of fire to separate us from the spreading darkspore. Though it faltered, within moments the blackness spread through the gaps.

"It's too damp!" she shouted. "There's nothing to burn. I can't hold it!"

Blackbird's form shivered beside me. Her eyes elongated and her hair spiked with static, her wings unfurled behind her like oily film forming on water. They blurred into invisibility behind her with a drone audible even over the dull thunder of the waterfall and she skipped up from the walkway up onto the railing behind, out of reach of the darkspore.

"You can fly out of reach, little one, but I only need to touch him once and the battle is over. My brother will pluck you from the air, then rip your wings off and drown you in this sewer like the insect you are."

"Niall, watch your feet!"

The darkspore surged towards me and I was forced to divert my attention from Raffmir to burn it away from my feet. As the gallowfyre touched the darkspore it flared white and vanished. She screamed at its touch, the shrieks echoing in the vaults. Raffmir pressed forward and with my attention divided I could not hold him back. He tore my defence to shreds and the darkness welled inwards towards me.

"*Trial!*" Blackbird howled out the word.

He hesitated in his attack.

"What?" I asked her.

"I call for trial," she repeated, loudly. She called down to Ben, "Smith. Cease the work."

I looked up at her, standing balanced on the handrail looking inhuman, her wings blurring behind her.

"What are you talking about?" I gathered my strength, ready to do my utmost to bring Raffmir to his knees, no matter what it cost me, but Blackbird stepped down from the rail, regaining her human form as her feet touched the gantry.

"You have to stop fighting. Forgive me. It was all I could think of." She sounded resigned. She had halted the attack, but she sounded as if she had accepted defeat.

"Stay your hand, sister," Raffmir called. "They have called trial and we are bound by it."

Warm laughter bubbled up from Raffmir. "You two really are full of surprises, aren't you?" His gallowfyre flickered and died, leaving them as uncertain shadows on the river bank.

"What is he talking about?" I asked her, searching her face.

"It is our way, an ancient way, to settle disputes among the Feyre. I don't think it's been invoked in centuries, but it still applies. I invoked a trial to determine the issue in dispute and all who are of the courts are bound to allow it."

"What about me? I'm not a member of any court. I don't have to follow any law."

"It's all I could think of. It's that or fight them."

"I can beat him." My words sounded hollow, even to myself.

"*We* would lose."

It took me a moment to realise that she wasn't referring to the two of us but to another "we", closer to her heart. I looked into her face and saw anguish laid bare. She had chosen to save her own life and the life of the child she carried, rather than fight and risk losing both. I could not judge her harshly for making that choice.

"It's OK," I told her. "We'll go to this trial, wherever it is, and make our case there."

"No, Niall. It's here, and now. It's not a trial by jury. It is a trial by ordeal, and they will choose the ordeal because I invoked it."

"I hope you know what you're doing," I told her.

"I'm doing what I must."

"What happens now?"

"There are formalities. We must all agree to be bound by the trial. If we survive the ordeal then we win and they will withdraw. If we do not, they win and we withdraw, or at least the survivor does. I'm sorry, Niall, I could see no other way."

I could see why she'd made her decision. At least this way she and Ben would not be harmed. My gallowfyre flickered and died and we were illuminated only by the meagre light from Blackbird's torch left discarded on the gantry floor. I stood in the darkness and understood the price she'd sold me for. I couldn't blame her. Had it been my daughter's life in the balance I would have chosen the same. It was all a gamble anyway. I didn't know if I really could have beaten Raffmir. I just knew I needed to win more than he did, and that maybe it wasn't enough.

"What's happening?" The shout was from behind us. Ben had seen the light fade and was trying to find out what the situation was.

Blackbird turned to the rail. "There's to be a test to decide what happens. The good news is you get to walk away at the end of it."

"And the bad?" he asked.

"The bad news is that if we lose, then the knife will not be remade, and the barrier will fail."

"And if we win?"

"They'll leave us in peace, at least for now," she confirmed.

"What do we have to do?" I asked her.

"We must exchange names," she told me, "so each is bound by the outcome of the trial. Those surviving will know the true names of each of the parties here, but must tell no one else, ever. It is only between those who take part. It means a great deal to have that power over another and it will bind us to the outcome. Each of us has the names of the others as forfeit, so balance is maintained. It binds us in enmity far closer than we would ever be bound in alliance."

A glow of blue-white light sparked into being above our heads. I tensed against some new attack, but this was cold and steady like fox-fire, and unlike the fickle glimmering of gallowfyre.

"I have taken the liberty of lighting our discourse." Raffmir crossed the gantry and shepherded his sister onto the walkway.

My dark adjusted eyes saw him clearly for the first time. It struck me suddenly that our magic was not the only thing we had in common. I knew he was tall and that his outline was slim. What I hadn't realised was that his facial features mirrored my own. The sharp cheek bones and wavy dark hair, the slightly sunken eyes and length of jaw were all things I recognised. In a roomful of people I would have picked him out as some long-lost relative, a distant cousin, perhaps. His dress was different and the long-cut black Edwardian jacket and white lace frilled sleeves would have marked him out as an eccentric in any company, but the similarity remained.

The woman I already knew. That cold pinched face with the harsh tight mouth.

She glared at me. "I should have eaten you the first time."

I answered her courteously. "Madam, you have failed to kill me twice before. I would think, having failed a third time, that you might give it up as a bad job."

Raffmir's laughter filled the vaulted tunnel despite the sound of thundering water from below. "Truly, my sister, he is of our blood. Like it or no." She turned her glare to him but he was immune to it.

"Mistress," he turned to Blackbird, "you have called trial and therefore you must lead."

Blackbird took a deep breath, as if steeling herself for what was to come.

"I am named Velladore Rainbow Wings, Daughter of Fire and Air, called Blackbird," she said, clearly.

"And I am named Cartillian, Son of the Void, Star of the Moon's Darkness, called Raffmir," he answered, bowing elegantly to her.

He turned to me.

Following Blackbird's example, I spoke. "I am Niall Petersen, from Kent, also called Rabbit."

There was a moment's shocked pause. Then laughter boiled up from him, bemusing me and causing his sister to give him another withering look. He clearly found it very amusing. I wasn't sure whether to be offended or not. I turned to Blackbird, the memory of a smile played on her lips, but she just raised her eyebrows and shrugged.

"This cannot be," Raffmir declaimed to the tunnels. "You may be a mongrel, but no half-brother to me or mine can carry a name like that into a trial."

Blackbird corrected him. "As I think you pointed out, Raffmir, he cannot have a formal name for he has not yet been received at court to claim one. These are the only names he has."

"Then I shall give him one. One fit for a brother to me, though the blood-ties are more tenuous than I would wish. If you are to stand trial, mongrel, I will not have you tested without a name. I name you Alshirian, Son of the Void, Brightest Star in the Heavens. A mongrel name for a mongrel Fey. Be welcome, Dogstar, into your heritage."

"Another name will be yours," Blackbird whispered, "when you have earned it." It was an echo of Kareesh's words and I tried to remember what else she had said. There was something about evading traps and wearing cloaks, but after all that had happened I could not remember her precise words.

"Now you," Blackbird addressed the figure in grey.

"Mind your manners, half-breed," she hissed.

"Come, sister," Raffmir said. "Would you rather forfeit than give up your name? Have a care. The laws of the Courts of the Feyre care nothing for the heritage of the tried."

"They are not even Fey!" she spat.

"But you are, and therefore you are bound by Feyre law, just as I am. Will you stand before our lord and master and tell him you have broken Fey law? Have patience. All will be as it should."

These last words sounded as an ominous reassurance of what was to come.

She folded her arms, stubbornly.

"There is sanction for those that refuse fair trial," he reminded her gently, "and that would be beyond my ability to protect you."

"Oh, very well. I am named Iriennen, Child of the Void, Nightshade's Daughter, also called Solandre. Satisfied?" This last was thrown at Blackbird.

She looked to Raffmir for confirmation and he nodded.

"It is nicely done," she confirmed. "Now it is for you to choose the trial." By her expression I could see she'd been dreading this part. They could choose anything they wished and I did not think they would make it easy.

439

"Very well," said Raffmir.

He walked to the rail and looked over, surveying the anvil and the figure below. Ben was sat on the anvil, and the ball of light floated out over Raffmir and into the vaulted space sliding dark shadows into the niches along both sides and revealing the dark lines in his up-turned face.

Raffmir surveyed the anvil and the smith beside it, the hammer resting on the dull surface.

"Since this concerns the making of a knife," he intoned, "the trial shall be this. The hammer must be taken by the one who stands trial from one side of the river to the other, simply that. See the rungs down into the water beyond the island. It must be crossed there."

The light floated obligingly out over the island and we could see from that vantage point that bars were set like rungs into the bricks on either side of the river beyond the island, possibly dating from its construction.

"Which of you will endure the trial?"

"It must be him!" Solandre pointed her bony finger at me. "He is the true abomination."

"No," said Blackbird. "It is ours to choose who endures. I will stand."

"You can't," I blurted. "What about–"

She grabbed me and pulled me aside, shaking her head in warning. "One moment. We must confer."

"What are you doing?" I whispered, once we had a little distance between us. "I thought I would do it."

"You can't even swim." She dismissed my argument.

"No one's going to swim carrying that." I pointed down to the hammer resting on the anvil. "It weighs a ton."

"You can't even bear to be near it, Niall. How are you going to carry it?"

"I'll manage somehow. You can't be serious. Not *now*." My emphasis of the word was not lost on her.

"This way perhaps we may all survive. I will carry it across." Her voice was filled with doubt.

"But water's not your element. You're fire and air, not water and stone."

"It is my responsibility. I was the one who called trial."

"No. I forbid it."

"You cannot forbid me." Her chin lifted and her eyes gleamed green in the dark.

"I've run out of visions, Blackbird. There are no more clues, no more mysteries to solve. All the pieces are played. My fate is decided here. You said I wouldn't make the dawn, but I did. If it was fortune that brought me here then it is my ordeal to be endured, not yours." I softened my voice so as not to be overheard. "I ask you. For my sake. For the child's sake. Let me do this."

"You must come to your decision," said Raffmir from behind me.

Her eyes suddenly filled. She shook her head. I pressed my hand against her warm cheek.

"I have an additional condition," I announced, turning to him.

"And what would that be?" Raffmir's voice held challenge.

"By the laws of trial, is it true that once the matter is decided then the parties are free to go unmolested and neither hunted nor persecuted thereafter?"

"The law says the parties may not cause each other harm by the knowledge they have gained nor contest the matter further," he agreed.

"I want my daughter and the smith included in the parties," I told him. "If I undertake your trial then you will let them be, whether my daughter shows her Fey lineage or not."

"That's highly irregular," he told me.

"You invoked my daughter's name here, Raffmir. You brought her into it and made her part of it. And if I succeed the smith must be free to complete his work without interference, threat, or fear of harm," I reminded him.

"Very well," he agreed.

"You cannot!" Solandre interrupted him.

"It doesn't matter," he told her. "He will not succeed. The barrier will come down and everything will change. We are simply agreeing that us two will not cause them harm or cause harm to come to them. But that only applies to you and me."

"You cannot set others to harm us either," I reminded him.

"That would be to cause harm. We will let them be. It is agreed, isn't it, my sister?"

"You presume too much."

"Once the barrier is down many things will change. Two girls and a renegade smith are like autumn leaves in the mouth of the storm. Let him have his way."

"Very well," she conceded. "But I will not fail again, Raffmir." She turned those mean colourless grey eyes on me. "I will have his soul."

"Then I will stand."

The look that formed on Solandre's face was something I will never forget. She was like a spiteful child who had stolen a sweet and got away with it.

I displayed a confidence I did not feel and smiled into the face of her spite.

"Peace, sister." Raffmir was all charm and smooth words again. "Retrieve your hammer, then, Dogstar, and we will see what transpires."

It was what I needed. By including Alex in the protection of the trial I had secured her safety whether I succeeded or failed. I could undertake the ordeal in the knowledge that Alex, Blackbird and the unborn child she carried would survive, whatever the outcome.

At least until the world fell apart.

TWENTY-SEVEN

I turned back to Blackbird, finding her drawn but resolved. "Are you absolutely sure you want to do this?"
she asked.

"It's not ideal," I told her, "but it's the best that we
can make it."

"Very well."

She leaned over the rail and called down to Ben, explaining about the trial and telling him what she wanted
him to do. "If Niall succeeds in getting the hammer
across the river then they will leave us and you can finish the work unmolested."

"And if he doesn't?" asked Ben.

She paused, glancing sideways at me, then spoke back
to the figure below.

"If he doesn't, get away from here as fast as you can.
Get back to your family. Keep them safe."

"What about you?" he asked her.

In my mind's eye I could see her, escaping to some
distant forest to raise her child, our child, alone among
the trees.

"I won't be staying." She shook her head. "I can't stay."

We agreed we would all remain on the gantry until
Ben had transferred the hammer to the bank near to

where it had been stored. Then he would return to the anvil to await the outcome. It was as near to safe as we could make him. I still had the memory of standing in Meg Highsmith's kitchen, trying to explain that the task was not without risk and that others might try to stop us. Warning her did not make me feel any less responsible. At least this way he would return.

"It's waiting for you," he called up to us, and then to me, "Are you going to be OK?"

I looked at Blackbird and she held my gaze. She would not look away.

"We're doing what we must," I told him.

Raffmir and Solandre were arguing on the bank next to the gantry. Raffmir's reasonable tone was underscored by her hissing and spitting. If he hadn't been there to hold her back then I think she would have gone for us, law or no law.

I trusted Raffmir's sense of honour. To him this was all a game. He liked it. He liked the play of it. That was why he had allowed me to include Ben and Alex in the deal. He was playing to win and it suited him to raise the stakes. He had not even considered losing.

I had come to understand that it was this unshakeable confidence that gave the Feyre their power. The magic was there, regardless, but like a razor edge it was inert until it had intent. For that they needed belief in themselves.

Solandre was different. I suspected that she was used to being feared and respected, but that had been thrown into doubt when she had failed to kill me and had been forced to excuse her failure with tales of a half-breed mongrel wielding gallowfyre. She'd told me in the glade that they had not believed her, that they'd said she was hallucinating or dreaming. She'd begun to doubt herself and that doubt had eaten away at her like the rot she had spread into my bedroom door. Doubt was not something the Feyre could afford.

I trusted Raffmir, but I feared his sister. I feared she was no longer sane.

I turned to Blackbird. "I don't trust her."

"Nor I, but the law here is strong. Her life is forfeit if she goes against the trial or its outcome and she knows that."

"I don't think she cares. She's not rational anymore."

"I'm not thinking about her," she said.

And there it was. The thing she had agreed I should do was the thing she believed would end me.

"I've been living on borrowed time, remember?"

She turned her face away, but I caught her chin and turned it back to me. Tears brimmed into her eyes, running carelessly down her cheeks.

"Have faith," I told her.

"I do," she whispered. "I'm so sorry. If I could think of another way…"

"There is no other way."

She pressed herself into my chest and I wrapped my arms around her, her head resting against my shoulder. I breathed her scent, which wrapped around me even in the foulness of the fetid tunnel. She was a private breath of sunshine and, for that moment, she was mine.

"Are you prepared?" Raffmir's voice was expectant, keen with enthusiasm.

"I am ready," I told him.

Blackbird hugged me one last time and I lifted her face to plant a damp kiss on her lips. I smiled for her. If we were doing this then I wanted it over with.

I climbed down first onto the bank where we had retrieved the hammer, with Blackbird climbing after me. I called my thanks to Ben. He'd left the hammer close to where the rungs were set, leading down into the dark water. As we approached it the hackles rose on the back of my neck and my senses jarred at it. Carrying it was going to be an ordeal, even without the water.

I wiped my palms on my trousers where they were greasy with slime and sweat. My spine was prickling and my head ached with the wrongness of it. I would try and make this quick. The less time I had to spend near the thing, the better.

Raffmir descended the ladder and produced a lace handkerchief to wipe the slime from his hands and from the edges of his sleeves. He was as fastidious as a cat and the expression on his face as his white hanky took on the green-brown stain was almost worth enduring the trial for.

Solandre stood at the top of the ladder. I knew it was petty but I looked forward to her getting her hands dirty. Instead, she stepped lightly off the gantry and floated gently to the ground, her skirts billowing around her legs. Another benefit, I supposed, of not being entirely anchored to reality.

Disappointed, I turned back to the hammer.

I could not escape the sense that it was somehow alive, brooding darkly, waiting for its opportunity to hurt me. It would not have long to wait.

Ben had secured a sling around it with some blue nylon rope. I blessed him, as it would mean I could descend into the river without having to hold the hammer at the same time.

Raffmir objected. "You cannot have the rope. You must carry the hammer across yourself," he asserted.

Blackbird corrected him. "Actually you said it must be taken by he who stands trial from one side to the other. You did not specify the means by which it should be carried."

He hesitated, and then allowed that it was what he'd said. He didn't look happy about it, though. "Very well, but he may not throw it or pass it across. He must take it across the river himself."

"Agreed," I confirmed.

I had never liked water. Not since the day I had almost drowned. I claimed I'd never had the time to learn to swim, but the truth was that I could always think of something else to do rather than that. With the hammer, though, swimming was not going to be an option. It would weigh me down like an anchor.

Ben had bound the rope around the head and down around the end of the handle forming a sling of sorts. It looked well-tied and secure.

"Which way up do you want it?" Blackbird must have been steeling herself because she looked relaxed as she went over to it. Whether this show was for my benefit or theirs I could not say.

"Put the head at the bottom. That way it will be easier to manoeuvre."

"Just don't touch it by mistake, OK?"

The worst part was picking up the hammer. Blackbird helped me, even though it must have made her flesh crawl to do it. She slipped the nylon rope over my head and shoulder so the hammer was slung across my back. It made my bones ache, my nerves jangle and my muscles cramp and twitch, but I would bear it. I was determined to see this through.

My stomach knotted and twisted and I comforted myself that it was not the thought of the river turning my guts, but the proximity of the hammer. As I stood, finally prepared, Blackbird brushed my hair back from my face in a gesture I understood. It was enough to raise the ghost of a smile, though in truth I was feeling sick from being so close to the hammer. There was nothing left to say.

Looking down at the flow, I was sure that if I simply tried to cross the stream then I would be swept away. The current had risen while we were there, fuelled by the rain from the world above, and the whole width of it would be treacherous. For a moment my mind filled with the thought of it invading my nostrils, choking my mouth, slipping dark and cold into my lungs until it starved me of oxygen, leaving me scrabbling for air.

"Ready?" Blackbird's voice broke into my thoughts.

I nodded once, telling myself it would be OK.

"May fortune smile upon you."

Fortune was all well and good, but I was not intending to leave this to chance. I smiled back at her, not daring to linger or I would give myself away.

I had come up with a plan.

I could try and explain to her, but it was better that she didn't know. I wasn't quite sure whether what I intended was within the strict laws of the trial, but it would meet the conditions that Raffmir had set out and I was relying on his sense of honour to hold back his sister when, and if, I endured. I was not without hope, but I would keep my secret to myself.

If my plan worked then I would carry the hammer from one side of the river to the other. However, it was important it looked right, otherwise there might be room for them to contest the validity of the ordeal. I had to make this look good.

Crossing the stream physically was not part of the plan. Once I was under the surface and out of sight, I would put my hand on the sixty-first nail which was tucked into my pocket and use that to create a path through the void to the other side. As long as I could stay focused, the slight time delay would give the illusion that I had struggled across and then I could emerge victorious with the hammer.

They would have to allow it. As Blackbird had said, they had not specified the means or the manner of my crossing the river, only that I must carry it across myself. I was tempted to do it from the bank. He hadn't said I had to use the rungs or even enter the water, but I did not want to leave room for doubt. I would suffer the brief torment that carrying the hammer down into the water would inflict to make sure there was no room for them to wriggle out of their promise.

I sat down on the cold bank, hanging my legs down over the edge. The damp seeped into the cloth of my trousers. No matter. I would be wetter and colder shortly.

Being careful to mind the hammer I leaned back and rolled over so I could drop my legs over the edge and seek with my foot for a toe-hold. There was no hand-hold at the top and I guessed the rungs had only ever been intended for emergency. My hands were aching where I held the wooden shaft of the hammer so it would not slide over the edge and drag me backwards into the water.

After a moment my toe found what I thought was a rung. I tested my weight on it and it held. Below it was another. I scraped backwards slowly, easing myself over the edge. I let the sling take the weight of the hammer and let it swing free behind me. It pulled into my shoulder and banged back against my leg, momentarily numbing my thigh muscle.

I eased back and down, and when my head was level with the bank, Raffmir said, "Farewell, little brother." The look of smug satisfaction on Solandre's face made me even more determined to make my plan work.

I stepped down again and felt the first touch of water around my feet. The damp bricks had been chilled, but this was icy. I lowered myself further. The current tugged at my ankles and calves. It got harder to find the footholds with the water pulling at my trousers. I told myself it would not be for long. Twisting around, I looked across the gap of twenty or thirty feet to the other bank, the line of rungs descended there into the water. I fixed in my mind the clear picture of the other wall so I would be able to find it through the void.

The water came up to my waist now, chilling the whole lower part of my body. The hammer swung slightly as the head was buffeted by the current. Water soaked into the bottom of my shirt. I took another step down, and another, holding tightly to the rungs to keep from being swept from the wall. At chest height in the water, I lowered myself again, wondering how deep it was and how much further down I could descend. The water swirled against me, dark and oily. It smelled of rain-stormed streets and flushed gutters. Pieces of litter were swept by along with darker, less identifiable flotsam. I was just a head above water. It was now or never.

I looked up one last time, hoping to catch Blackbird's eye. Instead Solandre's face leaned over, watching me. I did the only thing I could think of with both hands clinging to the rungs. I stuck my tongue out at her.

The expression of outrage on her face as she turned away to tell Raffmir was worth the moment of bravado. He would see the joke and it meant she would miss the moment when I slipped below the surface. I was glad of that.

I filled my lungs with air and descended two rungs, making sure I was well below the surface where they could not see what I was doing. The freezing water swirled and tugged around me and I began shivering almost immediately. Fine bubbles steamed from my mouth as my body immediately started to shake with cold.

Being careful to avoid accidental contact with the head of the hammer, I released one hand from the rung. The current swung me sideways as I let go and the water pressed me at an awkward angle. My wrist scraped against the roughness of the bricks. I found my pocket and fumbled with rapidly numbing fingers for the nail. Weed slipped across my face. At least I hoped it was weed.

My fingers wormed their way inside the sodden pocket and my hand found the metal of the nail. I wrapped my hand around it, feeling the answering echo of the void within it, sensing it fall into blackness in my hand.

Already running short of oxygen, I focused on the nail and formed a link with the core of darkness within me. The universe parted for me and the many overlapping and intertwining worlds were there, but there was something different, something wrong. There was a weight, an anchor holding me to the world I was in. The iron of the hammer would not come through.

I twisted and pulled in the water, pulling the hammer around in front of me. I wrenched at the void and it

450

answered, distorting space around me. But the hammer stayed. It was solidity where everything else was fluid. It would not move.

I had a choice. I could try to cross without the hammer, or stay with it and drown. My chest ached with the need to draw breath and I hadn't even started to cross. Without the hammer, I knew there would be no point to any of it. With my lungs already bursting from lack of oxygen, I shoved the nail down into the pocket and pulled the hammer around in front of me, letting it drag me down to the bottom. I crawled away from the wall along the bottom, using the hammer to stop me being swept downstream.

The current was stronger away from the wall and swirled about me, tugging at my clothes. I opened my eyes briefly, trying to get some sense of distance. It was pitch black. I could feel the pull on the sling as the hammer swung underneath me bumping along the bottom. The river bottom was littered with junk. Objects embedded in the silt, sharp and blunt, scraped my hands and knees. With my numb fingers I clawed my way along, pulling myself forward. I reasoned that as long as I kept the force of the current to my left I would be heading in the right direction, though how I would find the rungs at the far side, I had no idea.

My lungs burned and I ached to take a breath, but I knew that was death. Spots swam before my eyes and I began to feel light-headed. Bubbles of precious air escaped from my nose and ran up my face, wriggling like worms.

I hauled myself along, scrabbling at embedded fragments of rusted metal and slithery weed with both hands. The hammer caught on some unseen snag and I wrenched it free. How much further could it be? The strength in my arms deserted me and cold panic pooled in my gut. I hated water. Why had I agreed to do this?

The current twisted and pulled, tugging me around. It was a fight not to get swept sideways. I needed to breathe. I kicked upwards with futile twists trying to reach the surface but the hammer stuck resolutely to the bottom. My vision blurred, filling my closed eyes with warm tears.

I tugged myself along. My head swam with lack of oxygen. I couldn't find the way. I was lost. I coughed and the deathly cold water flooded my mouth and nose. I retched at the foul taste of it, the spasm pulling water into my lungs. I kicked listlessly for the far bank, feeling consciousness began to slip from my grasp.

I did the only thing I could think of. I shoved my hand in my pocket, grasped the nail and *linked*. The world slid apart and I crawled into the edge of the parting, still tethered to the hammer and unable to enter fully, but grateful for the moment of respite. The void held neither air nor water. I drifted in it like the weed in the current, coughing and retching, my mouth filling with sour bile. My vision blurred, unable to focus on the non-space surrounding me. The sounds of voices echoed distantly around me.

"How long do you wish us to wait?" It was Raffmir's voice, drifting past me like the flotsam in the water.

"Not yet," Blackbird said, her voice cold and hollow.

"How long?" he repeated.

"Just wait."

I released the nail and kicked back into the water. The hunger for air returned, my oxygen starved muscles screaming with cramp and fatigue. I pushed myself backwards along the bottom using my heels for traction. I got a few feet before I had to grab for the nail again.

This time the void spun around me. My oxygen-starved brain whirled the fractured worlds in kaleidoscopic dizziness.

I could hear Solandre giggling to herself. That bitch was barking and her brother knew it.

Within me, I could feel fingers of the void spreading into me, the cold echoing that of the water. I had not called it but it had come. My hold on it was slipping.

I had a brief flash of Blackbird, standing on the bank looking into the dark roiling water. Her arms were wrapped tightly around her. She held herself stiff and inert, Raffmir waiting at her shoulder. Then blackness clouded my vision and pulled me away with lazy strength. It whorled and turned, responding to some unseen current, fed by an unknown source. My mind drifted, unable to face the water again. The void swirled within me, echoing the water. It sent an exploring tendril out and upward, coiling around my heart and then, tenderly, pricked it.

Pain exploded in my chest. I wrenched myself back into the world, fleeing in panic from the acid touch. The water gushed into my mouth and I coughed, desperately trying not to breathe in. I wrenched and grasped at anything to draw me from that dark embrace. The black coils stayed with me, sliding inside my arms, feeding from the burning ache in my cramped muscles, tasting the pain.

My hand punched into something solid, sending a jolt up my arm, further numbing my senses. I tried to scramble past but something was blocking my path. In a moment of clarity I realised it was the far bank. I was there. The prospect of air had me skidding my hands across the wall while my chest felt like it would burst apart. My numb fingers skittered across the broken bricks searching for a handhold. A vertical edge found me a metal rung and I hauled myself up while I choked and coughed, inhaling water and slime, my vision swimming with spots and strange lights until finally I erupted out into air.

I slid my forearm through the highest rung I could reach and hung there, retching and spewing, while the current still tried to pull me free and carry me downstream. My head swam and the world spun around me as my chest tried to pull air into my waterlogged lungs. I felt curiously detached. The pain seemed distant and otherworldly. My vision swirled and the void within me

453

writhed and coiled. Somehow I was out of myself. I was up in the vaulting, seeing the wretched bedraggled figure hanging from the rung, the hammer still dangling in the water behind, while the figure spasmed and belched muddy water.

Blackbird's voice drifted up to me. "Don't die now. Not now."

Then the body twitched again and it hauled itself up another rung, more by reflex than intent.

Solandre's expression was pure disbelief. She shook her fists and shrieked. "Noooooooo…"

Her voice dissolved into a whisper like the wind through dry grass. Her body seemed to fade slightly and then expand. Her arms drifted out over the water towards the sodden figure hanging from the rung.

"Solandre! No!" Raffmir's voice held a note of command, but the fading figure ignored him.

"Stop her," Blackbird told him. "Stop her now!"

"I cannot," he said. He turned back to watch his sister reaching out across the water towards my body.

"Well, I can." Blackbird stepped behind Raffmir towards Solandre, being careful to avoid the indistinct floating cloud as her body drifted apart.

She slipped her hand into the pocket of her skirt and pulled out the Dead Knife. Immediately, its colour began to rise, a deep blush rising in the metal. She focused on it and the metal roared into flame.

"Solandre!" she shouted. "This is for Niall."

She shoved the burning knife deep into Solandre.

There was a flash. A sound like the slamming of a great door rolled around the vaulting. A giant hand picked Blackbird up and slammed her back into the wall behind her. It went pitch black.

After a moment there was coughing and choking. The air was filled with smoke. A hesitant light flickered into life down the bank away from her, throwing elongated shadows into the clouded air. Tiny particles of floating ash drifted aimlessly in air currents, mimicking the

454

eddies and swirls of the river, dimly illuminated by the floating light.

Blackbird pushed herself up against the wall, her limbs slow to obey her. She looked around for Solandre and Raffmir. He was pulling himself onto his knees, from his position sprawled, legs half over the edge. There was no sign of his sister.

Blackbird spat the ash from her mouth and raised an arm weakly. A sudden breeze swept the smoke and floating ash spiralling up over the gantry and away. The air cleared and the light steadied.

Movement in the water caught my eye. Ben was in the water, swimming towards the rungs where the figure still clung. Blackbird looked around, still confused. Raffmir pulled himself to his feet, pushing his long hair back from his face in a habitual gesture. He was smeared with soot and ash and he looked more like a ragged street urchin than the gentleman he affected.

Blackbird climbed to her feet, leaning against the wall for support and stood to face him.

"You killed her," he said.

Ben swam to where my body hung from the rungs. I was pulled down from the vaulting and back into my body as he clambered over me then hauled me up onto the ledge. I coughed again, spewing water onto the bricks. The air in my lungs fought with the dark tide in my core. I spewed water onto the bricks, retching and gulping air into my lungs.

Reluctantly the dark tendrils unwound from my heart and I slid back into unconsciousness.

TWENTY-EIGHT

A thin sound entered my awareness. An alarm clock beeped and beeped, incessantly and I tried to summon the effort to hit the snooze button. My limbs felt like lead and even a small effort was too much. I dearly wished someone would turn the damned thing off.

Gradually I became aware of other sounds. There was a rattling rasp, rhythmic and almost regular, which waxed and waned with the pain in my throat and, under that, the low hubbub of activity in a distant room. Aches drifted into focus, my arms, my chest, my legs all throbbed with dull persistence.

Then I remembered. The water, the hammer, the cold. It all came back to me in a wash of recall. I struggled to open my eyes, finding the light blurry. A voice spoke to me.

"It's all right, you're safe."

It was an effort to turn my head towards the sound. Her face moved into my field of vision and resolved slowly into focus. Her lips curved upwards slightly and she laid a cool hand on my forehead.

"Sleep, Niall. Let your body heal."

Whether through some magic of hers, or simply because I was too weak to hold onto consciousness, I slipped back into dreamless sleep.

When I next awoke, it was quiet and the lights were dim. The beeping noise had gone and my eyes fluttered open to see Blackbird curled in the chair beside my bed, asleep. The chair, the room and the bed told me this was a hospital. There were the small noises, murmurs and rattles percolating through the fabric of the building, telling me it was night. I didn't have the heart to disturb her; she curled around herself with her spiralled curls falling over her face, her hands tucked under her chin. I closed my eyes and let the sound of her breathing lull me back into sleep.

Sunlight woke me next. A bar of white resolved itself into a gap in the curtains as I blinked and stretched, my muscles protesting and joints cracking as I shifted position. I groaned and rolled onto my side away from the brightness. She was resting her chin on her forearms on the side of the bed, watching me, her eyes sparkling green in the light.

"Hello," she said.

"Hello." My voice sounded hoarse, even to myself. "What time is it?"

"It's nearly eight o'clock. How do you feel?"

"Sore," I admitted. "Like I've been on wash, rinse, heavy load, intense cycle, with repeat."

"You're getting better."

It was good to know the aches and twinges accompanying every movement were a sign of improving health.

"What happened? Did we make it? Did Ben finish the knife?"

"It's all handled. Don't fret. You made it across and he finished the knife. It's all taken care of."

"But we have to get it to Claire." I pushed myself up onto one elbow, making my head swim and precipitating a thumping headache.

She leaned over and pressed me gently back down, the weight of her hand outweighing my meagre strength.

"It's being done today, in a few hours. The preparations are all in hand." She smiled. "We did it, Niall. We beat them."

I collapsed back to the bed, confused. "What day is it?"

"It's Tuesday. I thought you were going to sleep all week. Are you hungry?"

My stomach growled in response. "Starving."

"I'll go and see if I can rustle up some food for you."

She made to stand, but I caught her hand, despite the tubes taped to my arm. "Stay."

She eased herself down again and I rested my hand on hers. Just the touch of her was a kind of therapy.

"I was sure I'd lost you," she said, quietly.

"I had a plan," I told her. I explained how I had planned to slip beneath the water and then use the sixty-first nail to transfer the hammer across beneath the surface of the river and emerge victorious on the other side.

"That would never work. The hammer is iron. It's about as antithetical to magic as you can get."

I let her explain what, for her, must have seemed like an elementary mistake, mainly just for the sound of her voice. She was amazed that I been stupid enough to try it.

"Well, how else did you think I was going to cross?" I asked her.

As soon as the words came out, I knew it was a question I should have left unasked. It silenced her and the shadow of it moved behind her eyes like something lurking in the depths. The answer was simple. She hadn't.

I squeezed her hands under mine and she did not look away.

It struck me that she had let me make my decision and been prepared to live with the consequences, but still she had waited, hoping against hope for a miracle.

Perhaps I had been granted one.

"What happened in the tunnels?" My memory of it was fragmented and strangely unreal.

"After you went into the water, we waited for what seemed like an age. Raffmir started pressuring for me to call an end and I kept trying to put him off. It was getting to the point where I was going to have to concede when you appeared on the other side. After you pulled yourself up the rungs on the far bank, Solandre lost it completely. She faded into spectral form and reached across the river towards you. Raffmir tried to stop her but she was obsessed. She was going to kill you. I did the only thing I could think of. I pulled the Dead Knife from my pocket and made it as hot as I could and then stabbed her."

"I thought she couldn't be hurt physically."

"I thought so too, but the heat might have hurt her enough to get her attention away from you."

"And did it?"

"It did more than that. Ben told me that if powders get spread into the air at a certain density, they can ignite. Fire spreads though them like a chain reaction, superheating the air and causing a shock wave. Effectively, she exploded."

I tried to take in what she was saying.

"What about Raffmir?"

"There was nothing he could do. He was hurt slightly in the explosion; nothing lethal, unfortunately, but by the time he realised what had happened it was all over. His sister had broken the laws of trial and he knew her life was forfeit. He was forced to accept the outcome and the fate of his sister, though he didn't like it."

"Did he say anything?"

"Very little. He conceded the trial and said he would honour the outcome. Then he said that if the formalities were concluded he would take his leave. He's such a prig. His sister's just been blown to bits and he's discussing formalities."

"So he left."

"Her ashes either drifted away on the water or blew away on the breeze. He just climbed back up onto the gantry and vanished into the dark. I expect he'll have some explaining to do when he returns to his world, but they will have to honour the outcome as he has. It's our way.

"Ben had been thrown into the river by the force of the blast but fortunately for you, he can swim. He climbed up the rungs after you and hauled you up onto the side. He pumped as much water as he could out of your chest and put you into the recovery position. It was all he could do. By that time I'd crossed the river and could take over."

The shadow reached her eyes again.

"What?" I asked her.

"I made him finish the knife, Niall. I want you to know that. I couldn't carry you out of the tunnels alone, but I made him finish the knife before we carried you up together and called an ambulance." Her eyes were dark and haunted by the decision.

The security we had all fought for was dependent on finishing the knife and restoring the ceremony. Without that, every sacrifice would have been meaningless.

"It's OK. I would have done the same. And I'm still here, aren't I? You can't get rid of me that easily."

A little of the haunted look dissolved. There was a hint of a smile and I smiled back. She leaned forward and pressed her warm lips to mine in a long languid kiss. I shifted, sending shooting pains down my back and grunted at the pain. She stopped and drew away; worried she had hurt me.

"Don't stop," I whispered.

She kissed me again, this time warming me in a way that was completely incompatible with my physical state. When she stopped, her eyes were filled with promises. She squeezed my hand.

"I really should let them know you're awake. The policeman let me stay in here on condition that I promised I would let him know as soon as you woke."

"Policeman?"

"We brought you up out of the tunnels, but I couldn't revive you. Your lungs were still waterlogged and I had no idea how long you could hang on for. Your glamour had completely faded and you looked like you did when I first met you. That worried me more than anything else."

I put my hand to my cheek, feeling the stubble where I was unshaved, knowing my face was my own.

"We called an ambulance and Ben told them he'd dragged you out of the Thames from one of the piers. He's a convincing liar when he has to be. The ambulance crew found your wallet and your driving license on the way to the hospital. By the time I'd caught up with you at the hospital, they knew who you were and the police were here waiting for you. There's been an officer on the door ever since."

"Can we slip past them? Get away before they realise I'm awake?"

"Well we could, but I think your daughter might be upset if you did."

"Alex?"

"The police called Katherine and told her you were in hospital. They returned yesterday morning and came to see you while you were still unconscious. Alex was very grown up about it, but you could see she was worried. I don't think you can just vanish without seeing her."

"But what about the police?"

"If you run now, they'll never leave you in peace."

She stood slowly and left me with that thought while she went to tell the officer I was awake and to try and rustle up some food for me. As soon as she'd gone, the officer came into the room, nodded once to me and then stood by the door, looking blank and impersonal.

"Am I under arrest?" I asked him.

"Not at the moment, sir. But the senior officer would like to speak with you regarding our enquiries."

"So I can leave if I want to?"

"I think it would be better if you stayed, sir. There's a doctor coming to check you over and the investigating officer is on his way."

I rested back against the pillow, trying to organise my thoughts ahead of the interview I knew was coming.

The doctor arrived before either Blackbird returned or the police arrived. She was a well-groomed, middle-aged Asian lady who spoke with a light Birmingham accent.

"I'm Dr Agraval. I've looked after you since you were brought here on Sunday. How are you feeling?" She held a torch up to look into my eyes.

"Not bad considering."

She took my hands in hers and turned them over, looking at the palms of my hands which were criss-crossed with a lattice of newly formed scar tissue. "Do you always heal this quickly?"

"Not usually," I answered truthfully.

"Hmm. Any headache or disturbed vision? Do you feel nauseous?"

"If I turn my head too quickly, my head thumps a bit, but apart from that, no."

She felt under my chin and around my neck. "Your glands are swollen."

"Is that bad?"

"Not necessarily. With the amount of water you took in, your immune system has gone into overdrive." She put a temperature probe into my ear and read off the digital display. "Your temperature's within the bounds of normal. Can you open your shirt please?"

She held the metal end of her stethoscope in her hand to warm it while I struggled with the unfamiliar buttons of the pyjamas they had provided for me, just as Blackbird returned with a plate of sandwiches.

"I leave you for a moment and you're taking your clothes off for another woman," she remarked casually. The doctor ignored her. I guess she'd heard it all before. We went through the routine of breathing in and out while the doctor pressed the stethoscope to various parts of my chest and then my back. I eyed the plate of sandwiches, my stomach making alarming noises. "There's nothing wrong with your appetite, then?" she said.

I shook my head.

"You can have those after I've taken your blood pressure. Eating will affect the result."

She slipped the armband up around my arm and began inflating it while Blackbird removed the cling film and put the cheese sandwiches on the table by my bed. After a few moments the doctor released the arm band and declared open season on the sandwiches. They were plain white bread and plastic cheese, but I wolfed them down. They tasted wonderful.

"Anything else bothering you? There are no broken bones, but sometimes a ligament strain can be just as painful."

"I feel a bit bruised," I told her around a mouthful of sandwich.

"Remarkable. I have patients who take months to make this much progress and you've only been here a couple of days."

"I guess I'm just fortunate I didn't take in much water."

"When they brought you in you were unconscious. Your lungs were full of foul muddy water and you were a hair's breadth from dead. We had to drain your lungs and give you oxygen to keep you alive."

"I'm just lucky, I guess." I exchanged a look with Blackbird.

"Beats me," she stood up and tucked the stethoscope into a pocket of her white coat. "Maybe it's something in the water. Maybe we should be bottling it and selling it as a treatment."

"That might not work," I said, chewing sandwich.

"I've seen stranger things, but not many," she said. "Are you up to talking with the law? They're hopping from foot to foot outside waiting for a shot at you. I told them I would see you first, but frankly there's nothing wrong with you that rest won't cure. I'm more worried about them than you. They look like death warmed up."

"I suppose I had better see them."

She nodded and stood up. "If you get any dizziness or nausea I want to know immediately. I've written you a prescription for painkillers, so ask the nurse if you need them." She turned to leave.

"Can I go home?"

The doctor turned back. "I would prefer to keep you in for observation, but I can't keep you here. See how you feel after you've spoken to the police. You may find you tire pretty quickly. Your system's repairing the damage and you may not have much energy for anything else."

She went to the door and opened it. "You can come in now." She nodded to me and left the door open.

Two men entered. The first was short for a policemen, but wide with it. He stepped into the room sideways, more out of habit than need. His mid-brown hair was cut short and his dark jacket looked as if he might have slept in it. The second man looked innocuous next to the forcefulness of his colleague. He regarded the room with a passive expression taking in the bed, the chair, Blackbird and me in one sweep. I suspected that if you asked him in a month's time what was in that room, he would be able to describe it all.

"We would like to talk to you about an incident at your flat last Thursday night," the second man said, without preamble.

"Sure. Come in." They were already in, but I wanted to make the point that this was my room, at least for now.

"We would like to speak with you alone, please. Constable, would you take the young lady for a coffee or something. You can take a break. We'll come and find you if we need you."

"Sir." The constable held the door open for Blackbird and they filed out, closing the door quietly after them.

The stocky man went to the side table and put down a small handheld tape recorder. He pressed Record.

"Recording, one, two, three." He stopped the recorder and rewound it, then pressed play. His voice repeated itself from the machine. He rewound it again and pressed record.

"This is Detective Sergeant Bob Vincent with Detective Inspector Brian Tindall." He looked at his watch and then timed and dated the interview, naming the hospital and the ward. "DI Tindall leading."

He turned and sat in the chair by my bed and took out a notepad. The chair was too reclined for him. He perched on the edge of it, looking uncomfortable.

DI Tindall walked up and down in the meagre space at the end of my bed. He stopped and looked at me. "Would you state your name, please, sir, just for the record."

"Petersen. Niall Petersen."

"Age?"

"Forty-two."

"Residence."

"I live at one hundred and forty-five Cromwell Road, South Ealing." DS Vincent noted this in his book.

"Mr Petersen, we would like to know what you can tell us about the events of last Thursday night."

"Very little, I'm afraid." I needed to keep this to a minimum. I knew I would find it hard to lie and that they would probably be able to tell if I did.

"You were discovered running down the street in tracksuit bottoms and a T-shirt at oh-four-seventeen. You were carrying a rucksack."

"As I told your colleagues, I was going away."

"One of my colleagues is dead. He was attacked by a virulent biological agent in your back garden. His face was eaten away to the point where if we didn't know who he was, forensics would have a hard time identifying him."

"I'm so sorry."

465

"Sorry? You hear that, Bob? He's sorry." He strode around and leaned over the bed, grabbing a handful of pyjama and hauling me within inches of his face. "He had a wife and a four month-old baby. She isn't even allowed to see the body. Shall I let her know how sorry you are?" He shoved me backwards onto the pillow and stared down at me. He was breathing hard, trying to control his anger.

"There was nothing I could do. I wasn't even in the garden."

"You didn't see what happened."

"No."

"Or hear?"

"Well, I could hear some of it. They were on the radio. But I didn't know—"

"I quote: 'Tell them not to touch it. Tell them!' That was you, wasn't it?" He leaned over me. "Why did you say that if you couldn't see?"

"I didn't know. I was guessing."

"Guessing!" His face was inches from mine and spots of spittle landed on my face. I daren't raise my hand to wipe it away.

"Is that your usual technique for interviewing key witnesses, DI Tindall?"

The voice was new and came from the doorway. Tindall stood slowly, fighting to regain his dignity as the colour in his face faded slowly. He wiped his hands down the front of his jacket and turned to the door. DS Vincent stood up.

"Only I don't remember reading any of that in the procedures manual and I wondered if I had somehow missed that part."

"No, sir," said Tindall.

I registered the uniform of the man standing in the doorway holding an A4-sized white manila envelope and wondered why Tindall was addressing him as "sir". Then I noticed that the uniform was immaculate. The buttons shone, and the shoulders and collar were covered in gold braid. It wasn't a regular constable's uniform.

"I think," said the man, entering the room, "they can hear you in the entrance hall, two floors down."

"Sorry, sir."

"And it may be that you need some emotional distance from this case."

"I'm fine, sir. Really."

"Nevertheless, I think you should withdraw."

"Sir? We were just getting somewhere."

"Really? Was that the part where you were leading the witness or the part where you were compromising the integrity of the evidence?"

There was silence. Tindall looked to Vincent for support, but Vincent wouldn't meet his eyes.

The new officer spoke calmly and reasonably. "I think it would be a good idea if you took a long step back from this case and regained some objectivity. I would like your report on my desk at oh-nine-hundred tomorrow."

"But, sir–"

"I've just come from seeing our dead colleague's family, detective inspector, and I am not in the mood to debate it."

DI Tindall's shoulders slumped. "Yes, sir."

"Get moving. DS Vincent will stay to assist me with the interview."

"You, sir?" said Tindall.

"What?"

"It's just that you don't usually take such a direct interest in a case, sir."

"I have a man in the morgue and another on extended leave for compassionate reasons. Two others are in shock and barely holding it together. That makes me four men down. Can you think of a more appropriate time for me to take a direct interest in a case, inspector?"

"No, sir."

"Good. I'll see you in my office at nine sharp with your report."

"Yes, sir." Tindall took one last look at me and then turned away. The new officer pushed the door gently closed behind him. After a moment there was sharp noise that might have been a bark or a muttered expletive. We could all hear the anger in the footsteps gradually fading beyond the door.

The new officer spoke. "DI Tindall leaves the room. Assistant Commissioner Mark Perkins taking over the interview. Do you mind if I sit?" He indicated the edge of the bed.

"No, er, help yourself."

I was unsure if this was a reprieve. Was having an assistant commissioner conduct the interview an improvement or simply a sign that things had just become a lot more serious?

He sat on the edge of my bed while DS Vincent sat uncomfortably perched on the bedside chair.

"I think it would help if you took us through the events of last Thursday night. From the beginning, please."

I went back to what I had said earlier, rehearsing the events in my head. Perkins hardly spoke, letting me give my own version of the story. I missed out the bit about my glow and using magic to seal the door, but apart from that I told it as it had happened. When we got to the part where they found the thing in my garden, I paused.

"Could I have some water?" I asked.

Vincent passed me the water and I took several sips. They didn't prompt me or pressure me to continue, but waited patiently.

"There was something wrong," I told them. "The power was flickering and there was this strange laughter in the garden. It was freaking me out. I told them not to touch it. I tried to warn them, but it was too late."

"It?"

"I know this is going to sound strange, but it had a man's voice but a woman's sound. Does that make sense?"

468

"You're not the only one to say that. Why did you warn them not to touch it?" Perkins prompted gently.

"Are you kidding? Have you seen the walls of my flat? It wasn't like that before. Whoever was in my flat did that. If they were in my garden then I was staying well away from it."

"Why didn't you warn them earlier," he asked.

"I don't know. They told me it was safe. They said it had gone."

"Does the name Gerald Fontner mean anything to you?"

"No."

"Are you sure?"

"Yes."

He opened the envelope and extracted a photograph. He handed it to me.

"Do you know this man?"

I studied the picture. The man was almost certainly dead. He was lying on his back amongst garden debris. He wore a suit and looked strangely peaceful.

"No. I've never seen him before."

"Are you sure? Take your time."

"I'm sure I would recognise him if I knew him. I don't."

"This is the man in your garden. His name is Gerald Fontner. He has – had – a wife and two children, lived in Hampstead. Company director for a car dealership."

"I don't know him."

"What kind of car do you drive, Mr Petersen?"

"I don't. There's no point in having a car in London. There's nowhere to park."

"Do you know why Mr Fontner came to your house that night?"

This was dangerously close to a question I didn't want to answer.

"Maybe that stuff made him crazy."

"Can you think of any reason that Mr Fontner would want to harm you?"

"Maybe he wasn't himself?"

"Do you know what the substance is, on the walls and ceiling of your flat, Mr Petersen?"

"It smelled like some sort of mould." I was dancing around the questions.

"It's mildew. Plain ordinary mildew. We've had it analysed. We had the lab drop everything so we could get early identification of the substance."

"Mildew doesn't do that, does it?" I asked.

"We have a number of theories, Mr Petersen. None of them are very satisfactory. Did you paint your walls with anything unusual?"

"No."

"Have you had any strange substances in your flat?"

"No."

"Was there mildew in it before?"

"No. It was freshly decorated before I moved in. I've only been there a year."

"We have a forensic team looking at your flat. They will find evidence if there have been drugs in the house. Is there anything you want to tell us now?"

"No. I don't use drugs. There's nothing for them to find."

He watched me for a long moment, assessing my reaction. "They tell me that you were dragged from the river, barely alive. How did you come to be in the Thames, Mr Petersen?"

"I don't remember being in the Thames," I told him, schooling my face. The river I had almost drowned in was the Fleet, not the Thames.

"Did someone throw you in?"

"Not that I know of."

"Then what were you doing in the river?"

"Drowning?"

He smiled slightly. "People don't normally go swimming in the Thames. If there is something you have become involved in that's got out of control, then maybe we can help."

"I haven't done anything wrong," I told him. "I haven't broken any law."

"You don't always have to break the law to end up out of your depth, Mr Petersen. The police are here to protect the citizens from harm and to keep the Queen's peace. If you are being threatened or intimidated…?"

"No one is threatening me." They weren't. Not now.

"Understand that you can talk to us if there's a problem. We may be able to help."

"Thanks, but I think I'm OK."

He paused for a moment, thinking, then stood up and picked up the tape deck. "Interview ends at…" He checked his watch and recited the time and date. Then he handed the recorder to DS Vincent.

"If you could get a transcript typed up for me for tomorrow, I can go through it with DI Tindall in the morning."

"Yes, sir."

"And you could find the constable who was keeping an eye on Mr Petersen for us and let him know he can go home."

"You're not going to arrest me then?" I asked.

"The police are not in the habit of prosecuting witnesses, Mr Petersen. We would like you to come down to the station and sign a copy of your statement, but apart from that we won't be needing anything else from you, unless there's something more you would like to tell us?"

"No. There's nothing else."

"Very well." He waited while DS Vincent gathered up his notebook and tape recorder and went in search of the constable.

"Do you play golf, Mr Petersen?"

"Golf? No, why?"

"The head of the CPS plays golf."

"CPS?"

"The Crown Prosecution Service. The people for whom we must gather the evidence and to whom we must make our case. The head of the CPS is responsible for deciding who gets prosecuted and who does not."

"And he plays golf?"

"Apparently he plays with some of the Queen's Bench Division at the Royal Courts of Justice. I believe you are acquainted with one of the masters there, by the name of Checkland?"

"Yes. We met quite recently." Was this another interview, without the recorder this time?

"I just wanted you to know. If I find out that you were in any way responsible for the death of one of my officers, it won't matter who you know or what favours you are owed. Do I make myself clear?"

I took a deep breath. "Yes. I understand."

"Good morning, Mr Petersen." He quietly pulled the door closed behind him.

After a minute or two, Blackbird reappeared. She was not alone.

"Daddy!" Alex threw herself onto the bed, wrapped her arms around my neck and hugged me fiercely.

"Careful, darling, he's still not well." Katherine, a few steps behind our daughter, was being Mum. "Sorry, she's been dying to come in here ever since she first heard you'd woken." She tried to ease Alex from around my neck.

She managed to move her from lying on my chest, but my daughter was not going to be parted from me so easily. She lay alongside me, her head on my shoulder, curled into the crook of my arm, her curls tickling my nose as I stroked her hair. Katherine gave up trying to separate her from me when I nodded it was OK. It was better to concede to being hugged than to have her fight to stay.

"How are you feeling?" Katherine asked.

"I've been worse," I reassured her, noticing Blackbird slipping out of the room past a man who was standing in the doorway, looking out of place. Tall and bearded, he was caught at the boundary, unwilling to enter, but also unwilling to leave. I looked curiously at Katherine.

"This is Barry," she introduced him. "Barry brought us over in his car."

My Fey hearing found the evasion in that sentence, and the look between Katherine and our daughter confirmed that there was more to this than they were saying. They were terrible at keeping secrets at the best of times.

I nodded to him. "Hi, Barry, you don't have to stand in the doorway. You can come in." He edged into the room, still looking uncomfortable, as if he didn't think he ought to be here.

Katherine took a deep breath. "Niall, you might as well know now. Barry is my fiancé, we're getting married."

I looked between the two of them, while my daughter hugged me extra tightly as if I might erupt. It took me a moment to realise that a week ago it would have sparked a deep sense of resentment in me, but a lot had changed in the past few days.

"Well, that's great news," I told them. "Congratulations, to you both. Really." Barry smiled at this positive reaction. I offered him the hand that didn't have a drip attached to it and he shook it gently, conscious of my debilitated state.

Katherine was more sceptical about my reaction.

"We've been seeing a lot of each other, but I didn't know how to tell you. Alex here has been sworn to secrecy, haven't you, sweetheart?" She reached over and ruffled her hair.

"Katherine, it's your life. I wish you every happiness together."

"Thanks," she said, and seemed to mean it. "And I'm not the only one with developments on the relationship front. I've met your girlfriend. She seems very nice. What an unusual name."

A moment of panic hit me when I realised I had no idea what name she'd given them. "Is it?" I said lamely.

"Yes, I've never come across a Blackbird before, have you?"

"It's kind of a nickname that stuck," I explained.

"Well you've been keeping her quiet, too. Where did you meet her?"

"I met her on the Underground and she insisted on taking me for coffee. We've not been together very long."

"Don't look so embarrassed, Niall. It's good that you've found someone, even if she is a lot younger than you. She's barely left your side, you know, and she's been worried sick about you. We've got to know each other over the past day or so. I like her."

"So do I."

Reassured that there wasn't going to be a row between her parents, Alex sat up on the bed, taking in the room and its contents.

"Dad, what do these buttons do?" She pointed to a row of buttons on the wall.

"I have no idea, sweetheart. Just don't press any of them."

Katherine interceded. "Barry, would you mind taking Alex and seeing if you can find something for her to drink? I think I saw a water fountain near the door."

"I don't need a drink. I'm fine," my daughter declared.

"Don't be difficult. You haven't had a drink for at least two hours and you know what you're like. You'll wait until there's no chance of getting one and then declare you're dying of thirst. Go on with you, you can come straight back to your dad once you've drunk it."

She reluctantly agreed to go on condition that she could come back and Barry guided her outside. She was comfortable with him and they had clearly spent a lot of time together.

"He's OK, your Barry," I told her as he closed the door behind him.

"He's a good man, Niall, a gentle man."

It was a remark I would have taken as critical before, but I took it as another positive sign that I could accept her assessment without inferring it as critical of me.

"So, did the situation you were involved in get sorted out? Is that how you ended up in the river?"

This was the question she had manoeuvred Alex and Barry out of the room to ask, and I wondered how I could explain the events of the past days without telling her things that would only raise more questions than answers.

"I think it's safe to say it got resolved, Katherine. I don't think there is a threat to you or Alex any more, but it's made me look at my life in a whole new light. Things are going to have to change, that much I do know. In many ways they already have."

"You do seem different," she remarked, "but I still don't understand how you ended up in the river. Did you fall from a bridge? Did someone throw you in?"

"No. It's very complicated and the less you know about it, the better, but you can trust me when I say I had no intention of ending up swimming in the Thames." I could say that in the knowledge that there had never been any possibility of swimming with the hammer slung across my shoulder – besides, I had been in the Fleet, not the Thames.

"I'm not sure I like these secrets, Niall, not when Alex and I are involved."

"You're not involved. I worked very hard to make sure you stayed out of it. And I'm not the only one with secrets, am I?"

"Well I just hope that there's an end to it, whatever it was."

Blackbird appeared, closely followed by a nurse who straightened the bed, took my temperature again and updated the chart on the end of my bed. Then Alex reappeared and I was treated to a full description of her trip abroad, including the aeroplane, the hotel, the city and all she'd seen and done.

The description was more of a monologue than a conversation, though both Katherine and Barry were solicited for opinions on whether something was "awesome" or simply "cool". She asked me about the needle in my arm and then asked whether Blackbird dyed her hair and then she got to wondering whether anything would really happen if she pressed the buttons behind the bed.

Eventually Katherine declared that I must be tired and, despite protestations from Alex that I couldn't be tired as I had only just woken up, she was shepherded out with promises that she could return the next day if I wasn't discharged.

"That," I remarked to Blackbird when they had gone, "is a real incentive to feel better."

"She was worried about you."

"Yes, I know. And I do appreciate her concern. But she's so full of life, sometimes, she wears me down."

"And she's only one," she reminded me, walking around to sit beside me on the edge of the bed.

I grimaced, but then smiled at the thought of what was to come.

"The doctor says the water has cleared from your lungs and with the amount of antibiotics they pumped into you, I shouldn't think you'll get any infection for years."

"I don't think it works like that," I told her.

"Really?" The corner of her lips turned up in that half-smile and she tilted her head sideways, slightly.

"Don't tease. I'm not up to teasing yet."

"Oh? And here was me hoping you might be up to a little more than light teasing in a day or so."

"I've only just regained consciousness," I reminded her.

"Actually you were conscious that night, for a short while. You've recovered really quickly. The doctors are already wondering at your rate of recovery. You were off the oxygen after twelve hours and have been improving ever since."

"Is that your doing?"

"No, water really isn't my thing. It's your body that's changing. Just look at your hands. When they brought you in, they were covered in cuts. They put several stitches into your fingers. That was less than two days ago. Now you would think the scars are months old. Fortunately, the nice lady doctor says some people stick together well, and you're one of them. Still, you've given even her pause for thought."

"Do you think I should play sick for a while?"

"No, I think you should get yourself out of their sight as soon as possible. You don't want to show them any more than you need to. Seriously, if I'd realised you would heal this quickly, I wouldn't have called an ambulance."

"Where else can I go? The flat is still torn apart from Solandre's visit and I doubt the police will let anyone near it until they've completed their forensics."

"Well, that's the other thing I wanted to talk to you about. I can't go back to being Veronica, other than for a short while to quietly sort out her life and give her an excuse to disappear. I think you know now that going back to your job isn't really a possibility."

"What am I going to do for money? I have Alex and Katherine to support, and if you're not going back to the university then neither of us has a job."

"What's that?" asked Blackbird. She tensed, suddenly deeply concerned.

A noise came from beyond the door to the corridor outside, like a pendulum tick, slowly increasing in volume. It had a sharp metallic quality and a frequency that matched a steady walking pace. It slowed as it approached my door and Blackbird stood, facing the door, body set. The door opened slowly and a tall gentleman wearing a dark grey jacket over a black T-shirt and charcoal trousers stood in the doorway.

His eyes swept the room before he entered, taking in each detail, reminding me of the way the quiet policeman had assessed the room, except he didn't look much like a policeman. He looked like a bouncer.

TWENTY-NINE

The tall man entered, stepping sideways, leaving the door wide and placing the wall behind him. His manner was professional and he carried an expression of faint amusement, as if he were aware of a private joke he was unable to share. His hair was short and his ears stuck out slightly. In his hand was a dark wooden stave, about as tall as his shoulder. The top was ornamented with a decorative silver cap and the base was shod with steel. It slid downwards through his hand, tapping sharply as the tip struck the tiles beside his feet. It was an easy movement showing long familiarity.

"You are Niall Petersen and Blackbird of the Fey'ree." It wasn't a question. "I am Warder Garvin. I bring you the felicitations of the Lords and Ladies of the Seven Courts and request that you stand before them before sunset today."

"A request?" I asked him.

"It's a formality," Blackbird said. Her stance said that she knew this fellow. "They want to see us today."

"Will you come?"

I looked at Blackbird.

"Where?" she asked.

"There's an address in Soho Square on this slip of paper." He untucked a scrap of paper from his pocket and leaned forward to place it on the bed. "Be there an hour after noon. We'll take you the rest of the way."

"We?" I asked.

"I brought reinforcements, in case there was trouble. Tate?" He smiled, tipping his head towards the door without taking his eyes from us.

The doorway darkened and in it stood a huge bear of a man. The way he filled the doorway reminded me of how Gramawl had filled the tunnel below Covent Garden. He had the same bulk, as if he had to lean down to pass through the limited opening. His long hair was gathered back in a clasp and he had a grizzled beard. Grey eyes regarded us from beneath bushy eyebrows. He also wore the dark uniform.

"Trouble?" he asked. His voice was resonant and low, rich like chocolate and not in the least bit perturbed. If there was trouble, he wasn't concerned.

Garvin glanced over at us and then shook his head. "No. We'll see you in Soho Square."

"What if we're held up?" I asked.

"Don't be late. Or we'll have to come and fetch you."

He turned, the bulk of Tate retreating before him, and they walked away back down the corridor, the rhythmic tap of the staff on the tiles sounding their retreat.

"Who were they?" I asked Blackbird.

"We're being summoned to stand before the Council of Seven Courts, the full council of the lords and ladies who rule all the Courts of the Feyre."

"Seven courts? I thought you said the Seventh Court wasn't part of that anymore."

"Their place is held open for them should they ever decide to return. The Council is where the rulers of the courts meet together to discuss matters affecting them all."

"So why are we being summoned?"

"I don't know. The Council usually acts to defend the independence and authority of each individual court. They resolve disputes between courts."

"So why do they want to see either of us?"

"I don't know, but you can't refuse. You have to go."

"What will happen if we don't?"

"They would send those two to bring us before the court and, believe me, it would be far better to go willingly. Or we could be ruled in contempt, just like a human court except the punishments are more visceral."

"There are only two of them," I pointed out.

"The Warders of the Seven Courts are a cross between court officials, bodyguards and court enforcers. They carry out the will of the courts, in blood if necessary. And there are six of them, one for each court."

"So they'll try to bring us before the court. We can stand up for ourselves, I think we've proved that much at least."

"The Untainted are bad enough to deal with but the Warders are different. If the Seven Courts decree an execution then these are the people who carry it out. They're specially trained to go up against the worst of Feyre society. They are the ultimate sanction of the courts. They work as a team and they make Raffmir and Solandre look like amateurs."

"They didn't look so bad."

"Delivering messages is one of their more pleasant duties. They probably regard it as a day off."

"Do you think we should go with them, then? Couldn't we run away, go somewhere remote?"

"You may be able to run, but I can't."

"Why not?"

"Niall, I am bound to the courts. When I am summoned I must go. I receive the court's protection, but I am also bound by its decisions. I don't have a choice. They'll always find me and, anyway, it's not really an option in my condition."

"You're definitely pregnant then?"

"You'll be a father again."

"Oh wow. That's incredible, really. I'm delighted." I drew her to me, intending to kiss her, but she resisted.

"I've never done this before. I confess I'm a little scared."

"I'll stay with you. It'll be OK. We can go to ante-natal classes together. I did it with Katherine."

"I can't go to ante-natal classes, Niall." She looked troubled.

"Why not? It's easy. It's just exercises and stuff. You'll be good at it."

"You forget, the baby is only partly human. Fey mothers carry their children for almost a year, not nine months. Don't you think people are going to be suspicious if it takes that long? It might not even come out looking human. I can't have a scan or let anyone see it, can I? I have to keep it secret."

"Don't the Feyre have midwives or something? Surely if they're so keen to have children they have something?"

"Kareesh will look after me when the time comes, but in the meantime I need somewhere quiet, somewhere safe for the baby to grow." She was looking more and more concerned.

"It'll be OK," I reassured her, "After all we've been through, we can deal with this. I'll think of something."

"There's more. I'm going to lose my power."

"What do you mean?"

"I'm going to lose my ability to use magic. It's already fading. Pregnant Fey can't use magic. It would be dangerous for the baby and my body won't let me. It'll close down for the duration. That's how I know I'm pregnant. What I did in the tunnels, I couldn't do any more. It's the way it should be, but…"

"But what?"

"Niall, I feel so helpless."

I opened my arms and she leaned forward and rested her head on my chest while I hugged her to me. She was trembling so I simply held her until the trembling eased.

After a while she lifted herself up and looked into my eyes.

"Tell me that it will be OK?"

"It'll be fine," I told her. "I promise." She rested her head back on my chest and we lay there for some time while the hospital murmured around us.

"I need help," I told her, after a while.

"What kind of help?" she asked.

"I need Claire, today, now. Can you bring her to me?"

"Here? Yes. What for?"

"We need Claire to help us. I'll explain it to you both when she gets here. But hurry."

"She's going to want to know why, Niall."

"Tell her I want her to be our insurance policy."

Blackbird and I reached Soho Square shortly before one and found the early afternoon drinkers were already established in the pub on the corner. The garden in the centre of the square was arrayed with office workers eating lunch. We found the address easily, an anonymous entrance in a row of doors. We were ten minutes early.

"They're not here yet," I remarked.

"Of course they are," Blackbird contradicted.

"I don't see anyone."

"You won't."

She looked around nervously, then ascended the short flight of steps and pressed the brass doorbell mounted by the door. No one came to the door. She waited a moment and then descended back to the pavement.

"They will know we're here now."

"I thought you said they already knew."

"Don't be picky."

We waited on the pavement in full view while people walked through the square on their way to meet friends, lovers or colleagues. We scanned each face for signs of our earlier visitors, but didn't see them approach. They appeared out of the random movements of passers-by. One moment there were a number of unrecognised people strolling through the square and the next they were there.

With them was a young woman with short, dark hair, wearing a pale grey silk shirt and trousers. Her eyes were as hard as glass. She had walked past Blackbird and then doubled back, cutting off the retreat. We knew she was one of them from the sword swinging from her hip which hadn't been there a moment before. The black lacquered scabbard gleamed with the dull sheen of constant handling. She watched us, and Garvin and Tate watched the square. Tate swung a long-bearded axe gently from one hand. It looked like a toy against his enormous frame.

"You're on time." Garvin's smile was noncommittal, as if it was all the same to him. "Tate you know. This is Amber. You will not call power unless it is directly requested, understand? Use power without permission and we will kill you without hesitation."

He moved down the pavement, staff tapping on the paving, away from the door where Blackbird had rung the bell. Tate and Amber moved in to flank us.

"Aren't we going inside?" Blackbird asked, gesturing towards the door where she'd rung the bell.

He shook his head. "There's no one in there. I checked."

He went down the row to another similar door, as anonymous as the first, and trotted up the steps. The door opened as he reached it and a fourth member of the team was waiting, wearing the same charcoal uniform. On his belt were two long knives, one on each hip. Like every other weapon they looked worn by frequent handling. He was shorter in build with a broad nose, a bull neck and shoulders that gave him the impression of being roughly square. His hair was ginger and he reminded me of someone I had seen recently. I was trying to recall who it was as we were shepherded inside. Then I remembered. He had the same broad flat nose and protruding eyes as Marshdock.

"Are they ready for us?"

"They're assembled," he said to Garvin. "But they have some other business to discuss. Fee is with them. She'll let you know."

Tate and Amber followed us inside. We were led through the house, past closed internal doors to what could only be described as a scullery at the back of the house. It had a range cooker that looked like it hadn't been used in decades and a large rectangular table in scuffed bare wood, scored with generations of service. A window looked out onto the back, but it was too shadowed between the buildings to see what was outside. Garvin didn't pause. He went straight to a side door at the back of the room and opened it.

"Down here," he said.

"What is it," I asked Blackbird as she descended the stairs behind Garvin, "about the Feyre and basements?"

"It's closer to the earth," she said, as if that should explain it.

The stairs had a bend in them and were quite difficult to negotiate, so that I wondered how Tate was going to get down them. They opened out at the bottom into two cellar rooms accessed through an open doorway. There was a faint musty smell and I noticed a tray left out on a chest with a number of wizened apples on it. They didn't look like this year's harvest.

Garvin strolled into the second cellar and waited for the rest to follow. Amber came down after us, followed by a scraping sound as Tate eased himself down the stairway and into the room.

"The courts are down here?" I asked Garvin.

He shook his head. "Follow."

He walked to the centre of the room, turned to face the back wall and stepped forward. There was a twist in the air, he shimmered and vanished.

"It's one of the Ways, is that it?" I asked Blackbird.

"There isn't a Way here," she said. "It doesn't go anywhere."

"Yes it does," rumbled Tate. "You next." He nodded towards Blackbird.

She stepped forward to the place where Garvin had been, orientating herself as he had done.

"Interesting," she said, then stepped forward and vanished.

"Now you." He nodded towards the spot.

I walked forward, remembering the last time I had tried this. I had become lost and had nearly broken my neck getting out again. Nervously, I turned to face the wall and then felt down below my feet. The sensation was different. When we had used the Ways before I had felt the flow of power beneath my feet like a raging torrent. This was more like a stream or a tributary, the same in nature but much less powerful. I looked at Tate, but he just nodded. Amber dropped her hand to her sword hilt for emphasis.

I reached down and felt for the connection. The Way swelled beneath me and rose. I stepped forward and felt it pick me up and rush me away. Unlike the wild ride of the other ways, this one had only echoes of the vast emptiness I had felt before and lasted mere moments. Then I was stepping into a brightly lit room which smelled neither damp nor musty. Blackbird was there with Garvin and I walked forward out of the Way across the stone tiles to allow the others to follow me. I turned around, noticing there were no windows, and realising there was someone behind me. The figure stood behind me was the size of a man. His pelt was brown like warm chestnut and his arms and legs were long under the dark grey cotton of his loose clothing. The long fur on his head fell forward over his face and there was the

486

bright glint of dark eyes under the stringy fringe. He smiled, baring rows of sharp pointed teeth in a grin far too wide to be human. He was holding a short spear with a long, double-edged blade, held so the point angled down towards the floor. The blade looked clean and sharp and he was poised, like a dancer.

"This is Slimgrin. He's here to make sure only invited guests arrive this way."

"Where are we?" I asked Garvin.

"Somewhere else," he said offhandedly. He turned to Slimgrin. "When the others come through, tell Amber and Tate to follow us upstairs and have Fellstamp help you here. Close the gate as soon as they've arrived."

Slimgrin nodded. The way they used names was arrogant, as if it didn't matter that we knew them.

Garvin turned and walked towards the bottom of a stairway, gesturing us to follow.

The stairs were wider than those we had descended and doubled back on themselves to rise to an open doorway. At the top was a grand hallway of the type that might have graced a small country mansion or an upmarket townhouse. The tall ceilings gave the building a Georgian feel, as if ladies dressed in bustles and panniers would appear at any moment. There was an open door into a sitting room with armchairs loosely arrayed around a large stone fireplace. The curtains had been drawn across the large windows and a couple of Regency-style standard lamps were left on, providing a soft and unobtrusive light. The fire had been set, but was unlit.

Garvin escorted us into the room.

"Sit here for a moment until they're ready for you. It shouldn't be long."

Blackbird went to an armchair and sat on the armrest. I walked to the fireplace and turned to face the room. I was too nervous to sit. Garvin stood next to the doorway, not blocking the exit exactly but making it clear that we were to stay.

Amber and Tate appeared together. Tate went to the chair opposite Blackbird, the wood frame of the chair making protesting creaking noises as he eased himself into it. He rested his head on the back of the chair, placed the axe across the arms and looked at ease. Amber stood inside the door leaning back against the wall, the sword in her hand resting against the side of her leg. She watched me like a cat watches a mouse-hole.

We waited in complete silence for ten minutes. I found myself listening to Blackbird breathe. The tiny sounds of the overburdened chair under Tate overlaid the faint nameless noises from the rest of the house. If I listened carefully I could hear my own blood pumping in my ears.

Approaching footsteps warned us of the arrival at the door before she appeared. In contrast to Amber, she wore a mid-length shift dress, in charcoal grey like everyone else, but it was short enough to show off her bare legs and clung to her curves. She was tall and pretty and moved with a lithe grace that said she knew it. Her hair was blond and fell in long curling ringlets around her shoulders. Strangely, her curls appeared to move on their own, even when she was standing still, giving her an unearthly quality at odds with her pretty girl image. In her hand was a short baton, thicker and shorter than Garvin's staff and polished with a glossy black lacquer.

She nodded to Garvin and smiled at us. "Hello, I'm Fionh. Blackbird, they will see you now." She stepped back from the doorway and waited for Blackbird to rise.

I stepped forward to go with Blackbird, but Tate lifted one hand. "Just the girl," he rumbled.

Blackbird came to me, turning her face up to accept a chaste kiss. "Good fortune," she whispered.

She turned and walked through the door, Fionh and Amber falling in behind, the footsteps fading as they went deeper into the house. There was creak as Tate shifted in his chair. Garvin didn't move.

I went to the armchair Blackbird had vacated and slumped into it. Her warmth lingered in the arm where my hand rested. I had hoped we would be able to see them together, to face them as we had faced other adversaries. We weren't being given that option. Still, Blackbird knew what to say if it came to it. We had no way of knowing why the council wanted to see us. It could be good news. They might want to reward us for the service we had performed, though somehow I doubted that. I had been summoned to numerous board meetings in the past and it was never to give you a pat on the back and tell you what a good boy you'd been.

I pushed my mind away from worrying about Blackbird to thoughts of my work colleagues and what they would say when I resigned. Would they let me resign or would I already have been let go? If I was lucky then there would be a settlement package waiting to tide me over until Blackbird and I had our lives sorted out. That was assuming we still had our lives.

The footsteps in the corridor brought me to my feet. Tate stayed in the chair until the last possible moment, only levering himself up after Fionh appeared in the doorway.

"They will see you now," she said.

"Where's Blackbird?" I asked her.

"She is being cared for, don't worry."

"If she is harmed…" I told them.

Garvin interrupted. "She won't be harmed while she's pregnant."

"How did you know about that?" I asked him.

He shrugged, a seismic movement. "I make it my business to know about the people I have to deal with."

Fionh led the way while Garvin and Tate fell in behind. We went back into the house, which was clearly a substantial property. We passed room after room, some with dust covers over the furniture as if they hadn't been used in years. We came at the end to a set of double doors facing us. Fionh opened one of the doors toward her, stepping to the side to allow me to enter.

"Garvin will go in with you," she said.

Inside, the room was dimly lit. I stepped through the doorway into a room buzzing with power. Outside there had been no trace of it, but within the room it was like walking through a cloud of static.

There was a large domed ceiling with a mural painted on it, like the ones you see in churches, except the angels had far too many teeth and the wrong sort of wings.

The room could originally have been a ballroom. There was a gallery at the far end where the musicians might have sat. In the centre of the floor was a pool of light within which there was a huge seven-pointed star.

"Come forward, Alshirian, called Dogstar, also called Niall Petersen, so that we may see you."

Arrayed in a semi-circle around the star were seven chairs, large enough to be called thrones and set back so they were in shadow. Six of the chairs were occupied, illuminated dimly by some unseen light source. The empty chair was dark.

Whether it was some distortion caused by the power in the room or a quality of the light, the figures in the chairs were isolated, picked out against the dark.

Some of the occupants had features I recognised. The strikingly beautiful blue-eyed lady wrapped in the deep blue cloak had hair that wound around the finials on the top of her chair of its own volition and was just as disturbing as Fionh's had been. The short fellow with the broad nose and the grumpy expression reminded me of Marshdock and Fellstamp. They shared common features in the way a son inherits his father's ears.

A delicate figure with finely boned limbs ending in long spindly fingers sat to my right. Her skin was pale as moonlight and her ears came sharply to a point. She had a small pert nose and a mouth wider than a human mouth would be. Her eyes were slightly elongated and shone green in the dark as she turned a yellow gold band on her left wrist. Next to her was a huge woman, her face broad and flat, her forearms the size of hams. Ivory teeth protruded from her bottom jaw, reminding me of Gramawl, but she was largely hairless and as pale skinned as her neighbour. Heavy silver rings dangled from each ear and she had a broad leather belt around her waist, pulled over a loose shirt with a great silver ram's-head buckle.

Next to her was a man who I would have not looked twice at if I had met him elsewhere. Dressed in a red silk shirt, he had a feral look about him that spoke of something predatory. He regarded me with cold malice.

For a moment, I thought the figure next to him was Slimgrin, the warder who had been waiting in the room downstairs, but the fur on his head had been caught into a topknot and he had a groomed, more cultured look about him. He also had a heavy silver chain around his neck that sat bright against the dark lustre of his fur.

They were clearly waiting for me, so I stepped forward into the circle of light and stood at the centre of the star. Garvin moved in behind me. The light caught the bright edge of a bare blade in his hand. His staff had transformed into a long slim blade and scabbard. I hadn't heard him draw it.

"Is that necessary?" I asked him.

"Not my decision." He shrugged lightly.

I turned back to the dimly lit figures in the seats.

"Is that it? Have you brought me here to slaughter me?"

I was greeted with silence. The power in the room was making my ears buzz.

"If not for that, then why am I here?"

"That's a better question," said the lady in the blue cloak in a light contralto voice. "I am Kimlesh. I speak for the Nymphine Court, the undines and the greyne. That's one of the things we are here to consider. Why you are here."

"You summoned me."

"I meant why you, a wraith, un-bound of the Seventh Court and part-human, are here."

"That, I don't know," I said honestly.

"Blackbird has told you, I'm sure, that the Seventh Court are not known for associating with humans."

"The fact I'm here means someone has been playing away from home, though, doesn't it?"

"Not necessarily."

"How else do you explain it?"

"There was a time, long ago, when the Feyre were not as you see us today. Each of us here holds a strand of that thread. Teoth, there, holds the office of High Maker, held only by the luchorpán and the nixies. Mellion is the Hordemaster, ruler of all the goblins and gnolls of the Goblin Court. These boundaries were made, though. They did not appear by accident."

"What does that have to do with me?"

"We, in this room, made a decision some time ago, to allow our bloodlines to mix with those of humanity and repair the damage that was done. We allowed, and in some cases even encouraged, a liaison between the races."

"I know. That's why the Seventh Court rebelled."

"The Feyre has become more and more specialised as certain traits only manifest themselves inside a single court. It has made us fragile."

"You don't appear fragile to me."

"I don't mean fragile as individuals. I mean as a race. We have lost the ability to reproduce because parts of our make-up have become unstable."

"But breeding with humans fixes that?"

"We took a calculated risk. We have known for a long time that the union between Feyre and Human was fertile and had the potential to restore the fertility lost to us. Humans spread like moss on a damp tree. If we could acquire some of their fecundity then we would be restored. That was a prize worth the taking. Human blood has the missing pieces, as far as we are concerned.

You are a demonstration of that. You already have a daughter and there's another child on the way."

"Blackbird told you?"

"We already knew. The prospect of a birth is important news amongst the courts of the Feyre."

"Then you asked me here to congratulate me?"

The answer was not a warm one. "The nature of the babe is uncertain."

"You mean it could turn out like me, wraithkin, rather than like Blackbird."

"It's more complicated than that. When we mixed our bloodlines with humanity, the capacity to have children was not the only thing altered. It was the risk we took when we allowed it."

"What else changed?"

"The Feyre are defined by physical form. Fey'ree are small and delicate like Yonna here," she gestured to the pale, slim figure with the green eyes, "whereas ogres like Barthia are much larger and stronger." She gestured to the huge woman, who accepted the complement with a nod.

I looked back at Yonna. I could see now the resemblance from when Blackbird had transformed herself in the room above the inn, when we were in Shropshire. The pale skin and the way the eyes were elongated. "I am Fey'ree," she'd told me. "A creature of Fire and Air."

Kimlesh continued. "Humans, though, do not inherit the full form of the Feyre. They can acquire aspects of it, of course, and some are more Fey than others, but none are quite like us."

"Is that a problem?"

"It makes it much harder to determine what gifts they have inherited, especially as human blood adds its own twist, bringing forth gifts that were formerly dormant."

"What do you mean?"

"I mean that your Fey forebear could have come from any court, not just that of Altair, our missing brother. Your human blood threw the dice and you are the result. Just because you are wraithkin and Blackbird is Fey'ree does not mean your child will be one or the other. Human heredity has thrown us back into the hands of fortune. Your daughter, Alexandra, could take after any of us. As could your unborn son."

"My son? It's a boy?"

"Did Kareesh not tell you? Yes, if Blackbird survives to deliver him, you will have a son. Be warned, though, birth among the Feyre is a hazardous business. Blackbird must be careful."

"I'll look after her."

"You?" It was the first time the feral man in the red shirt had spoken. "You're not leaving this room."

THIRTY

Teoth broke the silence that followed that remark.

"Unfortunately, Krane is right. We cannot allow you to leave."

"I'm sorry? Why not?"

"Blood price alone demands your heart," said Krane.

"We talked about this, Krane," said Yonna. "Fenlock initiated the attack. Even Carris agrees. She cannot claim blood price."

"It doesn't matter," said Krane. "He knows about the ceremony. He knows about the barrier and the arrangements we made. He cannot be allowed to leave this room with that knowledge. He could bring the whole thing down around our ears and there would be nothing we could do to prevent it. Are you prepared to set him free with that knowledge?"

"He has a point," said the deep booming voice of the ogre. "Our position would be significantly undermined."

"What about Blackbird?" I asked. "She knows as much as I do. What will you do? Wait until the babe is born and then kill her too?"

"Her position is different," said Yonna. "She is bound to the Court of Fire and Air. We have taken her word that she will tell no one else. It's her life if she breaks that oath and she knows it."

"Then do the same with me. Will you not accept my oath?"

None of them would meet my eyes. Even Krane looked away.

Barthia broke the silence that followed. "There is only one court that could have you, and that seat is vacant."

"Because I'm wraithkin."

"Even so," she said.

Claire Radisson looked up to the gallery of Court Four to see if she could see Ben Highsmith. At that distance and in this light her eyesight wasn't good enough to distinguish faces, even with her contact lenses. She smiled anyway, hoping he could see her and not realise how nervous she was. She and Jerry had conducted the Quit Rents Ceremony many times before, but it had never had the significance it had today.

When Ben Highsmith had appeared on Sunday, his clothes soaked through with river water, he had caused quite a stir. Security had refused to let him in and he had been threatened with arrest. It was only when he'd asked for her by name and they had promised to bring her to see him that he'd calmed down enough to allow himself to be led to a side room away from the busy entrance.

She'd found him standing in the security office, a grim smile on his face and the towel she had lent Niall in his gnarled hands. The knives had been wrapped in it. He'd told her what had happened and insisted the ceremony must go ahead.

Elizabeth had expressed her concerns. The grey tinge underlying Jerry's complexion worried Claire too, but Blackbird's message had been clear. The best protection for Jerry, his family, and everyone else was the restoration of the knife and the performance of the Ceremony of the Quit Rents.

Whatever Blackbird had said to Elizabeth in the hospital must have been enough because she acceded, though she could see her sitting in the front row, the set of her shoulders a testament to the enforced leave Jerry would be taking as soon as his duties were completed.

Behind Elizabeth, the two figures dressed in red grandeur stood with chains of office hung about their necks. These were the candidates for the Sheriff of the City of London and for Middlesex. They were being presented to the Queen's Remembrancer, in his role as representative of the monarch, for approval. Since the City of London had picked the wrong side in the conflict between Simon de Montfort and Henry III, they had been required by the reigning monarch to present their sheriffs for ratification. They would have been brought up the river from the Square Mile and then walked through the Inns of Court in procession with all the pageantry this group of wealthy middle-aged men could muster.

"And can you confirm for me," the Queen's Remembrancer called out in tones that carried up to the rafters, "that there was no repetition, when crossing Temple, of the disgraceful scenes of 1756?"

The Comptroller of the City of London, wrapped in his bearskin cloak, shook his head and smiled.

"I can assure Your Lordship, these fine men have behaved impeccably and were received with courtesy and respect wherever they walked."

The Comptroller went on to extol the virtues of the two men being put forward. One was an accountant for a big consultancy and the other was a tax auditor, but they each stood and listened in silence to their lives being described in bold terms. They certainly looked the part, even if the most dangerous thing they would be called upon to do was to decide whether to accept another glass of port or move on to the brandy.

She wondered idly whether the investiture also had some secret meaning, whether the City had its own reasons for conducting rituals lasting hundreds of years. She thought it much more likely that the office of sheriff had more to do with networking and connections in the world of high finance. She smiled as she realised people probably looked at her and thought she had a boring staid existence.

If only they knew.

The Comptroller completed his speech and recommended the two candidates for approval by the crown, which the Remembrancer granted. He looked gravely at them for a moment and then told them in a serious tone, that although there was an annual salary of three hundred pounds for each of them, due at the quarter-sessions of Epiphany, Easter, Midsummer and Michaelmas, they would receive not a single penny of it.

There was a ripple of laughter though the assembled audience of family members and colleagues, all turned out in their finery. They all knew these city gentlemen regarded three hundred pounds as small change and that they would probably spend more than that on champagne after the ceremony.

Rolled charters inscribed on vellum, one for each of them, were sealed with wax using the great silver seal of the exchequer, binding the ribbon interleaved into the document and making it official. It was a great honour to be made a sheriff and she wished them well of it.

Then was the moment she had been waiting for.

"End it now," said Krane, "before he causes any more trouble. Garvin?" I saw the flash as the blade came up.

"Wait," said Kimlesh. "He has earned our gratitude. He and Blackbird restored the barrier when without it all would have been lost. Surely that is enough to save his life?"

"You'd let him walk away, knowing what he knows?" said Krane.

"A boon then," said Kimlesh. "His life is forfeit but we

will grant him a boon for his service to the courts. We have much at our disposal. What would you ask of us?" he said to me.

"Are you offering me compensation so you can kill me without feeling guilty?"

"I regret this, truly, but I can see no other way. Come, what would you have from us?"

"I would have three things, then."

"Three? Oh very well. Name them."

"The first is for Blackbird. She needs somewhere safe and secure to live while she is pregnant. Somewhere with trees."

"It is done," said Kimlesh. "What else?"

"For my daughter, Alex. If she comes into her power then I want her to have a place in the courts, whatever her nature turns out to be."

"If she is wraithkin, then it is not within our power to grant," said the Ogre woman, Barthia.

"Aside from that, then. Will you take her?"

"We will," agreed Barthia.

"That leaves the third," said Kimlesh. "Three is the trick of it. What will you have?"

"And now we come to the rendering of quit rents in respect of two petty sergeantries held directly of the crown, one for the Forge in Tweezers Lane, just south of St Clement Danes ,and the other for the wasteland known as the Moors, in the county of Shropshire, formerly the county of Salop. The quit rent for the former is six horse shoes and sixty-one nails."

"I have them here, my lord," said the Comptroller, indicating the items laid out on the black and white chequered cloth of the Exchequer.

"Will you count them out?"

With exaggerated care, the Comptroller lifted each horse-shoe in turn, the huge size of them making his hands look small. He showed each of them to the assembled court.

"There are six, my lord, and the nails are here. Ten, twenty…" He laid bundles of nails, each tied in a bundle with blue ribbon, on the squares of black and white draped over the bench. "Thirty, forty, fifty, sixty and…" He patted his pockets absently, then more urgently.

There was a tense moment, but then he smiled and produced the final nail, the one Ben had pried from Niall's lacerated fingers and returned to Claire along with the knives.

"Sixty-one nails, my lord."

"Good number!" called the Queen's Remembrancer in response and cracked his gavel down hard on the bench.

"And the knives? Do they meet the test?"

This was her part and her stomach clenched as she went to retrieve the Dead Knife from its place. She picked it out of the box carefully, reminded of what had happened when Niall had held it. Reassuringly it kept the same dull sheen she had always known. She walked forward and placed the knife, edge up, against the bench.

The Comptroller walked forward, a length of green hazel twig, one year's growth in length, in his hand. They exchanged a nervous smile. There had been the time when a bumptious upstart from the City had usurped the Comptroller's place and decided to test the knives himself. Neither knife had broken the rod, despite strenuous effort on his part. The Remembrancer of the time had been forced to fine the Highsmiths for non-payment, and they had not been happy.

He held the rod on either side of the knife and pressed down. The rod bent over the edge but it did not break. The Dead Knife had done its job.

She turned back to where the box for the knives was placed and replaced the Dead Knife, retrieving the newly forged Quick Knife in its place. The broad leaf of the blade was dark metal, but the edge shone bright where Ben had sharpened it. She stepped forward again, holding the knife up momentarily for effect, and then placed it edge up on the bench.

Now came the moment of truth. This was the test. If the knife was remade then it would cut through the hazel rod and the barrier would be sealed. If not...

She looked around at the ranked faces in the benches craning to see. None of them realised how much would change if the knife failed the test.

The Comptroller stepped forward again with the rod. As he held the rod out, she realised his hand was shaking, very slightly. He couldn't possibly know the significance of this, could he? She looked up into his face and saw uncertainty there, and then he grinned.

He pressed the rod down on the knife dramatically and stumbled forward slightly as the knife cleaved through the rod as if it wasn't there. He'd pressed much harder than he needed to and his chin came unexpectedly close to the burnished edge. Claire whipped the knife away, concerned he would be cut. Her concern was not so much for the Comptroller but for the knife. Lord only knew what would happen if they got blood on it.

Regaining his composure, the Comptroller turned and held the two pieces of the rod high for all to see.

"The knives have passed the test, my Lord."

"Good service!" intoned the Remembrancer, banging his gavel down again. "That concludes the rendering of the quit rents." He smiled broadly at the assembly.

Claire carefully turned and replaced the knife next to its twin in the wooden case. She closed the lid and fixed the catch and then let out a long sigh. There had been no clap of thunder, no peal of bells, but she'd felt the knife in her hand after it had split the hazel rod. The tingle of power that shivered through it was all the confirmation she needed.

It was done.

* * *

"The third thing." I took a deep breath and released it slowly, then I told them. "I would have you know that if you take my life, here and now, then by the end of the week there will be notices posted all over Covent Garden, Leicester Square and random parts of central London describing the nature and reason for my death. They will detail the nature of the ceremony, the schism with the Seventh Court, the purpose of the two knives, the horseshoes and the sixty-first nail, and the fact that you have had me killed to prevent the knowledge from being discovered."

There was silence.

"I beg your pardon?" said Kimlesh.

"I think you heard me well enough."

"How?" said Barthia. "How can you achieve this? You'll be dead."

"The Queen's Remembrancer, who is also a High Court Judge, issued a court order this morning. Notices have been lodged with a number of London solicitors and are held in trust pending my disappearance. I don't know all the details, for no single person does, but if I do not present myself before the Queen's Remembrancer before the week is out then they have instructions to assume I am dead and enact the court order. The notices will be posted by agents throughout the city. Special arrangements have been made to make sure Marshdock gets one of the first notices printed. By the end of the week, everyone, Fey and human, will know what you did."

"This is an outrage!" shouted Krane.

"So is killing me to keep a secret."

A sound built slowly. It rumbled and bubbled up around us until it was near deafening. I realised, finally, that the ogre was laughing. By the time she had subsided and we could hear ourselves think, the realisation of what I had done had come home to them all.

"This is impossible duress," said Krane. "If we let him go then he could tell them anyway."

"If we don't let him go then they will certainly find out," said Kimlesh. "He's sending it to Marshdock of all people. You know what that means."

"I say kill him now and clean up the mess as we find it," said Krane.

"You're letting your heart rule your head, Krane," said Teoth. "This has been carefully constructed. I am impressed." He nodded to me and folded his arms, regarding me with new interest.

"I still say we cannot allow him to leave without an oath to seal his lips."

"Then I will give you one," I said. "Which of you will accept it?"

They looked at each other. "We cannot," said Kimlesh. "You don't understand."

"Then you'll just have to take my word for it," I told them.

"We cannot do that either," said Yonna. "It is too sensitive. It would leave you unprotected if someone were to try and pry it from you. There are those who would do so if they knew, and fragments of this may yet slip back from other sources."

"It would suit the wraithkin lord's purposes to see us squirm," Barthia agreed.

"You don't know what you've done," said Yonna.

"I think I've saved my own skin," I told her.

"Only for the moment. There are others who will not give you the clean death that we would have."

"I'll deal with that when it happens," I told her.

The long-limbed figure of Mellion uncurled itself from the seat and stood, proving himself a head taller than either me or Garvin. He spread his hands flat and moved them slowly apart. The others stopped talking. He pointed to the vacant seat, then held his hands over his eyes. Then he dropped his hands and walked around to Garvin and held his hand out. Garvin looked confused until Mellion gently prised the scabbard from Garvin's hand and offered it to me.

"What does he want me to do with it?" I asked Garvin.

"I think he's offering you a solution," said Garvin.

"He wants me to kill myself?" I asked.

"No," said Kimlesh. "Hordemaster Mellion has once again proved his tactical ability. My compliments, sir."

Mellion bowed and returned to his seat, leaving me holding Garvin's scabbard and wondering whether I could use it as a weapon in some way. One look at Garvin, however, changed my mind. He held his long blade with easy readiness.

I looked around the circle of faces, the blank looks among them reflecting my own confusion.

"Why am I holding this?" I asked Kimlesh.

"Mellion is suggesting you join the warders."

"Me? I don't know one end of a pointed stick from the other."

"I agree," said Krane. "A wraithkin warder? His loyalty would be questionable at best."

"But there have always been wraithkin warders, haven't there, Garvin. Tell them," said Kimlesh.

"This is true," Garvin said. "While there hasn't been a wraithkin warder since the separation of the Seventh Court, that's only because there have been no candidates. As you know, there were originally seven warders, one from each court. And their loyalty is to no single court. We carry out the will of the council." He made this point looking directly at Krane.

"I'm sorry, Garvin," he said. "I did not mean to imply—"

"I understand your concern, Lord Krane, but the warders swear their oath to the council, revoking any previous oath to their own court. They are bound to the council as anyone else is bound to their court."

"Are you... are you offering me a job?" I asked them.

"It is a way out of the dilemma, certainly," said Kimlesh. "We need your silence and you wish to survive. The two are not incompatible if you are a warder."

Garvin addressed himself to the council. "I would respectfully remind the council that you are going to be putting your lives in this man's hands. Is that what you want?"

"Can you train him?" asked Teoth.

Garvin looked me up and down, assessing me like a piece of meat. "I can make him competent. Whether he has any true ability remains to be seen."

"He's already proven himself far more resourceful than any of us would have credited," said Teoth.

"And it is better to have him bound close to us than running around loose, don't you think?" Kimlesh looked around the circle.

"Warders can get killed," said Krane. "If he dies in service then we still risk exposure."

"I can ask the Remembrancer to rescind the order," I told them. "If you will all swear not to harm me or mine then it can be withdrawn. It will take a few weeks to unravel, but it can be done."

"You misunderstand," said Kimlesh. "We would not harm you. You will be our protector, our bodyguard and our servant. A warder has never, ever been harmed by the council."

"Nevertheless," I looked at Krane, "that's my condition."

He sat back in his seat, while everyone looked at him. "Very well," he said. "Swear him in. The sooner this is done with, the better."

"Do you each swear that you will do me no harm, either directly or indirectly?"

"I swear that we will treat you like any other warder, with no preference or privilege, nor any wish for harm," said Kimlesh.

"So say I," said Yonna.

"And I," said Teoth

Mellion pressed his hand over his heart and nodded solemnly.

Barthia agreed, "The same for me."

Krane looked around the faces, then nodded. "I'm going to regret this, I just know it," he sighed. "I too will treat you as any other warder with no preference or privilege, nor any wish for harm. Is that enough?"

I nodded.

"Give Garvin his scabbard back and then take off your jacket and kneel," said Kimlesh. "Garvin?"

Garvin took back his scabbard and moved to the side of me while I dropped the jacket in a bundle on the floor and knelt in the centre of the star.

"Put out your right hand and bare your wrist," she instructed.

I hesitated just a moment, then pulled back the shirt from my wrist, exposing the skin. I held out my wrist and Garvin's blade flashed down. I flinched, but the blade stopped, just above the veins of my wrist. He withdrew the sword.

"A test?" I asked. Then I noticed the blood welling out of the cut across my wrist. I hadn't even felt it touch me.

"Taste it," said Kimlesh. I sucked the blood, feeling the coppery tang of it in my mouth.

"By your blood, will you serve the will of the council until released of your service," she asked.

"I will." The coppery taste got stronger.

"By your heart, will you hold the life of any member of the council above your own?"

I looked at Krane. "I will." I could feel the blood on my tongue.

"By your mind, will you seek to preserve and protect your fellow warders even at risk of your own life?"

"I will." Its taste thickened.

"By your power, will you keep the secrets of the council, even to your own death?"

"I will."

"Stand, Warder Alshirian, called Dogstar, also called Niall Petersen, and bow to the council."

I got unsteadily to my feet. Garvin watching me, then turned to the council and bowed slowly.

"Garvin will take you to Blackbird. I imagine you will want to tell her your news."

Garvin wiped down the blade with a plain white cloth. Then he nodded to Kimlesh.

"Go then. We will see you again, Warder Alshirian."

I turned, but Garvin caught my eye. He turned and whirled the blade around in his hand, sheathing the blade with a soft hiss in one smooth movement, then he placed his right hand over his heart and bowed slowly to the council. I mimicked his bow.

He turned and escorted me to the door.

"Send in Fionh, please, Garvin."

He held the door while I stepped through and he stepped through after me. Tate and Fionh were waiting outside. Fionh's eyebrow went up when she saw me.

"You're to go in directly, Fee. Tate, you're with me."

"What happened in there?" asked Fionh.

"I'll tell you later." He looked me over. "We're going to have our work cut out. See if you can find out how long they're going to be. Mullbrook will want to know if they are dining."

Fionh slipped back into the room, pulling the door quietly closed behind her.

Garvin walked away down the corridor with Tate stepping in behind. I stood there for a moment, bemused, unsure of what I should do.

Garvin paused and slowly turned back to me. "First lesson," he said. "I can lead, but you have to follow."

They strode away. I gathered my wits together and trotted after them.

"Are you going to tell me what's going on?" asked Tate as we neared the room where we had originally been taken.

"You and the rest of the team," said Garvin. "But first we need to return Warder Dogstar here to his love."

We entered the room. Blackbird was standing by the fireplace. She took one look at me, then ran and threw herself into my arms, wrapping her arms around my neck and pressing her warm lips to mine.

"Warder Dogstar?" said Tate from behind us.

"Come on. We need to get the others together." He waited until Blackbird released me and then pointed at me and then at the floor. "Stay here. Do not leave this room until I come and get you. Consider it an order."

"Yes, sir," I said, grinning at him.

"Learn to follow them. It'll keep you alive."

"Yes, sir."

"Tate. Get the others. Team briefing in five."

"Yes, sir," he rumbled.

Garvin looked steadily at him. "Don't you start," he said.

Tate grinned at me, then left to gather the others together. Garvin nodded to Blackbird and pulled the door closed behind him, giving us our privacy.

"Warder Dogstar?" she said.

"It was the price of freedom, though I'm not exactly free. They swore me into service." I showed her the cut across my wrist where the blood had smeared and was already clotting.

"She knew, Niall. All that time, she knew. When Kareesh offered you the sight of something she said 'courts', plural."

"I thought they would let us go, that they would have to. They nearly didn't."

"It's enough, Niall. What will you do now?"

"Garvin said he'd train me. He sounded like he wasn't going to enjoy it."

"Will you stay here?"

"I don't know. I think they were as surprised as I was. Mellion suggested it and I don't think Garvin could find a way to turn him down."

"You don't mess with Mellion," agreed Blackbird.

"And what about you?" I asked her.

"I had to swear to keep the secret," she said. "If I tell another soul it will kill me and the baby."

"Our son."

"I know, they told me too. They have offered me a bursary, an income to help me through the months ahead in return for my silence."

"You accepted?"

"There wasn't really much of a choice."

"They offered me a boon. I asked for somewhere for you to live that's secure while you're pregnant and for them to accept Alex into the courts, when and if she comes into her gifts. That was before they swore me in as a warder, though."

"Did they agree?"

"They did, yes."

"Then it is done. They will not go back on their word."

"So you have somewhere to live."

"*We* have somewhere," she said, pressing her hand to my cheek. "I don't want you too far away."

That possessive glint had appeared in her eye.

"Don't say it."

"Why not?" she said, turning her face up to be kissed. "It's true."

I kissed her, and she laughed, throwing her hands around my neck. I pressed my lips to hers and whirled her around. It didn't stop her though. I had to release her eventually.

She stood before me, breathless but determined, eyes full of green fire.

"Mine," she said.

ABOUT THE AUTHOR

Mike Shevdon's love of Fantasy & SF started in the 1970s with C S Lewis, Robert Heinlein and Isaac Asimov, and continued through Alan Garner, Ursula Le Guin and Barbara Hambly. More recent influences include Mike Carey, Phil Rickman, Neil Gaiman and Robert Crais, among many others.

He has studied martial arts for many years, aikido and archery mainly. Friends have sometimes remarked that his pastimes always seem to involve something sharp or pointy. The pen should therefore be no surprise, though he's still trying to figure out how to get an edge on a laptop.

Mike lives in Bedfordshire, England, with his wife and son, where he pursues the various masteries of weapons, technology, and cookery.

www.shevdon.com

ACKNOWLEDGMENTS

A story is not created alone, and there are many people to thank for the help and guidance they have offered in the creation of this book.

Firstly, Scott, who when I sent him my first raw efforts, simply requested more. That quiet encouragement kept me writing, dude, so you have only yourself to blame.

Thanks and hugs to my test readers: Ameen, Bob & Tina, Jo, Juliet, Kev, Lauri, Rachel, Sarah, Simon and Tor. You are to me what every writer needs and few have. You rock. Also, thanks to Aggy for the donation of the little computer so that I could write on holiday in Italy. It worked like a dream, mate, and I still use it.

Particular thanks to Andrew and Joy of the Welly Writers who pulled no punches and left no page unturned. Your frankness, your openness, your ability to be objectively critical and still be positive are a credit to you both. You made me look at my writing in new ways. Good luck with your own projects, may the muse be ever there for you.

Special thanks to Jennifer, my agent, for a sharp critical eye, spot-on feedback and rock-solid representation, and to Marc at Angry Robot, both for having the nerve to publish the monster and for solving the conundrum around the finale. You're both a joy to work with.

Thanks to Jane Follett of the Royal Courts of Justice for permission to use the quotation from the booklet concerning the Quit Rents Ceremony and to the staff of the RCJ for the courteous and dignified way they dealt with my rather odd enquiries about the workings of the Royal Court of Justice. It's appreciated.

And to my whole family, who have been unshakably supportive throughout this journey. You have kept faith with me when the odds seemed insurmountable and put up with endless hours of anti-social typing, moody plotting and faltering drafts. Bless you all.

Finally, huge thanks to my wife, Sue, and my son, Leo, for their patience, wisdom, insight and love. You are my world. Without you I would not be able to be who I am.

THE QUIT RENT CEREMONY

It has been said many times that truth is stranger than fiction and this book is, in some ways, a reflection of that. I came across the Ceremony for the Annual Rendering of the Quit Rents during research for this novel, as a reference in a book on English folklore. The ceremony itself is entirely real and is the oldest legal ceremony in England with the exception of the Royal Coronation. The ceremony has been performed annually since 1211 between the feast of St Michael and St Martin, usually early in October.

The origin of the ceremony goes back to the time of William the Conqueror. The county of Shropshire, then known as Salop, was granted to Roger de Montgomerie, a senior counsellor of William, in 1071, along with many other holdings. Roger was 1st Earl of Shrewsbury and lived until 1094 when he was succeeded by his younger son, Hugh de Montgomerie who became 2nd Earl of Shrewsbury and died without children.

The land then passed to Hugh's older brother in Normandy, Robert de Bellême who had a reputation for starting wars and kidnapping his neighbour's children. Robert de Bellême was exiled to Normandy in 1102 after conspiring to depose Henry I and the land in Salop was forfeit. The majority of this land was granted to men loyal to the king, but a piece of wasteland, known as the Moors, just south of Bridgnorth, was retained and held directly of the Crown.

The earliest record of a tenant is of Nicholas de Morrs who occupied 80 acres of land, 20 acres of meadow and 80 acres of pasture from 1211 upon the rendering of two knives, one blunt and one sharp. The purpose of the knives was to create tally sticks for the receipt of taxes where a hazel rod of one year's growth (roughly the length of a man's forearm) was notched with the blunt knife to represent payment. The sharp knife was then used to split the rod in two, forming two corresponding halves of a receipt.

In 1521, the obligation to provide the knives passed to six Mercers and then in 1556 to Richard Mylles. In that year one of the city men attending for the confirmation of the sheriffs attempted to perform the service with the knives. Neither knife would cut the hazel rod and Richard Mylles was fined ten shillings for contempt.

At some point the two knives were replaced with a hatchet and a bill-hook (a hedging tool) and the hazel rod with faggots, small logs of wood. A hatchet and bill-hook used for the ceremony at this time can be seen in the Northgate Museum at Bridgnorth. They were probably made specifically for the ceremony as they are plated, possibly with silver.

Nowadays, two knives are made each year, commissioned by the Worshipful Company of Cutlers for the City of London, and sometimes displayed afterwards in the exhibition cabinets in the main hall of the Royal Courts of Justice where the ceremony continues to this day.

The role of the Queen's Remembrancer (or King's Remembrancer, if the monarch is male) dates back to 1164 when Richard of Ilchester, Archdeacon of Poitiers and later Bishop of Winchester was asked by the King to stand alongside the Treasurer and "Put the King in remembrance of all things owing to the King". There was also a Lord Treasurer's Remembrancer whose role was to "Know and keep all the secrets of the Kingdom", a post first held by Master Thomas Brown a former Lord Treasurer of Count Roger of Sicily.

Around 1830, the tax gathering element of these roles was transferred to the newly formed Treasury under the new Chancellor of the Exchequer. The word Exchequer is derived from the chequered cloth laid over a counting table where debts were set into the squares on one side and then, as they were paid, transferred to the other. Inns that bear the name "The Chequers" were often where the tax collections were held and the Prime Minister's country retreat is still called Chequers, possibly due to links with the Exchequer.

In recent times, the ceremonial elements of the role of Queen's Remembrancer remain with the senior master of the Queen's Bench Division of the Supreme Court who still wears the tricorn hat of a cursitor baron on top of a full wig when presiding over the ceremony. A photo of the Queen's Remembrancer, fully robed and wearing the wig and tricorn hat, with a horse shoe in one hand and one of the knives in the other may be seen in *Keepers of the Kingdom, The Ancient Officers of Britain* by Alistair Bruce, Julian Calder and Mark Cator (Weidenfeld & Nicolson, 1999).

There is some debate around the circumstances of the establishment of the forge in Tweezers Alley, but it is likely that the forge was originally erected as a temporary facility in the corner of the tournament fields of the Knights Templar, who had the land close to the banks of the Thames near where Tweezers Alley now stands. The tenant, Walter le Brun, was allowed to go quit of the rent for the forge in return for the provision of six horseshoes suitable for a Flemish war horse and sixty-one nails, ten for each shoe and one extra, perhaps, as a spare. The rent is first entered into the rolls of the Exchequer in 1235. This continued until 1361 when the rent was commuted to eighteen pennies, provided that the tenant, Emma of Tewkesbury, provided shoes for the ceremony to continue. The shoes she presented are still in use today and are the oldest horseshoes known to exist in England. I have not discovered what purpose the Queen's Remembrancer would have for the horseshoes and nails; some things will always remain a mystery.

London is, of course, famous for one river, the Thames, but in fact has many. The Fleet river is one of the major tributaries flowing into the Thames and comes out at Blackfriars just near the Mermaid Theatre. The river used to flow openly and was navigable in its lower reaches, but became increasingly silted up and was used more and more as a sewer as London grew. It was eventually built over completely and now runs above ground from its source in Hampstead down to Kings Cross where it is channelled underground. I cannot say whether there is an island with an anvil or not.

Finally, during the writing of this book, it became necessary to invent a hammer in the story so that the Quick Knife might be remade. You can imagine, therefore, how delighted I was to learn that there are two hammers used in the ceremony of beating of the bounds of the parish of St Clement Danes, just across from the Royal Courts of Justice. They were used to keep order at the feast which is held after the parish bounds had been walked and were presented by Elizabeth I in 1573 and 1598 respectively. Each hammer is mounted with silver, and has a Tudor rose and the letters ER upon it, together with the anchor of St Clement Danes. This is recorded in *Curious Survivals* by Dr George C Williamson (Herbert Jenkins, 1923), along with many other curiosities. The hammers are still used ceremonially today.

The Quit Rents Ceremony, along with the confirmation of the Sheriffs for the City of London, is conducted every year at the Royal Courts of Justice and members of the public may attend, though the number attending may be limited by space. In 2011 it will celebrate its eight hundredth anniversary.

Mike Shevdon, 2009

COMING SOON

The Road to Bedlam

Here is a brief extract…

Kayleigh was running out of places to look. It wasn't like Alex to skip lessons like this. Well OK, just that once, but they'd done it together, scaring each other with the prospect of getting caught in town when they should be at school. This was different. They had arranged to meet before Geography so that they could swap ideas on the homework, so where was she?

She went through the outer doors, peeping around the wall in case a teacher lurked there. The playground was empty, no teachers and no Alex. She was about to go back into the building when she heard a noise from the PE block. It was more of a yell than a scream and it wasn't Alex's voice, but there shouldn't be anyone in the PE block at this time.

She checked the playground again and ran across the tarmac, praying that the teachers in the rooms facing the playground were now engaged with their mid-morning classes and too busy to be looking out the windows. She reached the side door to the gym and slipped through, breathing hard. The echo from her school shoes on the wooden floor where outdoor footwear wasn't allowed made her walk around the edge rather than crossing the open space. She stopped and listened. There were raised voices coming from the girl's changing room.

She tiptoed quickly down the passage and stopped. The voices were louder. She leaned on the door, pushing it open slightly. She recognised Tracy Welham's voice and the unmistakable smell of cigarettes. She was about to ease the door closed again and leave them to coat their lungs with tar when she heard Alex.

"I won't tell anyone, honest, but you have to let me past."

"Have to, do I?" challenged Tracy. She was in the year above them and had a bad reputation.

"You'd better let me go now," Alex asserted, "or something bad is going to happen."

"Yeah," Tracy said. "Something bad is going to happen. Grab her."

It was the sound of the scuffle that made Kayleigh push into the changing rooms. Two other girls, mates of Tracy's, were holding Alex, pushing her into one of the cubicles. At the sound of the door, Tracy turned to face Kayleigh.

"You'd better let her go or I'm gonna get the teachers." Kayleigh raised her voice, keen to make sure the others heard her.

"Get out of here now, horse-face," said Tracy, "or you're getting the same."

They crowded Alex into the cubicle and she could hear the grunts and shoves of Alex struggling against the two older girls.

Tracy tossed the cigarette into one of the sinks and made a grab for Kayleigh's long hair. Kayleigh evaded her, slipping back past the changing room door and pulling it closed behind her. Tracy's arm came around the gap and Kayleigh trapped it in the door.

"You little sod!" Tracy's hand grasped for Kayleigh. "I'm gonna rip your hair out."

"Kayleigh!" Alex's voice sounded hollow in the tiled room. "Tell them to stop, tell them I can't hold it. It's getting free. I can't hold it!"

Kayleigh's mind raced.

"You have to let her go!" she shouted through the door at Tracy. "She's not herself. You don't understand. She's really going to lose it."

"Oh yeah, we're really scared about that." Tracy shouted to her mates, "Drown the little bitch." With a sudden tug, she pulled her arm back and slammed the door closed on Kayleigh.

Kayleigh pushed at the door, her shoes sliding on the smooth floor as she shoved against Tracy holding it shut from the other side.

"You don't understand. You have to let her go!"

From behind the door came the sound of burbling and then coughing and retching.

"Drown the bitch!" Tracy urged them.

The sound of burbling resumed, but underlined by another gurgling sound. Kayleigh hammered on the door, screaming for them to stop. The gurgling deepened to a low rumble, the sound vibrating in Kayleigh bones, making her teeth ache. The temperature dropped suddenly, the chill sending goose bumps down Kayleigh's arms.

There was a moment of silence.

Then the rumbling returned, building to a crescendo until everything burst at once behind the door. Kayleigh hammered on the door, screaming for them to open it before it was too late, pleading with Tracy. Water started streaming out from under the door, pooling around Kayleigh's feet. Suddenly the pressure on the door reversed and it was Tracy trying to pull it open.

Water crashed into the gap, the weight of it pressing the door shut. Tracy was screaming for her to push, just push. Her hands were white against the edge of the door as water and sewage from the drains pressed the gap closed. Kayleigh tried to wedge her foot in it but the flow was too strong and it was pushing her aside. The door slammed shut, trapping Tracy's fingers. Kayleigh heard her yank them free with a bone-popping wrench.

The screams turned to hammering as the changing room rapidly filled with foul-smelling water. Kayleigh could hear them, shouting and yelling as the water swirled around them. Water streamed under the door, spraying round the edges as the pressure built. She could see the door handle rattle and then jerk as hands were dragged away, screams gulped off as they lost their footing and were swept under. Their cries echoed, rising and fading as the water began to turn, the screams turning to gasps as they tried to swim against the turning current. Her imagination conjured the vortex, tugging at their clothes, pulling them into the centre, dragging them under.

Kayleigh turned and ran down the passage and out through the gym screaming for someone, anyone, to come and help. She ran across the playground, tears streaming down her face, shouting until her voice cracked, knowing it was already too late.

The story of Rabbit and Blackbird continues...

Nine months after the events of SIXTY-ONE NAILS, Blackbird is heavily pregnant. They don't know when the baby will come, only that it will be soon. Niall is beginning to adjust to his new life. His daily training as a warder of the High Court of the Feyre leaves him covered in bruises that fade by dawn, only to be replaced with a new set every following day.

Then he gets the news no parent ever wants to hear. *There's been an accident. It's your daughter.*

THE ROAD TO BEDLAM

ANGRY ROBOT

Teenage serial killers **Zombie detectives The grim reaper in love** Howling axes **Vampire hordes** Dead men's clones   The Black Hand Death by cellphone **Gangster shamen Steampunk swordfights Sex-crazed bloodsuckers** Murderous gods Riots **Quests Discovery Death**

Prepare to welcome your new Robot overlords.

angryrobotbooks.com

> MOXYLAND
> Lauren Beukes
> "A TECHNICOLOR JAZZY ROLLERCOASTER RIDE INTO A DAZZLING..." —André Brink

SLIGHTS
KAARON WARREN

ANDY REMIC

KELL'S LEGEND

TIM WAGGONER

Introducing Matt Richter Private Eye. Zombie.

Nekropolis

"An atmospheric and exciting mystery" —SF Site

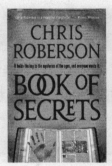

CHRIS ROBERSON

It holds the key to the mysteries of the ages, and everyone wants it.

BOOK OF SECRETS

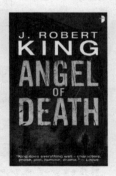

J. ROBERT KING

ANGEL OF DEATH

"King does everything well - characters, prose, plot, humour, drama." —Locus

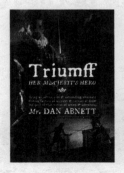

Triumff
HER MAJESTY'S HERO

Mr. DAN ABNETT

WINTER SONG

COLIN HARVEY